PYROGENS
International Red Aid Clinic, not far from Gerrikaitz, Spain
Friday 23 April–Saturday 24 April

—Swallow each and every one, or your cock will fall off.

—Wait, what?

She rattled the bottle. —You have gonorrhea. These sulpha pills will shoot back up your throat and taste like bile. Unpleasant, I know, but you must take one every eight hours until they're gone.

He squinted at her. —Nurses don't wear trousers.

—I do. Now, for the crabs. This ointment will smother them, and it will soothe the kerosene rash, too. Please don't use kerosene again. Stand too close to a fire and you might become a lamp.

He took the ointment. —Petroleum jelly?

—I'll fetch you a nit comb. What's your name, comrade?

Kostya fastened his trousers. Despite weeks of drill, he still spoke Spanish with a Russian accent. His friend Misha spoke much better Spanish and never lost a chance to remind Kostya of the fact. Then Kostya considered the common rumours — rumours he knew to be true — of the heavy presence in Spain of NKVD, the Soviet secret police. NKVD agents hunted, tortured, and killed members of POUM, an anti-Stalinist communist faction that ignored and defied orders from Moscow. Disobedience caused disunity, and so POUM must be purged. Even as NKVD destroyed POUM one bullet at a time, Moscow sent arms and food for the republican side of the Spanish Civil War, the side on which the communists all fought.

Kostya decided this nurse hardly needed to know he worked for NKVD, not yet. So he lied. —Tikhon. I'm a journalist.

—Just Tikhon?

—Just Tikhon.

Considering how her nurse's uniform had never materialized —just another of the administrative cock-ups plaguing the cash-strapped British Secret Intelligence Service — Temerity also lied. —Well, Comrade Just Tikhon, you may call me Mildred Ferngate.

Kostya studied her. Brown eyes, curly brown hair, petite: not his type. Quick, confident, almost serene: irritating. —You're British.

Ignoring how her patient adjusted his holster, Temerity focused instead on his jacket, khaki canvas boasting many useful pockets, and then on his dark hair and beard. Both needed a trim. His skin, while burnt by wind and sun, still looked soft, and his strong cheekbones, she thought, gave him away as Russian as much as any accent. *That,* her handler Neville Freeman would say, *and his apparent inability to smile. You can always spot a Russian. Not got much to smile about, what?* Temerity had asked her father about that. *Nonsense, Temmy. Your mother smiled all the time. Your smile is very like hers.*

She considered smiling now, if only to test this Tikhon's belief in her nurse cover story. Instead, she decided to remain brisk. —English, to be precise. Here, take this.

Kostya studied the comb's long metal teeth. His mouth twitched, as if he wished to frown, or laugh. Then he tucked the comb in a pocket. —Where's the doctor?

—He'll be back later. Now, let's see that bad toe. Are your boots the right size?

Kostya pried off his right boot and exposed the foul *portyanki* wrapped around his foot, the cloth stained yellow and green around the big toe. Blushing, he plucked away the cloth. Gonorrhea and pubic lice he considered inevitable. An abscessed toe? Well, that came down to poor hygiene. —My boots fit fine. I've walked most of the way from Madrid.

The odour of long-unwashed feet, the abscess of an ingrown toenail, some of that nail pried loose from its bed: Temerity almost gagged. Her medical knowledge consisted of Girl Guides' first aid and whatever she'd crammed into her head on the voyage from London. The clinic's doctor, Cristobal Zapatero, had, for reasons of his own, accepted the Nurse Mildred Ferngate story. He did say that he hoped they'd never have to perform surgery in the clinic, adding that he worried as Franco's fascists gained ground. *Hell marches north, Comrade Ferngate.* Temerity had nodded, hiding her recognition that, in a medical crisis, she'd be almost useless, if not dangerous.

An ingrown toenail, however, she could handle. And the Russian attached to it. Surely.

Thinking about how this Tikhon had limped from a lorry, which then drove on, Temerity decided to shake loose some information.

—Madrid? That's quite a walk.

—Most of the way, as I said.

—Oh, so the man who brought you here in the lorry picked you up between here and Madrid? When is he due back from Gernika?

Kostya neither flinched nor blinked. —Gernika?

—That's the direction he drove in.

—He won't be long.

Temerity nodded, then turned to a shelf of medical supplies. Her orders while in Spain: observe and report on Dr. Cristobal Zapatero and any other POUM members, and observe and report on any possible NKVD activity. The arrival of an armed Russian — perhaps two, counting the fair man who drove the lorry — not long after Cristobal left on a bicycle trip to Gernika? With Tikhon's colleague in likely pursuit? Well, one must observe. And hope to report. NKVD rarely left witnesses.

Releasing the catch on a leather case, she expected to find a set of lances. Instead, dilatation rods and a speculum glinted in the light. She stared at these instruments a moment, imagined their touch, shut them away.

Then she opened the correct case. —I need to boil this lance. Wait here.

Ignoring the instruction, Kostya followed her from the main room, crowded with cots, shelves, and medical gear, to the clinic's tiny kitchen. He discovered a kerosene camp stove, a sink equipped with a hand pump, piles of coiled rope, a spade, a hammer, and a five-litre can labelled with an *O* and a minus sign. He crouched before the stove, a German model called a Lichtträger ringed with a narrow cooking surface marked in German, Spanish, Russian, French, and English. The stove could, with some strategy, cook food for three or four adults, but boil enough water for an influx of wounded? Unlikely. The inventory of bandages, ointment, medicines, and gear, and the smell of disinfectant, created a layer of legitimacy. Yes, Kostya told himself, this place could function as a clinic, but the chaotic storage in the kitchen might signal a hurried setup. He considered the clinic's distance from Gernika: far enough to make a walk or bicycle ride long and tedious but not impossible, not if one needed the Gernika telegraph. So, a clinic, and also a communications corridor for POUM, those communications sent and received by his target, Dr. Cristobal Zapatero.

Temerity touched his arm. —Tikhon, are you all right?

He shook her off. —Dizzy spells. I really need to see the doctor. When will he be here?

How to answer? Lie and say Cristobal might be days yet, in the hope this Russian might give up and leave? A journalist might not waste time. An NKVD agent, however, would wait. Tell the truth and risk giving useful information, say she expected Cristobal tomorrow morning on his bicycle, again in the hope the Russian might get tired and leave? No. A journalist with dizzy spells and a sore foot would not want to leave, knowing the doctor would return soon, and neither would an NKVD agent. Back to lying. Yet if she lied, and Tikhon was NKVD and then discovered the deceit…

Blasted blasted bloody hell. —I expect him back tomorrow morning.

Kostya pointed to a bare cot in the far corner. —Fine. I'll wait. I can sleep here tonight, yes?

Temerity's pulse seemed to thud in her ears: run now, run now, run now. *Run where?* She moved to the sink. —I'll get you a blanket once we're done with your toe. I'll need some water.

Metal squeaked. One sink, one pump, one small woman to work it: Kostya almost laughed. Instead, his voice rapped out a command. —Step aside.

She stared at him.

He slipped off his jacket and rolled up his sleeves, exposing wiry muscles. —So I may pump the water, Comrade Ferngate.

—I am quite capable, thank you.

—Yes, I'd guessed that much. I can also guess the pump is difficult. So I will do it.

Unsure why, she took a few steps back and acquiesced. —Thank you.

Kostya leaned into the pumping. —I'm lucky I found you. This clinic, I mean. It's in a strange spot.

Temerity heard her father's voice, how he would calm her when she was frightened: *Steady the Buffs.* —I believe it was a storehouse. No one uses tinned blood anymore. Some of those gauze bandages are from before the Great War, I expect, and Cortez himself surely sent back those pots and pans.

Wincing, Kostya pumped harder. *She must have arms like iron bands.* —Nothing so grand as the British imperial cull.

—I beg your pardon?

Kostya hid his smirk. —The Elgin Marbles? The Koh-i-Noor?

She stood very straight, shoulders back. —Those treasures represent pinnacles of human achievement and civilization, and they belong where such pinnacles can be recognized and celebrated.

—In Britain, the greatest pinnacle of them all?

She just stopped herself from snapping *Of course* as she lit the stove. Then she asked herself why Tikhon was teasing her. —In a museum. Where everyone may see them. Well, not the Koh-i-Noor, that's locked away. But we've got the marbles on display, as you must in Russia with the treasures liberated from the tsar.

He looked up from the pump in surprise. —What?

—The Amber Room? The Orlov diamond? No? Give me about a cup of the water so I can boil the lance, and you take the rest in that bowl outside. The light's better. Wait, pour in these Epsom salts, but don't soak your foot just yet. I'll join you in a moment.

Outside, sitting in the dust and propped against a clinic wall, Kostya relished the heat of the sun on his face. He sighed, avoided looking at his foot, then gave himself permission to doze.

—Tikhon?

Sunlight glinted off the metal bowl, blinding Kostya a moment, and he cursed himself for letting this woman sneak up on him.

Pinching a lance between finger and thumb, Temerity knelt before him. —Now, let me see that abscess.

He studied her trousers, how they flowed off her waist yet clung to her thighs. A small object bulged in her right pocket: a folding knife, perhaps. To his surprise, he felt at once proud and protective of her. She could look after herself, it seemed, yet she was so small.

Reminding himself this woman was his enemy, he looked to the lance. —Will it hurt?

—Only if you laugh.

Hand near her shoulder, she held the lance as though hoisting a tiny harpoon, and hesitated.

Smirking, Kostya spoke in English. —An indecisive Britisher? Don't look so surprised. I speak seven languages.

—English is not your strongest, then.

He resumed speaking Spanish. —Apparently not.

—I could cut that accent with a knife and fork.

—English is an ugly language, hardly worth the effort.

—Nonsense. A poet can make English sing. Listen:

Take all my loves, my love, yea, take them all;
What hast thou then more than thou hadst before?
No love, my love, that thou mayst true love call;
All mine was thine before thou...

Well, you get the point.

—No, please, finish it.

Temerity almost smiled. Perhaps Tikhon hadn't lied. Perhaps he really was a journalist and not an enemy. —Very well.

All mine was thine before thou hadst this more.
Then, if for my love thou my love receivest,
I cannot blame thee for my love thou usest;
But yet be blamed, if thou this self deceivest
By wilful taste of what thyself refusest.
I do forgive thy robbery, gentle thief,
Although thou steal thee all my poverty;
And yet love knows, it is a greater grief
To bear love's wrong than hate's known injury.
Lascivious grace, in whom all ill well shows,
Kill me with spites, yet we must not be foes.

The silence between them felt suffocating.

Then Temerity sounded brisk again. —Shakespeare, sonnet forty. Now lie back. I'll get beside you and lean over your legs, so you don't kick me.

Unsure what else to do, Kostya lay on the ground. The press of belly and breasts on his legs startled him. —Is this really the best way?

—Little pinch.

—Fucked in the mouth!

She knelt up and wiped away wad after wad of bloodied pus. —You Russians have the best profanity.

17

—You speak Russian?

Had to show off, didn't I? She continued in Spanish. —I hardly need to speak the language to understand that you just said something foul, but yes, I've picked up a few words. Hold still.

She manipulated the abscess, squeezing out the last of the visible pus; Kostya hissed and winced.

—All right, Tikhon, I've got about as much of the corruption as I can manage. Epsom salts will draw out the rest. Then we can see about rooting out that nail. For now, I want you to sit up, lean against the wall there—yes, well done—and soak your foot.

Confused, pained, charmed, he could say nothing.

Temerity looked up, frowned.

Jaw clenched, Kostya followed her gaze.

Temerity shook her head. —I thought I heard planes. It's just sky.

Reaching into his jacket, Kostya nudged a book and retrieved cigarettes and matches.

Temerity noticed. —I'll have one.

Face stern, Kostya switched to Russian. —Stunts the growth, little one.

She heard the challenge, polyglot to polyglot, and, as Kostya lit two cigarettes at once, she answered in Russian. —Very funny. Thank you. Next time, don't stick my cigarette in your mouth first. Germs, you know. Oh, wait here.

—Where else might I go?

On her feet again, she smiled down at him.

Delighted by the sudden imperfection of her crooked teeth, he smiled back.

The sun shone so bright.

She returned, offering some blur of colour, swirls of green, white, red, and blue playing against a light bronze: a cloisonné cigarette case.

Kostya stroked the case with the pads of his fingers, then turned it over and read the Cyrillic engraving on the back: *Viktoria Ivanovna Solovyova*. —It's lovely.

—Empty, I'm afraid. My mother's, before she got married.

—So your mother taught you Russian.

Temerity tugged at her trousers. —I don't remember the sound of her voice. She died in 1918. Flu.

—Did you have it, too?

—Yes. Terrible fevers.

—Savage.

They sat in silence, smoking. Kostya offered Temerity a second cigarette.

She nodded. —Thank you. I'm sorry I teased you about your accent when you spoke English. I can only imagine what mine sounds like in Russian.

—I could listen to you speak my language all day. All night, too.

The flirtation's frisson sharp, Temerity almost complimented Tikhon on his technique. Then she chided herself for giving away so much, her mother's name for God's sake, while gleaning so little.

The water in the bowl splashed as Kostya shifted his weight. —So how did you learn Russian?

—I always wanted to, I suppose. My father would translate fairy tales for me out of one of my mother's books, and I loved the Cyrillic alphabet.

—Which fairy tales?

—Oh, so many of them. It's been a long time. *Narodyne russkie skazki*, that was the book.

Kostya felt tension leave his neck and shoulders. This woman smelled delicious, honeyed musk and peppery sweat. And she spoke Russian. —I like 'The Maiden Tsar,' the hero saying he does things by his own free will yet twice as much by compulsion.

—I remember that. And 'The Frog Princess.'

—'Go I Know Not Whither and Fetch I Know Not What.' And 'Vasilisa the Beautiful.'

Temerity looked to the ground. —I remember the illustration.

—You're blushing.

—I shoved the book away. My father was partway through the story, the bit where Vasilisa's stepmother gives her the impossible task, and I just shoved the book away. Knocked it to the floor.

Kostya lit another cigarette. —Willful child.

—No. I was scared.

Temerity surprised herself, saying that.

Kostya gave her a long look. —Of what?

—The task. Vasilisa was too small. She couldn't win.

—Go back and finish the story. She finds Baba Yaga, or is it Baba Yaga finds her? Anyway, Baba Yaga gives Vasilisa her blessing and some holy fire. Then Vasilisa finds all the bones in Baba Yaga's yard, chooses a skull, and turns it into a lamp for the holy fire. Off she goes, completes her quest, happy ending.

—She gets out of the boneyard?

Kostya nodded. Then he wondered why he'd earlier thought this woman irritating.

Almost unaware, Temerity switched to English. —Holy fire. My father's got a print of the Novgorod Gabriel in his study.

Kostya followed her to English. —My grandparents had three copies of that ikon on their beauty wall. I stared and stared at it. The angel's eyes were so big. But you must use his correct name: Gavriil.

She studied him, that serious face, those green eyes, and laughed. Then she returned to Russian. —Gavriil it is. All the archangels are Russian, I suppose?

Kostya refrained from laughing, though he did smirk. —As Russian as Baba Yaga and Koshchei the Deathless, and just as ridiculous. You know Koshchei, right?

She wanted to hear the story in his voice, how he'd tell it. —No.

—Koshchei is a terrible old man, a tyrant, and he's managed to hide his soul away, so if anyone should strike a killing blow, he will not die, because his soul is still intact. He rapes, he kills, he steals what he wants, and no one can fight him, only serve him. One day, Ivan, who's only heard stories of Koshchei and doubts the old brute even exists, sets out on a quest. He bumbles through the woods for a summer and a winter and comes out of it starved and chilled and bloodless from fly bites. He meets a woman, Marya Morevna, who's looking for something. She's a warrior. She takes a liking to Ivan. Maybe she pities him. They fall in love, get married, have a big party, and then a messenger brings Marya Morevna some news. Marya tells Ivan she must go, but he'll be safe in her castle. She and her knights gather weapons and food, put on their armour, saddle their horses, and instead of telling Ivan she loves him, as he expects, Marya warns him not to go into the cellar. Ivan asks why. Marya begs him to trust her, then kisses him goodbye. Soon he hears someone cry out from the cellar. It's a dry old voice begging for water. Ivan is not heartless. He immediately brings water to the cellar, and he finds this old, old man, starved and foul, chained to a wall. Ivan is angry with Marya for her cruelty, and he helps the old man drink until he drains twelve barrels of water. Then the old man stands up, breaks his chains, knocks Ivan over, and runs up the steps. He's gone, and the servants tell Ivan it was Koshchei the Deathless. Marya Morevna had captured him and then starved him to keep him weak while she looked for his soul. How's my toenail? Soaked long enough?

Temerity peeked in the bowl. —Almost.

—Ivan sets out to find Marya and her knights and warn them, maybe even help them. He finds all the knights dead except one, who says on his last breath that Koshchei has taken Marya. Ivan buries the knights, then sits down in despair. He has no idea what to do. Baba Yaga finds him, tells him what a fool he is, and then, because she likes Marya Morevna, gives Ivan a magic horse which will take him to the island where Koshchei has hidden his soul. Baba Yaga says Ivan will recognize the spot when he sees it, because every child knows where Koshchei keeps his soul: under the oak tree and inside a locked chest. And in that chest waits a rabbit, and within the rabbit waits a duck, and within the duck waits an egg, and within the yolk of the egg lies a needle, and in the eye of the needle rests the soul of

Koshchei the Deathless. This is a very long story. Are you sure you don't remember it?

Nodding, she moved a little closer to him, close enough to feel his body heat, not quite enough to touch.

Kostya noticed a line of ash on the ground next to him; he'd not smoked much of his last cigarette. —I'll make this quick. The horse gets Ivan to the island, and Ivan finds the tree, digs up the trunk, so on and so on, gets the needle, and rides back to where Koshchei keeps Marya. Koshchei is a giant now. The wizards are already fighting him with lightning, and the steppe shakes and burns. Oh, I forgot: Ivan died before he found Baba Yaga, when he tried to attack Koshchei on his own. The wizards brought him back to life. I can't remember why. Anyway, the wizards are losing, but Ivan holds Koshchei's soul. First he finds and frees Marya Morevna, and then he shows her the needle. She recognizes it, and she takes it, and she breaks the eye. Koshchei falls to the earth, and the wounded wizards blast him with lightning, all together, and with one long scream, Koshchei the Deathless dies. Ivan and Marya return to her castle and have many children and live a long and happy life. For all her days, Marya wears the two broken pieces of the needle around her neck. When she dies, one piece of the needle is buried with her, while the other is taken far out to sea and thrown at a wave. To this day no one knows where Marya's bones lie, or where that other piece of the needle sank. Another cigarette?

—Yes, please.

This time he gave her the cigarette first, then lit a match and held the flame to her face.

Inhaling, Temerity leaned back. —You stare at me like I've got three heads.

—You have freckles on your eyelids. It's beautiful.

She hurried to stand up. —Keep your foot in the water for another ten minutes.

—No, no, please. I didn't mean—

Brushing dust off her trousers, she refused to look at him. —I'll come back and check on you shortly.

—Wait.

The clinic door clicked shut.

The cloisonné case, left on the ground, seemed to stroke his fingertips.

Kostya shifted on his haunches and drew harder on his cigarette. Still touching the cloisonné with his left hand, he patted his jacket with his right till he found the weight of the book: a copy of Turgenev's *Fathers and Sons* with certain passages underlined to use as code. When Kostya sent his superiors a message that read *As Turgenev notes, first we've got to clear the ground,* it meant *Target found.* When he sent the message *As Turgenev notes, even nightingales can't live by song alone,* it meant *Target liquidated.*

He considered the British woman, her languages and nerve, her Russian mother's surname.

Solovyova meant nightingale.

He flicked his cigarette butt to the ground next to the bowl of water and scowled.

They passed a tense night, both vigilant, and Kostya also sore from using the nit comb. He'd almost convinced himself the British woman might truly be a nurse, despite the business with the lance, and Temerity had almost convinced herself this Tikhon just might be a war correspondent. Not enemies, then, but two people meeting in events neither could control. Such fictions would make the day easier.

After a meagre breakfast of rice and beans, the clinic's food rations low, and after a long and tumbling conversation about languages and fairy tales, Kostya walked a short way south to bathe in the river. Temerity took a sketchbook and box of pencils from beneath the pillow on her cot and sat at the table. She glanced at her portrait of Cristobal, then turned to a fresh page. The sound of her pencil marking the paper soothed her.

An engine approached from the northwest, all rumble, rattle, and squeak. *Tikhon's colleague?* Temerity closed her sketchbook, patted her pocket to check for her folding knife, and then stepped outside, where she rounded the corner to the north wall. She found a lorry parked there, the same lorry as yesterday. Sunlight glinted off the windshield; a tarp rippled over the back.

Bloody hell, where's the driver?

Right behind her. Pressing the muzzle of a gun in her ribs.

A male voice spoke in accented Spanish, his breath hot on the back of Temerity's neck. —Where's Zapatero?

She answered first in English, then Spanish. —What? What?

He grasped her arm, wrenched her around to face him. —By the wall. Now.

She walked backwards, palms raised. —This is an International Red Aid clinic. Everyone is welcome here.

The breeze stirred the second Russian's fair hair, blowing it in to his eyes, then out again. He stood about the same height at Kostya, and his face wore the same stern expression. —Where's Zapatero?

The outside wall of the clinic met her back. —Gernika. I expect him back any moment. Oh, is that him over there?

He looked away, and she struck the side of his neck with the edge of her hand, interrupting blood flow to his brain. As he staggered, she rammed her elbow into his sternum. The gun clattered to the ground. So did he. Temerity whirled round to find Kostya running towards them. She ran into the clinic, latched the door, and pressed her ear to the hinges to listen.

The second Russian stirred, groaned. —She said Zapatero was over there.

Kostya sounded disgusted. —You fell for that?

—And then she hit me. Hard! Listen, Zapatero left Gernika early this morning. On a bicycle. Can that nurse speak Russian?

—Fuck, no. Zapatero is here? You sure?

—Those trees, over by the river. You look terrible.

—The nurse gave me sulpha pills. I fucking belch brimstone.

—Take more care where you stick your cock next time. See that, the shirt in the trees?

—It's him. Go. Go.

They ran off.

Temerity ran from the door and wrenched open the haversack she kept near her cot. She took her passport and tucked it into her brassiere, then flinched as a fist beat on the door. The plea came in Spanish. —Let me in!

She unlatched and opened the door, stumbling as a man wheeling a bicycle shoved her aside. —Cristobal?

Eyes wide and dark with fear and fatigue, Cristobal stared straight ahead as he dropped the bicycle, grabbed Temerity's arm, and hauled her to the little kitchen. He wore no shirt beneath his jacket, and he clutched something in his left hand as he whispered in rapid Spanish. Then he pointed back at the unlatched door.

She whispered back. —Wait, wait, I don't understand. The latch—

The door slammed open.

She had no idea what the two Russians yelled. It didn't matter. Only the guns mattered.

The object fell from Cristobal's hand and clattered at Temerity's feet: rosary beads.

Kostya aimed at Temerity. —Misha, get Zapatero outside.

Misha grabbed Cristobal by his right arm, marched him off.

Temerity stared at Kostya, recalling how he'd told Misha she could not speak Russian. She spoke in Spanish. —Let me bring him the beads.

—Pick them up. Then give them to me. Slow.

She did so.

Outside, Misha shouted at Cristobal, who shouted back.

Kostya rubbed a bead between forefinger and thumb, then dropped the beads into a pocket. —Into the kitchen. Stand by the Lichtträger and face the wall.

—Tikhon, please.

—Move!

As they passed the table, Kostya picked up the sketchbook. Pages flipped. Then he shoved the book over Temerity's shoulder and held it before her face, open to the newest drawing. His voice sounded younger, less certain. —Me?

Mouth dry, she nodded.

Fascinated by the portrait, he just stood there, right hand aiming his gun at the British woman's back, left hand holding a sketch of himself.

Outside, Misha's voice rose as he demanded something. Then he fired, and Cristobal screamed. Temerity clenched her jaws and stifled her own cry.

Kostya shouted over his shoulder. —What the barrelling fuck? Did you *miss?*

—You should get out here, Nikto.

—Yes, I'd guessed that much.

Staring at the Lichtträger and the tin of O-negative blood, Temerity mouthed the name to herself. *Nikto? It means nobody.*

Misha sounded flippant, even cheerful. —Thigh. He lunged at me. Anyway, he can't run now.

Kostya shoved the sketchbook into a pocket. —Can't fucking walk, either.

—Then he'll be ready to talk to us.

Kostya's left hand clamped on Temerity's shoulder; the gun muzzle touched the back of her head. —Kneel.

The floor scraped her knees.

His boots squeaked as he took a few steps back. Then he fired. Wide.

The concussion of the shot, so close to her ears, left Temerity deaf, and blood sprayed from the can labelled O-negative. Kostya kicked

Temerity with the side of his boot, just hard enough to knock her off balance. As she fell and rolled onto her back, she saw spatter stains on both the walls and Kostya's clothes, and an expression on his face she could not read. He gestured with his free hand, and his mouth worked, English: —Stay down. Stay down.

Then he snatched several rolls of bandage and ran.

Noise filtered past the ringing in her ears: rapid Russian conversation, Cristobal's pleas to pack the wound, the slam of lorry doors. The engine roared, stalled, roared again, and faded toward Gerrikaitz.

Dizzy, Temerity sat and wiped her cheek with the back of her hand, smearing tinned blood across her face. The clinic door, left open and stirred by the breeze, rapped against the wall.

She hadn't screamed. Wondering why, she recalled her Aunt Min's advice a few years before, on their long trip through India. *Steamer trunk, Temmy, my dear. Organize your mind like your steamer trunk, all those layers of clothes and little drawers and the false bottom, and finish the task at hand. There'll be time for tears and laughter later. Remember Nelson's signal and you'll be fine. Say it with me: England expects that every man will do his duty.*

Temerity spoke aloud. —England expects that every man will do his duty. Right.

She stood up, brushed dirt from her trousers, kept still for a moment, then ran outside, knelt in the dirt, and vomited. Quick, efficient, she strode back inside, hoisted the haversack on her shoulders, picked up the dropped bicycle, and wheeled it outside.

—Lovely day for a ride.

She gripped the handlebars hard to stop the shaking in her hands and mounted. The bicycle frame too big for her, she faltered and slipped off the seat.

—Oh, God. Oh, my God. Right, Nelson's signal, you'll be fine. Just get to Gernika and the telegraph. No cringing. Off we go, then.

She found her balance, pedalled.

The bicycle squeaked.

[ ]

Kostya glared at Misha over the top of Cristobal's head. —I don't see why you get to drive.

—I found the lorry, didn't I?

—You've also found every single bump in the road.

—He's slipping. Move closer. Keep him propped up between us.

Kostya peeked at the dressings on Cristobal's wound; they'd gone almost purple with blood. —Why in hell didn't you kill him?

—Because I want you to hear him talk.

Kostya sighed. —We don't need an interrogation. Look, he's suffering.

—Since when has that bothered you?

Kostya nodded, acknowledging the point. —It's messy. Follow orders next time. Bullet to the head, done, walk away.

—Like the nurse?

—Yes.

Between them, Cristobal shook.

Eyes intent on the road, Misha steered around a rock. —Is he convulsing?

—Crying.

Misha switched to Spanish. —Not long now.

Cristobal looked at Kostya and his blood-spattered clothes, then shut his eyes.

Bilbao Docks
Monday 10 May

Temerity noticed his sling first, then the tattered khaki sleeve and the bright wounds on his left ear and neck. She told herself to ignore him. A chance resemblance, nothing more.

Besides, she had a task. She needed to blackmail her prime minister. At least, it felt like blackmail, this succinct yet emotional report on conditions in Bilbao she'd written for Leah Manning, the British politician struggling with Consul Ralph Stevenson to evacuate Basque children. Manning and Stevenson worked in the thick stink of the crisis, Manning, like Temerity, even caught in the Gernika bombardment. Temerity relished her work for the evacuation, as much as it tired her. The work, she acknowledged to herself, hardly lay in her purview as an agent; she considered it more within her moral duty as a human being. Britain's government had relented and agreed to accept Basque child refugees but only to age twelve, and with the caveats that the children be privately sponsored and Francoists must also be evacuated. Temerity and the others had recognized an immediate problem: the girls. The age cut-off left adolescent Basque girls vulnerable to invading soldiers, whose presence now was only a matter of time.

Seeking a particular British boat and the captain who'd agreed to ferry her report back to London, Temerity glanced back at the injured man. He disappeared within a cloud of delousing gas pumped by a stocky man in a peacoat. As the gas dissipated, the injured man pointed to himself with his good arm, then to the line of boys before him, the boys aged from maybe four to fourteen and wearing cardboard discs around their necks. Temerity could guess what he said. *You see? The gas did me no harm. Now it's your turn.* One of the boys stepped forward. Soon a cloud of delousing gas covered him, and he coughed.

Three Basque mothers recognized Temerity and hurried toward her. Surrounded by drawn and worried faces, by tearful pleas to convince England to take their daughters, Temerity wanted to scream. She listened to the mothers' words, nodded in understanding, and reminded them the committee would do everything in its power, and now could you please excuse me?

Ducking into the crowd, Temerity continued to seek the British boat. She told herself the hunger pangs would settle soon.

Behind her, the injured man called out in Spanish, then in French, his voice almost lost in the dockside racket. —I need someone who can write Russian. Can anyone write in Russian?

She knew the voice. No denying it. As she turned to face it, the speaker surveyed the crowd for a response. His beard, longer now, seemed to sharpen his cheekbones — perhaps that was hunger — and his wavy dark hair stirred in the wind off the sea. The boys stared into the crowd with him.

Kostya called again. —Please, my shoulder is hurt, and I can't hold the tags. Can anyone write in Russian?

Lost to his sight in the crowd, Temerity strode toward him, approaching the dock as he dug in his jacket for a pencil. Two of the boys pointed at her, and Kostya turned around.

His big eyes shone with pain; the wounds on his left neck and ear flushed a darker red. Staring, he wanted to ask Temerity how she'd reached Bilbao, ask how and why they'd met again. He knew he should demand her silence about the clinic, make some quiet threat to finish the job. He didn't bother. Such conversations belonged to that time, brittle now in retrospect, before bombardment.

Gesturing to the boys, Temerity spoke in Russian. —Evacuation?

—To Leningrad.

—So few? And only boys?

Kostya pointed behind him to a small fishing boat, its name in Cyrillic letters. —It's all I can do. And I don't trust the captain around girls. There'll be other ships. Soon. They may even get a Royal Navy escort from you British. Solidarity, comrade.

—Just give me the pencil.

He did so, and Temerity knelt before the first boy, reading his name. She switched to Spanish. —Good day, Enrico.

Kostya stood behind her, just to her right, speaking first in Spanish, then repeating his sentence in Russian. —Enrico, you are now Genrikh.

Holding the name tag in her left hand, Temerity wrote the Russian name above the Spanish name with her right. —Next.

Kostya gestured for the line of boys to move. —Eduardo, you are now Eduard. You see? Russian's not so strange.

Eduardo tried to read his disc upside down, frowned.

The next boy came to Temerity, and Kostya said nothing.

Temerity spoke instead. —Miguel, you are now Mikhail. Perhaps they'll call you Misha.

Kostya muttered in Russian. —Hurry up.

The twelve boys re-named, Temerity stood up and gave Kostya back his pencil. —This needs sharpening.

Perceiving a tension between the two adults, a tension he could not understand, one of the older boys giggled.

Temerity pointed to her own ear, neck, and shoulder, mirroring the path of Kostya's wounds. —Gernika?

Voice bland, workaday, he spoke as if commenting on the weather. —Gerrikaitz. The Luftwaffe bombed us first, then Gernika in the afternoon. Were you in Gernika?

—Yes.

—Hurt?

She tugged her hair out of the way and exposed a scabbed bruise on her forehead. —Nothing serious. Cristobal Zapatero?

Kostya shook his head.

—Well, I expected no better.

Kostya stared down at the dock, at the water visible between pieces of wood.

As Temerity turned to leave, Kostya surprised them both by calling to her. —Wait, please.

She faced him, crossed her arms.

He stepped closer. —It's a long way to Leningrad, and I don't want to run out of stories. Tell me an English story, so I can share it with the boys later.

Temerity hesitated. —Tam Lin. He fell from his horse, and he should have died, but the queen of fairies caught him, kept him prisoner, and then he lived for hundreds of years. He never aged. One day, the queen of fairies got tired of him and gave him a castle, and he lived there in silence until Lady Margaret, the local lord's daughter, picked his flowers. After an argument, Tam Lin and Margaret fell in love, Margaret fell pregnant, and the fairy queen got angry. She turned Tam Lin into a snake, a bear, a lion, a wolf, all to frighten Margaret off. Margaret held Tam Lin tight, and together they broke the spell. Then they grew old together and died.

—That's it?

—That's not enough?

The man in the peacoat called out to Kostya. He called back acknowledgement, then grasped Temerity's upper arm, too hard at first, and stared into her eyes. —I have to go, Marya Morevna.

—I doubt Marya Morevna had freckles on her eyelids.

—She had courage. Like you.

She shook him off. —Take care of those boys.

The man in the peacoat bellowed again.

Kostya rolled his eyes. —Yes, Comrade Captain, yes, I'm coming! Fucked in the mouth, I hate sea travel. I won't be able to eat for days.

Temerity almost laughed, then stepped away, calling back over her shoulder. —Don't let them forget their Spanish names.

Kostya ducked into the wheelhouse, giving no sign he'd heard.

[ ]

FEME SOLE 1
London
Monday 24 May

—A pity you're missing Empire Day, Miss West.

Here in a windowless brown office that she compared to the dead end of a bowel, Temerity studied the man she and her father had privately called a fool. *Freeman,* Edward West liked to complain, *bloody Neville Freeman. How he ended up in charge of field agents, I shall never understand. The man can't think his way out of a compound sentence. The Service is full of incompetence.* Once Temerity's private language tutor and now her handler, Neville Freeman looked timid and plain. He cultivated this impression. In his mid-forties, he combed his thinning brown hair over to one side and oiled it in place. His deep-set blue eyes seemed to hide behind his round spectacles, those lenses glinting in the light. Each word he spoke either sank or puffed his cheeks, and air whistled through the gap between his two front teeth.

Temerity's mouth felt puckered and dry from too much gin the night before. —One hardly expects holidays in the Service.

—Quite. Please, sit down.

She did so, glancing at the isochronic map on the wall. Holidays? A nice little sea voyage, Bilbao to Southampton on the *Habana,* a ship built for eight hundred and carrying four thousand, rough seas and resultant mess, and the decorations at the Southampton docks, pennants and ribbons and flags left over from the coronation of George VI, pennants and ribbons and flags gone limp with rain and now leaking dye, thought to signal a sufficient welcome for child refugees. After all, the decorations had been good enough for a king. Oh yes, a holiday to remember.

Neville pulled out his desk chair, scraping it on the floor. —Please, let me offer my condolences on the death of your father.

She busied herself with her cigarette case; the cloisonné felt so cool and smooth beneath her fingertips. —Thank you.

—Our Russian cryptanalysis won't be the same without him. He had an astonishing gift for languages. I rather admired him for refusing to use the title. 'Just call me West,' he always said. And you, too. I should call you Lady Temerity, yet it's Miss West who sits before me. I always said of your father, even when we disagreed, and we disagreed rather a lot, that he was a man who understood his debt to the empire. Your grandfather made his fortune on Darjeeling and Simla tea, wasn't it?

Temerity's eyes glittered. —Tea, prostitution, and opium. And for that, he was made a peer.

—Yes, well, that was a long time ago. Was your father ill before you left for Spain?

Temerity told herself not to think of her last conversation with her father. —Run down, I thought. We had Spanish flu in '18, not long after my father came back from overseas. My mother and my brother died. It damaged my father's lungs. He was prone to pneumonia, came down with it every few winters.

—You look rather run down yourself, Miss West. When did you last eat a decent meal?

—Lamb chops and asparagus were hard to come by, I admit, Spain being a war zone and all.

Neville raised his eyebrows. —Quite.

Eyes on her handbag, Temerity lit a cigarette. She knew Neville expected her to lean in so he could light it for her. She'd not got the patience for such games, not today. —Do you know who had the gall to send me flowers?

—Half the men in London, I would imagine.

Temerity decided to ignore that. —A sympathy bouquet, I mean. William Brownbury-Rees.

Neville gave a reassuring smile. —Yes, that was a bother, but surely it's all sorted out now.

—Freeman, did you hear me? He sent flowers to my flat. He knows my real name, and he knows where I live. How did he find me?

—*Burke's Peerage*?

—Very funny.

—Perhaps he's just smart.

—Certainly not.

—Then he had help. The British Union of Fascists has members in distressingly high places. All the more reason MI5 needs to keep an eye on them.

Temerity recalled the thud of her head bouncing on the floor as Brownbury-Rees pinned her and called her a treacherous whore, the taste of his blood when she bit through his lip, the high scream as she managed to grasp and twist his scrotum. She exhaled a long stream of smoke. —I want to bring charges.

—Not wise.

—I beg your pardon?

—First, it will draw too much attention to Five's activities, and Five won't be in a mood to help, not after you transferred out to join us in SIS. Second, you were in a compromising position. How did you describe it in your report? 'He's eating out of my hand.' Perhaps that's why it didn't sound quite like what you said. And spare me the hard-as-nails act. I knew you when you had spots.

Temerity shut her eyes. Neville's gaze, that steady gaze of evaluation — a butcher deciding where best to cut meat — could still unsettle her. Polyglot Neville Freeman had, during a self-imposed exile from the Service, worked for Edward West as a modern languages tutor, instructing adolescent Temerity. Delighted with her own gifts for languages, Temerity had sacrificed Roedean and returned home to Kurseong House for intensive study of German, French, Italian, and Spanish, with some headway into Danish. Neville admitted defeat when Temerity announced she wished to learn Russian. Edward, with some help from Five, found an impoverished White Russian émigré, one Count Ilya Ostrovsky, happy to offer lessons in exchange for a room of his own and something decent to eat. He got both at Kurseong House. As Temerity progressed in Russian, nearing sixteen, she felt like the main character in a play about to start, the audience murmuring just beyond drawn curtains. Her father, her Aunt Min, Neville Freeman, and Count Ostrovsky all seemed to expect her to follow a clear path — clear to everyone except

Temerity. Then Neville muddied the view one spring afternoon by reaching across the table to grasp his student's hand and stare at her in blatant desire. Frightened and repelled, Temerity snatched her hand back, upsetting the loose pages of her latest German composition. Edward and Ilya walked in on this situation, their quiet but intense conversation in Russian falling silent. Neville Freeman left Kurseong House the next day. The Secret Service had welcomed him back, polyglots always in high demand, and Temerity, like her father, felt only irritation and not surprise when, years later, she found herself reporting to Neville Freeman. *The man's a damned fool,* Edward often said, *and he's a symptom of everything that's wrong with the Service: not enough training, not enough cash, and not enough brains. No, we've got the likes of Neville Freeman wasting our best resources on risky operations. He seems to think capable polyglots grow like rhubarb. How he got to a position of command, I'll never know.*

Glass clinked as Neville poured whisky into two glasses and passed one to Temerity. Then he pronounced his judgment on the matter of Brownbury-Rees. —We shall do nothing. Chin-chin.

Temerity just stopped herself from telling Neville to go to hell. The words had reached her tongue with frightening speed. Raw. She felt raw, as if all courtesy, all restraint, had burned away.

In those Gernika fires, perhaps.

She took a good swallow of whisky.

—Miss West, I could put you on bereavement leave. There's no disgrace in that.

—Disgrace?

—We'll come back to that. For now, you must have arrangements to look after.

She shook her head. The new inheritance laws meant that she, and not some absurdly distant male relative, now owned Kurseong House and the small estate in the Kent village of Prideaux-on-Fen. —I've already sent word to keep the house in dust sheets. I need to work.

—Are you quite sure you're up to it?

—Of course.

Neville topped up their drinks. —Good, because we really must discuss the manner of your return to England. It's caused some confusion here in the department, as your last orders said to stay in Spain until recalled. It looks rather like when you hopped on the *Habana*, you abandoned your post.

—Children, Freeman, we evacuated *children* from Bilbao, and they needed chaperones.

—Children change nothing.

—Really? Perhaps the ancient Romans are more to your taste. They said war changes everything. God knows, the Luftwaffe rather upset my plans. Should I have stayed at the clinic and reported on developments by power of mental telepathy? Or should I have stayed in Gernika and hidden in the ashes? Did you care nothing of me when you learned Gernika was bombed?

—You're an agent, Miss West. I care about your results. But about Bilbao—

—Where else could I go? I finally got to speak with our consul. He was frantically busy organizing prisoner exchanges, for God's sake, with the Francoists. He asked me to help Leah Manning and then that silly vicar we've got posted there with the evacuation donkey-work, so I could do something useful whilst I waited for orders from London, and it was so hard to get any food, and I was surrounded by frightened people, and after all that fire in Gernika, the Francoists are marching closer, and then all those parents in Bilbao begging me to get their daughters to safety, and we finally get some children out, almost four thousand of them, and it's nothing...

She closed eyes and rubbed her temples.

—Miss West? Oh, please don't cry. I can't bear sadness in women.

—I'm not sad. I'm bloody angry!

Neville stood up and turned his back while Temerity blew her nose. —Tell me again what happened in the clinic. It's an extraordinary story.

—Story? POUM defies Moscow. Should we not be better friends with POUM? By standing aside and just watching, we betrayed Cristobal Zapatero and every other POUM communist. There's your *story*. God's sake, are we to sacrifice our allies?

Neville watched Temerity light and almost drop her second cigarette. —Britain is not officially involved in the Spanish war, so we can hardly speak of allies. As for Zapatero, however unfortunate his end with the NKVD, he knew what he'd signed up for, and if he didn't know, he quickly learned. Strange bedfellows and all that. But I'm not worried about Zapatero. I'm worried about you. Now, we've got a chance to calm any concerns about you deserting your post in Spain.

—I deserted nothing! That NKVD agent—

—Missed, yes, so you said. From such a short distance. And him a professional.

Temerity's fingers twitched as she rubbed her cigarette case. —I've told you the truth.

—All of it?

—Of course.

Not sure why, she'd omitted the business with the name tags. Now she asked herself if helping that same NKVD agent with refugee children mightn't be some sort of treason.

Treason to whom?

Sweat dampened her underarms.

—Please understand me, Miss West. Another handler might worry about your emotional state, but I know to cut a woman some slack. What matters here is not so much the truth as what we believe to be the truth. I suffer no doubts when it comes to your loyalty. I believe it to be true. And that makes me your greatest protection.

She said nothing.

—Your father always wanted you behind a desk in decrypt. He thought you'd be safe and still using your gifts for king and country, still doing your duty. But you wanted to be in the field. Is that still true?

—Yes.

Neville stood up from his chair and gestured to the isochronic map on the wall above a case of leather-bound books. Blobs of colour, fading and darkening in zones, spread from one country to another, indicating travel times by steamer and rail. Stroking the pads of his fingers from Leningrad to Moscow, Moscow to Odessa, Odessa to Vladivostok, Neville looked over his shoulder at Temerity. —One thing we've noticed in the Russian decrypt is bullets. The Bolshies use rather a lot of bullets. At the same time, Stalin has hauled this immense union of states from a medieval existence to what he calls a radiant future. Electrification, paved roads, metros, and radio: how have they done it so fast? Is it like St. Petersburg—sorry, Leningrad — built on the bones of slaves? We need more agents on the ground, Miss West. We need to know what the hell is going on.

On the ground. Temerity thought of the giant fowls' feet of Baba Yaga's cottage tramping up dust.

Neville jabbed his finger at Moscow. —Redemption, Miss West. You've got the language.

—Will I have any contacts?

—Ah, well, it seems we've run into some difficulty there.

—What?

—People disappear in Russia.

Temerity took a deep breath. —Passive listening, observe and report?

Neville pursed his lips, licked them, clicked his tongue. —A little deeper. Short romance abroad, that sort of thing. An NKVD man would be ideal.

She gave a start. —Freeman.

—You're not going to tell me you're worried about your virtue? I am well aware you've obtained precautions. After all, you didn't want the pitter-patter of little Brownbury-Rees feet.

The doctor's disdain as he'd fitted Temerity for a cervical cap, his cynical comments on the loose wedding band she wore and on his own burden of conflicted conscience: *Department-issued ring? It keeps me awake at night, you know, granting contraception in the name of king and country to unmarried women who then defile themselves.*

Cheeks burning, Temerity forced herself to look Neville in the eye. —You think some battered old Chekist will risk a bullet to the head for thirty seconds between my legs?

—Men have risked far more for such a pleasure.

She stared at her glass.

Then she nodded.

Neville clapped his hands together. —Excellent. Steamer to Leningrad, rail to Moscow. Write nothing down, not even in cipher, because you'd not want to be found with ciphered notes in Russia, now, would you? Our cryptanalysis shows regular interference with the post, so letters, even to the embassy, are out, except as a very last resort. You'll have two passports but only one set of matching travel papers. They'll be in the name of Margaret Bush. Oh, I did have fun inventing her. Margaret Bush is not on speaking terms with her family except for her dear Auntie Agatha. So write to auntie once you've arrived to let her know you're settled in, and, if things do seem to be going a bit wrong, get word to the embassy about coming down with flu.

—Flu? But you just said—

—Oh, don't goggle at me like that. Get in, charm some poor bastard until he tells everything he knows, get out. We'll have your return tickets booked. By the time you come back, any concerns here about you leaving your post in Spain will have blown over. Yes, yes, I know, you did your best. Just keep your Margaret Bush travel papers and passport separate from your Temerity West passport. If worse comes to worst, you might need your real self. The Bolshies don't know one end of a British passport from the other, but our own embassy wallahs might spot the fake, and if you need their help, then you'll need that real passport. Of course, it won't come to that. I don't mind saying, I jolly well wish I could go, too, if only to snap a few photos of St. Basil's in Red Square. Do you know how Ivan the Terrible kept the architect's secrets? He ordered the man's tongue hacked out and his hands cut off.

Temerity knew that to be apocryphal nonsense. She also knew that Neville had mispronounced *Ivan*. Too weary to argue, she faked interest by nodding.

Neville smiled, pleased to get such a reaction. —Chin up. You'll be fine. Just mind your own hands and tongue. That's a joke, Miss West. Perhaps you'll appreciate it when you're feeling better.

[ ]

DOG'S HEADS AND BROOMSTICKS 1
Moscow
Tuesday 25 May

Grey and green, grey and green, grey and green: the colours of the room looked like phlegm coughed up during flu. The walls, the ceiling, the floor, even the bench where he slouched stripped interest and desire from Kostya's mind and seemed to press, press, press. This tedium only sharpened the pain in his shoulder. Several hours now with no food, no water, no cigarettes, no toilet, no one to speak with, nothing to read: just him and this locked room at Moscow-Leningradsky Station. It didn't look like an office. Or a broom closet. Or a tiny canteen for workers to eat meals. It looked like an interrogation room, and waiting here, for the first time the prisoner and not the secret police officer, fake identification confiscated, all certainties upended, reminded Kostya of how he felt the day he nearly drowned as young child. He'd not understood that he was drowning. Bubbles surrounded him, wobbling in their ascent to the surface, and as he followed their path, he saw tree branches and sky. When he reached for a bubble and missed, his fingertips now ten, twenty, thirty centimetres from the surface, he recognized first the reversal of expectations and then his peril. *I can't touch the air,* he thought, *and I can't feel the bottom. Is this dangerous?* Then, as he panicked, a fury of bubbles flew past his face and broke the surface, and his grandfather reached into the water and hauled him out.

For what seemed like the hundredth time, Kostya pushed his long hair out of his face and combed through his beard with the fingers of his right hand. His left arm, out of the sling but still weak, lay close to his side. His body and clothes still smelled of delousing gas, and his skin felt itchy and bitten.

Time slugged past.

Despite his fears, he dozed.

The scrape of a key in the lock woke him up.

An NKVD captain entered, his tailored uniform obscuring his growing paunch, his body language speaking of old discipline and graceful strength. His close-cropped hair, blond with some grey, looked as coarse as beard stubble; his hazel eyes, surrounded by squint lines, seemed gentle. He carried nothing in his hands.

Kostya stood up and saluted.

Boris removed his cap and placed it on the table. —At ease, Konstantin Arkadievich. Sit down.

Startled by his first name and patronymic instead of surname, this captain a stranger, after all, Kostya obeyed.

—I'm Boris Aleksandrovich Kuznets, and I'm sorry. I meant to be here hours ago.

—Am I under arrest?

—Whatever for?

—Comrade Captain, I—

—We're alone. You may call me Boris Aleksandrovich.

Kostya had never invited a prisoner to call him by name and patronymic. —Ah, thank you, Boris Aleksandrovich.

Boris studied him. —Are you ill?

—I'm fine, just concerned.

—Why?

—My recall from Spain.

Boris shook his head. —Your gift with languages was recognized and put to use. Later, it was felt you'd served long enough and deserved to come home. It's been ten months. You did want to come home?

—Of course.

—Very good, but keep it all quiet, for now. Consider your little evacuation a rehearsal.

Kostya blinked several times. —With respect, we got children free of a war zone. How is that theatre?

—Now we know Spanish children, or at least the boys, will survive the journey this far north. Some of our scientists thought a Spaniard with his southern blood might freeze to death on the way. There are still concerns about the winter, but now that we know they're hardy enough to travel we can save many more of them and show the Western powers how to treat refugees. I don't understand why you're upset. It got you home.

Kostya felt himself bare of old expectations. NKVD agents did not form emotional connections. If they did, they could not best perform their duties. Admitting why he felt upset meant admitting a weakness. He said it anyway. —I didn't say goodbye.

Boris leaned forward, eyes concerned. —Goodbye?

—I sailed with those boys for two weeks. I got to know them. I told them stories, I taught them to say Russian phrases, and I started them on the alphabet. And I told them that no one, no one, has the right to call them *bezprizorniki*, because a human being is not now, not ever, a stray dog. When we got to Leningrad, NKVD officers separated us. I got searched, and the boys got marched away.

—Anyone who returns get searched, Konstantin Arkadievich.

—It wasn't the search. I just…

—You're tired. Do you need a moment? Tell me about the injury to your arm.

—Shoulder. Almost a month ago. Gerrikaitz.

Boris held out his hands, asking for more.

—The twenty-sixth of April. The Luftwaffe bombed Gerrikaitz in the morning, then Gernika in the afternoon. It's in my preliminary report. I know it's brief, but it's hard to write at sea.

—That's fine. And Minenkov?

Kostya traced his fingertip around a whorl in the table. *Misha.*

—Konstantin Arkadievich, I know what you wrote, but I need to hear you say it. Where did you last see Mikhail Petrovich Minenkov?

—Gerrikaitz. The morning of the bombing.

—And after the bombing?

Kostya shook his head.

Taking a deep breath, Boris shifted his weight on the bench. —I need you to come into Lubyanka tomorrow, for a more formal debriefing with myself and another captain. Paperwork. As for me, I'm quite satisfied. Your father's waiting outside.

—Who, Balakirev? With respect, Boris Aleksandrovich, Arkady Dmitrievich Balakirev is not my father.

For just a moment, Boris looked alarmed. —The way he speaks of you, I assumed he was.

—Many people do. He's looked after me since I was twelve. I was a *bezprizornik*, after all.

—But you told the boys—

—Not now, not ever, a stray dog. Yes, I told them that. Just like Arkady Dmitrievich told me.

Boris placed his cap back on his head, and Kostya admired the shade of blue, familiar, yet alien. He owned two such caps. Like the rest of his uniform pieces, they waited in a closet at Arkady's house. Sitting here, detained for interrogation, however gentle, he felt that he'd never worn such a cap. He had, of course, almost every day for thirteen years now, yet that past self felt as distant as the sky, as the surface of the water on the day he'd nearly drowned.

Boris looked stern. —A word of advice, Konstantin Arkadievich. You've endured hardship in the name of duty, but this is no excuse for allowing emotions to flood the mind. I can tell from your manner of speech you've been abroad. You sound loose, and—

—I—

—And you interrupt. Don't.

After a moment, Kostya nodded.

Boris reached into the pouch on his *portupeya*, took out a red leather wallet, and slid it across the table. —Now, let me be the first to welcome you home.

Kostya picked it up, opened it: his true identification, not the Tikhon fakes. —Thank you.

Boris tapped on the door to signal to the guard outside to open it, and as they emerged into a larger office, Kostya caught sight of a big man in an NKVD uniform with major's insignia hunched over in a chair. Thighs almost filling his *galife* pants, belly harassing the confines of his *gymnastyorka* and *portupeya*, Arkady held his cap in his wide hands. His fleshy neck claimed his jawline, and oval spectacles magnified his brown eyes. He'd gone bald on top. The remaining hair, trimmed short on the back of his head and over his ears, showed scattered white hairs in the dark grey. So did his heavy moustache. His eyebrows remained black.

—Arkady Dmitrievich?

Arkady looked up, and Kostya almost cried out. Kostya called Arkady *old man* in his thoughts, had done so since they'd met. Today, Arkady looked the part: sorrowful, worried, worn.

Arkady pulled on his cap and strode to Kostya, arms wide. —Welcome home, Little Tatar, welcome home.

Speech fled as the floor crashed into Kostya's knees.

Arkady called to Boris. —Kuznets!

Already hurrying to his next appointment, Boris did not look back. —Tell him ten o'clock tomorrow morning, my office.

Kostya noticed a buckle-worn spot on Arkady's *portupeya* and recalled how amber worry beads once hung there. Then he noticed nothing at all.

[ ]

BEDSIDE MANNER
Friday 28 May

Arkady Dmitrievich Balakirev loathed doctors. His friend Vadym
Minenkov once stated as a scientific fact — after too much vodka
— that Arkady felt this way not only as part of the class struggle
but as a personal penance. Arkady's father had been a doctor who
then married a wealthy woman, and they'd raised their one child in
some luxury. Vadym had further mused on patronymics and how one
would hope to love or at least respect one's father, for one could never
be free of his name. Arkady then told Vadym he was full of shit. In
truth, Arkady feared doctors, not for their own sake — what, those
pathetic intellectuals, those arrogant parasites? — but as signals of
mortality and so often helpless.

Arkady shifted his weight in the wooden chair and looked down
at Kostya, dosed with morphine and bromides and receiving fluids by
an IV. Tucked away in this private room, Kostya had slept and slept,
almost three days now. *Rest,* every doctor consulted had said, *he needs
rest.* Dr. Scherba, standing on the other side of Kostya's bed, had not
uttered anything so facile, so obvious. Not yet, at least.

Dr. Efim Scherba, a short man with bright blue eyes, nearly bald
with tight greying curls round his ears and the back of his head,
studied an X-ray film and did his best to ignore Arkady. This Major
Balakirev, his case officer while seconded to Moscow for medical
research, reminded Efim of a wild boar: cunning, self-interested, dangerous. The X-ray film, an image of Kostya's left shoulder and upper
arm, showed many tiny pieces of shrapnel, some of it embedded in
bone. Efim could guess the patient also suffered from muscle and
nerve injury. Sighing, he looked up from the film.

Arkady raised his heavy eyebrows. —Well?

Pretending not to hear Arkady, Efim held the X-ray at a different angle and considered his arrival in Moscow a few hours before. He still felt dizzy with the speed of it all. He'd expected to travel to Moscow later in August, with his wife, Olga. Instead, Leningrad NKVD had knocked on his door, told him the new job started immediately, to pack his bag and please hurry. Olga had also grabbed clothes from a closet, only to flinch when an NKVD officer placed a hand on her shoulder: *Not you, only the Comrade Doctor.* In those last moments of privacy, the NKVD officers kind enough to wait in the hall, Efim and Olga whispered about obedience and risk. *It's morning,* Olga pointed out, adding socks to Efim's pile of undershorts, *not night, so it's not an arrest, and if the university in Moscow needs you now, then you must go.* Efim tore shirts from hangers, asking *Then why no letter or telegram? Why* NKVD *at the door? Is it the abortions?* Olga tried to fix Efim's collar, reminding him thousands of doctors had performed abortions when the procedure was legal, so why would NKVD object to that? Neither of them mentioned the several disappeared colleagues and friends. Then Olga insisted she'd be fine, as safe as anyone else in Leningrad. Efim hardly found that comforting. *It's Moscow, not Kolyma,* Olga had said as the officers, sounding less polite now, warned Efim they had only a few minutes to catch the train. Olga's last whisper: *Spare me a martyrdom. Just be a good doctor.*

When Efim's train pulled into Moscow, NKVD officers gathered on the platform. Holster flaps open, they made no attempt at subtlety. One of them, a heavy man in his fifties perhaps, or hard-worn forties, some old Chekist with a thick moustache, and in command — Major Balakirev — spoke with a train guard, and the train guard pointed to Efim's carriage. As the officers boarded, Arkady scanned the crowd. He spotted his prey, pointed at Efim, then made a chopping gesture with his other hand. The other officers shouted for the passengers to leave, which they did, shoving one another aside in their hurry. Once rid of the passengers, Arkady ordered the other officers to leave and stand guard outside at the carriage doors.

Arkady then settled himself in the seat next to Efim and asked to see his papers. Before Efim could produce them, Arkady waved his hand and explained that asking for Efim's papers was just a little joke. *I know who you are, Dr. Scherba. Welcome to Moscow. Now let's get you settled in at Laboratory of Special Purpose Number Two. No, no, it's not part of the university.* Neck cold with sweat, Efim objected, pointed out the mistake. Arkady dug out a wad of folded papers from the pouch on the belt of his *portupeya*, pressed it flat with his hand, and pointed at a signature. Efim's signature. Well, a competent forgery signalling his acceptance of the position of senior medical officer at the Laboratory of Special Purpose Number Two. *Number Two?* Efim asked. *Yes, Number Two,* Arkady said, *plenty of special purpose in Moscow. We need to stop by the hospital first. You'll find life moves faster here than in Leningrad.*

Now, a few hours later, standing in a room of a Moscow hospital where he had no privileges, his suitcase near the door, Efim stared at an X-ray film and prepared to offer advice.

Scraping the chair on the floor, Arkady heaved his bulk and stood up. —You've had long enough. Tell me what you think.

—The patient has sustained shrapnel injuries, and he's exhausted. He can be treated here first, then moved to a rest home.

Arkady took the X-ray film. —A rest home?

Efim almost asked for the film back, to confirm the patient's name, which he must have misread. *Nikto?* —Proper convalescence, recovery in fresh air and sunshine, plenty of *kumis* to drink, and no physical strain until he is ready to resume work.

—He's ready now.

—He's unconscious. And he's got fourteen pieces of shrapnel in him.

—Splinters.

—If nothing else, the strain on his nervous system—

—His nerves are fine.

—If you're so certain, Comrade Major, then why do you ask my opinion?

Arkady strode to the hand-washing sink and turned on a faucet. Then he took out a lighter, ignited a flame, and held it to the X-ray film. —He needs to work. It's as simple as...shit!

The nitrate film burned and melted faster than Arkady expected. He manoeuvred the remnants beneath the water stream. Smoke rose.

Efim decided not to warn the major that his actions could well clog the drain. Instead, he tried to fan smoke away from the patient. —What do you want from me, Comrade Major?

—Help. First, however, I will help you. I've found you a flat. I'm sure you'd prefer that to sleeping at the youth hostel. Moscow's housing shortage is worse than Leningrad's, but you were promised a flat as part of the job.

A nurse opened the door and peeked in. —Comrades, why do I smell something burning in here?

Arkady ignited his lighter. —I smoke.

She studied him, then backed away and let the door ease shut.

Efim thought he noticed Arkady smirk as he tucked his lighter into a pocket. —Major Balakirev, when can Olga join me?

—Who is Olga?

Efim suspected, hoped, dared not believe, that Arkady teased him as he had on the train. —Olga Nikolaieva Aristarkhova, my wife.

—Kept her own name, then? A modern woman. And Scherba: Jewish?

Blaming the stench of melted film and not his clammy fear, Efim thought he might vomit. —Latvian.

—Pardon me. Doctors and the like, I thought...

—Secular Latvian.

—Secular Latvian it is. Scherba is also a kind of soup. Dr. Soup. It might go well with *doktorskaya kolbasa*. Never thought to change it to Scherbakov?

—No.

—Why won't you treat Nikto with phage therapy? You're an expert.

Now Efim felt dizzy. Did official interrogations progress so, like some map with palsy, borders twitching? And who the hell was this patient called Nobody? A prisoner? —Phage therapy is no use here. The patient has no infection, by some miracle.

—Miracles ceased to exist in 1917. And what has infection got to do with it?

—It's what phage therapy fights. *Phage* means devour. What preys on a bacterium? A virus. What drives a virus? Reproduction. And they're hard to kill, if they're even alive. A virus can lie dormant in permafrost until thawed and still swarm a patient. So we learn the language of the virus, whet its appetite for specific bacteria, inject it into the patient who's already ill, and let it hunt the infection.

—Civil war in the patient's body?

—The end result is a cure.

Arkady nodded. —Justifies the means. Can you set these phages on a different target? On healthy cells, for example?

Efim saw the teeth of the trap. Oh, this Major Balakirev understood phage therapy well enough. —In theory, yes.

—But in your heart, no?

—Comrade Major, I'm a doctor.

—A doctor assigned to Laboratory of Special Purpose Number Two. A specialist in your field.

—Now, wait—

—What did you say your wife is called?

Shutting his eyes, Efim thought he could smell Olga's perfume, Krasnaya Moskva. He didn't bother to answer.

Arkady spoke, and the borders twitched again. —Tell me, is it true about you and the train?

—Is what true?

—You served on a medical train in the civil war?

—Yes.

—And made it a point of honour to treat any patients you en-countered, Red or White?

—When I could.

—Once jumped off the train to do so?

Efim opened his eyes and met Arkady's gaze. —Well, it hadn't got up to speed.

Arkady laughed, the way he might at a precocious child who'd interrupted a party to share wisdom, and the sound woke Kostya, who, too weak and drugged to move, simply lay there, working to open his eyes. Neither Arkady nor Efim noticed.

Efim waited for Arkady to finish laughing. —You mentioned a flat.

—Yes, yes, the housing shortage. I've looked into your case, and I made some arrangements. Twelve square metres per person is the ideal, and we can't always meet that. At first, Comrade Doctor, they had you listed to share a sixty-square-metre flat with a family of six. Here, take the chair, you look like you need to sit down. As I said, sixty square metres with six other people, make it seven in total, that's, oh, just over eight square metres per person, less walls and furniture and the rest of it. I flagged this in your file as unacceptable. Your work will be difficult, and you will need your rest. So I've found you a ninety-square-metre flat, new building, fresh paint, partly furnished, two bedrooms, a front room, a kitchen, a bathroom with a shower and hot running water, which you must share with only one other person.

—One other person being my wife?

—No. Don't go so pale; it's not me. It's him. And now that I've helped you, here's how I want you to help me. Look after this man and keep him fit for duty.

Efim glanced at Kostya, then looked back at Arkady. —I can't do that.

—Why not?

—He's ill, exhausted, and injured. He needs to convalesce.

—I've just explained, he needs to work, and you need a flat where you can rest. All I want is for you to keep your doctor's eye on the one person, one, with whom you share these ninety square metres. Understand me yet?

You don't give a damn about my rest. You want me to run a creche. Despite telling himself to shut up and not antagonize the NKVD major, not get himself shot, Efim continued. —If he's so precious, then why can't he live with you?

—He did, once. We argued.

—Is he your son?

—No.

Efim took a deep breath. —And my wife?

—We can discuss it again in a few months, if your work goes well. Arrangements for Aristarkhova would be out of my hands, though I can put in a word. Meantime my colleagues in Leningrad will keep an eye to her. She's alone there, I understand. Her sister died not long ago, and, of course, you have no children.

—You know all of that?

Arkady raised his eyebrows, tilted his head to one side.

Embarrassed, Efim nodded and acquiesced. —There was a mistake on the X-ray film. What's his name?

—Nikto.

Efim took a deep breath, said nothing.

Kostya still couldn't open his eyes or speak. *It's true,* he tried to say. *My name is Konstantin Arkadievich Nikto, and I can't fucking move.*

He managed a grunt. The sound got lost beneath Arkady continuing to instruct Efim on the pragmatics of Moscow life.

[ ]

HOMO SOVIETICUS
Friday 4 June–Sunday 6 June

Standing before a dozen children aged five to twelve in a tiny room in Moscow's Hotel Lux, Temerity spoke in English. —Dismissed.

The students stood up in unison, inclined their heads to their teacher, and replied in English. The accents of their parents faded more each day. —Thank you, Comrade Bush.

Courtesy and discipline displayed, the class broke into two groups, girls and boys. The girls gathered to talk among themselves, while the boys ran off, shouting of games. They'd all switched to Russian, obeying the standing order, sometimes dipping into German or French for this word or that, and improvising a new vernacular. This had long been the hope: the children of Comintern unified in their ability and desire to overcome language barriers. When first gathering at Hotel Lux, Comintern members wasted no time setting up language classes. The Kremlin regarded these classes with increasing suspicion. For now, the children's language studies could continue, so long as the children spoke Russian outside class.

Restriction after restriction: many of Comintern's hopes had stalled. Comintern members had come together from all over Europe, devoted to the ideals of revolution, ready to work for economic justice and world peace. Herded into Hotel Lux, which soon became its own tiny world, they met their comrades from other countries, shared stories of the struggle to get to the Soviet Union, of terrible fights with their families and financial ruin. Yet for all their conviction, their devotion to world socialism, restrictions now fell on them like snow, until Hotel Lux earned a nickname: the Golden Cage of Comintern. Security reasons, comrades. It won't last long. It's all for your own safety. Comintern members accepted these restrictions, sometimes with grumbling, sometimes with a shrill or hissed reminder of the dangers of traitors and spies. Radio Moscow assured listeners that the Kremlin reeled from act after act of treason, espionage, sabotage, and other depravities fit only to file under the shameful labels of Trotskyism and anti-Soviet activities, and so the Kremlin must, with both sadness and steely resolve, examine loyalties. The members of Comintern — now called not comrades but foreigners — found themselves high on the list. Day by day the air in Hotel Lux seemed to sour. Hotel staff, so many of them, appeared from corners and shadows, saying nothing, just listening, their faces often stern.

For all the sternness, Temerity also saw emotion, mostly fear, flicker in the hotel workers' eyes, and she wondered what the penalties for hotel staff might be if Comintern members misbehaved. She'd gone outside the hotel herself only twice since arriving on the thirty-first of May, both times to visit the nearby food store Gastronom, and both times facing many questions from hotel staff when she returned.

Grateful for the open door and some fresher air, Temerity collected the exercise books. *Go*, she wanted to tell the girls, *run, play*. She thought of their parents. The adults often gathered in the communal kitchen and talked, standing around, sometimes drinking tea — mostly women, far fewer men. Rumours among the Comintern members suggested that NKVD considered fathers the easiest prey, docile in prison and submissive under interrogation, all to protect wife and children.

Radio Moscow broke past her thoughts. Speakers blessed every hallway and room, and these speakers lacked a switch. Until the station signed off at night, one could only reduce the volume, never extinguish the sound. Temerity had just taught a class on various English greetings over a muffled yet insistent report on oppressive conditions in the British Empire. Now, the announcer gave the time and introduced a Tchaikovsky recording. Temerity rolled her eyes. This huge country and its embarrassment of riches when it came to composers, and yet Radio Moscow played Tchaikovsky, Tchaikovsky, Tchaikovsky.

A child collided with her and then spoke startled English as he retreated a few steps. —Comrade Bush, I am sorry!

Mikko Toppinen, Temerity's brightest student, and, if she must choose, her favourite. Aged ten, Mikko already spoke excellent Russian alongside his native Finnish, and he could manage good French. He craved language the same way Temerity did, breathed it, and in his spare time he worked on a large drawing of a complex series of staircases that curved, intersected, overlapped, and sometimes twisted into diacritical and punctuation marks. *Babel Interior*, he called it.

—Comrade Bush, are you hurt?

—No, I'm fine. You carry on.

He ran off, joining the other boys in a noisy game.

A hotel worker, carrying linens in her arms, gave Temerity a long look.

Temerity nodded acknowledgement. —Comrade.

Ursula Friesen emerged from behind the hotel worker and greeted Temerity in loud Russian. Strands of her greying blond hair fell loose from her bun and framed her face, and her Berlin accent, which strengthened when she got tired, reminded Temerity of childhood visits to the *Weihnachtsmarkt* and, therefore, ginger cookies. When Temerity told her this, Ursula had first frowned, then chuckled. *So I am a Britisher's gingerbread woman?* —Margaret, there you are. All done with language class, comrade?

Temerity offered Ursula her arm, and they walked together down the corridor to the stairwell. They didn't bother trying the tiny yet stylized lift that Temerity called the art deco coffin. It rarely worked.

Ursula, almost the same height as Temerity, leaned in to murmur in her ear. —Laugh when I finish, as though I'm telling you a joke. Tell Mikko he must take greater care and speak only Russian outside the classroom.

Temerity gave a soft laugh, hoping it sounded genuine.

Another hotel worker watched them until they passed the threshold to the stairwell.

On the stairs, Temerity thought Ursula looked old, much older than forty, tired, and starved for sunlight. She'd not ventured outside Hotel Lux for almost three months.

—Ursula, Mikko was just showing off.

—Yes, and it could get us all in trouble. He should understand that. If he doesn't, then you must make him understand.

As Temerity opened the stairwell door, she revealed yet another hotel worker, standing there as if by design. The three women nodded acknowledgement and continued on their paths.

Ursula sounded cheerful. —Shall we freshen up and make some supper?

The communal kitchen, where diapers might boil in one pot and fowl in another and still not cut through the lingering stench of vinegar, cabbage, and lard, left Temerity with little appetite. —Not hungry, thank you.

—At least have a cup of tea. You Britishers always want some tea.

—The samovar baffles me.

—I'll do it. You go sit down, maybe write some letters.

Temerity almost laughed. —So I can give the hotel staff something new to read?

Ursula pretended not to hear.

Temerity told herself to be more considerate of her friend's fears. —Thank you, Ursula. I'd love some tea.

NKVD Garage Number One. Same old spot, same old racket of execution's gunfire, same old cars, Ford Model As, manufactured under license in Moscow, painted matte black and nicknamed ravens. Kostya nodded to the older officer in the passenger seat, Gleb Denisovich Kamenev, checked his watch — shortly before two in the morning — and eased the vehicle into the night.

Kostya's latest argument with Arkady, days old now, still rattled about his head. The old man murmured about the machinery of revolution, gears loose and cogs jammed, purges misled. Arkady dared not mention the arrest of former NKVD chief Genrikh Yagoda, and Kostya, feeling at once loose and jammed himself, ignoring his memories of Spain, craved order and refused to think of Yagoda. He wanted to bury himself in work, as he'd always done, so he might silence not just Arkady's sudden doubts but his own. *You're getting paranoid,* he told Arkady. *I'm out of hospital, and I just got a promotion. No one is out to get me. Or you.*

Under the car's wheels, asphalt surrendered to cobblestones. Contradictory signage, warning of construction and offering impossible detours, interrupted the headlight beams.

Kostya braked the car and peered through the windshield. —What the barrelling fuck is this?

Gleb gave the barest of grunts. Nonsensical road signs, an everyday occurrence, merited nothing else.

—That's no help, Gleb Denisovich.

Shadows fell on Gleb's thin face, hiding his drunkard's flush. —If we turn left and take the alley behind the . . . no, wait, it's blocked at one end.

Kostya closed his eyes and bowed his head. —Signs should make sense. I just want the signs to make sense. Am I asking too much?

Gleb grunted again, his tone disapproving. Smart officers knew better.

Kostya accelerated. Ignoring Gleb's warnings of rough road and narrow ways, his doubts of just what punishment the car's suspension could take, Kostya drove around the various signs and navigated by memory. Apart from knocking over a detour sign shaped like an arrow, he encountered no difficulty. Either the workers had completed the signalled construction, or, more likely, they'd not yet begun. Perhaps they waited on a permit.

Gleb studied Kostya a moment. He'd known Kostya Nikto for years, teaching him as a cadet. He'd considered young Nikto a most promising student then and a most promising officer now, and he'd remarked several times this week that he felt no surprise at Nikto's promotion to senior lieutenant. The wounded ear and shoulder, the sunken face: Nikto had earned a reward. Besides, Gleb now added to himself, sneaking a nip from his flask and tasting his limp moustache, with NKVD in such flux, the ranks might yet change again, and an experienced and overlooked longtime sergeant like Gleb Kamenev should soon find himself drawing more pay and respect.

Kostya accepted the scrutiny and ignored the flask. Gleb's dedication, loyalty, and, above all, results meant no one wished to examine his drinking. Besides, it seemed all the old Chekists drank.

Gleb checked his watch as Kostya parked. —Two o'clock. Dead on time.

—We are, yes. Where the hell is the rest of the squad?

Ursula tapped on Temerity's door. —Margaret? Are you awake?

Temerity flicked on a lamp, relieved to find electricity still flowed. Then she checked her watch, which read two in the morning, and freed herself of the bedsheets. —I am now.

—I can't sleep. Would you play backgammon with me?

Ursula had extended this same invitation on Temerity's second night at Hotel Lux, explaining how backgammon calmed her. *Many nights I don't sleep well.*

None of the hotel residents slept well. While one could almost smell NKVD paranoia, one could not predict a date for the raids, only the likely time: the hours of deep sleep, between one and four in the morning. Those left behind by the arrest of a loved one, sleep wrecked, might then sit up for the rest of the night or stumble back to bed and doze, fear now shot through with relief and guilt: not me, not me, not me.

Temerity freshened her perfume. Despite the warm and stuffy air, she felt chilled. She recalled a night during her first social season in London when she'd ducked the supervision of her Aunt Min and joined several other debutantes to visit a nightclub. The clock struck two as she sneaked back into the family's London flat, and Min, still sitting up, provided a thorough tongue-lashing. That night, too, had been warm, and Temerity had shivered in dread, though not, she told herself, of Min's anger. She shivered the way she had when, as a child, she'd pushed the book of Russian fairy tales from her father's hands. When the book fell to the floor, pages up, Baba Yaga's hut, half-hidden by trees, still lurked behind Vasilisa. Something, it seemed, waited for Vasilisa and Temerity.

Ursula called again. —Margaret?

—Give me a minute.

Down the hall, in a room not used by Comintern guests, a telephone rang, rang, rang.

Scowling, Temerity rolled on her stockings and recalled Neville Freeman's definition of a Londoner: born within the sound of Bow Bells. Temerity, he would add, being born on the Kurseong House estate, could not call herself a Londoner. Moscow, like London, had once kept time by church bells; Moscow's bells belonged to memory. Shoved from belfries, many bells cracked, even shattered. Some survived their crash. The condition of the bells hardly mattered past the gesture, the theatre of the fall. The rougher pragmatics of fire took over as smiths melted the bells and reforged them into more useful items, like parts for locomotives and strong locks for heavy doors.

Temerity opened her door; the telephone's jangle fell silent.

Temerity started in German and finished in Russian as she followed Ursula into her room. —I'm sorry. I was thousands of miles away.

Closing the door and pointing to a rickety table where the backgammon game waited, Ursula smiled. —I'm glad you enjoy backgammon. I thought I wouldn't find another partner.

Ursula's first backgammon partner had disappeared, arrested by NKVD on the last night of May, the same night Temerity had arrived at Hotel Lux. Ursula spoke of her friend's arrest in a roundabout way, almost a code, because she feared hidden microphones. *How else,* she'd argued in fierce whispers, *could* NKVD *know so much?*

Temerity wanted to scoff, yet as each day passed, she, too, could believe more in the hidden microphones. Ursula preferred hidden microphones as an idea, as an article of faith, to any acknowledgement of NKVD using torture. Her adherence to communism an exercise in intellect and empathy after the spectacular worldwide failure of capitalism in the early 1930s, Ursula struggled to avoid the gall of truth: revolutions betrayed. The Great Purge, she reasoned, cleansed away only the guilty, the traitors, the filth of society. Those who disappeared must, on some level, deserve such treatment. Otherwise, nothing made sense.

Struggling with these thoughts, Ursula sought distraction. She found it in Temerity's wafting perfume. —You smell so nice.

Temerity smiled as she dropped dice into the leather-edged cup. Before leaving London, she'd purchased a bottle of Shalimar perfume and a Stratton compact, both luxuries, as potential bribes. Now, she wanted to keep them, wield these expensive pleasures in — what, defiance? No, certainty of self, or at least an attempt at it. She'd worn Shalimar back in England, if against her father's wishes; she would wear it in Russia. The chip in the stopper, a souvenir of rough seas, hardly mattered.

Ursula tapped a pencil, rhythms random, against the table edge. This action, she'd explained, disrupted sound waves; any eavesdropper must struggle to listen. Temerity doubted the power of a pencil against eavesdroppers and hidden mics. Still, like Ursula, she now kept a pencil in her handbag.

Temerity rattled dice in the cup.

Ursula dropped the pencil.

Temerity shook the dice some more.

On her knees, Ursula retrieved the pencil and used it to point to the east wall, where she suspected microphone placement. Then she stood up and commented in a clear voice on how much she'd enjoyed the sugar in her coffee. Temerity agreed, yes, the sugar had been lovely, too bad it's been scarce, but surely next week the hotel would have plenty of sugar.

As the dice clattered on the table, Temerity considered how best to ask a cold and cynical question: did NKVD have quotas? Could these arrests and disappearances, supposedly the workings of law and justice, of crime and punishment, truly be nothing more than a tool of terror? Too soon, she told herself. Even if Ursula suspected quotas, she'd dare not say so. Not yet.

Ursula pitched her voice a little too high. —Good roll.

Temerity nodded, smiled a little, then moved her token.

Ears keen, ready for car engines and booted footsteps, for knuckles and fists on doors, they played the round.

And then another.

Kostya lit a cigarette and glanced up at the building, a block of flats, unusually high with its seven floors and only a few years old, much like the one where he now lived. Arkady had bribed, or threatened, the right people. Arkady himself still lived in a two-storey house inherited from his parents, and he'd raised Kostya there from age twelve. Never married, Arkady now lived alone. When first released from hospital, Kostya had stayed with Arkady, sleeping in his old bedroom, these days made over into a study that Arkady never used, and he felt great surprise at how much he wanted to stay. He could not explain it. Not long before leaving for Spain, he'd argued with Arkady, both men shouting, about his need to live on his own, free of Arkady and Vadym's supervision. Now he wished to return to this house and bask in its familiarity.

Change, Arkady said over and over, things had changed while Kostya was in Spain, deep and drastic change. Arkady's new anxiety, the way he cautioned Kostya against vague menace and then deflected questions, the way he ordered that poor bastard Dr. Scherba around, all made Kostya worry about the old man's sanity. Then again, Arkady treated all doctors and intellectuals with a Chekist's contempt. When Kostya demanded concrete examples of this mysterious change, Arkady changed the subject to Kostya's new independence and flat, throwing Kostya's own words back at him. *You're thirty-two years old, Tatar. You should have moved out long ago. You don't need me breathing down your neck.* When Kostya learned that Dr. Scherba, of all people, would also be his flatmate, Scherba no doubt under pressure to report to Arkady, Kostya gave Arkady an exasperated look. Arkady shrugged. *It's a complete coincidence,* he'd said. *Well, you both need a place to live, don't you?*

So, Kostya reassured himself, after a detention, a hospital stay, and a recovery, he now had a modern flat just a few minutes' walk from Vasilisa Prekrasnaya on the new metro line, a promotion with a raise in pay and prestige, and a promise that the Spanish boys would be looked after. Life looked good. At his new Lubyanka desk, one with a locking drawer, Kostya had faced his first task with vigour, then irritation, then rising dismay: the review of junior officers' paperwork. He corrected spelling and grammar. He double-checked quotas. He asked himself how reliable NKVD records could be with so many errors. He also chewed his nails down to the quick and discovered he could not sleep for visions of ink-smutched forms spewing like steam from the wounds in his shoulder.

After a few days of this disorienting misery, of new questions and doubts about NKVD procedure and possible reasons for it, Kostya had scraped up the courage to ask the acting department head — the second man to fill this position in a week — when he might expect a return to more active work. Within the hour, he received an order to report for night duty. Arkady, visiting Kostya's office when the order arrived, read it and just shook his head. *Be careful what you wish for, Tatar. At least it's not* poligon *duty.*

Night duty: a tiresome chore and one which did not rotate across departments as often as it should. Junior officers carried out much of the work of raid and arrest under the supervision, often nominal, of a slightly senior officer, while the more senior officers relished their day shifts of paperwork and interrogation assistance. The younger and fitter men did much of the physical work in an interrogation, though exceptions occurred. Sometimes an old Chekist took over, eager to prove, if only to himself, his vigour and zeal. Kostya, as yet unsure what his injured shoulder could handle, had told himself to hide behind his new rank and order subordinates to carry out the beatings. Besides, his expertise lay elsewhere.

Still staring up at the block of flats, Kostya sighed, and a long stream of cigarette smoke wafted round his head. Electric lamps burned in various windows, giving the block the broken appearance of a censored document. In some of the lit rooms, people stood behind curtains, reduced to shadow and silhouette. Some shapes darted away; others kept their place.

Guardians, Kostya thought.

Gleb took another swallow from his flask. —Did I tell you about the ass I hauled in last week? When I knocked on the door, he greeted me with a smile so big I could see his tonsils. 'Where have you been, comrade?' he said to me. 'Why, I've been waiting for weeks now, my bags all packed and ready to go.' I played along, asked him what he'd done. 'Nothing at all,' he told me, 'which is precisely why I've been expecting you.'

Aware that Gleb might be shot for such a careless utterance, such a recognition and acknowledgement of the absurdities of the Purge, Kostya feigned distraction. Another NKVD car arrived, and two more officers joined Kostya and Gleb. The last shapes at the lighted windows flitted away.

Kostya tapped his watch. —You're late. And you left the garage first.

—Construction, Comrade Senior Lieutenant, detours.

Gleb smirked.

Kostya took papers from the pouch on his *portupeya* and passed them around. —Here are your lists. They're…

He noticed a pattern: even-numbered floors, odd-numbered flats. *Coincidence.*

Such a pattern, if it existed, would signal, in a written record, a deep and hurried cynicism: citizens arrested to fill a quota.

Quotas he double-checked.

No, we've not fallen that far. No.

Gleb's voice reached him. —Nikto, we've got more names here than room in the cars.

Kostya lit another cigarette. —So I see. Just pick one each. We'll send the other names back for another squad.

Gleb noticed a tremor in Kostya's hands and spoke in his old manner, teacher to student. —You smoke too much.

Exhaling, Kostya looked Gleb in the eye and then mimed drinking from a flask. —You have a better regimen?

—At least I'll die old and well-preserved. Those little chimneys of death will kill you before you're fifty.

—Make it forty. I'll take the top floor, Gleb Denisovich. I wouldn't want you to get winded on the stairs.

Gleb raised the back of his hand in mock-threat. —Get out of my way, child.

The other two officers looked mystified. That old workhorse Kamenev, pretending he'd strike a commanding officer, even in banter? What a night, what a night.

Grin fading, Kostya yanked open the lobby door, noticed the absence of a watchwoman — it was so often a woman, older, perhaps widowed — resumed an expression of stern officialdom, and loped up the stairs. His boot soles gave a gentle tap. Harsh smoke trailed behind him.

At the fifth floor, glad to be alone, Kostya slowed down to catch his breath. A pit of pain yawned open in his bad shoulder, and little jolts shot down his arm. He leaned on the railing, almost bending too far back to keep his balance — not that he recognized how he nearly fell. Pain stupefied him. He reached into the pouch on his *portupeya*, fearful he'd forgotten Arkady's long-ago gift of the amber worry beads. Amber met his fingers, reassured him, and as he rubbed the beads, his heartbeat slowed and his shoulder pain eased.

Below, his colleagues banged their fists on doors.

Kostya walked the final flight of stairs and emerged from the stairwell. Dim lights burned in the ceiling, naked bulbs dangling from shoddy fixtures. A third of the way down the corridor, the builders had run out of wallpaper, and the papered section ended on a crisp line: a border. Beyond it, the exposed plaster, grimy from the touch of many hands, seemed to shimmer in the poor light. It reminded Kostya of fever dreams, and he fell into the long stare. That's what he called them now, those spells when he seemed to sleep with his eyes open. One of the doctors at the hospital said Kostya had suffered concussive shocks from bombardment and must expect difficulties as his brain adapted. *Breathe,* the doctor instructed, making it sound so easy, *always remember to breathe, because you start to hyperventilate in this state. Pinch yourself, bite your lip, break the spell. Stay in the present. Your past is your enemy, and your enemy attacks you. Do not surrender to your enemy.*

The racket of his own heartbeat cramming his head, he pinched his left forearm. Hard.

Electricity hummed.

Stay in the present, good, good. The list, what did it say? Even-numbered floors, odd-numbered flats? Oh, just pick one.

He dropped the beads into his pouch and raised his fist to knock on flat number sixty-seven. Something seemed to shift in the air, as though several people moved at the same moment in the start of a dance.

Five bangs of his fist: he beat the tattoo. —Comrade!

Lights flicked on within number sixty-seven.

—Comrade, please, don't make me knock again. I've no wish to wake up the entire floor.

A small man in his fifties wearing striped pyjamas opened the door.

Kostya showed his identification, an extra step he considered a basic courtesy. Last year, before he left for Spain, his peers mocked him for such behaviour when, surely, the uniform sufficed. Kostya had insisted, saying there was no need for incivility. He now lowered his voice to a murmur, arrest, for all its theatre, being private, intimate. —Come with me.

Eyes glittering, the man looked up. —Why?

—A small matter. It shouldn't take long to straighten out.

—But why? What's the charge? What is it you think I've done?

—If I make a note of belligerence in your file, then the other officers will be harder on you.

—Wait, please, my granddaughter just moved in with us. Her mother has disappeared. My daughter. Please don't do this to us.

—Get dressed and pack a small bag.

—A bag? How long...

Kostya's voice took on a comforting tone, one a nurse might use with a seriously ill patient. —Just a few things, comrade. Then come outside. I'll wait here. Please, I don't want to disturb anyone else.

Nod slow, automatic, eyes wide and fixed on the wall behind Kostya, the man eased the door shut.

Waiting, Kostya smoked a cigarette.

Raised voices, male and female, reached him from the flat as he tapped ash onto the floor. Adults spoke quickly in raised voices. A child asked a question. Then all voices ceased.

The flat door opened. Clutching the handles of a tatty overnight bag in both his hands, the man emerged. He wore a tan coat atop striped pyjamas, and his bare ankles showed over the edges of his shoes. Someone else closed the door behind him.

Kostya took him by the upper arm, and they descended the many flights of stairs.

Outside, Gleb waited by the car. His prisoner, a pretty woman of maybe twenty, sat in the back, head bowed. Kostya guided his prisoner to the seat next to her, then climbed in behind the wheel. The woman shifted and writhed; Gleb told her to keep still. The other team of officers sat in their car, engine idling, waiting for Comrade Senior Lieutenant Nikto's signal.

Ignition, headlights.

Car doors slammed outside Hotel Lux. Ursula, fiddling with backgammon pieces and no longer trying to play, cried out.

Temerity spoke in English. —Steady the Buffs.

Not understanding the words, Ursula raised her eyebrows. Then, parsing the tone, she smiled.

Temerity smiled back, though her mouth twitched. *And what shall you do, the Right Honourable Lady Temerity West pretending to be Margaret Bush, if NKVD knock on Ursula's door? Protest? Scream? Demand a cup of tea?*

Machinery rumbled and squeaked.

Temerity rolled the dice. —At least the lift is working again.

Ursula stifled a giggle.

Down the quiet hall, to the right of Ursula's room, NKVD officers knocked on doors. Their low voices carried, and though walls and doors muffled the words, Ursula and Temerity knew the script. First, the naming ritual of Are you Comrade So-and-so? Then, the quiet orders to get dressed, pack a small bag, and wait in the hallway for the officer to return.

Two rooms to the right now, five bangs on a door, where the French couple with the baby boy who smiled at everything lived. The husband answered the door, and the NKVD officer ordered him to pack a small bag and wait outside his door.

Boot soles tapped; the officer strode past Ursula's door.

Temerity closed her eyes, only then aware of the dryness, the grit.

Ursula tightened her hand over the mouth of the dice cup.

An officer knocked maybe three doors to the left.

Temerity's room lay four doors to the left.

No one answered it.

Another door opened, and a high and girlish voice, speech rapid and pressed, answered the officer: Nina Fontana. She'd welcomed Temerity to the floor, showed her how the plumbing worked, asked if she needed anything. The night of her husband's arrest, she'd cried in Temerity's arms.

—No, I am not Comrade Bush. The Britisher hides in number twelve with the German, Ursula Friesen, right there.

Ursula scowled as Temerity struggled to understand.

Boots soles tapped, and a fist banged five times on Ursula's door. —Comrade Bush, are you there?

Ursula rose from the game table. Still, a moment for hope, and a moment within that moment as she opened the door: a mistake, perhaps? Voice polite and a touch surprised, as if ready to calm a lost child or a savage dog, she greeted the officer. —Yes, comrade?

—Are you Comrade Bush?

Flushed in the face, Temerity stood up and plucked her handbag from the back of the chair. —I am.

—Come here.

Ursula stepped aside; Temerity walked to the threshold.

The NKVD officer, tall and thin, the shoulder sling of his *portupeya* buckled on the last hole, *galife* pants baggy at the knees, looked her up and down. A flicker of regret revealed itself in his eyes. Perhaps the light played tricks. —Good, you're already dressed.

—My things are in my own room. Down the hall. We were playing backgammon.

—Wait here.

—But my things.

His voice sounded steady and certain. —You've got your papers.

—Yes, in my handbag, but—

—Then you will wait here. That is all.

Temerity stepped into the hallway, and, behind her, Ursula shut the door. The tall officer conferred in murmurs with his colleagues.

Temerity sagged against the front of the door, unaware that Ursula did the same against the back. Ursula sobbed; the door shook.

Temerity took a deep breath. Field training in the Service had included mock arrest and interrogation. Three times Freeman ordered such exercises for Temerity, without warning her. The arrests themselves — abductions, really, once from a train platform — offered little violence, more a menace of body language and words. The interrogations might not even start for hours. Temerity would have no idea how much time had passed, because her captors always confiscated her wristwatch. After a long confinement in either darkness or bright light, the questions began, voices perhaps soft and polite, or brutal and cold from the first words. As taught, Temerity accepted the disorientation and so managed to root herself. She clung to her cover stories, answering contradictions between what she said and what her interrogators said with feigned confusion.

She'd passed. Done rather well the third time, Neville admitted.

She'd cheated. Standing now in the Hotel Lux hallway, Temerity saw how. She'd never lost sight of the exercise as an exercise, of her tormentors as her teachers, of the rehearsal.

The tall NKVD officer? No ally there.

As the huddled NKVD officers continued their conversation, Temerity counted five other Comintern members also standing outside their doors, holding small suitcases, staring at the floor. Told to keep still, they kept still. *Obedience,* Temerity told herself, *internalized and perfected.*

Electric lights buzzed; radio speakers hissed.

The tall officer seized Temerity's upper arm. —Come with me.

The grip that would leave a bruise, the ride down the crowded lift, the tap of the officers' boots, the glimpse of Lauri Toppinen, Mikko's father, climbing into another car, the click of doors not slammed but instead shut with care — all so stifled and polite beneath beautiful and indifferent stars.

Shoved into a back seat, Temerity groped for balance and told herself to sit up straight. A large man sat on her right, the French father of the smiling baby. Her arresting officer climbed into the front passenger seat. His colleague, wearing too much Troynoy cologne, took the driver's seat, addressed the tall man as Ippolitov, and then teased him about a double shift. Ippolitov grumbled and reminded his colleague his turn for a double shift would come soon enough.

The Frenchman moaned.

The driver demanded silence.

Ignition, headlights.

Back at Garage Number One, Kostya checked his watch and then noted the time of the car's return on three different forms. He'd already delivered his prisoner to one of the collection windows and retrieved paperwork from the intake clerk. Paperwork for the car, for his prisoner's dossier, for the night's plan, and for the other officers under his command, kept Kostya busy at his desk until four thirty. Then, after locking away his ink and blotter — such items prone to disappearance — he descended to the detention cells to check and sign yet more paperwork, this time the clerk's report. Officers' delivery reports might, at any moment, be compared to clerks' intake reports, and a discrepancy could be dire.

His boot soles tapped on the stairs, and the grid-wire overhead threw sharp shadows in the electric light.

At the intake bay, near the cells, he queued with other officers on the same errand for a good quarter hour. Once he reached the window, the clerk needed to check with a colleague at another window. The clerk then reviewed Kostya's forms and said that all paperwork concerning his prisoner looked in good order.

Kostya thanked the clerk, and the paperwork disappeared into a file. He'd declined, in the end, to note any belligerence in his prisoner, and in a rash moment he later blamed on pain and fatigue, he wished he could tell the prisoner so. He'd not likely see the prisoner again. Other officers would interrogate him, in shifts, to prevent the prisoner's attachment to one man. A familiar face sparked hope; hope lent resilience; and resilience impeded interrogation, which only added to the burdens on overcrowded, overtaxed Lubyanka.

I played along, Gleb had said, *asked him what he'd done. 'Nothing at all,' he told me, 'which is precisely why I've been expecting you.'*

Sighing, Kostya checked his watch: hours to go before the end of his shift. The sloth of time. Target practice? No, not with so much pain in his shoulder. He climbed the caged stairs and returned to his desk. A new crooked stack of paperwork that threatened to slip and spill onto the floor now awaited his review. He'd asked for an in-tray. Many times. Given up.

Thoughts wandering to the constellations he'd glimpsed earlier in the night, Kostya told himself to focus on his work. He unlocked his desk, retrieved ink and blotter, took the topmost papers from the pile and reviewed them. He worked until almost seven, looking up as officers from one of the morning shifts arrived and passed by the hall. As he wrapped the reviewed forms in red tape and attached a note stating *Ready*, the two colleagues with whom he shared his office entered together. For now, they worked shifts opposite Kostya's, but one day, Kostya reminded himself, all three of them could be working the same shift and need the office at the same time. Dreading that, Kostya wished his colleagues a good morning, locked his blotter and ink away once more, deposited his taped paperwork on the secretary's desk, and signed out in the ledger.

Outside, the gentle air smelled reedy, as from some great river in a fairy tale: the forbidden Puchai, perhaps, where Dobrynya Nikitich bathed and thereby encountered Zmei Gorynich. Recalling this story as he descended to the metro, Kostya promised himself a long hot shower. He fell asleep and almost missed his stop. He scrambled then, aware that he amused the other metro riders, not that they'd dare show it: the uniformed NKVD officer so clumsy, so human? He wished he could laugh aloud at himself, laugh with the others as they all left the metro car. Instead, here in Vasilisa Prekrasnaya, before a stunning mosaic version of Ivan Bilibin's Vasilisa, the girl standing outside the fowl-footed hut of Baba Yaga and shining a lamp she'd wrought from a skull and holy fire, he tugged his uniform straight.

He ascended to the street and strode to his block of flats. *Eighteen hours to call my own.* Civilians, seeing the uniform, made certain to step out of Kostya's way. Kostya ignored them. By now, he reasoned, Efim Scherba would be getting ready for his workday, and Kostya would soon have the flat to himself. He greeted the old watchwoman in the lobby, noting the contrast between her white hair and black dress, and tried to remember her name. She was one of a very similar pair; they took turns. Once out of her sight, Kostya frowned. The women had only one task: to sit and watch. Not sew. Not read. Just watch. *All these widows,* Kostya thought, not acknowledging his relief at the lack of grid-wire enclosing these stairs. *Where did we get all these widows?*

Noise interrupted his thoughts. Tape. Someone ripped long pieces from a wide roll of strong tape.

Reaching his floor, Kostya glanced over his shoulder. Three of his colleagues worked to seal the flat of someone, or perhaps multiple someones, arrested overnight.

Reading Kostya's insignia, the NKVD men hurried to tug their caps back on. Kostya almost said it aloud: *I don't fucking care about uniform infractions at this hour.*

Still, they expected a response: a rebuke, perhaps a threat.

After a moment, Kostya nodded. —Good morning.

—Good morning, Comrade Senior Lieutenant.

Postures stiff and hinting at the goose step, they tore off more tape.

Kostya wrenched off his boots the moment the flat door closed behind him. Eyes aching, he walked down the short corridor to the large kitchen, turned left, and tossed his cap onto what he and Efim used as an eating table. The surface worked on a hinge and could nest in an alcove in the wall when not in use. The eating area led to a small front room, where the *stenka*, a high cabinet fitted with shelves and drawers, stood near a wall. A radio perched on one of the *stenka*'s open shelves, and a cushioned armchair, the only such chair in the flat, faced the radio. The new pine floors and the white walls reflected what little daylight came through the small windows, and the high ceilings made the flat seem bigger. Yes, Kostya acknowledged, a good flat. True, one must overlook the frailty of the plumbing, the inconvenient placement of light switches, and the nuisance of the telephone mounted on a strip of wall just outside the bathroom. Still, ninety square metres was ninety square metres.

Efim emerged from his bedroom. —I'm glad I caught you. Take off your shirts, and I'll look at your shoulder before I go. At the table. The light's better.

Glancing at the sink and faucet, recalling the strain to pump water in that clinic in Spain, Kostya placed his *portupeya*, shoulder sling, and holstered Nagant next to his cap. Then he eased off his *gymnastyorka* and undershirt and exposed his wounds. Fatigue pressed on his shoulders and neck; despite his hospital stay, he still felt drained.

You are resilient, Gleb Kamenev once told him, *resilient and adaptable. You'll go far.*

Efim manipulated Kostya's shoulder, then studied the scars. —These are healing well. Never any infection?

—I was full of sulpha pills when the bombs fell.

—Lucky man. When I turn the arm like that: better or worse? Any difference?

—No.

Efim drew the pads of his fingers over Kostya's scars, debridement craters and shrapnel's demented paths. —Any new pain here?

—No.

—The scars on the ear?

—They're fine.

—When I turn your arm like this, what do you feel?

—Nothing.

—Nothing at all? Nikto, strange as it is, I'm your doctor, and you need to trust me.

—I don't trust anyone. It's against regulations.

Each man looked at the other and almost smirked.

Then Efim pressed some of the scars. —Now what do you feel?

—It tingles, and it hurts. It always tingles and hurts. Look, would it not be your medical opinion that a man who's been working all night should go lie down?

—Well, yes, but—

—The only obstacle between me, a hot shower, and my bed is you.

After a moment, Efim stepped aside, commenting on his need to get to work, and deciding not to inform his flatmate that the building's plumbing had, once again, proved insufficient for demand. Nikto's shower would be a cool trickle.

Outside the flat, Efim avoided eye contact with the NKVD officers now finishing their work. As he headed for Vasilisa Prekrasnaya, thinking of how trains now ran underground, he collided with memories of the hospital train he'd served on in 1918.

Served at gunpoint.

In the station, he paused to study the mosaic of Vasilisa in Baba Yaga's yard. His eyes, however, took in not the tiles but the darkness between them.

Coerced on the hospital train then, coerced into Laboratory of Special Purpose Number Two now. He shook his head. *At least in 1918, I could still call myself a doctor.*

The metro train rumbled in approach.

The telephone's ring collided with the jolt of pain in his shoulder and the shatter of glass in his dreams. Kostya clutched his wounds, at once protective and surprised. He'd dreamt that his scars hosted a flower, some cross between a rose and a geranium, petals fleshy, stalk veined and erect, roots tangled. It smelled of iris. Efim Scherba marvelled at this growth and refused to cut it out. *Too deep*, he said, which Kostya could just understand, but then, much worse: *too beautiful*. Kostya shouted at him, insulted him, called him a country doctor. The wound had yawned wider and wider until glass broke and bells rang.

Grateful for the interruption, Kostya staggered down the hall and snatched the telephone receiver off the hook. —Yes? Yes, this is Nikto.

An operator from the Lubyanka switchboard connected him with the secretary for his new department, Evgenia Davidovna Ismailovna. —Comrade Senior Lieutenant Nikto, I apologize for disturbing you. Comrade Senior Lieutenant Ippolitov cannot come to work today. We need you to take his place. You can take the sixth off instead.

Kostya almost smiled. —Weaseling out of a double shift, is he?

—Yes, this line is bad. I said, Comrade Ippolitov cannot report in, and we need a senior lieutenant for the paperwork.

Kostya deciphered the warning: Ippolitov had been arrested. —Of course, Comrade Ismailovna. I'll be there soon.

Evgenia thanked him and ended the call.

Kostya glanced at his reflection near the edge of the bathroom mirror: dark circles beneath the eyes, sharp frown lines at the mouth. *I look like hell.*

He recalled shaving at the hospital before a tiny mirror and the startling moment of not recognizing himself. Long hair, black beard, strong cheekbones, chapped lips: yes, his face. Scars on his left ear and neck pointed to the deeper scars on his left shoulder. His big green eyes had looked like those of a prisoner, a man arrested, beaten, and, with his full knowledge, about to be shot.

This morning his eyes looked calmer: not panic, but vigilance.

The tap water ran with ferocity now, almost too hot for Kostya's hands. He swished the shaving brush over the soap, then over his face and throat, and graced the blade over his Adam's apple, thinking of Pavel Ippolitov's two sons, twelve and ten. Ippolitov bragged about them all the time. Now? Sometimes adolescents followed their parents to the camps, or to the *poligons* to be shot — acorns falling close to trees, enemies of the people, a family affair, everyone shot. And yet the state also prepared to welcome many more Basque refugee children, to keep them safe.

Why Ippolitov?

Kostya rinsed his face, checked for missed stubble, slapped on some Shipr cologne.

This makes no damned sense.

The Moscow Metro engineers had encountered strange difficulties building Dzerzhinskaya: an underground river, and the forgotten dead. Some said a medieval church and graveyard once stood there, before layers of dirt elevated Moscow closer to the sky. Pressure from the river, and then from the dig, destabilized the earth, and so migrating bones seized the engineers' time. The startled engineers, aware of circled days on the calendar and the brutal truths of Soviet schedules, pried loose the dead. Then they added reinforcements and filled the ancient graves with rocks and mud. The hurry and extra expense to finish Dzerzhinskaya resulted in less money and attention spent on final decoration. Compared to the other stations, opulent in lighting, design, marble, and gold, Dzerzhinskaya felt bare. Kostya, thinking of paperwork, strode from the train car and hurried up the steps.

Once inside Lubyanka, Kostya discovered he'd lost his way. The building, overcrowded and designed for an insurance firm, blended turn-of-the-century elegance and decorations with utilitarian purpose. Many corridors looked the same. Taking a wrong turn in Lubyanka had become such a cliché that most department heads refused to accept it as an excuse for tardiness.

As Kostya stopped walking, imagining a compass and seeking north, a man's voice, bass, rich and clear, sang out: —Now we fell the stout birch tree!

NKVD choir practice.

Kostya followed the voice as the singer performed the second verse of 'Ey, Ukhnyem.'

> *Yo, heave, ho. Yo, heave ho.*
> *One more time and once again.*
> *Yo, heave, ho. Yo, heave, ho.*
> *One more time and once again.*
> *On the bank we run along.*
> *Ay-da, da, ay-da.*
> *Ay-da, da, ay-da.*
> *To the sun we sing our song!*

Kostya slipped into the practice room, too small for so many men, and, as he expected, he recognized the conductor. Annoyed, that officer turned to face the interruption keeping his hands in the air. Then he smiled. —Kostya!

The singers, eyes and mouths wide, held their note.

Laughter soft and apologetic, Vadym Pavlovich Minenkov lowered his hands and gestured to the choir to relax. His blue eyes shone, and, as one of the mysterious Lubyanka drafts blew, his fluffy white hair, protruding from beneath his cap, stirred and fell. —Final verse. Comrade Kuznets, if you please.

Kostya felt surprise, then told himself to keep it from his face. The soloist: that beautiful voice belonged to Boris Kuznets. The choir roared behind him, louder and louder, as the men, rhythm and progress certain, reached harmonies at once delicate and robust: *Hey, haul the towline! Haul the towline!*

Vadym laughed in joy. —Excellent, excellent. We'll stop there today, comrades. I can hear a big improvement on enunciation, but we still need to work on the rhythm for our other showstopper, yes? That phrase, *Yezhov's iron fist*, it's causing us some difficulty. The new metre. If we sing with faith, we can overcome any flaws and limitations of earlier versions. When you practise on your own, remember: strength, yes, but above all, clarity. Dismissed.

As the men filed out of this tiny room, Boris giving Kostya a nod, Vadym picked up a clipboard and filled out a form, and Kostya apologized for interrupting. —It sounded wonderful.

Vadym laughed again, very pleased. —The new soloist drives the others to sing harder. He's a treasure. Just give me a moment so I can finish the paperwork. The form's changed again.

Kostya felt the old surprise at standing tall enough to see the crown of Vadym's cap. When they'd first met in 1918 at the train station, Vadym's hair, already white, looked so strange against a face so young, and Kostya, burning with fever, wanted to pull Vadym's hair from his head. Then, despite some stifled small voice warning him to keep quiet, Kostya told Vadym how the train carriage had transformed into Baba Yaga's house, the racket of the rails caused by the running of fowls' feet, a racket which in turn became a chant, and Baba Yaga's voice filled his head: *Welcome home,* bezprizornik, *welcome home.* But home was Odessa, Kostya continued, and in Odessa they kept Baba Yaga contained and confused in the catacombs. Then Kostya glanced up past the worried faces of Arkady and Vadym to study a clock. A terrible man stood beneath it. The second hand on the clock thunked into place, a slow heartbeat, and the terrible man adjusted his sleeve, exposing black feathers on his arms. Arkady and Vadym hurried Kostya along, Arkady muttering about unwanted quarantine. Kostya remembered nothing after that until he awoke in someone's bed, propped up on pillows and drenched in sweat. Vadym sat beside him, introduced himself, and explained how Kostya and Arkady both had flu. Kostya asked Vadym his age, and Vadym laughed as he placed a cold compress on Kostya's forehead. *It's my white hair, isn't it? Everyone gets confused. I'm thirty-one. I had flu in 1890, when I was a boy, and I took such a fever that my hair fell out. It grew back white.* Kostya slept a long time after that, and when he woke next, Arkady sat beside him, dark-eyed and pale. Kostya slipped in and out of a fever dream of a train with no light bearing down on him in the Odessa catacombs as Arkady muttered a story about Fyodor Basmanov and the Oprichniki, how they decorated their horses' tack with dogs' heads and broomsticks, because the tsar's hounds would sweep the country clean.

When Kostya recovered, Vadym introduced him to his nephew, Misha, an only child. The boys became good friends and called each other brother. On the awkward nights when Arkady would host a party and send Kostya to spend the night at Vadym's flat, Vadym would also invite Misha over, and the three of them would play games and talk politics, music, and the irritating mysteries of girls. Vadym, very fond of the boys, invited them to address him as Dima. Arkady disapproved and insisted on the more formal and respectful Arkady Dmitrievich for himself.

Paperwork completed, Vadym slapped down the clipboard and embraced Kostya. —You're home. You're safe. Arkady's Little Tatar wins the day.

Kostya allowed himself a smirk. —I am not Arkady Dmitrievich's anything, little or otherwise. Not even to you, Dima.

—I don't like those scars. Lucky to keep your ear, yes?

—It's nothing.

Vadym shook his head. —You're too bony. Have you been ill?

Surprised, Kostya recognized that Arkady had told Vadym nothing of his return. —Coming around, thanks. It was a long trip home.

Vadym took the clipboard and tucked it beneath his arm, then poked Kostya in the ribs. —I'll have you and Arkady over for supper, put some flesh on you. I'm due back in my department. Walk with me?

In the corridors, Kostya and Vadym alternated the volume of their voices as they navigated past dozens of other people and struggled to continue their conversation about what Vadym might cook. NKVD officers, civilian support workers, military officers, and Party members proceeded in all directions, carrying dossiers, briefcases, boxes, and loose papers, intent on their own missions.

Stopping near the stairwell that led to his own department, Vadym wagged his finger in mock rebuke. —And tell Arkady I won't hear any excuses this time. The evening after next, yes? At my flat.

—I'll tell him.

Vadym opened his mouth to ask something else, thought better of it, and instead sighed.

—What is it, Dima?

—Let me embrace you again.

—Here?

—Please.

Kostya leaned in, and Vadym hugged him hard.

—Dima, are you all right?

Vadym murmured in Kostya's ear. —Misha's listed as missing.

Kostya's back stiffened.

Vadym let him go, patted him on the good shoulder, and started his ascent up the stairs. In seconds, so many people filled the space between them that Kostya lost sight of Vadym.

Then someone jostled Kostya's bad shoulder, sending that wretched pain down his arm. It felt like an electric zap. *Of course it does,*

Efim had explained. *Electrical impulses drive the human body. Think of your nerves as wires. Your nerves are damaged, like exposed wires, and the electrical impulses cause not spark but pain.* Then he'd added, voice calm, face serious, either mocking or supporting propaganda, perhaps both at once: *All the energy for the state comes from the human body. The New Soviet Man is a human dynamo.*

Kostya shut his eyes. The steady noise of conversation, the clicks and taps and shuffles and scrapes of shoes and boots, invaded his ears and annexed his head. Jostled some more, he surrendered, opening his eyes and navigating the crowd. After his solitude in Spain, he found the crowding in Moscow a tiresome study in how to suppress cries of rage: so many people in so many queues. *It's gotten worse,* he'd told Arkady. *You're imagining it,* Arkady had said.

A younger man, a sergeant, addressed Kostya by rank and surname. The new rank still sounded odd to Kostya, like a mistake, much as his surname no doubt sounded like a mistake to the sergeant. —Yes?

The younger man saluted. —I am Katelnikov, Matvei Andreivich Katelnikov. Comrade Ismailovna asked me to keep an eye out for you and remind you to check with her for paperwork.

—We've never met, yet you know me by sight?

Matvei pointed to his own left ear, then thought better of it and lowered his hand. —I...

Smirking, Kostya clapped Matvei on the shoulder. —I shouldn't tease. Good work, Katelnikov.

The scent of smoky tea guided Kostya to Evgenia Ismailovna's desk. Evgenia worked two jobs in one, both as a general secretary for the department and as a private secretary to the department head. Piles of paper and dossiers covered her desk and threatened avalanche, yet somehow she kept the paper moving. Shelves loomed behind her desk, shelves holding the samovar, a tea tin decorated with red stars, tea glasses and *podstakanniks*, and yet more paper and files. In her mid-twenties, Evegenia affected the stern maternal manner of some of

the older female Party members, and she would ask even the department head to wait in silence until she'd finished typing a sentence.
Many new officers tried to flirt with her; she tolerated none of it.
Experienced officers might take the new man aside and explain how
much power Evgenia could wield. She had the ear of the department
head, yes, of course, any fool could guess that. Far more important:
Comrade Ismailovna tended the paperwork.

A dizziness took Kostya, a sense of disorientation deeper than
what any day off or even a hospital stay might ease. He felt like he'd
woken up in the wrong story. Not quite solid, these floors and walls
of Lubyanka. Not quite right, the clock behind Evgenia reading
eight minutes after ten, nor these fever-bright colours: Comrade
Ismailovna's green eyes behind her black-rimmed pince-nez, for
example, and her purple crosstie, that little strip of silk she wound
around her buttoned collar. Shot silk, Kostya now noticed. At certain
angles, a jade green showed. He studied her face. Apart from one
small mole on her right cheek, she had no marks, freckles, or scars.
Nor did she wear cosmetics. She kept her hair in a short wedge bob
that bared the back of her neck, and that haircut, like the line of
dark down on her upper lip, only made her seem more feminine.
Kostya recognized in that moment how much he admired all her
contrasts. The old-fashioned manners and pince-nez, the short hair
and insistence on her equality with any man: for Kostya, she almost
shimmered.

—Comrade Senior Lieutenant, are you all right?

Kostya reminded himself to focus and then ask for Ippolitov's
paperwork without mentioning Ippolitov. —Not enough sleep. What
have you got for me?

She gave Kostya a thin dossier and stroked the back of his left
hand with her fingers, perhaps by accident.

Startled by the touch, Kostya jerked away, then told himself his
arm often twitched like that.

Evgenia clasped her hands together atop her desk. —Would you like some tea?

Some mornings, Evgenia took first pour, despite that privilege belonging to the department head. The latest head, however, not expected to last much longer, likely wouldn't arrive until noon, only then in a cloud of vicious words and wine fumes, and Evgenia saw no point in wasting good tea. When Kostya had asked Arkady about the department head and his deplorable state, Arkady murmured, *A Yagoda man*. Genrikh Yagoda, their former chief, languished in a cell beneath their feet, and his absence pressed them all. As Yagoda's imprisonment wore on, and time and expectation hauled him towards a show trial and brutal execution, other officers drank themselves to oblivion and choked on vomit, crashed their cars into walls and trees, jumped from windows, shot themselves in the head. Each officer understood the escalating brutality inflicted on prisoners because each officer practised it. If Yagoda could fall from grace, then so might any officer, policeman to prisoner at any moment, any moment. Dread, and truth.

Arkady had always spoken well of Yagoda. So had Vadym.

Yet they carried on as though nothing bothered them, and so must Kostya.

Tea. —Yes, please, Comrade Ismailovna. Strong.

As Evgenia got up, Kostya noticed the closed door of the office where a colleague —*Bogdanovich* — the one with the big grey eyes — *Bogdanovich, Maksim Maksimovich Bogdanovich, one year older than me* — had shot himself with his own weapon — *a Tokarev, fucking ugly pistol* — his blood and brain matter staining the walls. And his paperwork. The office, like the flat of someone arrested, had been sealed.

A pity, several officers had said, *we need the space.*

—Sugar, Comrade Senior Lieutenant?

Kostya broke out of his stare. —We have sugar?

A racket of steel buckets dragged over floors interrupted. Clutching the dossier to his chest, Kostya turned around. Three men armed with brooms, chemicals, brushes, and mops identified themselves as a work crew here to perform a Special Clean.

Evgenia held up a typed memo. —I didn't expect you until this afternoon, comrades. See? Special Clean, 14:10.

The foreman, a man in his sixties, spoke to Evgenia as though addressing the most troublesome pupil in the classroom. —Look, young comrade, I'm sure you mean well, but you must understand that we were told to come here right now. You requested a Special Clean, and Special Cleans are urgent.

—Comrades, I don't have a key to the office in question, and the department head's not yet here. Surely you can return after lunch?

Sighing, the foreman detailed the tasks in other buildings scheduled for after lunch and then, of course, the need to get any amendments to this schedule approved by the Special Tasks Committee, which did not meet for another three weeks, and the further need to report first to the Works and Procurement Committee in a special liaison meeting with the Central Schedules. —So you see, young comrade, if you do not let us in, then you cannot have a Special Clean.

—No, don't go. That office needs a Special Clean.

—Then show us where and get out of the way.

—I don't have a key!

Kostya recalled his own new keys, those tokens of promotion, one of them engraved with an initial: a master key? —Can I help?

Despairing over the folly of young people, the foreman shook his head. —We'd need a commanding officer, Comrade Sergeant.

Kostya passed the dossier back to Evegenia and showed his ID. —It's Comrade Senior Lieutentant.

After reading the ID card and peering at the insignia, the foreman cleared his throat and spoke with a new respect. —Which office, Comrade Senior Lieutenant?

—This way.

Boot soles tapping, face impassive, Kostya strode to the sealed door

Odour seeped past the tape.

The key fit; the lock turned. Some of the tape gave way, and the odour thickened.

Kostya nodded to the foreman. —You've brought some bleach, yes?

Ignoring Kostya, feigning deafness, the foreman studied the door and discussed with his workers how best to remove the tape and leave no residue on the door.

Kostya returned to Evgenia's desk to collect his dossier and glass of tea. Evgenia held out a small plate of hard sugar pieces cut from a loaf, picked up a piece with little tongs, and then dropped it into Kostya's hand. —Thank you, Comrade Senior Lieutenant.

He tucked the sugar into his mouth. —It's nothing.

In his office, relieved to be alone and away from the racket of tape, Kostya unwound the dossier's red string.

A confiscated wristwatch fell out.

He picked up the watch and rubbed the face between his fingers, noticing a brand name on the face in the Latin alphabet and feeling something odd on the back. Turning the watch over, he found two engraved initials, Latin alphabet, MB. He read Ippolitov's summary. Reason for detention: passport irregularity. Site of arrest: Hotel Lux. Comintern member, British passport.

Maybe I can practise my English.

Another officer passed Kostya's open door and called out a greeting: Matvei Katelnikov.

Kostya nodded acknowledgement and resumed reading. The sunlight through the window warmed the back of his neck, and he turned away from his desk. In this moment, with the sky so blue, the tea so sweet, paperwork didn't matter. His wounds didn't matter. Bogdanovich and Yagoda and the ever-changing department head, even Arkady's fears and the uncertainty of Kostya's own position in

NKVD, none of it mattered. A delicious lassitude took him, for lassitude it must be, some relaxation of standards and morals, and he wanted to share this pleasure of existence, of being alive.

You sound loose, Boris Kuznets had said.

The dossier fell from his hand.

Kostya took up the dossier again and then rubbed his eyes with the pads of his fingers. If he pursued Ippolitov's note of passport irregularity, then he would involve whoever at Intourist signed off on Comrade Britisher here, and then that poor Intourist bastard might get arrested for that connection with Ippolitov, and that would only make the case against Ippolitov worse...

The British passport peeked out from beneath page 3 of the arrest report.

Sipping tea, Kostya took up the passport, admired the cover, opened to the photograph.

Almost spat.

Swallowing the tea, telling himself he felt nothing, he compared the travel documents to the information in the passport, checked the translations: English and Russian all fine, no irregularity here. Ippolitov, like any other officer, had simply filled his quota and needed an official reason for the paperwork.

Kostya stared again at the photograph of Margaret Bush.

A simple explanation, he told himself, yes, everyone has a double, somewhere in the world.

He tucked the British woman's passport, travel papers, and wristwatch into the pouch on his *portupeya*. The last of his tea scalded his throat, and 'Ey, Ukhnyem' echoed in his thoughts. As he left the dossier with Evgenia, he refused to think about that British nurse in Spain, because thoughts of her invited thoughts of Misha.

Yet he could think about nothing else.

One of hundreds on an errand in Lubyanka, he descended to the cells.

—

The one electric light bulb in the cell, caged, cast feeble light and mocked time, stretching it so it split and surrendered all meaning. Two steady leaks ran down the walls and pooled and spread on the floor, leaving no spot dry. Temerity lifted her nodding head. Since arriving near three, she'd perched on a wooden stool, the only piece of furniture in the cell, with no idea of how much time had passed. She struggled to think past confusion and fear. Pain interrupted. Stool-sitting, a standard method for softening those already deemed co-operative, exhausted body and mind with minimal effort from an interrogator, and it left no marks. She knew how it worked. It still hurt.

An officer had confiscated her watch, as she expected, but had not, despite a pat-down, discovered the Temerity West passport in the lining of her blouse. As the night wore on, Temerity had cried, to her disgust, blown her nose on the inside of her blouse, cried again, reminded herself that her period had ended the week before, so some small comfort there, then reviewed her cover story in minute detail. She left the small circle of light to pace the floor to stretch her back and check if maybe this time a patch of floor looked dry enough to sit on. The leaks flowed, and liquid almost breached her shoes. She returned to the stool, repeating this cycle many times throughout the night. When she kept still on the stool, fatigue and sleep took over. The soft edges of dreams interfered with her thoughts, these dreams no less anxious than her reality. As her balance slipped, her head would jerk upright.

The heavy cell door swung open, letting in muffled yells, cries, thuds. Down the hall, another cell door opened, another woman screamed, and that heavy door banged shut. Kostya stood at the edge of the open door, obscured, he knew, by shadow. Here, at this moment, in this created space, the prisoner would squint and peer, struggle to see.

Temerity did so.

No supplication in her eyes. Confusion and fear, Kostya noticed, and anger, even outrage, but no supplication. The slouch in her back as she perched on the stool betrayed her pain and fatigue. Kostya could smell soured sweat and a tang very common in the cells: dread. He could also smell perfume, faint, something spicy and floral. Incense? Iris?

Temerity shut her eyes, hoping to soothe the dryness, opened them again. Shiny boots and *galife* pants, *gymnastyorka*, shoulder sling, *portupeya* and holstered weapon, and that cap, topped in a blue reminiscent of the sky reflected in a dirty puddle: her NKVD interrogator. Lubyanka remained true. This cell and her presence in it remained true. It was no dream.

The officer turned to the guard outside and murmured instruction. The guard questioned something. The officer repeated his instruction in an irked tone, and the guard apologized, addressing the officer as Senior Lieutenant. Then, still speaking to the guard outside, the senior lieutenant made his voice friendly, soothing. —At ease. Long night? You look like you'd kill your own grandmother for a glass of vodka. Best I can do is tell you to get some tea, yes? Lock me in, get your tea, and then just wait outside. I'll signal when I'm done.

She knew the voice. Denied it, dismissed the very idea.

The door thudded shut, the lock engaged, and the officer took off his cap and stepped into the light.

He'd lost the beard and cut his hair, short back and sides, plenty of length on top and swept back with pomade. The green eyes, the cheekbones, the voice: all unmistakable.

Kostya looked around the cell, stepped back into shadow, and gave a short sigh. —Nowhere for me to work?

—I am not in charge of furnishings, I promise you.

He put his cap back on. —You have no leave to speak. You may get down from the stool.

The assertion of authority: right on schedule. Temerity slipped off the stool, stumbled, got her balance, and avoided the worst of a puddle. She took no pride in recognizing patterns of interrogation, because right now the patterns didn't matter. In another country, this man had aimed his Nagant at her head, only to spare her. Then she'd helped him with evacuees. And now they'd met once more, in a Lubyanka cell. Questions, so many questions, tumbled in her mind. Giving them voice would only sharpen the danger.

Kostya opened the pouch on his *portupeya* and retrieved something that glinted. He held it beneath the caged light bulb, and the glare bounced off the object and into Temerity's eyes. —Is this yours?

—Is what mine?

His boot soles tapped and splashed as he strode toward her. —This British-made wristwatch.

Her vision cleared enough to let her see fear in Kostya's eyes, then the wristwatch lying on his outstretched hand. —I believe it is. My initials are engraved on the back, *MB*.

He softened his voice, sounding courteous. —A cherished gift?

—My father gave it to me when I turned sixteen.

—How old are you now?

—Twenty-two.

He almost murmured, as though sharing a secret. —Those initials look like they were engraved last week. Why are you here?

Disorientation, step by step: Temerity could have written the script. Her knowledge changed nothing. Margaret Bush, Mildred Ferngate, Temerity West, or by any other name? Trapped. And what a coup for an up-and-coming NKVD officer, to expose her.

Except he must then explain why he'd spared her.

Temerity decided to play her strength. She took the tone of an offended memsahib, an upper-class British woman appalled by widespread incompetence in a foreign land and tasked with putting things right. —Now listen to me. I was arrested for no reason, and I demand—

Kostya raised his eyebrows, then held up a hand. —No, no demands, just answers. Why are you in Moscow?

—As I told the officer who arrested me, I am with Comintern, and I teach language classes to children.

—I see. Back on the stool, please.

—Pardon me?

—Back on the stool!

She hurried to obey, and the night's familiar pain returned.

He lowered his voice but kept the tone sharp. —You speak excellent Russian. Now put your watch back on.

She did this, saying nothing.

Dizzy, feeling he stood on the edge of a great fall, Kostya reached for his cigarettes. He'd omitted the British nurse from his report. Now she sat before him, the only explanation for her presence being the obvious one: she was a foreign spy. Under a beating, she'd scream soon enough about meeting Kostya before, and while such an allegation would be considered ridiculous, it would be investigated, and well, look at that, Nikto was in Spain, and why have you not mentioned this woman before, comrade? Is it because you're both working together?

He shook out a cigarette and pointed it at her. —Comrade Bush, you're frightened. That makes me think you're guilty.

—This pretty picture would frighten Joan of Arc.

Kostya lit a match. —She burned.

—She did.

He shook his match dead. —Travelled abroad before now?

Words cluttered her mouth. This human contact, any human contact, after the arrest and the long wait, contact with someone she'd already met, even someone who remained a threat, felt crucial, even precious. It left her weak. —Of course I've gone abroad.

Kostya held smoke in his lungs, waited.

—I travelled to India when I was eighteen, with my aunt.

He exhaled. —India?

—My aunt thought I needed a husband.

—And did you get one?

—No.

—Why not? You're pretty enough.

She tapped her finger on her head. —I couldn't find a man to keep up with me.

—No, I suppose not.

Temerity almost smiled; once again, he seemed so disarming. —I've done nothing wrong, comrade. Can you tell me why I'm here?

He stared at her again. —Travelled anywhere else?

She stared back. His exhaled smoke obscured his eyes and, perhaps, the flicker of emotion there.

Kostya walked around the edge of the light spill. His stomach tingled. —Answer my question.

Temerity recalled Neville Freeman's voice: *People disappear in Russia.*

Dirty water splashed as Kostya strode though the puddles in a tight circle around the stool. Then he paused behind her. The insanity of coincidence now felt quite unexceptional to him, no worse than the insanity of queuing for necessities in a country claiming surplus and glut, no worse than the insanity of the entire Purge. He murmured, voice solicitous, pleading. —Don't turn around, and don't think. Just answer me. Have you travelled anywhere else?

—No.

Once more studying the back of this woman's head, Kostya felt his mouth work.

He strode back to the shadows and beat his fist on the door.

Temerity took a deep and shaky breath and discovered she was weeping. —Wait. Comrade Officer, wait. You've not yet told me why I'm under arrest.

The lock clunked, the door swung open, and the tap of Kostya's boot soles faded as he stepped out of the cell. Then the heavy door slammed shut.

As Temerity dried her face with the backs of her hands, she saw how a puddle reflected back the caged light.

[ ]

PARTY FAVOURS
Saturday 5 June–Sunday 6 June

—Because truly, comrades, life is more cheerful than ever before. And now, Tchaikovsky.

Temerity strode down the corridor to the communal kitchen of Hotel Lux, hotel workers staring at her. She wished she could rip the bolted radio speaker off the wall and leave it trailing torn wires like guts. Then again, Temerity reminded herself, at least the blare of the speaker meant the hotel's electricity still ran.

For now.

Just outside the kitchen, Temerity could hear many of the gathered Comintern women speaking quiet Russian. They had yet to notice her. In the middle of the crowd, the French mother with the smiling baby wept. After arresting her husband, NKVD officers had sealed the hotel room with padlock and tape. All of her clothes, her baby's diapers and blankets, and her travel papers lay in that sealed room. She could access the room again once her husband returned, and he would only return once proven innocent. For now, she must find someone willing to share a room and perhaps a bed with her and the baby.

On the edge of this circle, her situation just as dire, Mikko Toppinen's mother Kielo scowled. Next to her, Nina Fontana sobbed as she told the other women how she'd sacrificed her relationship with her parents and most of her friends to serve in Comintern and move to the Soviet Union. —We've done everything asked of us, everything. Why must this happen?

Temerity wanted to spit. *Loyal servants of the Revolution, and this their reward: loved ones and faith bloody torn away.*

Kielo noticed Temerity then, and flinched: a spectre, a fetch, a Lubyanka wraith. —Comrade Bush?

Nina gasped. —Margaret!

Temerity wanted to strike Nina full on the mouth, that mouth so quick to give her up to NKVD. *And yet,* Temerity asked herself, *what else could she have done?*

Sounding happy to see her, relieved, Nina took Temerity in her arms. —I knew all along you weren't a traitor. Some of us might think NKVD sent you back to spy on us, but that's nonsense.

The others seemed to consider the suggestion as perhaps, just perhaps, more than nonsense.

Anger fled, leaving Temerity numb. She patted Nina on a shoulder and eased out of the embrace. —Of course it's nonsense.

Kielo laid her hand on Temerity's shoulder. —Did you see Lauri?

Nina grasped for Temerity's hand, missed. —What happened to Marco?

Temerity glanced about for an escape. The other women filled her sightline.

—Jean-Pierre?

—Carlos?

—Dietrich?

—Olafur?

She cringed. *Don't touch me.* —I don't know.

The other women stared at Temerity, demanding a better answer.

She tried to give it. —They shoved us into different cars, and then I was in a cell by myself. I'm sorry, I'm sorry.

Nina wobbled and swayed. Temerity and Kielo caught her and helped her to a chair. The samovar hissed. Then Temerity noticed several of the children had gathered as well. They now studied Comrade Bush, their English teacher, arrested but freed and returned in under twenty-four hours, when some of their parents had been gone for weeks, with no word.

Temerity saw evacuees' name tags hanging from their necks. When she blinked, the name tags disappeared, some shred of a dream.

Ursula Friesen broke free from the crowd in the kitchen and shooed the children away, telling them to go review their language lessons, for she and Comrade Bush might set a quiz tomorrow. Then she embraced Temerity, whispering in her ear. —I feel like I hold a ghost.

As her vision greyed out, returned, Temerity felt no affection, no relief.

Just fear. A buzz of it, a steady whisper, like static in the speakers.

Arrest and disappearance: it had happened once, so it could happen again, at any moment. And to add to it: guilt, wretched, clammy guilt at being one who came back, and came back useless, with no information. If she had a drink, she'd raise a toast to NKVD. Not twenty-four hours' captivity, a gentle interrogation, a release, a drive back to Hotel Lux, and now a two-man surveillance detail parked outside, all so polite by NKVD standards, and yet she felt gutted, marked, pried in two with emotions wild and intellect bound.

Well done, gentlemen.

Radio Moscow fell silent as the electricity failed.

Ursula offered her arm.

Temerity first shook her head, then accepted, and Ursula guided her away from the kitchen.

Away from the others, Temerity murmured in Ursula's ear. —I'm sorry. I need to tell them how sorry I am.

—You're limping.

—NKVD forced me to sit on a stool.

—Is that all?

A fair question, Temerity told herself, yet she snapped her answer. —What?

Ursula held Temerity's gaze. —We hear of much worse. Really, I'm very happy to see you again. Let's get you cleaned up.

As Ursula and Temerity reached the next floor, they found children playing, five boys, eight to ten years told. Four chased one, and they made very little noise. One of the chasers, Mikko Toppinen, broke off, turned around, and ran towards them. He stood before Temerity and gave the little bow due a teacher. Then he stared up into her face, asking so much yet saying nothing.

She shook her head. —I don't know.

His reply in English sounded hollow and rehearsed, and he gave another little bow. —Thank you.

Then something changed with the other boys. As they strode to Mikko, calm, certain, and, after two steps, in unison, they seemed older. Faster. They surrounded Mikko, Temerity, and Ursula, and their voices, calm, even bored at first, soon trembled with something like desire.

—Are you Comrade Toppinen?

—I am.

—Pack a few things and come with us. It's a small matter.

Ursula's face flushed a deep red. —Stop it. Stop it now.

The boys all laughed, laughed at how the adults understood nothing, until Mikko cried out.

His friends crowded round him, rubbed his shoulders. —He'll come back, Mikko. Your father will come back.

—Mikko, it's all right.

—Mikko, it was just a game.

Eyes clenched shut, Mikko struck the others with fists. —Shut up. Shut up!

The boys stepped away from him, looked at one another, ran down the stairs.

Mikko squinted into the dusty light, saw only Comrade Bush looking down on him. He raised his right forearm over his face, as in defence, and he whispered in excellent Russian. —Leave me alone.

Ursula patted Temerity's shoulder. As they both backed away from Mikko, the electricity returned and all the lights burned bright, too bright. Filaments blew, and the electricity vanished again.

Mikko ran after the other boys. —Wait!

Temerity shut her eyes. —Ursula, I need to lie down.

—Your room's not sealed. Perhaps they forgot after arresting you from my room. They gave you back your handbag?

Temerity recalled checking the handbag at Lubyanka. All her

Margaret Bush papers, her Margaret Bush passport, her cash, her hundred-gram slab of chocolate, even the compact, perfume, and cervical cap, lay within. —I've no doubt they manhandled every little thing, but it's all there.

—Then you're being watched.

—Comrade Quiet and Comrade Subtle? Yes, they're parked outside.

No voices from the radio speakers, no voices from the rooms: the silence clung like ash.

—Margaret?

Leaning on the jamb, Temerity unlocked the door. —I'm just tired.

Ursula said something about returning in a few moments, so Temerity left the door ajar. Stooped, bent as if bearing a child on her back, she shuffled to the bed and, with some difficulty, perched there. *How can sitting hurt so much?*

Ursula returned, carrying a metal bowl, a cloth, and a scrap of soap. —The water's only tepid. It's the best I could do.

The lining of Temerity's blouse, weighted by the hidden passport, clung to her skin. —Please, leave me alone. Just for the moment.

—What is this? We shower together.

Light glinted off the bowl, reminding Temerity of Spain. *All right, Tikhon, I've got about as much of the corruption as I can manage.* —Let me undress myself!

Ursula took a step back. —Those pigs.

—No, nobody touched me. Just the stool. It's nothing. I'm sorry.

Ursula turned down the covers on Temerity's bed. —Stop apologizing. It's far more than nothing. Now let me help.

Temerity held up her hands, showing her palms, and Ursula could not quite read the gesture: submission, or warning?

Fingers trembling, arms slow, Temerity unbuttoned her blouse. Shook it out. Folded it. Placed it in the middle of her pillow. Chin high, mouth stiff, she reached behind her back and unhooked her brassiere, an item of clothing that had elicited some envy in the shower room. She leaned forward, and the brassiere slid to her lap, cups and straps in disarray. Then, in some echo of being a child at bath time, in some dull surrender to mercy, she raised her arms.

Ursula washed and dried Temerity's neck, shoulders, and armpits. Then she kissed Temerity on the forehead, whispering for her to lie down.

Temerity fastened her bra again and slipped on the soiled blouse, aware of its smell. Rolling down her stockings and prying off her shoes, she scowled. —How did my feet get so swollen?

—The stool-sitting. It's very bad for the circulation. I'll leave you in peace if you promise to lie down.

—I promise.

Eyelids heavy, Temerity walked Ursula to the door, kissed her on the cheek, and then, even as Ursula opened her mouth to say something else, shut and locked the door.

On the bed, she lay on her side, clenched her body into a tight ball, and tugged the covers up to her chin. Safety and solitude at last.

She wanted to scream into her pillow.

She couldn't make a sound.

Later, her dreams smelled of iron and copper and spice, of blood.

—How much have you had to drink?

Perched on the side of his bed, Kostya giggled, cleared his throat. He'd stripped down to his undershirt but still wore his *galife* pants, and they looked huge and absurd. —Rough day, Comrade Doctor. I took a few glasses as soon as I got home.

—And a few more before you got here? Alcohol thins the blood and interferes with the healing of wounds. Keep still. How bad is the pain?

—I'm fucked in the mouth and one-third demented. Quite mild, really. Just fix it.

Efim took a step back. —You need to rest.

—I'll rest when I'm dead.

—That attitude will not help you.

—Look, when you wear this uniform, then, and only then, may you advise me on my work. Not before.

Efim studied Kostya's face; the scowl lines cut deep. —Untreated pain wears down the mind. It's like grit in the gears, and the works seize.

—A startling insight. Can you help me, or not?

—Will you allow me?

After a confused moment, Kostya nodded.

—I'll be right back.

As his flatmate rustled in his bedroom, and then ran water in the bathroom, Kostya thought about electric lights. The switch for the bathroom light also operated a lamp on Efim's bedroom wall. If Efim turned off the lamp, then the bathroom switch wouldn't work at all. They had come to an understanding, if a reluctant one on Kostya's part. Night visits to the bathroom would be unlit. Not that this bothered Kostya. He'd long overcome his childhood fear of the dark, and he often worked at night, so why would darkness ever frighten him? He told himself he merely disliked how the unlit bathroom reminded him of sleeping in the Basque graveyard in Spain, and in the catacombs in Odessa.

Efim returned to Kostya's room and prepared the injection, brooding on the visit to the lab of one NKVD sergeant Yury Stepanov. After Stepanov's departure, Efim had discovered the disturbing absences of two batches of an experimental hypnotic drug. One version could be added to a drink, though it left a salty taste; the other formula would be injected into a vein. Each bottle's label gave clear instructions. The formulae, however, remained problematic. Stupefied prisoners, at first compliant, soon became too disoriented to give their own names and succumbed to a frightening state, walking in circles, sometimes able to answer simple questions and follow instructions but otherwise, even at gunpoint, talking nonsense. Six to twelve hours later, depending on dose and route of administration, the prisoners endured severe headache, vertigo, and vomiting. Afterwards, they remembered almost nothing.

And to whom might Dr. Scherba complain about missing experimental drugs likely stolen by an NKVD officer?

Efim tied a tourniquet around Kostya's arm. —My day was long. Make a fist. Release it. Make a fist again. You'll feel a pinch. Don't move.

Kostya hissed at the prick and the burn. The two men counted to sixteen, one-two, three-four, five-six, as though counting the beats of a heart. On seven, Kostya felt a lick of relief. On ten, he lay down.

Efim took his pulse. —Better?

—It still hurts.

—I gave you the full dose. Come home drunk again, and I'll leave you to writhe on the floor.

Kostya's head lolled on the pillow. —Such excellent bedside manner. What do you do all day, Scherba?

—I work.

—But what is it you do?

Efim disassembled the needle and syringe. —Is this how you question criminals, with such subtlety? How long were you in surgery with those wounds?

—I don't know.

—General anaesthetic can affect the memory.

—The clinic had no general anaesthetic.

Efim felt ill. He kept his voice mild. —Oh?

—Too many patients. They rationed the morphine, too. I got bromides. It still took two men to hold me down. I think I'll sit in the front room now. Thank you.

After a moment, Efim heard the radio. A tense female voice rapped out details of an ongoing trial. The accused had confessed to sabotage of equipment, sabotage of morale, plots to kidnap, plots to

murder, pedophilia, hoarding of food, smuggling of warm coats from
France...

—France? Why would they make better winter coats than we do?

Then Efim bit the inside of his lip, hard. One did not ask such
questions out loud.

The announcer concluded her report with the criminal's sentence.
Because the accused had cooperated with the investigation and given
NKVD further assistance, the state would grant leniency and commute
the expected sentence of death to twenty-five years labour in Kolyma.

Efim found Kostya sitting in their one soft chair, his body at a
sharp angle to the radio, as if he bowed to it. He seemed to listen with
great attention.

—Nikto, I'll be in my room. You should make an early night of it.

Jaw tight, Kostya nodded. Then he sat back in the chair, felt his
jaw relax, and dozed.

Temerity woke up, checked her watch: not long after six in the evening. She ached all over. *As if coming down with flu,* she thought, *oh,
wouldn't Freeman enjoy that.* Somehow, her room smelled like the
Lubyanka cell. She put on fresh clothes and tucked her Temerity
West passport into the special lining of the blouse. Then she opened
her curtains and peered out her window at Gorky Street. Two parked
NKVD cars. Four officers leaned against the cars, chatting, smoking,
and staring up at the Hotel Lux windows. Temerity recognized two
of the men: Comrade Subtle and Comrade Quiet, still there.

The room's stuffiness worsened.

Christ, I can't think in here.

When upset as a child and adolescent, Temerity would walk
the grounds of Roedean or, if at home, the Kurseong House estate,
perhaps soak her shoes in the fen or run until she got breathless and
then lie on her back on the ground. *Air,* her father said, *good fresh air.*

Cures anything. The greatest men in history have solved their problems while out for a walk. Just a short stroll along Gorky Street, as far as the Gastronom food shop, and then, if she slipped Comrades Quite and Subtle, she could stroll a little farther, yes, make it a good hike, cross the river Moskva and get herself the bloody hell to the British embassy and maybe, just maybe, NKVD wouldn't arrest her again before she reached the embassy doors.

How best to leave? A service entrance might help her avoid the NKVD tail out front, presuming she could get past hotel staff and their suspicious questions. Leaving through the main doors meant informing the desk clerk of one's plans and destination, and, of course, attracting the attention of the NKVD officers.

Temerity descended the stairs to the lobby and strode up to the desk clerk, a young man with brown eyes and spectacles. He glanced up at Temerity, then returned his full attention to his paperwork.

After a moment, Temerity cleared her throat. —Good evening, comrade. I need some air and shall go for a walk.

—Destination?

—The Gastronom food store at Gorky Street Forty, then back here.

He took up a pen to make a note in a ledger and checked the time on his watch. —Very well, Comrade Bush.

—Oh, the last time I visited Gastronom, I picked up some chocolate, one of those big slabs, but it's the wrong kind. Would you care for it?

The young man's eyes betrayed his desire for the chocolate and his fear of a possible trap. How much did one name in a ledger really mean? And really, how could any chocolate be the wrong kind? Yet…

—Is the wrapper intact?

—Yes.

After a moment, he closed the ledger without writing anything in it. Temerity gave him the chocolate, then strode outside through the main doors.

Three of the NKVD officers stared at a disturbance down the street, a quarrelling couple oblivious to their audience, while the fourth noticed Temerity.

Underarms slick with sweat, she kept walking.

The officer made no reaction.

The stench of that Lubyanaka cell still in her nose, Temerity found herself thinking of the Gernika fires, and then imagining a lecture from Neville Freeman about deserting one's post. *Have you no backbone at all, Miss West? First little upset and you gallop to the embassy? England expects that every man will do his duty. Are you really suited for this work?*

Then she saw her own reflection in a glass window, her head sliced off at the neck by the edge of small poster promising plenty. The poster shone, paper glossy, colours slick: tumbling sausage, cheese, bread. Behind the poster, the window showed many empty shelves. The sign over the door read Deli Number 12, and someone had painted a surname beneath that: Babichev.

The light had changed, darkened.

Temerity blinked a few times. *This isn't Gorky Street. Wrong turn?*

Her watch told her that almost two hours had passed since she'd left Hotel Lux.

I've seen this deli before. Haven't I? Did I walk in circles?

A car approached, all rumble and rattle of metal and screws, and Temerity, about to turn and seek a street sign, caught the car's reflection in the deli window: matte black. She dug her nails into her palms. Comrade Subtle and Comrade Quiet had followed her, after all.

The car stopped; two men climbed out. They wore civilian clothes, and Temerity did not recognize their faces. Just a coincidence, then.

A radio blared through the window of a flat one storey up: classical music, Mikhail Glinka, the overture to his opera *Ruslan and Lyudmila*.

Temerity glanced up and down the street and saw no one else. Then she resumed her study of the deli's display, watching the men's headless reflections. They closed in. As she turned to face them, one took her handbag while the other reached for her left arm. —Come, little one.

Instinct took over. Temerity grasped the reaching man's sleeve, embraced him round the back while getting her knee between his legs, lifted him, then turned and flipped him over her shoulder. The thud and gasp of him landing on his back on the street seemed too quiet, and the pounding of Temerity's pulse seemed too loud. So did the second man's command to stop, heavy with the authority of an aimed Nagant. Head slow, Temerity looked up. One tiny black hole pricked her vision, and she stared at the muzzle's narrow darkness in the utter opposite of gazing at a star.

She lifted her hands and showed her palms.

The music of Glinka continued, quite merry.

The man who aimed the Nagant snarled at his colleague to stand up. The fallen man, breathing hard and complaining of the dangers of unmuzzled bitches, got to his feet, and locked handcuffs on Temerity, too tight. When she cried out, he gave her a hard shove. She fell to her knees, scraping them open and ruining her stockings. The men hauled her up by the arms, and the three of them walked in a brisk lock-step to the car. A witness, an adolescent girl watching from a third-storey window, caught Temerity's eye and then darted away.

As the men forced Temerity into the back seat, she commanded herself to speak. Her angry voice, however, remained imprisoned in her head, where it echoed alongside long-memorized instructions in case of detention. *Keep quiet and observe. What you see and learn may be invaluable. If compelled to speak, recite in growing detail your cover story and thereby stall for time. Your duty at all times is to observe and then escape and make report.*

The driver started the car.

Blood trickling down her knees, Temerity leaned forward to ease the pressure on her arms and peered through the windshield. Tears blurred her vision, and she saw little of the drive until they turned onto Gorky Street and passed the Hotel Lux. Comrade Quiet and Comrade Subtle had left, but the other two uniformed officers still smoked and chatted. The men in the car gave the officers no signal, and the officers in turn only glanced at the car. Temerity felt cold. The men in the car, while armed, wore civilian clothes and had not demanded to see her papers. Nor had they identified themselves in any way as NKVD.

Her voice sounded small. —Wait.

The man she'd flipped whirled round, ready to strike her across the face; the driver steered with one hand and grabbed his colleague's arm with the other. —Don't bruise the pastry.

A pause, a snort, a lowered hand: the man faced front.

Temerity worked to crack the idiom. *Pastry? Like crumpet? Desirable young female?*

The driver caught Temerity's eye in the rear-view mirror. —No need to cry, girl. Just cooperate, and nothing bad will happen to you or your family.

She said nothing.

Eyes back on the road, the driver continued. —You love your papa, don't you?

Play along. —Yes.

—You don't want to be the reason why he gets arrested.

Temerity made her eyes wide and spoke on a dry whisper. —No.

—Then don't fight. Just keep quiet, and your family will be fine. Everything will be fine.

She memorized street signs, memorized the address of the house where they stopped: an older home, set back from the street, the front yard a thriving garden of flowers and shrubs.

The men discussed the risks of taking the cuffs off the pastry now versus the risks of a neighbour noticing two men leading a restrained woman to the house. The car doors opened, and the scents of flowers, turned soil, and sharp resin seemed to promise beauty and peace. The man she'd flipped reached into the back seat, wrenched Temerity around, unlocked the cuffs, and hauled her out of the car. Her hands tingled; her arms ached.

The front door of the house opened, and a man welcomed them. He stood about six feet tall, his body broad, muscular once, now turning to fat. Bald on top with greying hair over his ears, a heavy greying moustache, and black eyebrows, he wore dark trousers and an open-necked white shirt. —Come in, come in.

A large cat rested on an upper windowsill and stared down at them all.

Once inside, the host grasped Temerity's left forearm and ran his fingers over the mark of the cuff. Then he glared at the two men. —I thought I made myself clear: no samples, and no rough play. I want them as calm as possible.

The man Temerity had flipped answered. —With respect, Arkady Dmitrievich, she fought back.

—This little one?

The driver smirked. —Yes, she flipped him onto his back and would have chopped into his neck if I hadn't saved his arse.

The other man glared. —Shut up! It's not like she could have killed me.

—Yes, she could have. One good blow. Or did you miss that class?

—I didn't miss anything. I fight better than you any day.

The driver mimed drinking. —Only when you find some guts in a bottle.

Rolling his eyes, Arkady strengthened his grip on Temerity's forearm and hauled her to a large dining table, this table covered with a cloth, bottles, glasses, many plates of food, and several bunches of cut flowers. He spoke with solicitous respect. —What can I get you to drink?

She glanced around the room, struggling to understand the meaning of this house, these men, the table, and the smaller batch of bottles to one side.

Arkady picked up one of the flower bunches. —I cut these myself. Pretty, aren't they?

Temerity accepted the flowers in her free hand, almost dropped them, held them to her nose. —Lovely.

He let go of her arm.

The other two men blocked access to the porch, and the back windows offered a view of another beautiful garden. A breeze played with her hair, as from an open door or window just out of sight.

Arkady gave her a glass of red wine, then raised his own in a toast. —To the beauty of women.

Steady the Buffs. She took a sip: sweet and heavy with a tainted finish, just salty enough to make her want to drink more and so get rid of that taste.

Smiling, she placed the glass on the table. —Oh, it's too strong for me. You see, I don't drink. My father wouldn't approve.

—Would your father approve of you insulting your host?

—I...

—Drink it, please. I've gone to a lot of trouble to make sure your evening is pleasant.

She backed away, and sunlight glinted off her watch. Arkady grabbed her left wrist again, peered at the watch face, at the brand name: English. He threw her wrist down as though shaking off repulsive debris and craned his head to look at the other two men. —How old is she?

The men glanced at each other, shrugged.

—You're to check their papers! Eighteen's the cutoff. Give me the handbag. I'll do it myself.

His back to the other men, Arkady faced Temerity as he scanned the British passport and travel papers for one Margaret Bush.

He stared at her.

Feeling the breeze on her face, she stared back.

Arkady dropped the papers and passport into the handbag,

snapped it shut, and let it dangle on his forearm. —Let's not waste good wine. Drink.

Temerity kept still.

Outside, dogs barked.

Arkady took a step towards her. —Drink it. Last chance.

—No.

—Stepanov, get in here.

Temerity ran towards the source of the breeze and collided with another man. Short and slender, with a snub nose and receding hairline, Yury Stepanov seemed half-lost in the poor tailoring of his NKVD uniform. As Temerity staggered back from him, the two men who'd seized her on the street dragged her to an overstuffed armchair and forced her to sit. Dust rose. The man she'd flipped spat in her face. Metal clinked glass, and Arkady, still balancing the handbag on his forearm, looked tired.

Yury stepped in front of him, holding a needle and loaded syringe. He'd pursed his lips into an odd pout, one that Temerity recognized from photos of another man. Knowing or not, Yury Stepanov imitated the new NKVD chief, Nikolai Yezhov.

Yury studied the scene, surprised by how much this pastry struggled. Did she not know she was overpowered? —Keep her still. Now, hold her hand out to me. I said keep her still. Why can't we just force them to drink?

Arkady peered over Yury's shoulder. —Because they might vomit. Not too much. She's small. We don't want to kill her. She's still swollen from the handcuffs, so you should get a good vein. No, not like that. Wait, what the hell are you doing?

Yury almost shoved the needle at Arkady, then thought better of it. —With respect, Comrade Major, I'll ask you to do it.

His boot soles tapped hard as he strode off.

Muttering an insult, Arkady tugged the handbag onto his shoulder, read the label on the bottle, held the syringe to the light, and flicked his thumbnail at the glass a few times to burst bubbles. He depressed the plunger; a drop of liquid emerged at the needle's tip.

Temerity writhed. —Wait!

—For what?

Temerity could not answer him.

Without easing their grip, the other two men moved to give Arkady room. Arkady knelt beside Temerity, something Yury had not thought to do, and so wielded his delicate weapon with stability and balance. He leaned in close to her ear, as if to kiss her.

She froze.

Arkady nodded. —That's better. Now, not a sound.

He injected a vein on the top of her right hand, the prick and burn signalling defeat. Still, as much in anger as fear, she did scream.

It guttered out.

The flat was quiet except for the music from the radio, and Kostya smiled, unaware he did so. Then he cried out and got to his feet. He thought he might vomit, not because of the morphine, which no longer bothered him that way, but because of a sudden cold and desperate anxiety.

He'd forgotten.

The old man's dessert party. Shit!

In his bedroom, he hauled on civilian clothes. Snub Arkady and avoid the party? Unthinkable. *All those years,* Arkady would say, *all those years that you begged me to invite you, and now you forget?*

Kostya strode and swayed through the flat door and locked it behind him, and as his shoes swished on the steps, so much quieter than his boots, he thought of his veins and how they rose to the skin and announced their presence after an injection, never before. In the lobby he nodded to the watchwoman. She rocked in her chair. Then he ran to Vasilisa Prekrasnaya — with some grace, he thought — paid his fare, and descended the steps. The train rumbled its arrival, the driver looking skeletal though the shadowed glass. The tile mosaic of Vasilisa, all her many pieces, shimmered.

As Arkady eased through a haze of tobacco smoke, laughing at the end of a joke and swatting one of his cats down off the dining table, he spotted Kostya's arrival at the front door. Kostya nodded to him, then answered a hearty greeting from another guest. Fifteen NKVD officers, old Chekists and a few favoured up-and-comers like Kostya, filled the parlour; male voices shouted and laughed and cursed, told stories, made toasts. Glancing around at his house, at the decor unchanged since 1903, Arkady could not decide which felt more bourgeois: keeping all the frills and stripes and curving lines of his parents' youth, or spending time and money on new and plain decoration. Busy with his career and then with raising Kostya, Arkady had ignored the house. Many visitors commented on how Arkady's house felt like an old photograph, a refuge from sharp lines and paperwork.

The men glanced at the closed study door, then pretended disinterest. Knowing what waited inside the study, Kostya smirked. The study had once been his bedroom, and he'd completed hours and hours of language drill there. At fourteen, he'd announced to Arkady and Vadym that he wished to become a Chekist like them, and surely his gift for languages would be useful there, just as Arkady had said for two years now. Arkady made the plans and arranged for more language tutors. Some of those tutors had asked Kostya when they might expect to see him at the university, and Kostya had never known what to say. Just before starting as a cadet in NKVD, Kostya considered changing his mind and instead attending university, perhaps studying to become a translator or even a doctor, like his grandfather. He chased the thought away, hardly able to admit it to himself, let alone voice it to Arkady. So the plan remained in place, and Cadet Nikto graduated and took up his duty. No doubts then, he told himself, and tonight, standing in Arkady's house with other officers while confined women waited in his old bedroom, and no doubts now. He shook his head. *No, no doubts.*

He gulped vodka, and the alcohol soon collided with the morphine. He felt calmer.

Arkady embraced a friend and colleague, and then he called Kostya over. Others heard this, and the older men joined in to welcome Kostya home, to offer congratulations on the promotion, show curiosity about his wounds, and then congratulate Arkady on raising such a fine man. Kostya, silent in deference as Arkady thanked everyone for their compliments, took in the scents of cologne, sweat, tobacco, and wine. Then, at a nod from Arkady, Kostya remembered his role as assistant host, excused himself, and ensured other guests had something to drink. He swayed a little. No one noticed.

Some of the men sang now, something from a movie they'd all seen a dozen times or more because Stalin liked it. Kostya, grateful for the darkness in cinemas, had yawned his way through the tiresome love story. Sunburnt collective-farm workers, the men all clean-shaven, no hairy *kulaks* here, and the women all young and slim, broke into frequent song and dance involving rakes, scythes, and combine harvesters. No conflict, not even the smallest problem of a balky tractor engine, threatened the finally consummated celebration of harvest and collective. Teeth, Kostya had noticed, all the actors possessed strong teeth — so many smiles. Years before, watching *Battleship Potemkin* with Arkady, Kostya got dizzy with a sense of exile. Eisenstein's weirdly lit Odessa split Kostya's present, rubbing his face in the fact he was no Muscovite, no matter how much he might consider Moscow home. Kostya from Odessa? Another lifetime, another Kostya. At the movie's sequence on the steps, as the untended pram bounced away and the baby imprisoned within cried, Arkady had whispered in his ear: *That's you*. Kostya pretended not to hear. He much preferred movies set on the moon, or Mars, or in the safety of the past, like *Lieutenant Kizhe*. Of this, he said nothing.

Satisfied everyone had a drink, Kostya leaned in a corner by the kitchen, a spot where he used to sit and daydream. When he glanced up, he noticed Arkady striding toward him.

Arkady murmured in his ear. —You're in pain.

—I'm fine.

—You can't hide it from me, Little Tatar. I know you too well.

A bump and a crash: something fell over in the study.

Kostya stepped out of the corner. —I'll check that.

—Just let them out.

Kostya followed Arkady into the parlour and sidled over to the study door. Arkady cleared his throat and clapped his hands, begging his comrades' kind attention; the men looked only too happy to grant it. Some of the younger officers smirked and nudged one another.

At a nod from Arkady, Kostya unlocked and opened the wooden study door. He gave it too hard a swing, using the strength needed to heave open a cell. The study door smacked off the wall, and Kostya looked to the floor, wondering if the morphine had affected him more than he thought. The contents of the study, however, distracted the guests from his gaffe.

Twelve naked women stood there. Some had crossed their arms over their chests; others waited with their arms and faces slack. All of them stared into some middle distance. Kostya knew why. On arrival, the women had been offered drinks laced with calmatives, and those who declined the drinks received an injection. Arkady took deep offence at refusals of his hospitality and resented the need for injections.

For many years, Arkady had barred Kostya from these parties. His attendance, finally permitted after he completed his NKVD courses, came with an understanding that no one spoke of these parties, which did, from time to time, get out of hand. With luck, and with the female guests showing a bit of common sense, Arkady's parties could end well for the men. Work hard, play hard.

Two of the women hugged each other, twin sisters, their blond and frizzy hair fringed across the forehead and bobbed at the jawline in a style that Kostya disliked.

A man laughed in Kostya's ear: Boris Kuznets. —My first time here, and I am not disappointed.

Nodding, Kostya recalled Boris's nickname at Lubyanka: the Sound Man. Comrade Captain Kuznets so loved his work that he would take time away from his desk to assist in interrogations. Later he might attend a concert, or an opera. The subtleties of sound delighted him, and he explained this via comparisons. Fist to face versus book to face. Boots to ribs versus chair to ribs. Penis to vagina versus truncheon to vagina.

Boris laughed and pointed to the study. —Look at that gooseflesh. We should warm them up.

Kostya noticed the pile of women's clothing on his old bed, a terrible mess of linen and cotton and lisle, hems and stockings and frills. The shoes and boots lay in a different pile on the floor, up against the wall, and Kostya suppressed a sigh. The shoes made him feel sad, even lonely, and he could not explain to himself why. Then, remembering his role, he bowed to the women, wished them all a good evening, disciplined himself to look only at their feet, and invited them to join the men.

As the women passed before him, Kostya recalled an old fairy story, one his grandfather liked to tell: 'The Twelve Dancing Princesses.' He leaned against a wall, noticing how quiet, how still the women seemed.

Numbed. Distant.

What the hell did the old man use tonight?

Then he wondered at his own stillness. At previous dessert parties he'd get hard as soon as he saw a female face. Tonight, he hung limp.

As the other men made noises of enticement and approval, as they broke into smaller groups, bartered with one another, and prepared to choose, Kostya closed his eyes and breathed in deep. The pain in his shoulder grew tentacles, and the tentacles spread down his arm in stinging jolts. He took a last look in the study to make sure he'd missed no one, locked the door, and pocketed the key.

The women's voices stayed quiet, placid, resigned. Some of the women responded to guidance and suggestion and played with the men's lapels, stroked the men's faces. Others walked in circles until chosen, until touched, and then complied. Couples disappeared to shadowed corners or to other rooms. Arkady offered Kostya a cup of wine, a sweet Georgian red now in vogue, which he declined. Vodka meant a milder headache in the morning.

Then he saw her.

His first thought was to wonder what had happened to her knees. Even as he thought this, he denied what he saw, denied the recognition, and almost laughed.

Hair dark and curly, eyes hooded and sleepy: that Britisher, Margaret Bush, Mildred Ferngate, or whatever the hell her real name might be, here, in Arkady Dmitrievich's parlour.

Kostya changed his mind about the wine and poured himself a big cup of it. Gulped it. Poured a second.

Abducted off the street, of course, picked up like any of the other young women, a pretty piece of pastry for the old man's dessert party.

Kostya dabbed wine from his lips with the backs of his fingers and strode towards her. Some of the men now discussed sharing, fifteen to twelve, after all, while others finished conversations about office life. One small and slender man, the only one in uniform, touched the tablecloth as if evaluating the quality, then flicked at a stray flower and answered another man's small talk. —I did not claw my way back to Moscow from rural outposts to remain a sergeant.

Stepanov, Kostya remembered, *Yury Grigorievich Stepanov.* Yury had been a cadet with Kostya and Misha and tried to force his friendship on them. Kostya and Misha had, with some cruelty, declined the offer.

Yury glanced at the petite woman with the injured knees and stepped toward her. So did Kostya.

Then Boris called Yury over, asking if he liked little blondes with curly hair.

Temerity looked at Kostya: no recognition or compliance in her eyes, just despair. Then her eyes dulled again as she crossed her arms over her breasts and resumed walking in a circle.

Kostya placed his right arm around her shoulders and guided her to the study. None of the other men saw this, he felt sure, for they all had their own distractions. Arkady might later demand to know why Kostya had presumed to use the study and then lecture him on not abusing the privilege of keys. Such folly from the old man could wait.

He locked the study door behind them. So much might happen at these parties, did happen.

—Enough.

His own voice. Kostya recalled nothing of the thought, of the choice to say *Enough*.

Yet he said it.

Hands quick, he plucked the small Persian rug folded over the back of the desk chair. The rug, soft and light, and much too precious to leave on the floor, had kept Kostya warm as he'd studied far into many cold nights. He wrapped it around Temerity.

She spoke English, confident and loud. —Ready, aye, ready. Though I don't know where I turned.

He crammed his hand over her mouth and shoved her against the wall, and the fumes of wine and vodka from his breath wafted round them both as he murmured in her ear. —Not a sound, unless I ask you a question, and then you whisper. In Russian. Understand?

Her nod felt weak against his hand.

—I'll take my hand away, and you will sit down in that chair.

She nodded again, sat down.

—What's your name? Not Margaret Bush. I've guessed that much.
She shook her head, over and over.

—You will tell me your name.

Anger rose in her eyes; confusion dulled it.

Kostya took her right hand, spotted the needle mark. —Get your
clothes.

Limp and still, she spoke French. —Blouse.

—Russian. Only Russian. I'll get your blouse. Is this it?

Temerity sneered. —That sack?

Kostya picked through pieces of fabric until he thought he recognized something. He held the blouse by the collar. —How in hell
would I know? This one?

She took the blouse, hesitated as though trying to remember something, crumpled the fabric, patted it, and slipped the blouse on. Then
she just sat there, eyes vacant.

Kostya shook his head. —Stand up, come on. Arms out, wait,
fine, fine, button it yourself. Which skirt? This one?

—Stockings. No, knees. Brassiere, brassiere.

—Fuck the underwear! You want to live through this night, yes?
Then obey me. Where are your shoes? These? No, too big. These?
Right. Now wait and keep quiet.

Kostya swaggered out of the study, adjusted his fly, discovered
the morphine had not killed response, only delayed it, and eased
the door shut behind him. Discarded male clothing, ties and jackets
and trousers, littered the chairs and floor. The owners had retreated
with their prey to other rooms or unlit corners. Grunts, slaps, and
muffled female cries filled Kostya's ears as he took a *portupeya* and
pouch hanging from the back of a chair. He groped in the pouch, past
papers and something sticky, until he found metal. He plucked it out:
a car key, engraved with the number forty-two. Tucking the key into
a pocket, Kostya returned to the study and offered Temerity his arm.
She leaned on him, and they emerged into the front yard, just some
drunken couple leaving a party for home.

As Kostya drove, the streets widened into valleys, and the streetlights changed into ancient fires on sticks. Telling himself to remember these morphine-bent perceptions, wondering why the woman next to him cried out about him driving all over the road, Kostya sought Vasilisa Prekrasnaya. Only then could he be sure of home.

He parked near his block of flats, confident no one would ask the driver of an NKVD car to move. He offered Temerity his arm again, and they staggered into the lobby. The watchwoman, slumped in her rocking chair, snored.

Kostya smirked.

As they climbed the stairs, Temerity stumbled, fell against him.

Eyes heavy, Kostya kissed the top of Temerity's head. A night for fairy tales. First, he'd witnessed the parade of the twelve dancing princesses. Then he'd sneaked past the sleeping dragon Zmei Gorynich with a prize. What next, Marya Morevna's defeat of Koshchei the Deathless?

The clink of metal on the wood from his dropped keys seemed to slice into his ears, and he winced. As he bent over, the awakened watchwoman called up from the lobby. —Goodnight, comrade.

—Goodnight, Grandmother.

Temerity tried to stand up straight, then leaned against him again.

He unlocked his flat door. —It's no better to be safe than sorry. After you, Marya Morevna.

She mumbled. —That's not my name.

[ ]

NARZAN, WITH BERRIES IN'T
Sunday 6 June

—Nikto.

Go away.

—Nikto!

Kostya dreamt that bones fell from the metro tunnel's mud and shattered the windows of the train. The Spanish boys screamed; the bones exploded; clouds of powder and ash fouled the air. New bones whistled like falling bombs, and as Kostya gagged and sought the boys, he found only cardboard name tags.

Thirsty.

Hung over.

The bed rocked and squeaked, a rhythm to it.

The neighbours are fucking. No, it's my bed.

Someone yelled. To his right.

—Nikto, help me! She's choking.

The room had developed a terrible spin, as if impaled on a spike and then given a smack to set it in motion.

The bed slowed; a sharp and ugly odour rose.

Scherba?

Kostya sat up fast, and the light sliced into his eyes. That British woman sat in bed next to him, retching over his sheets. He jerked away hard enough to fall from the bed. As he staggered upright, hand over his crotch to cover himself, the fabric of his trousers rasped his skin, surprising him. He was still dressed in last night's civilian clothes when he usually slept naked this time of year, and he had no memory of bringing a woman home.

Certainly not this woman.

Dust motes fell across the beam of light separating him from Temerity. She still wore her blouse and skirt. Dark bags swelled beneath her closed eyes, and freckles stood out on her face like tiny stains.

Efim frowned as he held Temerity's shoulders. —Afraid of a little bile, Nikto?

—How the hell did she get here?

—Puff of smoke? What did she drink last night? When I got in here, she — easy, easy, let it come — she was choking on her vomit. Good thing you left the bedroom door open.

Kostya rubbed his eyelids with the pads of his fingers. —I did? I need some water.

—Throw it in your face and wake up!

Catching himself against door jamb and walls, Kostya stumbled to the bathroom. He glared at the telephone. It stayed silent. Cold water ran into his cupped hands, and it smelled of soil and wood and something sweet yet unclean. Three handfuls down his throat, one handful on his face, as the good doctor said.

A decision. He'd made a decision. *Enough,* he'd said, surrounded by drugged women and sweaty men. He'd said it in Bilbao, navigating crowds of refugees, and he'd said it again on the docks struggling to write the boys' names in Russian. He'd thought it when he'd disobeyed orders and left a witness simply because he found her attractive — a dire dereliction of duty — and now the witness lay in his bed. Under interrogation, she'd soon enough mention Kostya and how he'd shot wide in Spain and then let her go from Lubyanka. All good reasons to say *Enough* and get her out of that party, keep her from arrest, yet something else drove him: the knowledge that she'd suffer and die for no good reason.

Her, and how many others?

Enough. He said it to his reflection in the shaving mirror, except the idea writhed, and a different word split his lips. —Impossible.

Impossible he'd brought her home. Impossible he'd spared her in the first place. Impossible she'd turned up in Moscow.

Promising himself never to drink that wretched sweet wine again, he lurched back to the bedroom.

Oh, it's possible. And sick in my bed.

Fucked in the mouth.

Eyes still clenched shut, she spat, gasped in air. —Get me some water.

Efim nodded his approval, and Kostya found himself filling a glass before he questioned why he'd obeyed her. He decided to ignore how she'd said *Get me some water* in English. Hadn't she? Yes, Kostya told himself, Scherba must have missed it, if it had happened at all. Surely. He made no reaction to hearing a foreign language from a strange woman in his own flat. He had simply, in his medical concern, picked up on the general idea that someone hungover would need water.

Efim took the water and passed it to Temerity, then lifted her other wrist. —It's all right. I'm a doctor. Your speech is slurred. I want to take your pulse. Sip, just sip, or else you'll retch again.

She spoke Russian. —What day is this?

Efim peered at her, then placed his palm on her forehead. —Sunday morning, the sixth of June. When did you eat last?

—Friday. Sometime on Friday.

—It's not very wise to drink on an empty stomach.

She took a breath to speak, as if angry. Instead, she sipped the water. Then she looked up and saw Kostya.

As Efim dodged her flinch and steadied the glass, he noticed the mark on the back of her hand: a puncture wound. He sighed. His flatmate, not as clever as a man his age should be, needed some advice.

Efim bundled up the soiled sheet. —Don't lie down. Nikto, prop her up with pillows, then come see me in the kitchen. I'll drop the sheets at the laundry service on my way to work.

At the kitchen sink, Efim ran water and hoped it would cover the sound of speech. —A narkomaniac streetwalker? Gonorrhea will be the least of it. Get rid of her.

Nerve pain zapped, and Kostya rubbed at his left arm, unaware he did so. —No, she's...I met her at a party. Can you look at her knees before you go?

—Knees? Then you won't need sulpha pills.

—What? No, no, she fell. Her knees are skinned and bloody.

Efim dug around in his medical bag. —Any more patients for me? Stashed in the pantry, perhaps?

—Just check her knees.

—After I check you.

Kostya leaned away from Efim's touch. —I'm fine.

—No, you're not. You keep your bad arm limp and close to your side. You skipped yesterday's morning dose, and look how miserable you got by the evening. Then, after treatment, you ran off.

—The morphine will only wear off in a few hours and leave me where I started. I don't want it. Listen to me!

Efim assembled needle and syringe. —I can hear you just fine. And I have clear instructions to keep you fit to work, something you know perfectly well, so stay still, and we'll see if we can find better veins than last night. I am quite imprisoned enough here without adding a stray whore to the mix.

—She is not a stray anything. You will speak of her with respect.

Efim stared him down. —Should I get the police?

—*What?*

—Strange woman in the flat. You're in distress. She frightens you.

—Frightens me?

—Clearly.

—What can she do: vomit on me?

Efim whispered it. —Who is she?

Kostya scowled. *I will not submit to interrogation from you.* —I notice you're wearing a wedding band.

Wincing, Efim almost shook his head in admiration. —My wife is alive and well back in Leningrad. I'm seconded to Moscow for research.

—How many children?

The water pressure weakened. Efim turned off the tap, and the speed of his answer betrayed his sorrow and relief. —None.

Kostya sat down in a kitchen chair, his posture that of an interrogator's, confidence and ease, just a small matter to straighten out, comrade. —Seconded, you said. Army?

—I was working at a hospital. A Red Army group forced me onto an armoured train. The White Army seized the train for a while, then the Reds took it back. Two winters, 1918 and '19.

Unbuttoning his shirt, Kostya softened his voice. —Did you ever visit Odessa?

Efim recalled what he'd told himself when he declined a chance to escape the train. *Escape where? I don't know where I am.* —I've no idea. All I saw was people, sick and injured people.

Kostya held out his left arm; Efim gave the injection.

Not sure how this NKVD officer had just pried him open, Efim took great care organizing his doctor's bag. —Sit still a moment, while I check your mistress's knees.

Kostya's voice rose, fell. —She's not my mistress. Look, if you think so little of her, then why do you pick up your bag? Why help her?

The doctor stared at the secret policeman.

Kostya looked away first.

In the bedroom, Efim asked Temerity about her injury. —Did you fall?

She tugged up her skirt. —Pushed, I think.

Efim tweezed small stones and fibres from her wounds and then dabbed some disinfectant. —My name's Dr. Efim Antonovich Scherba. Yours?

Kostya stood in the doorway, face drawn, voice sharp. —Her name's Nadezhda. She'll be with us for a while.

Efim kept his gaze on Temerity. —Nadezhda...what?

Temerity grasped at a sheet to stop the spin of the room. It didn't help. —Nadezhda Ivanovna Solovyova.

Impressed, Kostya almost smiled. *Name number three. Or are we up to four?* Recalling the touch of the cigarette case, he used the fond diminutive. —More water, Nadia?

—Piss off.

—Pardon me?

Efim lost his smirk as gently pinched the skin on the back of Temerity's right hand, near the puncture wound, and released it.

The skin did not flatten right away. —You're quite dehydrated, Miss Solovyova. I know, it should be comrade, not miss, but I am old-fashioned. Drink in tiny sips, just not too much. That tap water's not fit for a stray dog. Nikto, get her some mineral water at the deli, Narzan, no other brand. And some bread, for later, once you're sure she can keep the water down. I'll sit with her while you're gone.

—It's a sixth day. The shops are closed.

—Babichev always opens in the morning of a sixth day, seven till noon. Now go. Doctor's orders.

Temerity glanced at her right hand, where Efim had pinched her. She stroked the spot, then looked up and caught Kostya staring at her.

Efim closed his medical bag and stood up. —If she's not better by suppertime, she may need intravenous fluids at the hospital.

—She'll be fine.

—Nikto, she choked on her own vomited bile.

—Then how fortunate you heard the retch, yes?

Efim gave Kostya a long look. —Please hurry. I'm due at the lab.

—On a sixth day?

Efim stifled a sigh as he struggled in his mind, once again, with the new Soviet calendar. —The world doesn't stop spinning just because you get to enjoy a rest. I need to finish a report. At least today I'll get some peace and quiet.

—I don't get sixth days off, as a rule. I had a shift change, and...oh, forget it. Narzan it is.

As Kostya left, Temerity held the glass of tap water away from her mouth. —It tastes terrible. What did you put in it?

Efim took the glass.

Too tired to ask anything else, Temerity shut her eyes.

When Temerity woke again, she found Kostya sitting asleep in a kitchen chair propped against the wall, his feet on the end of the bed. Eyes shut, he breathed with a slight snore, expelling noise and wine fumes. He held something small in one hand: a string of amber beads. Next to him, on a tiny bedside table, stood a green bottle of mineral water and a tea glass supported by a filigree *podstakannik*.

Temerity took the *podstakannik* by the handle, then by its body. A nickel alloy, perhaps, the colour of dull brass. The pattern of vines and leaves pressed her fingertips as she tightened her grip.

Hand out for the bottle, Temerity hesitated.

The paper seal on the bottle seemed intact.

Kostya woke to the stuttering clink of glass. —Let me.

She watched him tuck the beads into a pocket and then pour water. She accepted the drink and wrapped her hands around the *podstakannik* to hide the tremble. The filigree dug in. —It's good.

He smiled, then looked stern again.

Birdsong and fresh air floated through an open window. Someone in a neighbouring flat practised scales on a piano. Temerity made a quick study of the room as the water settled in her stomach: the small closet, the little bedside table, and the kitchen chair. —Where are we?

—My bedroom.

—In your flat?

—Well, I haven't got a bedroom in Lubyanka.

She sipped.

Kostya poured himself a glass. —We're told the tap water is safe. I don't believe it. The well for this block lies near a recent cemetery. A gas explosion, twenty-odd people died the same day, and what pieces could be found were buried quickly in a small public garden with a memorial stone. It's why the water tastes so sweet. A toast, then. To the dead.

She raised her glass to match his, then watched him drink.

Mumbling, he gestured to the walls. —I'll go turn on the radio. We don't need the neighbours hearing every word we say.

—What about tapping a pencil, to break up the sound waves?

He snorted. —It doesn't work. Stay there. You're not well.

In the front room, as he reached for the radio knobs, his right hand shook.

He made it a fist. *Remember who you are.*

Then he relaxed his hand: stillness and strength.

As the radio clicked on, a deadweight thudded to his bedroom floor. Exasperated, he rolled his eyes, then turned up the volume like any good Soviet citizen who wished to hear about the latest tally of new galoshes from the State Rubber Industry Trust, a glorious surplus which may now bring the shortage within measurable distance of its end, and strode back to the bedroom, where he crouched down to help Temerity up off the floor. —See? This is why I told you to stay in bed.

Once he had her settled, he shut the bedroom window, then sat back down in the chair. His closeness left her little room to leave the bed on that side; her weakness left her little chance to leave the bed on the other side.

She took a breath to speak, looked away.

Kostya smiled, the way a boy caught playing a prank might, and held out his cigarettes. Temerity declined; he lit only one.

Smoke hid his face. —I was not my best self last night.

—Who are you today?

After a moment, he retrieved a red leather wallet from his trouser pocket and held it out to her on the palm of his hand.

She took it, recognized it: a Soviet citizen's identification. Unfolding the wallet, she found a photograph and a much-initialled, much-stamped official form reading Nikto, Konstantin Arkadievich, Senior Lieutenant of State Security.

She peered at him. —Your name is really Nikto?

As he took the identification back, he sounded tired. —Many people changed their names after the Revolution. Look, I was twelve. I'd lost all my papers, and I didn't want the orphan's surname, Neizvestny. It seemed like a good idea at the time. It's not important. At least it's not a common name, like yours. What? What's funny?

—I never asked to be called Nadezhda.

He whispered. —Well, what was I supposed to do? Tell the good doctor that you're not a narkomaniac prostitute but a British spy?

—I'm no spy.

—Silly me. A tourist, then, just like in Spain.

Temerity rubbed her temples. —Wait, wait. You share the flat with that doctor?

—Yes.

—He thinks I'm a...what did you say?

Kostya mimed injection. —Narkomaniac. A drug addict.

—No, no, wait, he injected me.

—Scherba?

—No! The fat slob with the moustache, the one running the party.

—Ah, him, yes. He's no slob. He's an old Chekist who saved my life, once upon a time, and you will speak of him with respect.

—Respect? What did he do to me?

Kostya wanted to brush the curls from her forehead. —Just something to make you calm.

—I can't remember. I can't remember anything from last night. I left the hotel. Then it's blank.

Kostya said nothing.

Temerity drank the last of the water in her glass. —So when will you bring me in? Could we get it over with?

Kostya's stern expression fell away, revealing worry and fatigue. —I'm not arresting you.

—Then you'll shoot me here?

—No! I'm trying to help you.

—Help me? You held a gun to my head!

—You remember that just fine.

Her voice squeaked. —How the hell am I supposed to forget it?

—And do you also remember I let you go? Hey? Because here you are, in my flat, in my bed, alive, intact, and one hundred per cent not shot.

—Oh, yes, pardon me for overreacting. Clearly, everything's fine so long as I'm not shot.

—I spared you. This means nothing?

—I don't understand it. This entire mess. You. How can a situation mean something when I don't understand it?

Kostya took a breath to snap back an answer. Another thought interrupted him. —Fucked in the mouth, the car!

—What car?

He wrenched open the closet doors, shook uniform pieces off hangers onto the bed, and unfastened his trousers. —Even here, it must be the British way or no way at all, yes? A problem, a country, a people do not even exist unless a Britisher builds an empire around them, exploits them, and then says, 'Oh, dear me, I do not understand them.'

She kept her eyes closed as he dressed. —The British have not built an empire around the USSR.

—Then what are you doing in India?

—What? You've got the biggest land mass in the world. What are you Russians so afraid of?

—Invasion. Aren't you, on your little island? Open your eyes.

He stood over her, an NKVD officer once more, flawed only by a wrinkled collar and a missing cap. Then he touched her shoulder. —Look, I want to help you. I'll get your papers, and then we'll figure out what to do with you. But stay here until I get back. The bathroom's just down the hall to your right, and the mineral water's there on the bedside table. Promise me you won't leave. Please. It's much too dangerous to go outside without papers. I'll get them, I swear to you. Just stay here.

—I—

—Please!

She studied him. —Open the window? Just for air?

He did this. —Stay in bed, out of sight of the window, yes?

She nodded.

He tugged on his cap. —I won't be long.

A long day in the garden always soothed Arkady. He wore his ragged gardening clothes, and he'd not bothered to shave. Bringing shrubs back to life after winter, planting annuals, tending perennials: it all earned him some ribbing from his colleagues. Arkady only nodded when teased, and he relished the satisfaction of dirty hands, dirty with life.

His garden also allowed for disposal of anything awkward left behind at a party. He'd buried clothing in the larger garden behind the house, many pieces over the years, near a specific hedge. The bones of one accident lay buried beneath an iris bed. Other accidents had gone to the morgue. Only three in total over all those years, good odds, really. The bones beneath the irises belonged to a young woman he'd picked up for an autumn dessert party, many years ago. He got her to the house before any other guests arrived. She fought back, refused a drink, ran to a window and beat on the glass, and then, worst of all, said she recognized Arkady from a visit to her uncle's office at Lubyanka.

Arkady struck her head with the butt of his Nagant — too hard, he'd discovered an hour later, when he unlocked the little closet in the basement to check on her. He considered faking a crime scene in an alley, a common tactic, but he respected his colleagues too much to waste their time. So after the party that night, in the small hours, cursing the girl's uncle and his callous disregard for her innocence — letting a girl see the inside of Lubyanka like that, really — Arkady buried the body in a wild patch of his back garden. The following day, he planted iris bulbs there. Each spring these perennials bloomed anew, fragrant and beautiful.

Arkady suffered recurring dreams in which he must explain flowers strewn on his Lubyanka desk as Kostya stood in the office doorway, hesitant, amber worry beads dangling from his hand. Sometimes Misha stood behind him, grinning.

Refusing to consider the iris bed, Arkady reminded himself that Kostya, at least, had not attended that particular party, being too young and sent to spend the night at Vadym's. These days, Arkady pretended to be irritated when Kostya missed a party, and he would remind Kostya of all his adolescent pleas to be invited. In truth, Arkady felt relieved when Kostya declined. *I've tainted him enough.*

Arkady had scheduled last night's party knowing Kostya had to work early the next day and so would not come.

Then, schedules changed.

Captain Boris Aleksandrovich Kuznets, new to Moscow and still finding his way around, had asked Major Arkady Dmitrievich Balakirev about his rumoured parties. Arkady had long decided on the best way to deflect any implied threat from another officer, a threat to report these parties: an invitation. Arkady would then observe the new man's reactions at the party and decide from there whether to invite him again or blackmail him into silence. —Yes, Comrade Captain, a very selective list of guests.

—How might one get added to such a list?

—I put you there. Consider it done.

—Thank you, thank you, that's very kind. Call me Boris Aleksandrovich, and forgive my asking, Arkady Dmitrievich, but what do you do about noise?

Arkady almost wrinkled his nose at the presumption. As the older man and senior officer, Arkady should be the one to set the level of formality, not Boris. —All taken care of, Boris Aleksandrovich. A private house and, for the excitable girls, supplements.

—Sometimes the noise is the best part.

—Too much noise, and the neighbours might call the police, and what a pretty fix that would be.

Both men had laughed. Then Boris explained that his protégé, Yury Stepanov, could obtain supplements, good ones, to ensure not just compliance but amnesia. Arkady remembered Yury from Kostya's adolescence and time in NKVD school, how Yury had trailed Kostya and Misha with something like murder in his eyes, something like love.

Ah yes, such fine supplements Yury had fetched. Party guests had complained that the pastries kept falling asleep. Arkady interrupted Yury in his abuse of a frizzy-haired blonde to ask the little sycophant if he'd perhaps supplied a general anaesthetic? Tugging up his *galife* pants, Yury spat on the unresponsive woman and murmured about the experimental and therefore perhaps unpredictable nature of the medications at Laboratory of Special Purpose Number Two.

Arkady almost struck him. —Do you even know what they're doing at Special Two?

—Indeed I do, Comrade Major. Because I supervise. While also making time to assist at Lubyanka.

Finding Boris with another blonde one who bore a great resemblance to the woman Yury had spat on, sisters perhaps, Arkady almost complained, almost spewed his fury with Yury's incompetence, almost said that Misha and Kostya had been correct to treat Yury like a worm.

Instead, he asked Boris to take his pastry's pulse.

—She's fine. Just dozy.

—Finish up. We need to get rid of them.

Boris and Arkady rallied the men, bundled the women into the cars, and instructed the younger men to drop the women close to where they'd found them. Or in a park, whatever worked, just not too many together. Clumps of unconscious young women would alarm passersby.

Arkady had still not decided precisely what to do about the British woman.

Then Yury complained that the car he'd signed out for the evening, and its key, had gone missing.

Arkady checked with the other officers in each car, asking if anyone had Stepanov's key and vehicle by mistake. Doing so, he discovered two things. Not only had NKVD car number forty-two disappeared, but so had Kostya and the British woman with the injured knees.

Devout in his desire to not understand this development, Arkady quizzed Yury once more about his memory of the car.

Yury stamped his foot. —Yes, I'm certain! Car number forty-two, and it's gone! How shall I get Comrade Captain Kuznets home now?

Arkady drove both men home himself, in his own signed-out vehicle, as Boris assured Yury this business of the missing car would not affect him. —Someone took it by mistake. We'll get it straightened out at the office, once I see the Garage Number One records.

Free of Yury and Boris, Arkady knew he should drive by Kostya's block of flats. Just to see.

Then he'd reminded himself of construction in that area, of random signs rearing up in the dark, and declined.

After signing his car back in, and after thanking a young sergeant called Katelnikov for then driving him home, Arkady returned to the study and sifted the detritus of women. Many pairs of stockings, one set destroyed at the knees. Drawers and step-ins. A necklace with a hammer and sickle pendant. Several handkerchiefs. Some bloodied rags. A brassiere, this last garment very strange to Arkady, and one which refused to give up its secrets even as he dangled it in the air, high above his face. And that handbag, black leather, well made, almost as conspicuous to his eyes as the wristwatch with the English brand name.

Arkady dumped the contents of the handbag onto Kostya's old desk: a mirrored compact; a lipstick; a beautiful glass bottle of perfume with a tassel and a chipped stopper; a leather case about half the size of Arkady's hand, and, inside that case, a rubber dome, intimate and strange; a small amount of cash; travel papers and the British passport in the name of Margaret Bush.

He'd almost said it aloud. *Kostya, we get shot for less.*

Now, in the garden, Arkady did say it aloud, and the sound of his own voice, and then the soft and quiet impact of his dropped trowel adjacent the turned soil, made him feel sick.

I've saved him before; I can save him again.

Somewhere behind him, a car braked. Arkady finished patting the earth over the buried stockings as booted footsteps approached.

—Beautiful afternoon, Arkady Dmitrievich.

—Boris Aleksandrovich, how are you?

Boris, looking younger somehow in his uniform, extended a hand. —Sore in the head, but I'm in better shape than young Stepanov. I suppose Nikto's sleeping it off, too? Sometimes I despair of the next generation. Young people today.

Arkady accepted Boris's offer of a hand up and lumbered to his feet. —No Chekist like an old Chekist.

—Forged in the fire of revolution.

They laughed at the slogans, at themselves.

—Arkady Dmitrievich, you'll never guess how I got here.

—Troika? I admit, I heard no sleigh bells.

Boris grinned, acknowledging Arkady's wit. —NKVD car number forty-two.

—Found it, then? Poor old Stepanov. Had he ever signed it out?

—He had. Someone else signed it back in. Not too long ago, in fact. Still, overdue.

The sunlight seemed to burn Arkady's face; the rest of him felt quite cold. —Come inside for a drink.

At his desk in Laboratory of Special Purpose Number Two, beneath a huge red poster showing two joined rings and the text *Only Those Who Work Deserve to Eat*, Efim wrote a letter.

My dearest Olga, my Olyushka.

The pen spit ink in blobs, and Efim scowled at the paper. How to say it, how to consider one's audience: not just Olga, of course, but any of the NKVD agents who might, could, would, intercept and read this letter? How to say it, and yet make the letter sound innocent?

Every year on their wedding anniversary, he would ask, *You still love me, Olyushka? You still want to spend your life with me?*

Yes, she'd answer, looking out a window, *I suppose so. I don't see anyone better.*

He'd brush her fair hair aside and press his lips to her forehead in mock concern. *Are you feverish?*

You're stuck with me, Fima.

As years passed, she'd sometimes pat her abdomen as she said *You're stuck with me.* No matter what Efim said about biology and the unknowable workings of life, she blamed herself for the miscarriages.

He imagined another such anniversary conversation. *You still love me, Olyushka, even after I inject poisons into political prisoners, call it phage therapy, and study the results? You still want to spend your life with me, or do you want spit in my face?*

He heard Major Balakirev's voice, his casual threat. *What did you say your wife is called?*

Efim covered his mouth with his hand and moaned. The compelled doctor: he'd played this role before. A sensation of movement, of travel, overtook him, as the floor of his office seemed to become the floor of that armoured train. Forced away at gunpoint, he'd left wounded men to die in misery. Cold. Months on end of bone-deep cold, and one war and one calendar wore into another.

One dull morning, grasses exposed, snow receded to puddles, the train maybe half a kilometre on its way, slow, slow, a woman alongside the tracks dropped the handles of the cart she hauled, a grown man and a child lying there, ran to keep up, then stopped, her arms outstretched. That dull morning, Efim leapt from the train.

Sunday 6 June 1937. My dearest Olga, Olyushka, my love, I think of you every night.

The new radio sitting on a chair in the corridor outside the main lab, volume cranked high, spewed static and Tchaikovsky's 'Dance of the Sugar Plum Fairy.'

As I sit here and think on you, I also think on my great privilege to serve our country as I do. I have here, in Moscow, a chance to leave a legacy in medicine. Such...

He tapped his pen against his thumb, oblivious to the spatter of ink. Such what? Detailed work? Meaningful work?

Intimate work?

My research progresses well, and we approach a breakthrough, one that may reverberate around the world.

A woman cried out, her voice ragged. —Mercy!

A door slammed.

A colleague's shadow darkened the frosted glass panel in Efim's office door, remained there a moment, then disappeared. Women's shoes tapped on the hard floors.

Efim sighed. Even with an office and a closing door, he could expect little privacy. His thoughts slipped on oily fear. So many people. Which of them eavesdropped? Which of them informed? Which of them sympathized with his reluctance to harm people? The prisoner who'd just screamed for mercy and now made no sound: had she even existed?

One day soon, would someone ask the same question about Olga?

Olyushka, my miracle, my love. As I sit here and think on you, I also think on my great privilege to serve our country as I do. I have here, in Moscow, a chance to leave a legacy in medicine. Such work is a journey in honour. I look forward to a new letter from you. I enclose a little money. Buy a nice blouse, if you need one, or a new pair of shoes. All my love, Fima.

Garbage, he told himself, complete garbage, the letter so stiff and formal even as he used the diminutives Olyushka and Fima. No NKVD agent would believe Efim had written the letter with no expectation of interference. Even this tacit acknowledgement of interference with the post could get him arrested.

He rocked the blotter over the fresh ink.

Olyushka, what have I done?

Acid and brine and vegetable fibres: pickles crammed Arkady's mouth. In his parlour, staring out the back window at his garden, Arkady shoved little pickles between his teeth, one after another, and then crunched them down. He did not swallow, instead holding the chewed mess in the pouches of his cheeks. He always felt worse after eating pickles; his father had avoided them. He told himself that he enjoyed eating pickles: fill the belly, occupy the teeth, chew chew chew. Two famines and subsequent random shortages had stripped much of the pleasure of eating from Arkady, leaving him with only a grim instinct to devour. He swallowed the wads of pickle in three gulps, shoved a chunk of bread into his mouth, then groped for the bottles on his table. His glass of wine had done nothing to calm him after the visit of Boris Kuznets, and neither had the vodka. The drinks did, however, help him decide that Boris's three separate mentions of cronyism, the charge so often thrown at disgraced NKVD officers, meant nothing.

Almost gagging on the bread, Arkady poured more vodka. *If Kuznets wanted to threaten me with cronyism, he'd never have come to my party. He damn near insisted I invite him. He benefits as much from my generosity as any other officer. What is he playing at?*

Glass clinked; liquid dribbled; knuckles knocked.

Three knocks, not five like NKVD on a raid. Spitting the bread into a handkerchief and stuffing that mess into his pocket, Arkady stood up to his full height, strode to the door, and yanked it open.

Then he sighed. —You have a key, Tatar.

Kostya stepped inside and, by long habit, sat on the little bench and fixed his heel into a bootjack. —I didn't want to startle you.

—Leave your boots on. Just wipe your feet; the charwoman comes tomorrow. Why are you in uniform? I thought you had today off.

—I had to drop by Lubyanka.

Grateful he had his back to Kostya, Arkady shut his eyes and accepted the lie. *You mean, you had to return Stepanov's car to Garage Number One.* —And what brings you here?

—Brings me here? Arkady Dmitrievich, I grew up in this house. Do I need a reason to visit my...you?

Arkady took a bottle from the table. —I expected you to be home today, sleeping it off. You need the rest.

Kostya shook his head at the wordless offer of vodka. —I'm fine. Can I help you tidy before the charwoman comes?

—I've got it looked after.

—Anything left behind?

Arkady stood where the sun shone bright, knowing Kostya would have trouble seeing him there. —Really, Kostya? Am I now the decrepit old man whose bib you must tie?

—I apologize, Arkady Dmitrievich.

—Let's go to the park.

—What?

Arkady had to admit the utterance surprised him, too. —Yes, Gorky Park. Such a lovely afternoon. How often do we get the same day off anymore? I can't go on holiday, like you keep pestering me to, but I can go to the park. Wait here. I'll get dressed.

He left the sunbeam and ascended the stairs.

Kostya studied the older man's back, his hunched shoulders, his tight grip on the stair rail. Then, once he heard Arkady close his bedroom door, he turned to the study.

Sunlight poured onto the tidy floor, the little bed, the desk. The piles of clothing, the heap of boots and shoes: gone.

Kostya took a deep breath, and he caught the echoes of sweet musks and Krasnaya Moskva.

He took another breath, and this time he smelled only stale tobacco smoke and men's cologne.

A breeze played at the window, at his face, and it carried the scents of the early flowers in Arkady's garden. Birds sang.

Upstairs, Arkady dropped something heavy, grunting as he bent over to retrieve it.

Kostya hurried now, checking beneath the bed, in the drawers of the desk.

No wristwatch, no handbag, no travel papers, no passport.

As if she'd never existed. I should expect nothing less from an old Chekist.

Then he spotted the Persian rug, folded over the back of the chair. He picked it up, drew it to his face, breathed in.

Arkady's voice floated over the stairs, almost like a warning. —Kostya?

Kostya left the study, hurried across the parlour, and stood at the bottom of the stairs. —Yes?

—Are the boot hooks in the porch?

Where else would they be? Kostya checked the porch, picked up the hooks, and returned to the bottom of the stairs. —I've got them. Should I bring them to you?

—No, just stand clear.

Left, right: Arkady tossed his boots down over the stairs, and they landed at Kostya's feet. Then the man himself descended, in uniform, armed, carrying his cap. He gripped the railing again, as if fearing a push, as if breaking a fall.

Kostya picked up the boots, held them out. —Why did you bother with uniform for a walk in the park?

—Kostya, what the hell is the matter with you? Ever since you came back from Spain, you've acted the foolish *pochemuchka*, always asking questions, why-why-why, and when you're not asking questions, you refuse to believe what's right in front of you. Save it for the cells. You're even worse now than then you first came here from Odessa. I have bothered, as you put it, with my uniform because even without translating a calendar I can feel in my bones this is a Sunday. When I was a child, I always wore my finest clothes on Sundays.

Kostya watched the older man tug on his boots with the hooks and ignored the heavy breathing. How to say it, how to acknowledge crime after crime: *Arkady Dmitrievich, did you find a British passport and travel papers?*

And if he hadn't found them? If she'd lost passport and papers somewhere else?

If one of the other men had found them?

Arkady looked up from his boots and waved a hook. —This gets harder every day.

Not speaking, they rode the metro to the park. As civilians made room for them, Kostya wished he could explain that he and Arkady were not on duty. Yet there they stood, uniformed from cap to boots, major and senior lieutenant of the NKVD, unmistakable.

Mistakes, thought Kostya. *I've made so many mistakes.*

Arkady touched Kostya's bad shoulder, and pain zapped down the arm. —Our stop, Tatar.

Park Kultury station: pillar after pillar of variegated brown and tan marble, corners sharp enough to cut the air. No Odessa catacomb, this, yet Kostya felt trapped and hungry, as if hiding underground to escape the sleet.

He hurried up the stairs. On the street, he turned around, looking for Arkady, who called out to him to wait.

In the park, the men strolled a while, commenting on the gentle air, the beauty of the grounds, and the happiness of children.

—Arkady Dmitrievich, I should get back.

Face calm, patient, Arkady gestured to a bench. —Let's sit down.

Kostya noticed the parachute tower, its twisting exterior a mash of Pisa upright and Tatlin constrained. Park visitors might climb this tower and then, wearing a motley parachute with a point like a *budenovka* cap, jump.

Arkady gestured to the woman who stood at the top of the tower adjusting her parachute harness. —I never understood the appeal.

Kostya made to light a cigarette; his match broke. He flicked the pieces of his shattered match to the ground and plucked out a second. Silk rustled and snapped as air filled the leaping woman's parachute, and her scream warmed to a laugh as she descended in safety and grace.

Ignition, flame: Kostya drew on his cigarette. —She seemed to like it.

—Those scars on your ear, do they hurt?

—Yes, they hurt. Yes, they're ugly. Yes, they look like the work of a savage dog. I know. I know.

Arkady raised his eyebrows. —Such a tone with me?

Kostya exhaled smoke. —I apologize, Arkady Dmitrievich.

—Those scars also turn dark red when you're upset. That's a dangerous giveaway.

—Can I hide nothing from you?

Emotion broke Arkady's steady voice then: concern, dismay. —The sunlight...you've got grey hairs.

—Yes.

Arkady said nothing.

Songbirds landed near Kostya's boots. —We should come here more often, Arkady Dmitrievich. Take a lunch together, here, Solonki, any place where it's green.

—Such a scowl on you.

—My shoulder hurts.

—Learn to hide it.

—What do you know about it? Hey?

Arkady shook his head. *The pain's as bad as that?* —I'll speak to

Scherba. At least sit up straight. You're in uniform, and you slouch like some sneaky *bezprizornik*.

—Well, once I was a sneaky *bezprizornik*. Now I'm...

Kostya dug in his pouch for another cigarette.

I'm fucked in the mouth, that's what.

Arkady leaned closer to Kostya's ear. —You're a damned war hero. When I got the telegram from Leningrad saying you were home, I almost said a prayer of thanks. And I've not prayed since 1905.

Please, old man, shut up. Wait, I didn't send a telegram.

A new tone in Arkady's voice startled Kostya: not quite a whisper, not quite a murmur, just the safety of the blasé. —Tatar, listen to me this time. Please. Things...changed while you were gone. We tread new soil and pretend not to notice the graves. The chief's arrest upset everything. Even inside NKVD we've turned on one another. Secrets. Games. The guiltier the officer, the better the arrest.

Kostya said nothing.

—For the ones who make the arrest, I mean. They look brave, willing to confront the corruption—

—I know, Arkady Dmitrievich. I get the same memos you do, the same orders. I know.

Arkady's eyes followed the path of a songbird as it rose and fell, then disappeared within a tree. —We're Chekists, NKVD, the strongest guardians against treachery and rot, and now we're under suspicion, too? I don't...

At the crunch of footsteps, both Arkady and Kostya nodded to an elderly couple passing by, the woman leaning on the man's arm, the man, despite a limp, jaunty.

—Enemies without and enemies within, Kostya. I cannot even give you a list.

The woman at the parachute tower, on her second turn now, kept silent on this fall. She landed on her feet. Impressed, Kostya nodded as if she could see him, and he admired, too, her lovely hair, all those loose brown curls. Laughing, the woman struggled to walk, to stay upright. She fell to her knees, and the parachute enveloped her. Her shadowed form struggled, stumbled, beat at the silk. Kostya stood, ready to run and help, unaware he did so. Then the woman emerged from the parachute, throwing it off. She ran to a waiting man and embraced him.

As Kostya sat down again, fire stabbed his shoulder. A spasm in the fingers: his cigarette and matches fell to the ground.

—I'll get them, Tatar.

Arkady bent over to retrieve the matches; his own flesh got in the way. Snorting, Kostya bent at the waist with ease and grace, and Arkady wanted to punch him, perhaps in the small of the back, to teach him better manners. Kostya's left hand darted out, fingers scrabbling against grass and little stones, water and cardboard, guano. *Got it.* Another spasm in his hand: he almost crushed the matchbox.

He sat back up, tucked a cigarette between his lips, and permitted Arkady to light it for him.

Arkady studied his lighter. —Has anyone at Lubyanka noticed you twitch like that?

—No.

—Keep it that way. Better?

Kostya sucked in smoke. —Better.

—Remember when you taught Misha to smoke, and he coughed til he made himself sick?

—I don't want to talk about Misha.

Arkady recalled Vadym's shaky voice: *Misha is listed as missing. No one will tell me anything.* —Then do you remember what I said to you both that night, when Misha was so embarrassed that he could not smoke while you could? He felt powerless next to you. What did I tell you both about power?

Kostya could chant it; Arkady had said it many times, in many situations.

He said it now. —The steppe surrenders in patches to forest, and the forest surrenders in patches to tundra, yet in places where you see no change, all the differences blend. Power works like that, Kostya. Deep intersections, almost invisible. Survival demands recognition of those intersections, and some fancy dance steps. You can't always waltz your way out of trouble.

Grinning, Kostya tapped out another cigarette and gave the answer he'd not dared voice when an adolescent. —Can I mazurka instead?

—Nothing looks so good on a dance floor as a man's shiny boots.

—Arkady Dmitrievich, that makes no sense.

Arkady gave a half-smile. When he spoke again, his voice made his words sound as ordinary as falling snow. —Whatever happened with Misha, I'm sorry.

—Enough. Enough with the interrogation games. I'm not some prisoner.

—Do you know where he is?

Silence.

—Kostya, what happened to Misha? Vadym loves him as he would love a son.

—I know.

—Not knowing is sometimes worse than—

—I know! I know it hurts him, Arkady Dmitrievich. I know I can't trust anyone. I know, I know, I know. How can I not know what I know?

—You have orders to keep quiet?

Kostya leaned forward, elbows on knees.

Arkady placed a hand on Kostya's bad shoulder, took it away. —You smoke too much.

—I know that, too.

—I should get back and finish the cleanup.

Arkady waited a moment for Kostya to answer, to offer again to help, to tell him to fuck off, anything.

Kostya exhaled smoke.

Telling himself Kostya would find his own way home, Arkady walked away.

Kostya counted Arkady's footsteps and then the flowers in a nearby bed. Then he noticed how the light had changed, how ash defiled his boot, how his hands felt empty and cold.

—Comrade Major Minenkov?

Vadym looked up from the paperwork on his desk. —Comrade Captain Kuznets, good morning. How's my soloist today?

—You should not single me out at the expense of the others. A choir is greater and more important than an individual.

Vadym blinked a few times, amused by this orthodoxy. —Yet sometimes one man possesses a gift. Sharing that gift becomes his duty, and you have carried out that duty with admirable grace.

—Thank you.

—But you're not here to ask me about the choir. Oh, don't look at me like that. Your body language, Kuznets. You might control your voice and every sound you make, but muscles twitch beneath blushing skin, just a gentle blush, yes? Muscles twitch and tell me a story.

Boris looked sheepish. —I can't hide much from you.

—There no shame in it. I've done this work for a long time.

—I wonder, Comrade Major, what you might hide from me.

Vadym's fingers stilled, pausing in their paper-push for just a moment, just a shred of a moment, but long enough, he knew, to betray anxiety. —Presumption always lands as a sour note.

—I apologize. Comrade Major, I...this is irregular, even silly, but may I look out your window?

—Of course.

Boris peered down at the courtyard. —A perk of the senior Chekist. I hope to have a top-floor office myself one day. Right now, I feel like a piece of flotsam, up and down, back and forth. Comrade Kuznets, you're assigned to this department, no wait, to that one, oh wait, we need you over here instead.

Vadym made sympathetic noises.

—May I close your door, Comrade Major? And may I call you Vadym Pavlovich?

It sounded like the most reasonable request, a way to clear away the stuffiness of hierarchy and rank, just the sort of shift in tone that Vadym, as host of this little office, should have anticipated, indeed, already offered. —Yes.

Boris eased the door shut, then sat in the chair facing Vadym's desk. —I've also come to you as a courtesy, one officer to another. The level of corruption among the senior officers cannot continue.

Vadym stared at him a moment, then snorted. —Courtesy? Is that what you call it, this folly tearing the force apart? You want my history? You'll find my truth right here, on my desk: that beautiful photograph of the officers and Dzerzhinsky himself, all of us cheering, because that was the day we named the Cheka. That was the day we came into existence.

—Vadym Pavlovich—

—I know that because I was there. At Dzerzhinsky's side. And you, Kuznets? Where were you that day? Getting your diaper changed?

—History is not—

—If you think you've got the slightest taint of corruption, or cronyism, or too many urinal visits on me, then expose your mistake so I might correct it.

Boris stared down at the floor, as if Vadym's voice and gaze had become too much to bear. —I apologize, Vadym Pavlovich. I've chosen poor words.

—Words for another man, perhaps. Unless you're singing, I am deaf to you.

—Shall I sing of a party I attended last night? The host is a friend of yours: Comrade Major Balakirev. Perhaps not much of a friend if he didn't invite you.

Vadym signed a document. —Major Balakirev is a fine officer.

—Yes. Quite a service record. I may be on the wrong trail.

Vadym signed a second document.

Boris felt his voice get tight. —Cronyism is just one of the thousands of forms corruption may take. Such a subtle and grotesque corruption, one officer in a position of privilege and power helping another.

—Balakirev is quite discriminating about whom he invites to his parties. If you attended, then you knew what to expect, and, I have no doubt, you enjoyed yourself.

Silence.

Boris stood up. —You'll come see me if you learn anything?

—Let me get the door for you, Comrade Captain.

Just as Vadym grasped the doorknob, Boris looked into his eyes. —I'm sorry about your nephew, Vadym Pavlovich. Not to know...

Vadym said nothing.

—Missing in the line of duty. It must be difficult for your brother, too. I could pull some strings, try to find out more.

Vadym turned the doorknob, and noise from the hallway washed in.

Boris saluted. —Thank you, Comrade Major Minenkov. I look forward to discussing this with you again.

Monday 7 June

Water ran, pots clanked, and music played. Temerity lay in bed, bones heavy, head sore, ready to rip into William Brownbury-Rees for making such a racket and, no doubt, such a mess. *It's a service flat, you fool. Send down for breakfast.*

Wait.

Fresh white paint, dark green bottle: not her London flat.

A male voice spoke Russian. —Are you done with the water in the kitchen? I want to get in the shower.

The flow of water in the kitchen ceased. —Go ahead.

Kostya's voice got louder, then thinned out again as he walked past the bedroom to the bathroom. —Thank you. Let's see if I can get any hot water. I'd settle for tepid.

The shower ran.

Temerity sat up. A clean sheet fell away from her, and the other side of the bed looked untouched.

As she drank the last of the Narzan, she listened to Kostya sing in the shower. He started on what Temerity would call 'The Song of the Volga Boatmen,' cursed about the tune being stuck in his head, then took up a jaunty melody and sang about winning the heart of sweet Natasha, ah ha ha ha.

Bathroom down the hall to the right, he said. The rest of the flat must be left. Go left.

Efim sat at the tiny hinged table, eating buttered bread and a fried egg. —Miss Solovyova, good morning. You look better.

—Thank you. I feel much better.

—Some bread?

She took in the small front room with its high ceiling, one soft armchair, and a *stenka*. The open kitchen, by far the largest room in the flat, with its massive stove and three sinks, reminded her of the communal kitchen at Hotel Lux. A short corridor, narrow and dim, led to the flat's door. It had a two-key lock in the newer style: utilitarian, with long and slender keys. One could lock or unlock the door from the outside, and one could lock or unlock it from the inside with the same key. If one lacked the key, however, one could do nothing.

She faced Efim. —Not yet, thank you. Pardon my appearance. You must think very little of me.

I think you're lost. —Please, sit down. Can I get you anything at all?

—I'd love some tea.

—Ah. Yes, so would I. However, we've got neither kettle nor samovar. Nor tea.

—Oh.

Efim thought she might cry. He considered how else to speak with her when Kostya, wrapped in a robe, wet hair stuck to his head, strode into the room. —There you are, Nadia. Good morning.

He leaned down to kiss her on the cheek. Stiff, she tilted her face to accept. *Embarrassment,* Efim thought.

As Kostya completed the kiss, something metallic clanked against the wooden chair. Efim peered at the pocket in Kostya's robe. It bulged. *His service weapon?*

Efim stood up. —I'll take a look at that shoulder before I go.

As the two men retreated to Kostya's bedroom, Temerity buttered a piece of bread and told herself to eavesdrop.

A bedroom door clicked shut. Then it locked.

The musical selection on the radio changed: Tchaikovsky's 'Waltz of the Flowers.'

Voices loud and cheerful, Kostya and Efim emerged from the bedroom. Efim said he must fetch his suit jacket and hat, then get to the lab; Kostya mentioned his day shift and suggested he bring home something for supper from the deli. —It's a Monday. A *shashlyk* vendor stands outside Babichev's every Monday.

Temerity stood up, got dizzy. *Babichev's deli? I'm not far. Get to the deli, puzzle out the wrong turn.*

Efim sounded doubtful. —Cold *shashlyk*?

—No no, hot, though it would still be delicious cold. This old Georgian—

—The one with the big curling moustache?·

—That's him. He sets up his grill in front of the deli, and it smells so good. Whenever someone wants to buy his *shashlyk*, he says they must first pay inside. Once inside, of course, they're at Babichev's mercy for salad, bread, and cheese. Babichev and the Georgian split the profits.

Efim hurried into the kitchen now, hat on his head, suit jacket over his arm. —Yes, I've seen him. You sure he's Georgian? I thought he was a Tatar. Goodbye, Miss Solovyova.

Kostya called out. —If I'm not home by six, give up on me.

Efim smiled at that, not a happy smile, and Temerity watched him unlock the door with his long key. Outside, he locked the door again behind him.

Kostya, almost in uniform, his *gymnastyorka* unfastened, strode over to the *stenka* and turned up the radio. Then he beckoned.

Temerity kept still.

Scowling, Kostya walked over to her, then spoke in her ear. —I'll get your papers today.

—You've not got them now?

—No. That is why I must get them today.

—I need those papers and passport.

—Yes, I'd guessed that much.

—Yesterday. You said you'd get them yesterday.

Kostya strode away from her. —Do you like kasha? Of course you like kasha; everyone likes kasha.

—I . . . what?

Kostya measured water into a pot and set it to boil. —I've got some butter for it. No cinnamon though, so I can't make my grandfather's recipe for you, all butter and cinnamon and honey, or sugar. Honey's better. My grandfather would add extra honey to mine, when my grandmother wasn't looking.

Temerity struggled to speak.

Kostya took a sack of kasha from the pantry. Then he looked at Temerity, and emotion surfaced in his eyes, hid itself again: desire, perhaps, and mistrust.

Fear.

—Comrade Nikto—

—Call me Kostya. Please.

—Konstantin . . .

—Look, that's not my name. Well, it is, but no one uses it. No one who matters.

—Kostya. I can't stay here.

—This will take a few minutes. The bathroom's free. Use my soap, on the left. There's a spare toothbrush in the *stenka*.

When Kostya turned his attention to the stove, Temerity sniffed her blouse. *Play along.* —Where shall I find a towel?

—*Stenka*, third drawer on the left.

Thin towels lay in perfect folds. —You're very tidy with your linens.

—Laundry service.

Inside the bathroom, ceramic tiles of an odd shade of blue, like that atop an NKVD cap, shone on the walls. Grey splashes pocked the mirror, yellow spatters stained the base of the toilet, and beard bristles littered the faucet and sink. Pieces of newspaper, cut in squares with a precision she could only admire, lay in an ashtray. On a shelf over the toilet, within easy reach of the shower, lay razors and shaving brushes, toothbrushes, tooth powder, a bottle of Shipr cologne, a brush and two combs, a tin of hair pomade, and two soap dishes. The scraps of grey soap lay in congealed pools of their own melt. An improvement over Hotel Lux, she told herself. At least this bathroom afforded some privacy.

And a key in the lock.

Afraid of mirage, she touched it.

Cool. Hard. Steel.

Wrist quick, she locked the bathroom door. Then she took the soap and ran the water in the shower.

When she returned to the fold-down table, the butter had disappeared, and the kitchen smelled of turned earth and toasted nuts with a depth of bitterness: agreeable, even enticing.

Leaning against the counter near the stove, Kostya looked up from a section of Efim's newspaper. —Did you get enough hot water?

—It was fine, thank you.

—The bottom two drawers in the *stenka* are mine. Take anything that might help.

Temerity plucked her blouse away from a damp patch on her

skin, then took up another section of the newspaper, Friday's *Izvestia*.
—Thank you.

Bearing two bowls of kasha, he sat next to her, pulled his chair close. —I put lots of butter in here.

She whispered. —Why? Why would you help me?

He studied her face, found the freckles on her eyelids, and whispered back. —Still got that cigarette case?

—Where are my shoes?

Kostya said it aloud, making them both flinch. —Your shoes?

—I left Hotel Lux fully dressed and carrying a handbag. This morning I own nothing more than a blouse and a skirt.

—I got your shoes on your feet before we left.

—Then where did you put them?

He craned his neck to look at the dim corridor leading to the door, then got up and flicked on the light: his boots, but no women's shoes. —I don't know. Let me check my closet.

As she ate, he opened and slammed the closet door in his bedroom, cursed.

He returned with his cap. —I'm sorry there's no honey.

—It's fine. I quite like it.

He looked pleased. —Help yourself to anything else.

—Wait. My shoes.

—I've got to go to work.

—Now?

—Yes, now. I promise, I'll get the papers, and then we'll find your shoes. Just be patient.

She took in a long breath, let it out. Then she rattled *Izvestia*. —I'll cut this up when I've read it.

—Thank you very much. Here, I'll get you the scissors.

As Kostya stepped behind the huge counter to open a drawer, Temerity bolted for the door.

—Hey!

She snatched the bathroom key from her skirt pocket, stumbling as Kostya grabbed first the collar of her blouse and then her arms. His furious whisper filled her head. —What the barrelling fuck do you think you're you doing?

—Get off me!

Gentler, he thought, than he might be in a cell, Kostya wrenched her away from the door, turned her around, and shoved her against the wall. —You think you'll get past the *babushka* in the lobby?

—Who?

He pried the key from her fist. —Even if you do, this is Moscow, not a collective farm. We have discovered shoes here in the barbaric land of Russia. Bare feet? Someone will ask you questions, and you've got no papers. You speak Russian well, I give you that, but you miss idioms, and in the cell, when you were tired, you started substituting words from other languages. Sometimes your speech sounds like translation; you still *think* in English. So, a barefoot woman who speaks imperfect Russian and can produce no papers? Not suspicious at all.

—Let me go!

He released her arms but continued to block the door. —Go where? Please, I know this must be difficult, but—

Light exploded. A pulpy pain followed, and Kostya fell, seeing Temerity lower her knee. The wall felt cool and comforting against his scarred ear. On his first breath, he called on God. On his second, he called Temerity a bitch. On his third, he retched.

She strode to the kitchen. A drawer rumbled, some cutlery clinked, and, as she returned to stand over him, her voice fell, certain, deep, cold. —Get away from the door.

Electric light glinted on the blade of a meat knife.

Kostya's voice rasped. —Please put that down.

—I said, get away from the door.

Kostya heard footsteps on the stairs as a neighbour descended to the lobby, on his way to work. —You won't use that.

—No?

—Go outside barefoot and bloodied? You're not that stupid.

Muscles in her forearm tensed.

Shutting his eyes against pain, Kostya sat up and pressed his back against the door. *Revolution, civil war, and flu, two famines, two sea voyages, and someone else's civil war, all so I can get kneed in the balls and die at the end of a knife in my own flat?*

Cutlery clinked, and a drawer rumbled closed.

He opened his eyes.

Temerity stood behind the counter now, hands empty, arms crossed.

Kostya stood up, limped to the fold-down table, and sat in one of the chairs. Breathing hard, he examined the key he'd taken from her. —Besides, this is the bathroom key. It won't fit the main door. Different lock. Fucked in the mouth. Get me a cold compress.

She kept still.

—I won't hurt you.

She raised her eyebrows.

—Please.

At the *stenka*, Temerity selected a smaller towel, shook it out, and considered making it a garotte even as she admitted to herself that she'd not use it.

As she folded the towel again, her hands shook. *Steady the Buffs.*

Cold water ran in the kitchen as Kostya lowered himself to the floor beside the table and stretched out. Sitting on a chair had been a mistake. He considered how the neighbours might interpret this morning's noise. None of them had seen him bring a woman home, but they may very well have heard a female voice. A body's thud? Comrade Nikto of flat seven on floor six either beat his woman or fell down drunk. Neither would draw undue attention.

Arm outstretched, Temerity offered him the compress, snatching her hand back as he touched and almost dropped the damp towel. Kostya unfastened his pants, applied the compress, winced and hissed.

Temerity noticed his bitten nails.

Kostya adjusted the compress. —You're stronger than you look.

She snorted.

—Did you find his bicycle? That day in Spain, did you find his bicycle?

Her eyed widened, for just a moment.

—I wanted you to find it. I wanted many things that day.

She stared at the wall, the white, white wall.

He leant on his right elbow. —Have you not asked yourself how, or why, we've met, over and over? The chances. It's ridiculous.

She pushed her cuticles, refusing to look at him.

—Or is someone who hates me using you to trap me? The beautiful woman, oldest trick we've got.

—You think I'm a plant?

—I don't know what to think of you. Beyond purpose, I mean.

Her attention remained on her fingernails. —What purpose?

—Destiny. You're here for a reason.

—I'm here by accident.

—Well, I don't protect you by accident. You're some test for me, some gift. For my redemption. If I save you—

She glared at him. —Your redemption?

Plucking the compress away from his scrotum, Kostya rose to his knees. His pants slid down. —I mean...

The radio announcer, voice assured and self-important, if a little tired after the long manufacturing report, introduced a newscast.

Kostya hauled himself to his feet and fastened his pants. —The time. I can't be late. I'll get the papers. Look, I need to talk to some people first, and I need to do that very carefully. Be patient. And if anyone knocks, do not go to the door. Simple, yes?

She turned her back and strode away from him to stand before the front room window. Arms crossed, she tried to ignore the other building and focus on the sky.

Behind her, fabric rustled and boots tapped as Kostya got ready to leave. Then the door, and its lock, clicked shut.

At a urinal in Lubyanka, handling himself with some care, Kostya remembered that he'd not shaved. *Second morning in a row. Fuck.* He could, if reprimanded, plead shortage and ask a superior officer where he'd last found razor blades. *And who will hassle me about stubble today: Tsar Pyotr Velikiy? The department head won't even be awake yet.*

Evgenia's greeting made him feel a bit sick. —Comrade Senior Lieutenant, there you are. Did you forget to shave? The new department head wants to see you.

Kostya glanced toward the head's office. The door hung open, and outside, pressed close to the wall next to the jamb, stood several boxes. The former head: arrested, drunk, dead?

Evgenia poured *zavarka*, then added hot water. —The new head's name is Kuznets. Captain Boris Aleksandrovich Kuznets.

Of course it is.

—And he said for you to report to him the moment you arrived.

Distracted by the intricacy of the *podstakannik* filigree, its practicality and beauty, Kostya accepted the tea. —Should I bring this to him?

—He's got some. Piece of sugar?

—No. I think I'd better have my mouth clear for this conversation.

—With the Sound Man? You'll not get a word in edgewise.

Kostya sipped the hot tea to hide both his amusement and his fear. —Don't let him hear you say that.

Evgenia looked down at her paperwork.

Considering where to leave his tea, deciding to balance it on a stacked cardboard box, Kostya knocked on the department head's open door.

Boris's voice sounded mighty, yet detached, a man comfortable with his power and feeling no need to prove it: the theatricality of nonchalance. —Yes, comrade?

Kostya stepped inside, saluted.

Seeing Kostya, Boris stood up, and his voice sounded much kinder. —Konstantin Arkadievich, come in. No tea?

—I left it outside, Comrade Captain.

—Well, you can't drink it if it's outside. Fetch it, and then close the door behind you. Good. Sit down. Why do you limp?

—I pulled a muscle, Comrade Captain.

—As long as that office door is shut, you may call me Boris Aleksandrovich. And have you run out of razor blades?

Kostya lied once more, the ease of deception surprising him. —Yes, Boris Aleksandrovich. I apologize.

—My father spoke in proverbs. I would get so irritated with him, but now I find the proverbs useful. Look after your clothes when they're new, and look after your honour when young. Your face, I mean. Your uniform is fine. A raven won't peck out another raven's eyes; I'll overlook it this time.

—Yes, Boris Aleksandrovich. Thank you.

Boris described the location of the market stall where yesterday he'd found both sharpeners and fresh blades. Then he picked up his own tea from the crowded desk; condensation dripped down the glass. —Do you know that some departments use Western cups and saucers for tea? Here, in Lubyanka? I was astonished.

Kostya raised his eyebrows in sympathetic dismay. How far might this hostility to teacups go? Would one's loyalty be tested by tea? Could a man call himself Soviet if he preferred a cup and saucer? Samovar, *zavarka*, and *podstakannik*: signals of orthodoxy? In these difficult days, might a man's choice of how to drink his tea become the rubric which parted innocence from guilt?

It's just tea, Kostya wanted to say.

He knew better.

—You like your tea, Konstantin Arkadievich?

—I can take it or leave it, though I confess, Comrade Ismailovna makes it well.

—It's good to have women around. I can't get started in the morning without it. Sometimes I get quite indulgent and take it with jam. Tea, I mean.

Taking a deep breath to kill his chortle, Kostya smelled something floral in the tea, like roses, then honey. Then he smelled smoke.

Boris patted one of the dossiers on his desk. —You're an excellent shot, even by our standards.

—Thank you.

—Your wounds don't interfere?

—I've not done much target practice since I returned.

—Get to it. You've practised at the Butovo *poligon*, the shooting range. And such a privilege you enjoyed one day, that visit to, ah, well, our former chief's dacha.

Fucked in the mouth, he means Yagoda.

How to explain it, explain that beautiful spring afternoon in '33, Arkady dizzy with the honour of an invitation to the chief's dacha, Kostya tagging along in some dismay. He'd skipped his community work, broken a promise to the boys at Home of the Child of the Struggle Moscow Number Two Supplemental Number Three to visit and read stories that day, and he felt queasy, first with guilt over the boys, then with embarrassment as Arkady bragged about him to Yagoda. *No, not my son,* Arkady said, ready to explain, but Genrikh Yagoda cut him off and challenged Kostya to shoot as well as Arkady claimed he could — but with a new weapon, the just-released Tokarev 33 pistol. Yagoda pointed to a dry spot of earth and told Kostya to stand there. Kostya glanced at the targets, which stood anywhere from ten to seventy metres off, took the pistol, and looked it over. Shoot with this monstrosity? Then he looked up and caught the flicker of despair in Arkady's eyes. If Kostya failed to live up to Arkady's boasts, then Arkady would look a fool before the chief. Arkady knew it, and Genrikh Yagoda knew it.

Five targets, eight rounds. Yagoda called out directions. Target four, left shoulder. Target one, base of the skull. Target three, heart. Target five, base of the skull...

Five precise hits, three close.

Yagoda announced luncheon, and the three NKVD officers ate and drank until sundown, when Yagoda ordered his driver to bring Arkady and Kostya back into Moscow. In the car, Arkady had murmured in Kostya's ear. *Well done, Little Tatar, well done.*

How to explain that afternoon with Yagoda without incriminating Arkady?

Boris placed his tea on his desk. —I'm sure Yagoda hid his depravities well, Konstantin, but you did visit him, at his Butovo dacha?

Admit it. Confess. No doubt it's all in that dossier. —I did. Myself, and Arkady Dmitrievich.

—Balakirev. He is so proud of you. So what did you think of the Tokarev? Many officers prefer it to the Nagant, eight rounds to seven, faster to load, lighter recoil, easier to shoot.

Only if you're an ape who uses his fists before his mind. —The first weapon I ever held was a Nagant. I'll stay with it.

—I prefer the Nagant, myself.

Kostya nodded. *How many more tests?*

Boris sipped his tea. —Tell me what you like about the Nagant.

—Well, it's easy to clean. It fits well in my hand, the curving lines. The heavy trigger pull leaves no doubt, and the recoil feels like a kiss for a job well done. The Nagant looks like a weapon. The Tokarev looks like a deck of cards glued to a piece of pipe and painted black.

—I agree, with all my heart.

Dizzy, Kostya exhaled gently, telling himself not to hold his breath like that. *Then why,* he wanted to ask Boris, *did you call me in here? Why mention Yagoda? Why threaten me with my past?*

Why-why-why, Arkady had said, mocking him. *Ever since you came back from Spain, you've acted the foolish* pochemuchka, *always asking questions.*

Boris sighed, rubbed his temples. —In times of emergency, the work becomes so strenuous. I have a problem, Konstantin Arkadievich, and it might snarl your day.

—Please, tell me how I can help.

—I need a man who can shoot.

Yury Stepanov, early for his appointment with Boris Kuznets, meandered from Garage Number One to the basement shooting range. Boris expected a report on progress at Laboratory of Special Purpose Number Two, and Yury, thanks to the slack discipline of Dr. Efim Scherba, had little to say. Angry with Efim, and dreading Boris, Yury wished he could drink. Instead, he decided to shoot.

The racket of barrage pressed on his ears; other officers had the same idea. Sometimes gunfire interrupted an interrogation. When this happened, Boris liked to point out, the noise assisted.

So loud. It never seems so loud to me when I fire my gun.

Then again, Yury falsified his practice records.

The officer closest to Yury stood before a target, cap off, face stubbled, head bowed, grip on his lowered Nagant slack.

Him, like this?

As Kostya brushed something from his face, Yury took a few steps back, staying out of his line of sight. Kostya lifted his arms and took aim, the Nagant not an extension of his body but his body an extension of the Nagant. Four holes already tore the practice target, a figure of man, his back to the shooter: three holes in the skull, one near the heart.

Yury smirked. *So tense, dear Kostya?*

Kostya fired the remaining three rounds, and Yury winced at the speed. The target, tattered now where the head met the neck, fell apart.

Pale, Kostya strode to a little table holding a bowl of ammunition, a pencil, and a clipboard heavy with forms. He made a note, signed his name, reloaded, tucked the cardboard box of shells back together to keep it tidy, holstered his Nagant, and rubbed his left shoulder.

Yury shook his head. *Good with the paperwork, Nikto. So good that you signed in my car for me. Thrown together again, are we?*

In NKVD classes, Yury had struggled with grades, often a distant tenth or worse to top students Misha Minenkov and Kostya Nikto. Despite his assertions that they together made a perfect trio, Kostya and Misha would never drink or socialize with him. Misha would draw caricatures, clever and pointed, often cruel, of classmates and instructors and show them to Kostya, who'd then struggle to suppress a giggle. Several times Yury caught sight of some of these caricatures, caught sight by design, he now knew — himself, sketched in humiliating poses and captioned as Little Yurochka. After graduation, Yury found himself assigned to an undesirable rural outpost, hundreds of kilometres away from Moscow. It took him fifteen years and several backstabbings of colleagues to get back to the city, and he intended to stay. He'd not expected the unpleasant sight of Kostya Nikto already wearing a senior lieutenant's insignia while Yury remained a sergeant. Even thinking of it now, Yury wanted to kick something. Everyone treated Kostya like an ascending angel, and life looked so easy for him. His languages, his memory, his shooting — how could one man have so many gifts?

Oddly, no one spoke of Misha Minenkov. Yury decided he should discover why.

Then he noticed Kostya staring at him. For a moment, just a shred of a moment, something new shone in Kostya's big eyes. A plea. *Help me.*

Yury took another step back and collided with a wall.

Kostya blinked a few times, then rubbed his eyes and temples. When he lowered his hands, his eyes seemed alert, even feral. *Normal,* Yury thought.

Then Kostya noticed Yury and nodded to him as he strode for the stairs. —Stepanov.

—Nikto.

A charwoman, young and willowy, hair hidden beneath a scarf, retrieved the ruined practice target and hung up a new one. As she swept the floor, collecting the burnt scraps of paper into a hinged dustpan needing oil, scrapes and squeaks filled Yury's ears. Irritated, he gave a little snort. The charwoman looked up then, noticed Yury's stare, and flinched. He bowed in apology and sought the stairs that would guide him up out of the basement and to the office of Boris Kuznets.

Even angels fall, Comrade Senior Lieutenant Nikto.

Even angels fall.

Six storeys up, no fire escape, and no balcony.

Grateful for the fresh air, the slight twitch of the breeze, and the distant scent of a river, much like the Thames yet also very different, Temerity peered out the front room window. She noticed three other women in the facing blocks of flats also staring out windows or leaning on the rails of their balconies, regarding the world with anxious boredom. A thin voice called, reminding someone of work shifts and metro schedules. One by one, each woman turned away from her window or balcony and retreated inside.

Temerity switched her attention to the metro station, Vasilisa Prekrasnaya. She reached out her hand and pretended to touch it.

So close.

She turned away from the window walked to the kitchen. The floor creaked at every step of her bare feet.

Find the shoes.

Once more, she checked the locked door, the *stenka*, the bathroom, the kitchen, every cupboard, shelf, and drawer.

A well-stocked flat; a well-stocked prison.

She studied the knife she'd threatened Kostya with, snorted, put it back.

Efim had locked his bedroom door: no access there.

In Kostya's bedroom, she wrenched open the stiff doors to the tiny closet, finding another pair of knee-high leather boots, lined for winter, and a pair of men's black shoes. She stretched to reach the shelf, and she knocked a spare uniform cap and a furry winter hat to the floor. Her hand also brushed dust balls and what felt like a book, and she jumped, jumped again, got it: a 1936 Moscow telephone guide with the pragmatic if slightly intimidating title *Directory for All Moscow.* Telling herself the directory would be useful, Temerity placed it to one side and then examined the clothes hanging on the rod. Uniform pieces, light overcoat, a winter coat, each marked with insignia, two pairs of civilian trousers, and three white shirts. Far off to the left, in the shadows, hung a woollen winter coat, faded navy blue and too small for this Kostya Nikto, and one long black leather coat, too big.

A piece of dull khaki peeked around one of the black leather lapels. Temerity lifted the hanger from the rod, and the leather coat slipped off, burying her feet and revealing something else on the hanger, a long khaki jacket with many pockets. It smelled of sweat and disinfectant, dust and blood.

Swallow each and every one, or your cock will fall off.

The left sleeve hung in tatters.

On the radio, dreary music ended on a weak note, repeated four times as it faded, reminding Temerity of *Rigoletto*'s 'Va, va, va, va': complicity and defeat.

A woman's voice, warm yet firm, demanded attention. —Now is the time when good Soviet children settle themselves.

Temerity thought of Mikko Toppinen raising his arms over his face: *Leave me alone.*

—Children, are you ready to listen?

Temerity picked up the coat and hung it again over the jacket. Then she shut the closet and returned to the front room, where she sat in the one soft chair, faced the radio, and closed her eyes. *Stories,* her father had often said, *are keys to a culture. You can understand a national character, my girl, if you understand that nation's stories.* As a child, Temerity could not fathom what insight *The Wind in the Willows* might give a foreigner, though she later thought *Kim* might help. She always smiled when her father started to talk about stories and national character, because that meant he would then translate a Russian fairy story from her mother's old book, and Temerity could strain for a memory, any memory, of her mother's voice.

She never found it.

The woman on the radio began the story of Dobrynya Nikitich defeating the dragon Zmei Gorynich. —And Dobrynya's mother warned him, even as she made sure he wore his warm cloak, do not visit the Saracen mountains, do not step on baby dragons, do not rescue Russian captives, and do not bathe in the Puchai River. What do you think he did?

Temerity closed her eyes and remembered the portrait of her mother at Kurseong House, a petite young woman with dark eyes and hair, curls escaping the chignon, three-year-old Felix standing beside her, sporting his first haircut and pair of breeches, and infant Temerity on her lap.

The day she shoved the book from her father's hands, Edward yelled at her, demanding she show more respect for her mother's belongings, and Temerity stared at that portrait in repentance. *It's Vasilisa, not Mother. I'm not pushing Mother away. Vasilisa is too small.* Then she'd turned and run back to her father's lap. Edward held her and let her cry.

The woman on the radio continued. —Do you think Dobrynya

obeyed his loving mother? He did not, and soon he found himself facing the terrible dragon, Zmei Gorynich.

Temerity knew this story. Soon after the book-pushing incident, Edward had bought Temerity English translations of Russian fairy tales, and she'd devoured them — though she'd still avoided Vasilisa. Dobrynya Nikitich fought Zmei Gorynich for three days, aided by a magic helmet and guiding voice, finally winning his own freedom and that of a captive woman called Zabava Putyatishna. How might the ending change to better suit these Soviet times? Would Zabava thank Dobrynya and then chair a Dragon Re-education Committee?

The woman on the radio concluded the story. —Dobrynya Nikitich was a peasant, and this story happened long ago, so Dobrynya Nikitich gave Zabava Putyatishna to his noble-born friend and fellow *bogatyr*, Alyosha Popov.

Temerity rubbed her temples. *Gave her. Like a prize.*

Another voice took the mic. —Join us again this time tomorrow for *Children's Tales*. Next, a selection of music by Tchaikovsky.

Temerity stood up, straightened her clothes, and looked to *Izvestia* on the little hinged table. First, she checked the main door to see if perhaps the lock had slipped. Then she cut the newspaper into squares.

Arkady heaved himself out of the overstuffed armchair. —*Poligon* duty? You?

Kostya nodded.

Scowling, Arkady lit two cigarettes, and passed one to Kostya. —Who did you piss off to get *poligon* duty?

Kostya took a deep drag on the cigarette and stared out the window at the back yard, at the flower beds. —Special Squad is a man short tonight.

—Oh, and you believed that?

Comrade Senior Lieutenant Ippolitov cannot come to work today. —Well, I'm not about to ask precisely why they're a man short.

—Someone's fucking with you. Special Squad is for apes, not star officers who speak six languages.

—Seven.

—I'll go talk to your department head.

Kostya shook his head. —No. I can handle it.

—Vadym, he'll put in a word. And Boris Kuznets. Between the three of us—

—Kuznets is my new department head, and he gave me the order himself.

After a moment, Arkady tapped his cigarette pack against the table. —Kuznets stuck you with *poligon* duty?

—In his office. A few hours ago. Over tea.

—Oh. He didn't tell me he'd be taking over that department.

Kostya studied the pile of ash. —He might have only found out himself this morning.

Arkady smiled at the joke, recognizing its likely truth. —Your shoulder, Tatar. You're not fit to shoot yet.

—The hell I'm not.

—Pardon me?

Kostya took his revolver from its holster, placed it on the table. —Target practice.

Watching Arkady pick up the Nagant, examine it, sniff it, Kostya felt like he waited for the throw of a switch. Approval, or punishment. Yes, or no. Life, or death.

Arkady passed the revolver back, and his big hands descended to his *portupeya*. The gesture reminded Kostya of the first time he saw Arkady, the January day in Odessa. —Kostya, I can go over Kuznets's head. Go around him, at least.

—No.

—Kostya—

—I said, no. Leave it.

—Then why did you come?

To hear your voice. —To warn you.

—Me?

—It's a test, and I refuse to give Kuznets any ammunition.

—You're still hung over, can't think straight.

—I saw how he looked at you at the party, just little flashes of it. He'd crush your skull beneath his right boot to get a better view of a game of bandy.

Arkady patted his belly. —He's kissed my arse so much that he's chapped his lips. An invitation to one of my parties is not easy to obtain. Again and again he asks my opinion on how the departments should function.

—How did he even know about your parties? Arkady Dmitrievich, please. He mentioned...

Arkady kept still, hands in mid-air. He mouthed his response. —Mentioned what?

Kostya deferred to Arkady's fear and whispered. —The former chief.

Arkady whispered back. —Yagoda?

—Indirectly. Kuznets knows about the day we visited Yagoda at his dacha and I shot with the Tokarev. He told me he knows about that for a reason.

Arkady's face took on a matte and sickly cast, like cooled fat. —Boris Aleksandrovich Kuznets is nothing but a cockroach to cram down Trotsky's throat, and he thinks he can wrench my balls? He... oh, Kostya.

His voice wavered on the diminutive. He whispered it twice more, eyes shut.

Kostya stared at him.

Arkady beckoned Kostya closer, and his lips brushed Kostya's ear. —Please. Say what you must, do what you must, to keep Kuznets happy.

Both men leaned away; Kostya ground out his cigarette.

Arkady got up and fussed in his kitchen, calling out he would fetch those pickles he mentioned, and the dark bread, and oh, he'd still got some butter.

Smiling, Kostya shook his head. He and Misha had often joked about Arkady's almost pathological hospitality. Argument? Arkady offered food. Bad news? Arkady offered food. Good news? Food. Visiting girlfriend? Some wariness, yes, but still, food. Roof falling in, wolves tearing at your throat? Arkady Dmitrievich would empty his cupboards and offer food — to the wolves, as well.

Misha had teased Arkady about it once, and the tone of the gathering slipped from jovial to sour. Even Vadym frowned. Arkady fixed Misha with his cold stare. *Should I then lock my door to you in times of famine? Is that what you want, boy?*

Kostya had thought Misha might cry.

Misha...

As Arkady clinked and clanked items onto a tray, Kostya stood up, stretched his back, and adjusted the tiny framed photographs on the mantel. Arkady's parents. Arkady and Vadym in a posed studio shot in those long Cheka leather coats against a backdrop of painted mountains and meadows. Kostya at graduation. The charwomen always disturbed them. He turned and sat down again as Arkady's voice and the familiarity of his words soothed him.

—Eat, Little Tatar, eat.

Kostya smiled. *He is still Arkady Dmitrievich, and I am still Konstantin Arkadievich.*

Efim mopped sauce from his lips. —Delicious.

Gnawing a piece of beef, Temerity nodded agreement. The *shashlyk* Kostya had bought as promised that morning was redolent with garlic, vinegar, and pepper. The accompanying salad of boiled potato chunks tossed in sour cream and dill gave contrast, filled her belly, and dulled her fears. She'd only eaten a piece of bread since the kasha that morning, and now she eyed the remaining *shashlyk* with greed. She even forgot the reason for the odd and suffocating quiet in the building: an electricity cut.

Kostya sat back and gestured to the feast on the table. —Eat, eat. I'm sorry the *shashlyk*'s on brown paper. The Georgian wouldn't let me take his skewers. Oh, Scherba, I need your help before I go out.

Temerity gave Kostya a sharp look, then tried to hide it. —Out?

—I've got to work.

She said nothing to that. Efim had accepted this announcement without comment; perhaps she should as well.

Kostya poured vodka for the three of them and gave a long toast to the man who'd cooked the *shashlyk*. He knocked back his drink, poured another, and knocked that back, too. Then he pointed at a section of bare white wall. —Some people still keep beauty walls. Historical interest only, of course. No one prays to ikons anymore. Arkady Dmitrievich calls them fairy tales.

Efim licked the last juices of his fingers. —Who is he to you? You never call him father.

—He's looked after me since I was twelve.

Temerity thought of Spartan boys and their mentors.

Kostya offered Temerity a cigarette. —Here, let me light it. My grandparents had a beauty wall with three copies of the Novgorod Gavriil, small, medium, and large.

Exhaling smoke, Temerity thought of the ikon, a golden-toned medieval painting of the Angel Gabriel, as she called him, with plaited fair hair and huge brown eyes. Her father had kept a copy on a wall of his study at Kurseong House. Then she considered the stained-glass window her grandfather had paid for as a gift to the parish church: a blond and pale Christ not so much in agony on the cross as muscular repose, surrounded by panels of blue, yellow, and red.

She'd decorated her London flat in shades of blue, yellow, and red similar to that window.

And that other stained glass in the church, Judith on her knees, studying Holofernes's throat. Is that all I believed in back then, pretty windows?

She caught Efim staring at her; he looked away.

Kostya crammed some more potato salad into his mouth, stood up, and adjusted his *portupeya*. —I have to go. I hope the electricity comes back soon.

It did, at that moment, and the radio resumed its blare: another report on another trial.

He smirked. —If only all my wishes came true. Nadezhda, I'll bring you something nice. If I'm not too late.

—Too late for what?

He wanted to kiss her. Instead, he patted his holster. —Out too late, I mean. My day slipped out from beneath my feet. Scherba?

The men retreated to Kostya's bedroom.

When Kostya returned, alone, his eyes seemed dull. He stroked Temerity's face, then tangled his fingers in the curls of her hair. —Kiss me goodnight? Your mouth, this time, not your knee? On my face, I mean, not...

She shoved his hand away.

He took a few steps back and bowed to her. —Pleasant dreams, my sweet angel of Comintern.

Smirking, he left and locked the door behind him.

Efim returned with pen, ink, and paper. —Do you mind if I use the table, Miss Solovyova? I wish to write to my wife.

Temerity stared at the corridor leading to the door for a moment, then faced Efim. —Please, call me Nadezhda Ivanovna.

—Efim Antonovich.

She pursed her lips, then nodded. —May I keep the radio on?

—Yes, of course.

As Temerity sat in the front room facing to the radio, Efim drew ink into his pen. *You'd think mine are the first friendly words she's heard in days.* He glanced at her as she crossed her bare legs at the ankle. *Why is she barefoot?*

—

The chugging lorry, cab covered in a tarpaulin, idled before Lub-yanka. Dusk bent the light glaring off Lubyanka's windows into beautiful pinks and gold. The lorry driver pitched the remains of his cigarette as he picked out the dark shape of an NKVD officer: the graceful lines of *gymnastyorka, galife* pants and peaked cap, and the confident walk, shoulders back, left arm perhaps a little stiff, right arm swinging while still covering the holster. As the officer emerged from the shadows, the colours of his insignia showed.

The driver saluted. —Comrade Senior Lieutenant, good evening.

Kostya nodded to the driver and, as a courtesy, showed his identi-fication. He could have signed out a car and driven himself, perhaps even requested a driver. *No,* he'd decided, *better to keep my head down.*

At Kostya's feet, the ember of the driver's discarded cigarette cooled from orange to red, the heat of it winking twice before a sur-render to black. Kostya recalled one of his own discarded cigarettes, the embers fading on Spanish ground, where blood pooled.

The driver read the identification, blinked, and gestured to the tarpaulin. —Full and ready, Comrade Senior Lieutenant.

Prisoners travelled to the *poligons* in such trucks. Under tarpaulin. Bound, sometimes gagged.

This tarp rippled and bulged.

Just the wind, Kostya told himself.

A male voice escaped the tarp: tenor, his tone as clear and crisp, Vadym might say, as water about to freeze. —You can come and go at a country inn as in a fickle woman's cunt…

A drinking song. Kostya recognized it; characters sang a politer variant in the movie *Lieutenant Kizhe.* Soon five other voices joined in.

The driver shook his head, in fondness. —Special Squad Number Three in there. Those guys can sing all night. Must be fun at a party.

—Let's go.

As they pulled onto the street, the driver attempted small talk: the weather, the state of the roads, the sudden availability of lemons. He soon gave up and joined the song. The sky darkened as they crossed the eight-lane Bolshoy Moskvoretsky Bridge, smooth asphalt and painted lines pointing to the Soviet promise of a radiant future.

Kostya looked up. *The sky looks bruised.*

The men sang and sang.

They continued south, Kostya oblivious to their progress until the brakes squeaked and the engine stopped.

As he hopped out of the lorry, the smells of the *poligon* reached him: diesel, sweat, earth, and dogs. Then he saw the wooden barracks, a separate stone cottage, and the range itself, gated and fenced like a courtyard with guard towers at each of the four corners. On each guard tower stood an electric searchlight. The dogs sounded agitated, even frightened, barking with an urgency that made Kostya frown. A tractor engine idled.

Inside the barracks, in what looked like a dining hall made over into a maze of men and desks, Kostya presented himself to the man in charge, a master-sergeant, and wrinkled his nose at the reek of Troynoy cologne. The master-sergeant raised his eyebrows when he read Kostya's insignia and identification card, then snarled at his colleagues to stand up and greet the senior lieutenant. A little chill passed between the *poligon* regulars as they obeyed. No doubt this senior lieutenant had come to inspect them, to review their efficiencies.

To report.

Kostya nodded his approval. —Thank you, comrades. Carry on.

The photographer wrestled with his flash; his assistant attached a little wooden bracket stuck on the end of a thin steel rod to the back of a chair. A clerk knocked his overflowing in-tray to the floor; Kostya retrieved it. The dossiers, mostly tied shut, held their contents, no release here, and the clerk babbled his thanks. Then the clerk turned pale and backed away. Sweat appeared on his forehead, and he asked the master-sergeant to excuse him.

The master-sergeant shook his head. —Not now, you fool.

An odour of excrement wafted.

Kostya stared at the clerk. *Really?*

The master-sergeant struck the clerk upside the head, called him a pig, and dismissed him. The man walked backwards away from them, only turning when he reached a door. Then he ran.

The master-sergeant ordered another man to replace the clerk, then muttered he'd see the first clerk shot. Eyes to the ground, his subordinates laughed. A joke, of course. Just a joke.

As the rest of the men of Special Squad signed in, the master-sergeant picked up a piece of paper, a typewritten list. He read it, looked up at Kostya, read it again. —Your name is on the duty roster?

Kostya nodded. —I could have avoided it, but then I'd never get the taste out of my mouth.

More laughter, more downcast eyes.

And a little tug at the master-sergeant's own mouth. Senior Lieutenant Nikto must hover near disgrace. Sending such a man to the arse end of the city for *poligon* duty? An insult, surely. A whiff of demotion.

Kostya read these thoughts in the master-sergeant's eyes, sidled up to him, and spoke in a murmur. —I'm here because I'm an excellent shot, Comrade Master-Sergeant. What do you say: three rounds into the wall, one next to each of your ears and one just over the top of your head? Or between your legs, yes?

The master-sergeant inclined his head just enough to signal a bow. —Not necessary, Comrade Senior Lieutenant.

The photographer called out. —Ready.

From far within the barrack, prisoners queued, clothing rumpled, hair greasy, faces dirty and stubbled. One at a time, a prisoner proceeded to the first desk, sat down, and reviewed metriks with the clerk.

Surname, first name, patronymic.

Age.

Address.

Hair colour, eye colour, height and weight, ethnicity.

The prisoner proceeded to the second desk, here confirming the correct duplication of his metriks on the execution warrant. Surname, first name, patronymic. Age. Address. Hair colour, eye colour, height and weight, ethnicity. This time the prisoner also signed on a large piece of paper so the clerk could compare the present signature with the recorded one.

Third desk, to witness a third clerk stamp the warrant.

To the chair before the camera.

The assistant reviewed the stamped form and wrote the prisoner's name on a little slate with chalk.

—Place your head in the wooden bracket, comrade. Hold the slate up. A little higher. Good. Bright light. Turn to the side, please. Bright light. Thank you, comrade. Next.

The prisoner stood up, seeing only spots of yellow. His vision cleared, and an officer came into focus within swirls of smoke: a handsome man, wavy black hair, big green eyes, livid red scars on his left ear and neck. The prisoner reached for the officer, asked him for a cigarette. A hand on his elbow then: the photographer's assistant steered him to the doorway that led to the courtyard. The prisoner mumbled an apology. One did not bother secret policemen for cigarettes when shuffling towards death.

Dogs barked.

The camera flashed, flashed, flashed.

The master-sergeant stood near Kostya and cleared his throat.
—Special Squad is in the stone house. Would you like to see it?

Drawing hard on his cigarette, Kostya nodded. Then he followed the master-sergeant to the little stone house, unfurnished and unlit, and discovered some of the men of Special Squad drinking vodka from one of two barrels. The master-sergeant introduced him; the men of Special Squad responded with correct protocol, if little enthusiasm. Kostya moved to the other barrel, bent over to scoop some up in his hand, flinched — not vodka but Troynoy cologne.

His eyes burned.

Then he laughed at himself, making sure the men noticed. Cautious and deferential, they invited him to the vodka barrel. When he scooped up a drink in his hands, they nodded and smiled.

Search lights clicked on and illuminated the courtyard. Dogs growled and whined now; men snarled at them to shut up. The men inside the stone house lined up and marched into the courtyard; Kostya among them.

Seven prisoners now stood in the courtyard, facing a guard tower and a wall, the lip of a long pit at their feet.

Kostya followed the other officers to line up behind the prisoners. On a table to their right, the table tilted slightly on the uneven ground: boxes and boxes of bullets, one neat pile for the Tokarevs, and one neat pile for the Nagants.

As a tractor chugged, Kostya noticed how much soil in the courtyard seemed fresh beneath tire prints. The courtyard would soon run out of room for mass graves.

The Special Squad now stood in a perfect line about two metres back from the pit.

Voices murmured and whispered; prisoners bargained with the officers, bargained with God.

—Kneel!

The prisoners obeyed. Some also bowed their heads.

—Aim!

The officers pulled their weapons from holsters. Three of the men, Kostya noted, used a Tokarev, and the other three, like him, used a Nagant. Each man aimed at the back of a skull.

—Fire!

Dogs howled.

No one knelt at the edge of the grave.

The next seven prisoners marched to the lip of the pit.

Prisoners knelt.

Officers aimed.

—Fire!

Again, again, again, again, again, until those using Nagants called for a pause to reload. Those using Tokarevs smirked and made loud complaints about the slowness of revolvers, about shooting one's load too early. After all, a Tokarev pistol carried eight rounds, clearly the superior weapon, comrades.

Seven prisoners at a time, thought Kostya. *How many in total? And why the hell can't the Tokarevs just load seven rounds in the magazine?*

When the Tokarevs had to pause to reload, they informed the Nagants that loading a magazine felt much like thrusting inside a woman.

Kneel.

Aim.

Fire.

Kneel, aim, fire, fire, fire, fire...

When the Nagant users called for a second reload, everyone took a break. The chained dogs snarled at any man who came too near, and the air stank of soil and blood.

Back inside, men scooped up Troynoy to splash on their faces; red tendrils stained the liquid. At the other barrel, they scooped up vodka, some in tin cups, others in their bare hands. The vodka, too, reddened. Cocaine appeared, thick lines of it. Left arm almost numb, Kostya refused the first offer, instead drinking more vodka. The second offer? Yes, comrade. Head nodding in a sudden and desperate need to sleep, he sniffed a line off the back of someone's bloodspattered hand. Lights brightened; laughter sharpened; pain calmed.

Clarity. Purpose.

—Kneel!

Kostya laughed at the sky.

—Aim!

Tears ran down his face, his jaw.

—Fire!

Seven bullets, four in joy, two in doubt, one in despair.

A prisoner died yet failed to fall into the pit. He had to kick her corpse.

Reload.

Insult the Tokarev-lovers.

Kneel, aim, fire.

Pause for the Tokarevs.

Kneel, aim, fire.

Five more rounds.

Reload.

Curse the dogs.

Threaten to shoot the dogs.

Another line of cocaine as the man offering it spoke of strawberries growing in places like the fertile *poligon*, so lush, so sweet...

Kneel, aim, fire.

They sang 'Yablochko,' over and over.

> *Ekh, little apple, where are you rolling?*
> *Right in my mouth. Now I have got you.*
> *Ekh, little apple...*

More vodka. Crying out as he moved his left arm, grateful no one noticed, Kostya now understood why they stood so close to the prisoners. He could not shoot straight from any distance now even if someone aimed a gun to his own head.

And if I can't shoot, then these apes...

Kneel, aim, fire.

He drank bloodied Troynoy by mistake. It packed a better hit than the vodka.

The dogs snapped and snarled. The men dropped ammunition as they tried to reload. The shooting postures changed and changed again: two-handed grip, one-handed grip, left hand behind the back or left arm slack, as the officer preferred, or as he needed so he might keep his balance.

Everyone laughed.

Ekh, little apple, where are you rolling?
Right in my mouth. Now I have got you.

The Nagant so warm, so heavy...the stink, the stink...

Kostya noticed him then, over behind the vodka barrel. Taller than the others, quite slender, long golden hair tucked up beneath his cap, like a woman in some pathetic disguise in a bad play, he drew his weapon: not a gun, but a sword. His huge eyes fixed on Kostya, eyes of flame.

Gavriil?

Kneel.

No, wait, the ikon...

Aim.

Gavriil stood beneath the beam of a searchlight and shone the brighter.

Fire.

—I said, fire!

Kostya flinched: only his prisoner remained, screaming, screaming in animal terror, worse than the dogs. He staggered forward, jammed the muzzle of the Nagant in the base of the man's skull, fired.

Spat.

Told himself he'd been stupid to bother with a clean *gymnastyorka*.

Sought Gavriil, failed to find him.

A call for a break to let the guns cool.

Two of the men found a strawberry patch and soon praised the fruit, so lush, so sweet. A third clapped Kostya on the good shoulder and offered him yet more cocaine. —Here, I've got the good shit. Stay sharp, Comrade Senior Lieutenant. We've got four hours to go yet.

[ ]

THE BUTTER PRINCE
Tuesday 8 June

The radio announcer gave a time check. —At the tone, the time is fifteen hundred hours, or three p.m.

The lock clicked.

Temerity looked up. She sat in the front room, gnawed by fear's fatigue, with the 1936 *Directory for All Moscow* splayed open on her lap. *Efim Antonovich home? At this hour?*

She'd paced the flat for much of the night in Kostya's absence, checking the lock every few minutes, just in case, because maybe this time, this time, it would release. When she did sleep, dreams thieved any rest, dreams of exile and flight. She'd struggled to read a map in the last dream, a map on which borders writhed and legends blurred.

Now she struggled with the tiny typeface of the telephone directory.

God's sake!

Kostya lay asleep, in his bedroom. He'd returned home around five that morning, loud and staggering, almost incoherent, waking both Temerity and Efim. Beneath waves of Troynoy cologne, he gave off a terrible odour: sweat, cordite, blood. *Unclean,* Temerity had thought. Kostya had then complained of pain in both his shoulders, ache of heavy use in the right, usual mess in the left. Done with that, he cursed about the tepid trickle of the shower. When Efim asked Kostya how he'd irritated his shoulder, Kostya shouted that Efim enjoyed no right to question him, and neighbours beat their fists on the walls. Then Kostya had laughed, low and steady. *I couldn't shower with those apes. I'm a senior lieutenant.*

The two men had disappeared, Efim emerging a few moments later to the front room where Temerity sat. He seemed angry with her. *In the animal kingdom, Nadezhda Ivanovna, it's adapt or die. How much longer will you be with us?*

So, on hearing the lock click and the door open, Temerity expected Efim, and she expected him still to be in a foul mood.

Instead, a different footfall, and a lower voice, almost melodious. —Kostya?

Temerity kept still, waiting for Kostya to respond.

Silence.

The man eased the door shut behind him, pried off his boots with the wooden bootjack, and padded into the kitchen. —Kostya, it's just me. I don't want to startle you.

Temerity hurried to put the phone book down before this man rounded the corner. —He's asleep.

—Oh?

A man who looked to be in his fifties, shorter than Kostya, fluffy hair snow white, eyes bright blue, peeked into the front room. He wore NKVD uniform and took off his cap. —I am Vadym Pavlovich Minenkov, an old friend. And you, dear?

Temerity walked towards him. —Nadezhda Ivanovna Solovyova.

Vadym held out his hand, as though ready to accept something; Temerity held out hers. He kissed it, thinking how this petite woman with her dark hair and round hips looked nothing like Kostya's previous willowy blondes. If well fed, she might run to a pleasing embonpoint. The eyes, the cast of her face, yes, compelling. Then he noticed her bare feet: a vulgar display. *New days, new ways,* he told himself, retrieving a brown paper package from the pouch on his *portupeya.* —Here, my dear, take this. I found dried mushrooms. Our Kostya adores mushrooms.

—Oh, so do I.

—He likes the agarics in a soup, a beef broth if you can manage it, and the puffballs and reindeer antlers sautéed in butter and black pepper and served on toast. Have you got any butter?

—Ah...

—Run out and get some butter. What about bones? Have you got any bones to make a broth? Shall I fetch you some?

—I'll wait and see what he'd prefer.

Vadym kissed her hand again. —Keep being good to him, yes? Delighted to meet you, dear.

Still holding the packet of mushrooms, Temerity walked Vadym to the door and watched him haul on his boots. When he opened the door and exposed a dim hallway of other doors, she almost lunged.

Right, tell one NKVD *officer how I wish to escape another. That would end well.*

Vadym prepared to lock the flat again from the outside. —Please don't trouble yourself, dear. Give Kostya my love when he wakes up, the lazy cat. Goodbye.

As the door closed and the lock clicked, Temerity held the packet to her nose and smelled earth. Then she strode to the bedroom, where, curled on his right side and naked beneath a sheet, Kostya remained asleep. His holster and the amber beads peeked out from beneath his pillow.

Temerity coughed, cleared her throat.

Kostya shifted onto his back, opened his puffy eyes, and tugged the sheet farther up his chest.

Temerity shook her head. —I've seen it before, remember, when it dripped with gonorrhea. Here, Minenkov brought you mushrooms.

Kostya tore a corner of the packet, sniffed it. —Dima? Oh, my God. Mushrooms. I've not gone mushroom hunting in years.

—Your God is a little fungus on a rotten log?

—If you ever ate these cooked properly, you'd consider them sacred.

—I do know what a mushroom is, thank you.

Laughing, he swung his legs over the side of the bed, the sheet draped over his belly and thighs. Then he patted the mattress to his left. —Yes, of course you do. Britishers know everything. Sit here.

She did, unsure where to look: the hair on his chest and forearms, the stubble on his face. —Your toe looks much better.

The scars on his ear, neck, and shoulder flushed deep red, and the skin over them seemed very thin.

—Are the scars painful?

He gave a half-smile. —Hurt like hell. At least, what I used to imagine hell to be, back when I could study a beauty wall. Now, these mushrooms. Wait, I told you not to go to the door. How did he get in?

—He had a key.

—Dima has a key? Then Arkady Dmitrievich loaned it to him. Fucked in the mouth, can the old man not even give me this much peace? Loaning out a key to my flat so he can check on me. I don't loan out my key to his house. I suppose all of fucking Moscow can get a key to my flat. Has all of fucking Moscow got any butter?

—Minenkov suggested bones.

Kneel, aim, fire. —What?

—For broth.

—We need an onion.

Temerity rubbed her temples. —An onion.

—Yes, an onion. What's wrong with that? Do you not have onions in the British Empire? If the onion turns blue in the broth with the mushrooms, then we've got poisonous ones, and if you eat them, you'll die frothing at the mouth, like this, fffffff… are you all right?

—Fine, fine.

—I'll get some butter, and some wine. We'll feast tonight.

He placed his left arm around her shoulders: heavy, stiff.

Warm.

Temerity kept still.

Kostya took his arm back.

Temerity shifted her weight. —Onions, butter, and bones. Does Minenkov always bring you groceries?

—We've all gone hungry. We shared everything during the last round of food difficulties. Look, Vadym Minenkov's lovely, but don't assume that means he's weak. And he can tell you stories about Dzerzhinsky himself. Just don't ask him; you'll be there all night. Now, butter. What are you smirking about?

She dropped her voice to almost a whisper. —I once saw the Prince of Wales made of butter.

—Who?

—Edward VIII, before he was king.

Kostya waited for her to stop giggling. —The one who abdicated?

—Britain's better off without him. He has no understanding of duty. Back in 1924, at the Empire Exhibition, the dear Canadians sent us a life-size statue of the Prince of Wales made of butter.

Her laughter broke free, and though he loved the sound of it, Kostya squinted at her. —Wait, a statue made of butter?

—The Canadians are farmers, wide open prairies and whatnot, dairymen, lots of milk. Sturdy children. Like your Ukraine, I expect. They're certainly proud of their butter. And so, the Canadians' gift: Wales, in butter. Life-size, with a horse. Three thousand pounds of it.

—That's just over thirteen hundred kilos. What happened to it?

Temerity dragged her thoughts from a memory of the Duke of York, now George VI, stammering and gagging through his speech to close the exhibition. —Ah, well, we got a replacement statue, I know that. The exhibition lasted for some time.

—No one ate it?

—I don't think so. I expect the butter turned rancid.

Kostya discarded the sheet and rushed off the bed, all muscle and speed. Then he bowed with great flourish and straightened up, grinning. He did not look happy. —Should I not be taller?

—What?

—Thirteen hundred kilos of butter, Nadia. In 1924, two years, two fucking years after the...food difficulties, when I was nineteen years old, I still wore the same size clothes as when I was twelve. I had a growth spurt at age twenty-two. And you greedy and arrogant British propped up your empire with art made of butter.

Her cheeks burned as she thought of her grandfather's wealth. Looking down, she straightened her skirt. —Please put some clothes on.

Sighing, Kostya sat beside her and covered himself with the sheet. —Truce. Dima is right. Butter and broth are the best things for these mushrooms.

—Very thoughtful of him.

—He's good that way. He nursed me through the worst flu I've ever had.

—What, 1918? You told me the truth about that?

—I told you the truth about many things. How much have you lied to me?

—Not about that flu. I did dream about skull lights as nightingales sang, and the fever locked me in a trunk and threw me in a river.

Kostya could smell the disinfectant in the clinic in Spain. —Like Svyatogor's wife when he punished her for adultery.

—Yes, except I escaped the trunk. When I did, I found that my mother and brother had died.

—Nadia, that's terrible. I'm sorry.

He means it. —Thank you.

Kostya made to kiss her forehead, stopped. —How many languages?

—Now, why would I tell you that?

—I'll go first. Seven, including Russian.

—I find that hard to believe.

Kostya sounded younger, like a boy eager to prove himself. —No, really, I told the truth. Spanish, Italian, and French but then if you've got one of those, you've got them all. German, Ukrainian, some Kazakh...

—Kazakh?

—And English.

—And where did you hear all those tongues?

—Odessa, to start. Oh, and some Yiddish.

—Lucky you.

He leaned close, and his stubble scraped her cheek. —You'd get French at school, yes, nice British girl? French is the gateway.

—Indeed, it is not. Latin is the gateway.

—You've got Latin?

—Ancient Greek, too.

He snorted. —Spare me the talk of the dead.

—You're jealous.

—The languages people speak now, Nadia.

—The word *gonorrhea* is Latin. It means flow of the seed. Of course, it's not semen that leaks out of the head of your cock but pus.

He stared at her a moment, then laughed. —Nurse, pedant, and polyglot, the girl of my dreams.

Jolly him along, she thought, and she gave a half-smile. —I had tutors before I left for school, and then again when I came back.

—What do you mean, left?

—Boarding school.

—Your father sent you away?

—It's not like that. And I didn't stay. I was a bit of a troublemaker. So I came home, and my father hired tutors. French, Spanish, Italian, German, and some Old High German. I can read some Danish, too, but it's very difficult for me, some rock in the fog, just out of my reach. I suppose you really want to know about the Russian?

This time, he did kiss her forehead. Then he said yes in every language he knew.

Sweat broke out on her neck, and she forced herself to smile. —My maternal grandparents emigrated to England in 1891. Part of the Russian flu, some people said. They were academics, he a linguist and she a chemist. They only had the one child, my mother.

He drew his lips over her hair.

Temerity struggled to concentrate. —In the end, I learned Russian from a lovely old count who emigrated in 1917. Very aristocratic. You'd shoot him on sight.

His lips touched her cheek, and he hesitated, giving her a chance to pull away.

She kept still.

He kissed her, just below the cheekbone.

Soft.

Then she got up, strode to the front room, turned up the radio.

Eyes shut, face red, Kostya let out a long breath. He tugged on civilian clothes, and, still buttoning his shirt, followed her.

She sat in the soft chair, body turned to the wall. Under the racket of a loud female voice rapping out arrest statistics, Temerity spoke in quiet accusation. —You've not got my papers.

—Look, I had a bad night.

Rubbing her cheek with the heel of her left hand, she gestured to the radio with her right. —Is that it, then? I'll disappear?

—I'll get them.

—Why couldn't you get them last night? What in hell were you doing?

Surname, first name, patronymic. —Paperwork.

A recognition hit her. This menacing NKVD agent, her one link to freedom, didn't know where to look.

He knelt beside her. —Please, don't cry. I'll find them, Nadia, just give me time.

—I've not got time! God's sake, why have you done this? Why did you bring me here?

—Spain.

—Spain. I see. What was it, then? The sunny skies?

—No.

—The warm breezes, the shortage of clean water?

—No. Listen—

—The beautiful music of bombardment?

—Shut up!

She flinched.

Still on his knees, he'd tensed and now seemed ready to leap at her. —Is this some competition for you, woman? Which of us had the worse time in Spain? You want bombardment? Try Madrid, over and over, and fucking Gerrikaitz!

She said nothing.

The radio report on arrest statistics finished, and another announcer introduced a short musical selection: the 'Garland Waltz' from Tchaikovsky's *Sleeping Beauty.*

Kostya stood up, grabbed Temerity's arms, and hauled her to her feet. —Shall we dance?

—No. Let me go.

Kostya led with vigour and grace; he murmured near her ear. —Ah, sunny Spain, Nadia: espionage, bombardment, and gonorrhea. I know you share the first two. You can travel. I can't. Another country? Strange dirt and foreign water can only poison me, infect me with Trotskyism or worse, imperialist Western decadence. One soaks up treason from the very air. But I got to see Spain. Another country. I got to see it. I love Russia, and I got to leave Russia. My orders to go to Spain were a gift. You dance well for someone wearing no shoes, my sweet angel of Comintern. I saw another country. In a civil war. I knew something about that, the confusion, and the fucking hunger, always hunger, everyone. And I added to it. I hurt people. I called it interrogation. Then I killed them.

He made a misstep, corrected it.

I lost Misha.

He took in a sharp breath. —And then I fell in love with you.

Her body slackened in his grip. —What?

He tugged her along in the waltz. —I told myself love at first sight, true love, whatever one calls it, is just decoration for fairy stories. I did believe in it once. Wandering Ivan meets Marya Morevna, they fall in love, and he joins her on some difficult quest. Perhaps they even defeat Koshchei the Deathless, and then they live happily ever after. I believed it when I was a boy, and then, as a man, I forgot it. NKVD work knocks sense into you. Humans are flawed, we learned, and NKVD must root out and destroy those flaws for the good of everyone else. It's a kind of love. Like when Arkady Dmitrievich would beat me. For my own good. He saved me, so I have to listen to him. How do I ever pay him back for saving me, hey? Or Vadym Minenkov, how can I repay him? I decide to serve them by serving my country. I do well, just as Arkady Dmitrievich predicted. *Languages,* he always said, *your gift for languages.* When he first tugged me up from the ground, I cursed him out in four different languages. Later he said he could see the future of the country in me. Why was Chekist Arkady Dmitrievich Balakirev, the Muscovite's Muscovite, fourteen generations on his mother's side, ten on his father's, even in Odessa in January of 1918? Why did Arkady Dmitrievich happen to find me on the ground and think to help me up, just so I could curse him out like the *bezprizornik* I pretended to be? Great forces we don't understand, Nadia, can't understand. I surrender to that idea. I do. I submit. Arkady Dmitrievich was meant to find me, and I was meant to find you, first in Spain, then in a Lubyanka cell, and finally at Arkady Dmitrievich's house. I love you. I am meant to love you. I submit.

The waltz ended.

He let go of her waist, took a step back, kissed her hand, and bowed.

She kept still. His voice at the clinic, so cold as he ordered her to kneel. *Down. Now!* Yet he'd fired wide. —You're in love with me?

Kostya gave her an exasperated look.

The radio announcer urged all good Soviet children to get ready for a special treat today, a recording of Comrade Prokofiev's *Petya and the Wolf.*

Temerity's hand tingled where Kostya had kissed it, near the injection site. —And if you'd left me at this Arkady Dmitrievich's house?

—Let me fix up some food, yes? Then I want to tell you a story.

As Kostya worked in the kitchen, Temerity stared at the radio.

I never tried to charm him. God's sake, his beautiful face...

Prokofiev's songbird asked the duck: What sort of bird are you that can't fly?

Help me.

And the duck asked the songbird: What sort of bird are you that can't swim?

Kostya and Temerity ate eggs and potato in silence until Kostya pushed his plate away, and the scrape of heavy glass across the wooden table seemed too loud. —I don't know how Arkady Dmitrievich found me. I don't even know how Odessa fell, and I was there. Early 1918. I was twelve. First the Reds took Odessa, then the Whites, then the Reds again, and any moment the Germans might roll in. I lost track. The Germans did take Odessa, after I got out, and years later Arkady Dmitrievich showed me a photograph of how the Germans cleaned the streets of *bezprizorniki*. Hanged them. I knew some of those boys. The one facing the camera as he tried to keep his balance on the gallows was called Timofei, Timofei Boykov. We sat next to each other in school. One day, I had the desk all to myself, and the teacher asked us all if we knew why Timofei had not come to school. None of us knew, yet all of us knew, even the teacher, because we all saw Timofei standing in queues for hire or huddled on the corner begging for coins and cigarettes. I heard him say that the next time a man offered to pay him for a blow job he'd cut the bastard's Achilles tendon. When I saw him again, he was wiping his mouth with the back of his hand, and when he saw me, he looked so angry, like the whole mess was my fault. When I became a *bezprizornik* myself, Timofei got his revenge, and I took a beating. Down in the catacombs. 'You pretended not to see me,' he said. 'Your grandfather gave me cigarettes and kopeks, but you pretended not to see me!' I hated him, and I was afraid of him, yet when Arkady showed me that photograph years later, I wanted to be sick. He was just twelve. Fucked in the mouth.

He paused to offer Temerity a cigarette.

She accepted, leaning closer so he could light it.

Wincing, Kostya rolled his left shoulder, then drew on his cigarette. —Do you remember when you told me your mother died of flu? I can't remember my mother, either. She died in the 1905 uprising. I was a baby. Her parents raised me. My grandmother died when I was eight, and then it was just my grandfather. I'm illegitimate. The patronymic gets tricky for us. My father abandoned my mother, that's all I know. I liked to pretend he was a sailor, not a sailor in the Navy but the kind who owns a ship and has adventures, and I'd make up stories about him and how one day he'd come back to Odessa and save me. Anyway, my mother had the right to give her child any patronymic she pleased. It might be for the father, or it might be to honour a man who had helped her after she fell pregnant. My original patronymic was Semyonovich. I don't know if that's for my grandfather, Semyon Berendei, or if my father was a Semyon, too. When I got older, I wondered how my parents met. Were they in love, some sort of forbidden affair? Was it just one night? Did he rape her? Am I walking around because of a rapist?

—So your name's not really Nikto.

—I told you, I changed it.

—And the patronymic?

Kostya tapped ash from his cigarette. —Arkady Dmitrievich took me to a clerk to get new identity papers. I was still dizzy and stupid with the flu. I could walk, that was all. The clerk made things difficult, asking if I'd made a thorough search for my papers. Arkady Dmitrievich got angry and asked the clerk if we should go back to Odessa and ask the occupying Germans to help us find the papers. I only wanted to vomit and lie down. I couldn't even manage my date of birth. I said 14 April 1905, and the clerk said 26 April 1905.

Arkady Dmitrievich had to explain to me Lenin had changed the calendar. The clerk kept asking my name, and Arkady Dmitrievich started shouting, and I couldn't stop him. I was sweating, and then when the clerk asked me for probably the fifth time for my name, I said Konstantin but froze after that. Arkady Dmitrievich supplied the Arkadievich. Then the clerk started to praise Arkady Dmitrievich for getting his bastard son out of a war zone. The old man tried to explain we're not father and son, but the clerk wouldn't listen. He was in charge now, able to push around a Chekist, and he would not give that up. The clerk looked at me then, and demanded I give him my surname. He even made up some horseshit about the papers being invalid if someone else supplied my surname. I had to say it. I froze again. I wasn't even sure this whole thing was happening. The clerk kept his voice steady, and the politer he sounded, the more frightened I felt. 'Tell me your surname. Tell me your surname.' I started to cry. I kept thinking about the orphan's surname. I didn't want to be a Neizvestny. But who was I? 'Nikto,' I said, 'I am *nikto, nikto*, no one at all.' And the clerk wrote it down. So there I was, reborn as Konstantin Arkadievich Nikto, and as we left, Arkady Dmitrievich promised me he'd have the clerk arrested.

Temerity stroked her fingers over the back of Kostya's hand. —So, who were you in Odessa?

Kostya sounded impatient. —Konstantin Semyonovich Berendei. I just told you. I left it behind. Fuck, if you'd been there... When history took a shit in 1918, it made a big dump in Odessa. I only had my grandfather, and he was exhausted. We couldn't get enough food or coal, and none of his patients could pay him, but he kept treating them. Then one night in January, it was bang-bang-bang on the door and frantic shouts for Dr. Berendei. Grandfather told me he had to leave. He walked out of the house, and I never saw him again. Then the schools shut down. I stayed in the house alone. I only left to queue for bread. I'd queue for hours. No one else in that line asked me about Grandfather or checked on me in any way. I was already invisible. After a few days of this, the baker said he could not keep a tab for me when he extended credit to no one else, and when would Grandfather come and pay? I couldn't answer him. He was a decent man, in the end, and he broke off some of his own loaf and sent me out the back door. I bolted it down, almost choked on it. It was like eating sand. Adulterated flour. And then sleet started, and I wanted to get inside, so I ran. And of course I slipped. I fell, smacked my head off a curb, and when I got up again and back to the house, I found strangers living there. I still don't know who they were or how they took over. A family of four, a middle-aged man the size of a bear and his two grown sons, scarred from the Great War or the Revolution or who knows what, and a cook. They had all these crates piled up outside the doors, and they'd even changed the locks. They stole my grandfather's house. I couldn't believe it. I would knock on the door, explain myself, ask to come inside, and they'd shout abuse at me. They wore me down. Finally I asked just to be allowed in to get a favourite book and my other warm coat. They looked about to relent, when I pointed to a painting near the beauty wall, a watercolour of the Odessa Steps. 'My mother painted that,' I said. 'Look, that's her signature in the corner.' One of the sons picked me up and threw me off the porch. Their cook called out to me after a moment, and she gave me buttered bread on the condition that I never come back.

I tried to ask people who knew my grandfather for help. Many had been his patients. I got nowhere. When I could get people to listen, they would shrug and remind me life was difficult for everyone now. I don't think they believed me. Perhaps they just didn't want to believe me. I slept outside, in empty buildings or in the catacombs. Odessa is not Moscow, but it's cold enough. I got so dirty, and the days got so long. Adults chased me away, called me rat, thief, *bezprizornik*. That last one still galls me. I fell in with the other street kids. I had to. My voice cracked and dropped and whistled and cracked again, so I could hardly get a word out. One day I caught my reflection in a window and saw how my eyes had gone wide. I hardly recognized myself. I had this burnt feeling all the time, like I'd had too much sun. All that mattered was food and sleep and cigarettes.

I counted the days. On day sixteen, I was walking by the waterfront when I saw the battleship *Dobrynya Nikitich* had docked. Captain Kastalsky knew my grandfather, so, I thought Captain Kastalsky would help me, surely. I'd gone aboard that ship many times. Sometimes Captain Kastalsky might visit my grandfather in his house. More often he would send word, and Grandfather would visit Captain Kastalsky. He'd take me with him. I got to know the boatswain, Shlykov. He taught me how to tie knots and curse in different languages. I always say he was my first tutor. Shlykov saw me through the fog. 'Your coat is dirty,' he said. 'Brush it. And I see you've gotten taller.' An officer came round to see whom Shlykov addressed like that, over the side of a battleship, and his shoulder boards seemed about to slide off his coat. Shlykov explained I was the grandson of the captain's great friend in Odessa. Fog rose like smoke, and *Dobrynya Nikitich* faded in and out of sight. Sailors loaded provisions, and I almost followed them aboard until I remembered I must wait for the captain's permission. After a long time, during which Shlykov had to carry on with his duties and could not talk with me, the skinny officer returned with the captain. Kastalsky looked faded, blurry somehow, like a bad photograph. His skin had gone grey, and his hair and beard had gone white. He stepped with new care, as though worried he might fall, until he reached the side and could look down on me. He called my grandfather's surname, and when I answered, my voice whistled and cracked. Kastalsky peered into the fog and said, 'Konstantin, is that you? Where is your grandfather?'

I said I didn't know.

I noticed how the sleet ticked the sides of the ship, and Kastalsky stared into the fog. Finally he asked, 'When did you see him last?'

I told him it was a few weeks, and I expected that any moment now, any moment he'd invite me on board so I could warm up and explain.

Then the fog closed over Kastalsky, and his slow footsteps receded. I called his name, over and over, but my voice cracked out, and the docks were noisy. Even Shlykov lost sight of me. 'Konstantin, are you there? Are you still there? Take care, boy.' A dockworker chased me away, threatened to beat me with his cargo hook, and then he called me a *bezprizornik*. Shlykov likely heard it. I felt my face burn, and then I leapt at the dockworker. If I'd had a knife, I'd have stabbed him. He threw me off like a rag. I got to my feet and made my way through the fog. I managed to beg a few cigarettes. The man who gave me the cigarettes lit the first one for me, and I lit the next from the embers of that one. Then I found myself at my grandfather's house once more, and maybe this time I could explain how the house belonged to Dr. Semyon Mikhailovich Berendei.

I should have stalked them better. I should have watched the house and learned the men's patterns so I'd know when they might be absent. I knocked and knocked on the back door and pleaded to be let in. Then I smelled the roasting pork. Where in hell had they gotten pork? It didn't matter. My mouth filled with froth, and when I swallowed it, I almost vomited.

The cook dragged me inside and let me sit on a wooden stool, the one my grandfather used when he wanted to reach a book on a high shelf. I saw the woven rug and the dark spots on the beauty wall where the ikons and my mother's watercolours once hung. The cook filled my pockets with bread and bits of pork and told me to let it cool. I begged her to let me stay.

The men heard us. They ran into the kitchen. The father told his sons to get me out, and they picked me up, one on each side, and they threw me outside. I landed on stones and ice. I scrambled to get back up, and the two sons were staring at me, eyes huge, and their father picked up a bucket. It was wastewater from the kitchen. We had indoor plumbing in that house, so it could have been worse. Anyway, he drenched me with it, and warned me again to stay down. This time I did, and the sleet turned to snow. The soaking took the fight from me, and it seemed easier to give in. The cold started to change, and soon I felt warm. A boot nudged my ribs, very gentle. Then a hand shook my shoulder, and I cried out for whomever it was to get the hell away from me. I rubbed ice from my eyes and got them open, and I saw the boots, the hem of a long black leather coat layered under a shorter coat of fur, the amber worry beads dangling from the belt, and the peaked cap.

A Chekist. He had a beard like Lenin's, and I was stupid and sleepy now with the cold, so I thought he was Lenin, bigger than I'd imagined from the photographs, and he'd come to tuck me into bed. The beads clicked, and the Chekist reached out his hand. 'Get up,' he said. I didn't take his hand. I told him to leave me alone and let me sleep. He hauled me up to my feet. 'You will get up,' he said, and that's when I called him a son of a syphilitic bitch in four languages. He stared at me a moment, and then he laughed. He took a flask from his coat and held it out. It was vodka. I choked on it. He took it away, and he said, 'I am Balakirev of the Cheka, and you will come with me.' I thought he would put me in jail, but he saved me. By his own free will, he saved me.

Temerity studied Kostya through whorls of cigarette smoke. —It reminds me of another story.

Kostya smirked. —When Baba Yaga smells the Russian hero. She complains of it, and then she asks, 'Are you here of your own free will, or twice as much by compulsion?'

—Is it true?

—Baba Yaga?

—You.

He reached over and stroked her hand the same way she had stroked his. —I'm here, aren't I? And I saved you. How the hell did you even get to that party?

—I don't know.

—Please don't cry.

She sniffed back tears. —I'm not crying. There were two of them. Armed. Not in uniform.

—Did they show identification?

Temerity shook her head. —I flipped one of them before I saw the Nagant. Jiu-jutsu.

Kostya stared at her a moment, then laughed. —And you wonder why I love you.

—You hardly know me.

—Sometimes, Nadia, it might be a person, or an idea, or, I don't know, a scrap of cloth, but what the cloth means, or even the existence of the scrap and how it came about: it's precious. To be cherished. Worth saving. Look, I've participated in those parties. I've chosen a woman and taken her. I'm not proud of that. But you, first in Spain, then in Lubyanka, finally at that party, three times, Nadia, three impossible times. Not only are you something to cherish, but you are meant to be cherished. You are meant to be here, and I am meant to save you, just as Arkady Dmitrievich was meant to be in Odessa and save me.

She shut her eyes. —Twice as much by compulsion.

—Do you believe me yet?

When she opened her eyes, tears fell, and she laughed, a hard and hollow laugh. —Believe you about what?

—That I won't hurt you. Think, woman. You kneed me in the balls, and I didn't strike you back, and believe me, I wanted to. Everything I've told you is a weapon you can hurl back at me. You tell another officer even half of it, and I'll be arrested in less time that it takes to say my name. In Lubyanka, we've got these special cells. The floors are sloped towards a grated drain. The walls above the drains are battered and pocked. We've got a spigot and a hose in the corridor outside. If I fuck up, that's where I die. And yet here I am, Senior Lieutenant Nikto of the NKVD, who wants to save a British spy.

—I'm not—

—You are, and if my colleagues knock on the door—

—Then I'm dead.

—Interrogated, brutalized, raped, and then yes, dead. And I'll go with you.

She sneered. —How gallant.

—No. At gunpoint.

She said nothing.

Kostya stayed close, kept his voice low. —The good doctor will be home soon enough. You need to convince him that you want to be here, that you're fond of me. At least a little. I can sleep on the bedroom floor, but we must both sleep in the bedroom.

Temerity shut her eyes. *Your duty at all times…*

Eyes still closed, she extended her hand for him to shake. —Fine.

Instead, once more, he kissed it.

Vadym and Arkady strolled Red Square. Both in uniform, both on duty, they'd claimed old Chekists' privilege and announced to their respective department secretaries a need for fresh air. Vadym had appeared at Arkady's office door, and Arkady, already too distracted to focus on a report from Boris Kuznets on Laboratory of Special Purpose Number Two, had smiled in relief.

Vadym struggled to remember the last time he saw Arkady smile.

Outside, as they kept their voices low and their faces calm, Arkady with less success, Vadym addressed his old friend with his usual term of endearment. —You grumpy old goat. You snubbed me. The invitation to my flat for supper.

—What invitation?

—Ah. Kostya forgot to tell you.

Arkady clicked his tongue and looked to the sky. —That boy will be the death of me.

Vadym chuckled. —Such a boy, such a remarkable boy, thirty-two years old.

—Fine, fine, he's a grown man. It hardly means I'll ever stop worrying about him. Do you know where he was last night?

—His bed, I hope.

—*Poligon* duty.

—Kostya?

Arkady nodded.

Vadym recalled his own days in the civil war as a Red Army executioner. He'd shot deserters. He'd hunted them, too, and often, as the deserters passed their final night, he sat up with them. Vadym considered it a duty, a deathbed vigil. Sometimes deserters confessed to guilt and shame. Sometimes they remained sullen, or defiant. Sometimes they shook. Boys, many of them, fifteen, sixteen. So many boys. At dawn, he shot them, in the head. —Wet work. Still, it must be done.

—Must be done, Dima, but by a man like him? It's artless slaughter. Any knuckle-dragging ape can shoot someone in the head.

Vadym changed his stride to imitate a gorilla's.

Arkady almost laughed. —I didn't mean you, Dima. I'm sorry. I'm not...we all shoot...I can't think straight. Some days, I hate humanity.

—Only some days?

—When we see something strong and beautiful, we want either to possess it or destroy it. Kuznets rides my back, thinks he's sniffed out treachery. Then he spots Kostya, who's one of our best officers, and he recognizes that, so boom, he must either possess Kostya or destroy him.

—Arkasha...

Arkady shut his eyes. The diminutive's sting of affection: only Vadym called him Arkasha, and then in moments so scarce they hurt. —And one reason Kuznets would possess or destroy Kostya is just to make a little sideshow as he pursues me, because I once said good things about...a man who's no longer working. Of course, I said good things about him. He was the fucking chief.

They walked in silence for several minutes.

Vadym took a key from his pocket and passed it to Arkady. —Kostya was asleep when I dropped by with mushrooms.

—Good. He needs the rest. And thank you for checking on him. He's been avoiding me. Mushrooms?

—At the fruit market where I found the lemons. Did I tell you about the lemons?

—Lemons are only good for keeping cats out of the flowerbed.

—The rest of us like them. Remember the first time we took the boys mushroom hunting, and I cooked mushroom soup in the woods? Misha turned up his nose, and Kostya stole Misha's bowl and licked it clean.

Pocketing the key, Arkady chuckled. —Yes, I remember that. Was he civil when you woke him?

Delighted to see his friend laugh, Vadym also laughed. —I let him sleep. I left the mushrooms with his girlfriend.

—*What?*

Vadym gazed up at St Basil's, at the beautiful domes he'd viewed, what, thousands of times? He sighed. —Ah. He's not told you. Now I have embarrassed you both, yes?

—A girlfriend? Living in the flat?

—Calm down. He should have married long ago.

Arkady softened his voice. —I'm worried about the *propiska* regulations, that's all. How did he get her registered to live there so fast?

—Well, I'm not about to start an official inquiry.

—What does she look like?

Vadym thought about it. —Petite, dark curly hair, not his type at all.

—And her name?

—Solovyova, Nadezhda Ivanovna Solovyova. From Leningrad, maybe? Her speech is a touch old-fashioned, now that I think on it, a smack of the aristocrat. She's lovely. I'm quite charmed.

—I can tell.

—She'll be good for him, if he holds onto her. Not got much of a record with women, our Kostya. That last girlfriend: Sofia, yes? She didn't last long.

—A complete whore. I could see that the moment I met her.

This time, Vadym looked to the sky. Sofia, like Yulia, Tatiana, Sonja, and the others, would not, or could not, withstand the words and scrutiny of Arkady Balakirev. —When will you learn to trust Kostya? He won't get entangled with a whore, complete or otherwise. He's not that stupid.

Breathing hard, Arkady slowed his stride. —Fine words from a man who never got married.

—I can't burden a wife with the work I've done and must yet do.

—Neither can I. So I serve my needs as they arise.

Vadym gave him a long look, long enough to lose sight of the street and stumble.

Arkady grabbed his arm, kept him from falling. —We should get back.

—Promise me you'll consider Kostya's feelings and be gentle with this one? Civil, at least?

—I am always civil.

—No, you're an iron-bound old Chekist who treats every encounter as an interrogation.

Arkady looked at Vadym in some confusion and hurt. —I do no such thing.

—You just did it to me.

Arkady ignored that. —If she's worthy of him, if she truly loves him, then she'll not be frightened off by me.

Neither man spoke again until they'd reached the Lubyanka doors.

Vadym looked Arkady up and down. —Are you sure you're all right?

Face sweaty and pale, Arkady nodded. —Never better.

—I'll reschedule supper, yes?

—That would be best.

Emerging from the shadows by the door, Efim almost dropped his large burden and so embraced it the harder. An electrical cord trailed behind him, plug knocking the floor, as he strode toward the flat's kitchen.

Kostya looked up from the cutlery drawer; he seemed to be counting.

Efim made it sound like a joke. —Are we missing a knife?

—No. What the hell have you got there?

—A samovar.

Kostya took it from Efim's arms and laid it on a kitchen counter. —I'd guessed that much. Where did you get it?

—The lab. I found it alone in a hallway just outside my office, toppled over on the floor next to the chair where the radio sits. I don't think I've ever seen this in operation. We've got a new one at the lab, massive thing, an absolute beast.

—So you stole this one.

—After working many hours of overtime, I contributed to a more just society and picked up rubbish from the floor. Or, if you prefer, I liberated it from the tyranny of sanitation engineers.

Kostya stared at him for a moment. Efim stared back. Then they both snorted and laughed.

The samovar squeaked as it tilted to one side.

Efim frowned. —Just needs a little support at the base. Some folded newsprint might do it. Ah, Nadezhda Ivanovna. You wanted tea earlier.

Kostya looked at Temerity. —You never told me that.

Efim kept his face neutral. *Not very observant for a secret policeman, are you?* —Now you may have such tea as you please.

Wondering why Efim seemed to be needling Kostya, Temerity

smiled. This womb-shaped machine, while smaller than the one at the communal kitchen in Hotel Lux, still baffled her. Surely, she could conquer it. —It's beautiful.

Kostya ran his fingers over the samovar's dim brass. —It needs a good polish.

Efim looked around for the best outlet. —Nikto, have we got any tea?

Kostya already strode for the telephone. —No, but I know where to find some.

Temerity studied the samovar. —Will it work?

—Only one way to find out.

Connected to Arkady's house, Kostya listened to the telephone ring and ring and ring. He ended the call and returned to the kitchen, where Efim and Temerity tested the samovar's balance on a narrow strip of counter near an outlet. —I'll be about an hour.

Temerity peered at him.

—You want tea, don't you?

Arkady stared at the stains in his toilet bowl. He recalled the day his father announced this renovation to the house, this indoor plumbing, flush toilet and shower bath. Arkady had been eleven, 1903, the same day he brought home failing grades in history, composition, French, religion, and music. Dmitri had wept after dark, when he thought Arkady had fallen asleep, wept and demanded of his wife why their one surviving child must be such an ignorant brute. Ekaterina defended her son: a big boy for his age who frightened the other children, no fault of his own. Perhaps he'd be an athlete one day, or a soldier. He'd find his place. Dmitri had disagreed: *I fear a place will yawn open for him, and he'll fall into it.*

The telephone rang: five, six, seven times.

Not now, Vadym.

The ringing stopped.

Arkady glanced at his shaving mirror. In his face, he took after his mother, except for the bloat. *Is it getting worse? No, I just had too much salty food today, the damned shchi and sausages at the cafeteria. Age. The face coarsens with age. I look nothing like my father.*

Dr. Dmitri Dmitrievich Balakirev had first blamed the Great War, then the Revolution, the Civil War, and finally the flu pandemic and all the resultant overwork for his depleted condition. One evening, while standing in this bathroom, looking at this toilet, he diagnosed himself. Oh, to be certain, Ekaterina later told Arkady, Dmitri consulted with a colleague; the other doctor only confirmed the guess. Yes, yes, very sad, and Dmitri's father before him. Dmitri Balakirev continued to work until the morning he stared at his stethoscope and did not recognize it. Then he took to his bed and died in great pain. Ekaterina died not long afterwards, and Arkady hid the strange bottles she'd discarded, perhaps dropped. His mother, Arkady told everyone, died of grief. The poison, he told himself, was just a tool.

She did not love me enough to stay. And I was helpless to stop this. Never again.

Downstairs, the cat flap opened and shut: one of three tomcats on his rounds. Sometimes the cats shat in his flowerbeds, and sometimes they perched on his higher windowsills, immovable sentries. When inside the house they scratched the furniture and woodwork but never soiled the floors. Arkady fed these huge cats herring and fowl and any other delicacies he might find, and they repaid him in dead mice and adoration, when they felt like it. They often got busy at dusk.

Arkady sighed. Dusk. His favourite time of day, once. When young Kostya asked him why, Arkady had said, *Change. Transition. So much happens.*

Tired, Arkady got into bed. Disgraceful, really, to laze like this so early in the evening.

His eyelids felt so heavy.

Disgraceful.

——

The metro train escaped the light of Vasilisa Prekrasnaya and rumbled northeast. Two stops, then a walk to Arkady's house to borrow some tea, which he'd replace when he next got to the shops. The old man wouldn't even notice. The lights flickered in the metro car, then steadied, and Kostya thought of wires, new wires drawing lines in the sky and cutting the wind till it whined. Then he thought of the boys at Home of the Child of the Struggle Moscow Number Two Supplemental Number Three, the nearest orphanage. Once upon a time, he'd visit every week. He called it community work; Arkady called it redemption.

Redemption from what, Arkady Dmitrievich?

Protection, then. You would protect those boys because no one could protect you.

Kostya would listen to the boys' complaints about food, teachers, lessons, silly rules, and then he'd tell them stories, often finishing with his own story as a child on the streets. *The wires cut the wind,* that's how he'd start, *the wires cut the wind, and it whined and howled one winter day in Odessa.* He'd told the Spanish boys on the voyage to Leningrad about the wind and the wires, about the family that stole his grandfather's house, how he had to move on. The boys had stared at him in stunned disbelief and then recognition, recognition of suffering, cruelty, and sorrows. *Don't let anyone call you a* bezprizornik, he told them, just as he'd told the Moscow boys. *A human being is not now, not ever, a stray dog.*

He sighed, and his eyes felt gritty. *When did I stop visiting the orphans? When did I stop telling stories? And why the hell did I tell Nadia about Odessa?*

The wires cut the wind, and it whined and howled one winter day in Odessa. That day the herring merchant boxed my ears, and Timofei had me beaten.

As the memory filled him with nausea and rage, the metro car filled with people, and Kostya shifted on the bench to make room.

All this time, and some herring merchant still hurts me? He's dead. Fucking dead. Since 1918. After Arkady Dmitrievich found me.

Once Arkady had pried him loose from the ground, Kostya slept at the Cheka depot set up in an abandoned store, where he and his grandfather once purchased sweets and *loukoum*. The dusty shelves lay in collapse and disarray, looted weeks before. During the day, Kostya continued to live on the street, scouting alleys and buildings, reporting back to Arkady and the other officers. The best method for such reconnaissance, however, was the queue. Kostya, like other street children, hired himself out to stand in line, to keep a place for someone else. Hours of waiting meant hours of eavesdropping. One evening, as Kostya complained of seized muscles and swollen feet, Arkady showed him how to massage his calves and reminded him how suffering yielded wealth. Kostya agreed, adding that other street children endured sexual abuse when hungry enough; his bed and supper at the Cheka depot prevented that. Arkady pounded a fist on the table, disgusted by the depravities of other men. One left the children alone. Then he commanded Kostya never to call himself or allow anyone else to call him a *bezprizornik*. *Do not accept such abuse, not now, not ever. You are far more than a stray dog. Is that clear?*

A few days later, Kostya had hired himself to a herring merchant in a line without a queue master, someone to write a number on everyone's hand and so maintain the order of the line, and he found himself next to Timofei Boykov.

—Kostya? Oh, you remember me, now that we're in the same queue.

—I always remembered you.

Timofei blew smoke into his face and signalled to a group of boys a few metres off. —No. You pretended not to see me. Your grandfather always gave me cigarettes and kopeks, but you pretended not to see me! Like I didn't exist. Kostya, I fucking exist.

—No, I—

Timofei spat at his feet. The other boys grabbed Kostya by the arms and dragged him from the line. Kostya cried out for help and mercy; Timofei turned his back. Others in the queue, if they deigned to notice at all, told themselves boys would be boys, so let them play their games in these difficult times, and besides, the fuss died down in no time.

Dragging Kostya into a nearby catacomb entrance, the boys kept a terrible silence; only Kostya's voice sounded, one thin voice. It cracked. In the darkness then, limestone glittering in the brief flares of a match light, the boys beat Kostya in the belly and face until he vomited and cried. Then, on a signal Kostya missed, they abandoned him. As he lay near a puddle, struggling to breathe, he told himself he knew the way out. He found the path soon enough and emerged — the street children called it going back up to heaven — to find the queue had both moved and grown, and the people between whom he'd stood might as well have vanished from the earth. No number inked on his hand: no proof of his place in the queue. Wrapping his arms round his rib cage, he shuffled to the end of the line. When the herring merchant found him there, he boxed his ears and struck his face. —Fucking useless *bezprizornik*!

Bloodied and bruised, Kostya explained his troubles to Arkady, and the following day at dusk, as Kostya settled into a meal of bread and sausage, Arkady strode in with the herring merchant.

Arkady and the other Chekists interrogated the merchant by candlelight. Kostya kept to the shadows, obscured, aware. The Chekists charged their prisoner with economic tyranny, bourgeois contempt, anti-revolutionary activities, and violent perversions. He denied everything, first with vigour, then with confusion, finally with indecision and growing fear. His anger, weak fire under sleet, surrendered.

In the morning, Arkady sent Kostya out to find some fresh loaves of bread, and Kostya took great care not to look at the prisoner still handcuffed to a chair. The prisoner spoke to Kostya, voice soft with petition and fatigue. Could the boy not explain matters to the Cheka?

When Kostya returned with a loaf of bread that looked like a charred brick, he discovered that Arkady's prisoner stood on the sidewalk before the boarded-up shop window, hands beneath his armpits, lips blue.

Stood there naked.

Arkady held his prisoner at gunpoint. As he called out the charges, he projected well and reached the edge of the crowd. His recitation became a priestly chant; he lacked only incense and bells. Other citizens peered through windows or watched in the street. Kostya told Arkady later that many of them seemed to recognize him: Dr. Berendei's grandson. They'd said nothing to Kostya when Dr. Berendei disappeared. They'd said nothing to Kostya when they saw him on the streets, sharp-boned and sad. They said nothing now as Kostya stood near the big Chekist for protection and warmth.

One older woman, wavy grey hairs escaping her hood, stepped forward.

Arkady kept his Nagant aimed at the prisoner and turned his head a few centimetres to include the woman in his line of sight. He stood with his feet maybe half a metre apart, shoulders back, knees steady. Snow marked the ground in whorls, like the skirt-hems of waltzing women, and the wind whistled round the wires.

Arkady addressed the older woman. —What do you want?

—Why are you doing this?

—He's guilty.

The prisoner shifted his weight from foot to foot. Arkady commanded the man to be still and resumed listing the litany of crimes.

A window from the flat above the depot opened. Arkady's colleague stuck his head out, studied the men below him, then lugged a large pot of water, almost a cauldron that reached to a grown man's knees, to the sill. He tipped the pot. Some of the water hit the prisoner's right shoulder, and it gave up vapour that froze like the breath behind the prisoner's cry. Arkady gestured with his revolver that the prisoner must stand in the puddle. He did so. The officer above poured some more, and the water hit the prisoner's head. He cried out again, then gasped, knees buckling, as though hit by a rock.

Arkady commanded him to keep still.

The prisoner obeyed.

Then Arkady ordered his colleague to slow the pour.

Many pots of water, some of it unclean.

Arkady explained it to Kostya. —We make an example of him.

—Frozen to the ground, like I was?

Arkady seemed not to hear him. —This would go easier with a hose and proper water pressure. Pots and pails will have to do. Here. You watch him. I need to go upstairs and take my turn with the water. Those pots get heavy.

Kostya accepted the revolver, held it in both hands, pointed it. He knew the make: the famous Nagant 1895. Curves stroked his fingers and kissed his palm. Kostya had often watched Arkady clean it, had studied the disassembled parts and begged permission to touch them. Arkady had refused. Now this sudden act of trust, this bounty, this privilege of the Nagant's beauty, jolted Kostya into a new strength, and a new understanding of that strength. A starving *bezpriznorik* held the life of a wealthy herring merchant. Was it so easy to obtain and exercise power, to solve problems, take revenge, soothe humiliation and pain?

It felt better than a hit of vodka.

The prisoner stared back at Kostya, eyes dull, teeth rattling.

Arkady's amber beads clicked as he walked away.

The prisoner's lips moved. Kostya thought the man might be praying.

Considering his own bruises, the pain of them, Kostya decided he cared nothing for the mystery of the prisoner's words. He shifted his gaze from the prisoner's face and stared instead at his hairy belly.

Water sluiced down, and another Chekist pried Kostya's fingers free of the Nagant. —Give me that, now.

By noon, a pile of sloping ice, about the height of a crouching man, stood beneath the broken window. Citizens avoided it, as they would avoid a deposit of debris.

The squeal of the metro train on its tracks hauled Kostya back to the present. The train slowed, approaching Krasnoselskaya, and Kostya rubbed at his eyes with the pads of his fingers. *Debris.*

A boy of maybe eleven, intent on his book, dropped a candy wrapper on the floor; Kostya ordered him to pick it up.

Eyes shut, Arkady turned over in bed and thereby escaped his itch, if only for a few moments. He considered the nerve signals and how itch ambushed him: intersections of power. He almost smiled. If he'd managed to pound nothing else into the boy's thick skull, he taught Kostya about intersections of power. A lesson had come the day they got Kostya's new papers in Moscow, though Arkady remained unsure how much the feverish boy heard. —The steppe gives up in patches to forest, and forest gives up in patches to tundra, yet in places where you see no change, all the differences blend. Power works like that, Little Tatar. Deep intersections, almost invisible. A clerk wields power over everyone in his queue, for they have come to beg, but he must remember to demonstrate his power, indulge in a little theatre, to manage the irritation and maybe anger of those in the queue. He must show his power and keep them near despair. So he keeps them waiting. In a queue for cheese, however, the people have power over the cheese-seller if he runs out. The power there tips much more quickly. Study the situation. Read and manipulate the emotions, and when necessary, do that to yourself. Find the intersections of power and adapt.

This memory of mentorship and its peace of certainty retreated, elusive as one of his cats.

Arkady sat up, refusing to scratch. *I felt so strong then, so well. And I didn't fucking itch at night.*

He stood once more over the toilet, produced nothing, and peered again into his father's mirror, hoping a better face would reveal itself in the failing light.

A distant click startled him.

It's fine, just the house settling.

Another click.

Cat flap.

A rustle: likely a cat leaping onto the table, despite Arkady's repeated assertions that he did not allow cats on the table. He'd shoo them down, and they'd leap back up again behind his back. The cats, Arkady maintained, understood him perfectly.

The itch rose, soles to scalp. *Let me sleep.*

The wall of the hallway outside the bathroom still bore the shadows and stains of bookshelves. Not knowing which of his parents' books might be considered bourgeois, dangerous, or illegal, Arkady had burned them all, and so kept himself and Kostya warm in the worst of that winter when it seemed easier to find gold than coal.

Kostya had wrinkled his brow the first time Arkady tore up a book for kindling. —Back in Odessa, my grandfather had lots of books.

—Did he, now?

—He was a doctor. Why did those people take his house?

—Leave that behind, Kostya. Those thieves will get what they deserve.

—When I'm grown, I'll go back and—

—It's out of your control.

—Shall I wait for God to set it right? God who no longer exists?

Arkady couldn't answer Kostya's question then. He couldn't answer it now. Sitting on the edge of his bed and leaning forward, he hid his face in his hands.

I stole him. I stole a doctor's grandson with a gift for languages. And if that doctor had lived, how would he have guided Kostya? Force him into medical school? No, Kostya was alone in this world. I didn't steal him. I saved him.

Maybe a week after the incident with the Odessa herring merchant, Arkady had received a message. He sat down on the cot next to Kostya and put his arm around the boy's shoulders. —I'm ordered back to Moscow.

—I won't eat much.

Arkady sighed. *You're quick, boy. Too quick.* —Kostya, I can't.

—I've got no one here!

—Go back to the catacombs. It's getting warmer.

Snorting, Kostya wriggled free of Arkady's protective arm. —The other street kids hate me. They will kill me. I'm the Chekist's lapdog now. You know this!

Arkady took off his glove and caught some of Kostya's tears on his fingers.

Kostya's voice sounded deeper. —Why did you even come here?

—Orders. Luck.

—Fucked in the mouth, then, aren't I?

Arkady said it before he'd even accepted the fact himself. —I would have to steal you.

—How can you steal me? I'm no dog.

—Correct. You are free, Kostya, free to live in the catacombs.

—Free to die!

Arkady tugged his glove back on.

—Steal me.

—Kostya...

The *bezprizornik* knelt before the Chekist, raised his arms and reached for the dangling amber beads. Then he rested his face on Arkady's knee. —Steal me.

Steal me, Kostya had said. Begged.

Arkady rubbed his eyes. *I am so tired.*

A cupboard hinge creaked, the cupboard where he kept salt and tea.

The cats couldn't open latched cupboards.

Already? No, we don't arrest until after midnight. It's not that dark. Is it?

Silence.

Despite the growing ache in his back, Arkady dared not move.

A rustle in the study: someone opened the closet.

Arkady's itch deepened as he imagined the path of the intruder. The clack of a light switch signalled his descent to the basement and furnace. Gentle clanks against the furnace wall and grate travelled throughout the house.

He even rakes the ashes in the furnace.

Then Arkady bit his lip. Those near-silent footfalls on the steps as the intruder ascended meant either a very good burglar or NKVD. Whoever crept up those steps knew to skip the final one, for it creaked.

The electric light switch clacked off.

Is that you, Little Tatar?

Of course not, Arkady told himself, refusing to consider the British woman or her handbag. Kostya had no reason to sneak around this house.

The intruder left through the front door.

Arkady counted to fifty, then stood up, wincing at the pain in his back and legs as he descended the stairs to the parlour and front door. He had locked the door earlier and taken the key. If his phantom existed, then he had his own key to lock the door behind him.

Arkady wrenched the knob.

Locked.

Either he'd hallucinated, or Kostya had just searched the house. Neither possibility held any appeal.

Weeping, Arkady poured a large measure of vodka. A cat returned, slipping through the cat flap and leaping onto the table, where he dropped his newest slaughter: a mouse. *No,* Arkady thought, tracing a finger along the dead animal's long tail, *a small rat. Still warm.* Praising the cat for his courageous efficiency, hoping the cat would then curl up in his lap, Arkady stared through the growing dusk at his telephone. He scratched the cat in his favourite spots, around his ears, at the base of his tail. The cat purred, rubbed his jaws against the side of Arkady's hand, and ran off.

The soil's freshest here.

Smelling lemon, pepper, and earth, Kostya placed the tea packet from Arkady's pantry to one side and dug his fingers deep into the soil near the hedge. Then he caught another scent he recognized, from one of the perennial beds: iris.

Her perfume at Lubyanka.

Years ago, Misha and Kostya would listen to Arkady drone on about flowers: perennials, annuals, patience, beauty, and roots. Both boys found the subject a painful bore, yet they listened, and, when quizzed, they answered. As Misha got older, he took up flowers as a small hobby of his own, learning how to please women with arranged bouquets. *Iris,* he told Kostya, *looks and smells like cunt.*

Dirty to his elbows, Kostya tangled his fingers in shredded silk stockings.

He glanced over his shoulder, back at the house. No lights burned. *The old man's still out.*

Engine. NKVD car.

Soil invaded Kostya's mouth as he struggled to hide himself. Explain digging in Major Balakirev's shrubbery at night? Not a hope in hell.

The officers drove past the house, their errand elsewhere.

Kostya buried the stockings again and got to his feet, smearing his trousers as he brushed damp earth from his legs. Then he patted a pocket to make sure he'd not lost his keys.

Upstairs, the bathroom and the old man's bedroom. Go back inside and search there.

He stared up at the study window, its curtains open, and his shoulder ached.

Shadow on the glass? Is he there?

Mating cats yowled and hissed; dogs barked.

Walking to the metro station, switching the packet of tea from hand to hand, Kostya wanted to spit at the quiet houses and peaceful blocks of flats. *You all sleep. How dare you sleep? You know nothing of night duty.*

Headlight beams caught him from behind: another NKVD car. The driver did not slow down, and Kostya thought he recognized the eyes reflected in the rear-view mirror.

Back in his own lobby, despite his quiet tread, he woke the watch-woman called Elena Petrovna.

—Comrade Nikto.

—Good evening, Grandmother.

Then he thought of his own grandmother. She'd never dressed like this, all black layers. She'd bobbed her hair, favoured white blouses and purple skirts, and wore perfume, lavender or rose. Wondering how old Elena might be, Kostya gave her a light bow.

—Why, Comrade Nikto.

—Yes, Grandmother?

—Whatever did you do to get so dirty? Dig a grave?

Aware of the weights of stolen tea and missing passports, Kostya ascended the stairs.

Yes, Grandmother.

[ ]

ALL THE TEA IN MOSCOW CAN'T HELP THIS HEADACHE
Wednesday 9 June

Accepting dossiers and a glass of tea from Evgenia Ismailovna, Kostya squinted in a sudden glare of sunlight, planned a careful return to his office through the heaving crowd behind him, and pretended not to notice the rapid approach of Yury Stepanov.

Yury would not be ignored. —Nikto, I need you.

—Join the queue. See this pile in my arms? The department is busier than Finlyandsky Station. Perhaps you've noticed?

—Who pissed in your kasha this morning? Down in the cells. I've got a Kazakh.

Kostya adjusted the dossiers in his arm. —Why am I worried about your Kazakh, Stepanov?

Weaving and dodging, Yury followed Kostya to his office. —He's a fucking Mongol who doesn't speak two words of Russian. How did he even get to Moscow? We've probably gotten eighteen different confessions—hey!

Collision.

Eight heavy dossiers flew from Kostya's arms and slapped against the floor. He managed to hold onto the *podstakannik* handle and so keep his tea.

A sergeant turned pale as he recognized not just Kostya's insignia but also his own offence: knocking dossiers from the arms of someone important. —Oh, Comrade Senior Lieutenant, let me fetch those.

The dossiers, like those knocked over by the clerk at the *poligon*, were tied shut and had released nothing. Kostya knelt with the sergeant, noticing hundreds of tiny scratches and dents in the once elegant parquet flooring. Other men's legs shading their vision, they collected the burden.

—I'm so sorry, Comrade Senior Lieutenant. I'm trying to find my way, all the corridors...

—It's nothing.

—Senior Lieutenant Nikto? It's me, Katelnikov, Matvei Andreivich Katelnikov.

—Yes, we've met. Pass me that dossier, yes, that one there, before it gets kicked to the wall.

Matvei did so. —I try to match your records in the basement.

—What?

—Target practice.

Kostya stood up, balancing burdens of dossiers and tea. —Oh. What's your weapon?

Still on his knees, Matvei grinned and patted his holster. —Tokarev.

—I use a Nagant.

Matvei blushed. —Oh. Maybe that's why you're so good. I mean...

Yury rolled his eyes. —Comrade Senior Lieutenant Nikto is busy.

Matvei got to his feet, stood aside, and, in his haste, knocked into someone else. This time, tea spilled. The bearer of the tea, another new man, uttered fierce apology as he and Matvei navigated a dance of power, rank, and a puddle.

Kostya wanted to shut his office door in Yury's face, but he knew that Yury would only open it and continue, unperturbed, implacable, steady as a river, clueless. Kostya dropped the dossiers on his desk, making the blotter rock, and suppressed a sigh. —Fine. Tell me.

—What's to tell? He's under arrest, he's guilty, and he speaks a language none of us understands.

—Well, what's he guilty of?

—Oh. Wreckage. At the Stalin Works.

Migrant labourer, Kostya thought. *Came to Moscow after the '33 famine.*

Yury leaned against the doorjamb. —Nikto, you speak Kazakh.

—Some.

—It's better than none, and I'm late for a meeting at Number Two.

—Number Two what?

Yury spat it out before wisdom could tell him that perhaps a fellow officer did not need that information. —Laboratory of Special Purpose Number Two.

Kostya kept his eyes on his dossiers and sipped some tea. *I must give Scherba my condolences.* —And what is your business at Laboratory of Special Purpose Number Two, Yury Grigorievich?

Wincing at his quick confession, Yury reminded himself that Kostya outranked him and so must be answered. That, in turn, made Yury's lips purse together into a tight little frown. —Supervision.

—I'll go see your prisoner once I get through these dossiers, after the department meeting.

Yury cleared his throat. —Meeting? At, ah, what time again?

—In ten minutes.

—Right. Yes, well, Special Purpose must wait. And, of course, Captain Kuznets did ask me to assist him with this meeting.

—Then perhaps you should check with him, yes? Wait, wait, before you tear off in a mad hurry—

—I am not in a hurry.

—Where will I find your Kazakh?

Shifting his weight from foot to foot like a prisoner denied urination privileges, Yury gave Kostya the cell number. Then he rushed toward the office of Boris Kuznets.

Kostya smirked into his tea.

The scents of stale tobacco, metallic sweat, vinegar, excrement, wine fumes, and resinous colognes filled Kostya's nose as he stood still, arms crossed so he'd not jostle or nudge anyone else, getting jostled and nudged himself.

Staff meeting.

The stink of men, Kostya thought, *always in the stink of men.*

Boris Kuznets spoke, his voice monotonous and huge, a cloudy sky on a winter day. He quoted figures, compared charts, heaped praise, demanded better. Soon, comrades, very soon, stern word would soon come from no less than the Boss himself, yes, Comrade Stalin, about increased vigilance and redoubled efforts, the ongoing need to root out and destroy the enemy, as many heads as Zmei Gorynich, cut off one and three more grow.

Kostya shut his eyes. The story of Dobrynya Nikitich and Zmei Gorynich in the Saracen Mountains: his grandfather had told it well, as he did the story of Koshchei the Deathless, adding new details each time, so that just when Kostya thought he knew the story, it grew. *Koshchei hides his death, his soul, buried beneath a green oak tree within a heavy iron chest fixed with many bolts. And within that chest lies a twitchy hare. Within the belly of the hare waits an angry duck. And within the duck waits an egg, and within this egg lies a needle. And within the eye of that needle rests the soul, the death, of Koshchei the Deathless.*

Boris droned on. —Innocent people will be hurt. This is regrettable. It is also unavoidable. When a building is on fire, and we are all desperate to escape the flames, someone gets bruised. Outside, when everyone is safe, the bruises no longer matter. Our job, comrades, is to make the Soviet Union safe. Right now, Mother Russia burns, and she screams for our help.

Jostled hard, Kostya opened his eyes and glared at his neighbour.

Boris picked up a final stack of paper, instructing Yury Stepanov to ensure each man in the room received his personal copy. The crowd rippled and surged as Yury navigated. The sheets lay filed alphabetically by officers' surnames; the officers stood at random. Each man got one sheet.

Boris announced dismissal. —Once you receive your new targets, you may leave.

Yury gave Kostya two sheets.

—Stepanov, wait.

Already wiggling through the crowd, Yury spoke in a sharp tone, much too sharp for a sergeant to a senior lieutenant. —What?

—It seems I have two sheets.

—Yes.

—Every other man received one. What, I've got twice the work now?

Yury shook his head and looked to the ceiling. —Your name is on both sheets.

Upper right corners: Nikto, KA. Yes, both sheets bore his name. Except the second sheet bore his name in ink, in handwriting, atop the crossed-out, typed name of another officer: `Minenkov, MP.` *Misha.*

Ignoring the tremor in his hand, Kostya shoved the second sheet at Yury. —Ismailovna typed this?

Yury shoved the paper back. —Get off me.

Boris called out. —Nikto, stay behind a moment.

—Yes, Comrade Captain.

Waiting for the crush of men to pass, Kostya got himself to a wall and stood there to study his two sheets of paper. Targets. Quotas. Timetables. Incentives. Well, the mention of incentives, no concrete details. Then he reported to his captain.

Boris sounded jolly. —Twenty years.

What, my sentence?

—Just think on it, Nikto. In December we'll celebrate twenty years of the Cheka.

Kostya nodded. —A milestone, Comrade Captain.

—We call ourselves NKVD now, but the soul of it, the reason our blood pumps: Cheka. There's talk of a party, you know, a big celebration. At the Bolshoi. When were you last at the Bolshoi?

—Ah...

—You should go. Concerts, ballets, it's good for you.

Kostya knew what that meant: good for him to be seen in the right places by the right people. Anyone of power, and most of those who desired such power, attended ballets, concerts, and plays at the Bolshoi. Sometimes they even enjoyed the event for its own sake.

—Here's what I want from you, Nikto. It's for the internal NKVD magazine, and for the department. We need some photographs, old and new, revolution, continuity, that sort of thing. I can't think of anything better than a portrait of you and Balakirev, new NKVD and old Cheka, flower and roots. Him seated, I think, and you standing to attention just behind his shoulder. Hope for the future.

The future?

—Nikto? You'll tell Balakirev?

—Of course.

—Warn him to expect a summons. For the photograph.

Place your head in the wooden bracket, comrade. Hold the slate up. A little higher. Good.

Kostya inclined his head to his superior officer. —He'll be flattered.

—So he wants us to pose for a portrait.

Voice blending into the general racket of the cafeteria, Kostya shook pepper into his bowl of *shchi*. Nothing fell.

Arkady took the pepper shaker from Kostya, gave it a hard rap on the table, and turned it upside down again. Still, no pepper fell. Snorting, Arkady knocked the pepper shaker on its side.

Vadym dipped bread into his *shchi*. —Balakirev, you photogenic old goat. Glory at last.

Arkady mumbled his answer around a piece of bread. —Kuznets just wants to blind me with the flash.

—If he did, the bloat in your face might go down. How long have you squinted like that?

Arkady looked to Kostya, pleading for intervention.

Kostya sat back in his chair and tilted his head to one side. —Whatever do you mean, Dima? Surely not that Arkady Dmitrievich looks unwell?

Now Arkady glared at him.

Vadym prattled on. —Arkasha, really, your eyelids should not be so puffy, nor your cheeks. Look, your hands are swollen. What about your legs?

—I could tap them like trees and drain off sap. What of it?

Kostya slurped soup and hoped that hid his alarm.

Vadym scowled. —Have you consulted with a doctor any time since, oh, I don't know, the Revolution?

Grunting, Arkady stood up. —I need to take a leak.

Vadym forced a chuckle as Arkady left the table. —I believe I've hit a nerve.

—You're right, Dima. He's not well.

—No, he can't be, not the way he looks and behaves. Kostya, he listens to you.

—Like hell he does.

—Can you convince him to see a doctor?

Not wanting to get nudged and brushed, Kostya leaned away from the men passing the table. Even here, in the cafeteria, where one might expect the noise to allow a more intimate conversation, one must acknowledge the press of other people, so many other people. —Maybe.

—I have to ask you something else.

Kostya waited. Guessed.

The words fell out of Vadym's mouth, a speedy confession. —I'm worried sick about Misha. I know he's missing.

Kostya knocked his glass of water against the side of his bowl. Hard.

Vadym took the hint and lowered his voice. —Did you—

Craning his neck, Kostya spotted Yury and Boris approaching the table. He tapped his glass against the bowl a second time.

Vadym turned to greet them. —Hello, hello, come sit down.

Kostya nodded and gestured to empty chairs at the neighbouring table. *Oh, the old man will love this.*

Yury and Boris approached their table, Yury bearing two full trays of bread and *shchi*. The soup slopped over the bowls. As Yury struggled to place the trays on the neighbouring table without further spill, Boris pulled a chair over to Kostya and Vadym's table. —Vadym Pavlovich, I owe you an apology. I missed choir practice this morning. Trouble in the cells.

—I guessed you were busy.

—Yes, teaching scales to a young woman. Not yet seventeen and stubborn as a woman of fifty.

As Vadym shut his eyes and sighed, Kostya noticed Arkady striding across the cafeteria, returning to the table.

So did Boris. —And you, Konstantin Arkadievich, did you tell himself about the portrait? Ah, as my father would say, speak of the devil.

Nodding to Boris, Arkady tugged his chair a little closer to Kostya's.

Boris glanced at Yury, who still stood at the other table. —Go ahead and start, Yury. Don't let your soup get cold. So, Arkady Dmitrievich, you'll pose for the photos?

—Why wouldn't I?

Yury winced as his soup burnt his mouth.

Boris winked at Vadym, as if sharing a secret. Then he dug in his pouch and gave an object to Kostya wrapped in a pristine white handkerchief. —Don't drop it.

Kostya parted the fabric and revealed a small bottle, heavy for its size, shaped in a fat oval and balanced on a pedestal, the blue glass cut with further perpendicular ovals. A tassel dangled on the bottle's neck. Such a strange object, strange and beautiful. It contained perfume, and it bore a name in the Latin alphabet: Shalimar.

Arkady loomed close enough to Kostya to throw a shadow over the remains of his lunch. He seemed to bite back his words. Even so, he sounded angry, betrayed. —What is this?

Boris laughed. —A little present for our Konstantin. Just a token of my admiration for his loyalty and hard work. Yury tells me it's a very fine perfume. French, of course.

Just catching sight of Matvei Katelnikov as he took a seat at Yury's table, Kostya removed the chipped stopper, sniffed, sniffed again, and then held the stopper under Arkady's nose.

Arkady sniffed. —Well, it's not Krasnaya Moskva. Similar. No, wait. Some rose, I think. Iris? That sweetness: lemon? Leather? Your nose is better than mine, Kostya. Ugh, something is ruining the flowers. It smells almost dirty.

Yury supplied the answer with his mouth full of shredded carrot. —Civet. Little animals, like wild cats. They secrete musk from their perineums. You can kill them and harvest the glands or keep them in solitary cages, near other civets so they can smell them. Then you can just scrape the secretions. The cages are a much better idea. Keep them alive and productive, well, until they die.

None of the other men had anything to say to that.

Watching Yury wipe up spat carrot, Kostya replaced the perfume stopper. *I know this scent.* Startled by this recognition, and by the recognitions hiding within it, he almost spoke. The briefest of warnings, surely just a trick of the light, flashed in Arkady's eyes. No. Kostya saw it. The old man knew where this perfume came from: a British woman's handbag. He'd found it and offered it to Boris as a bribe, and now Boris had given it to Kostya to prove something to Arkady.

Boris shook his head at Yury's mess. Then he looked at Kostya again. —Should you wish to please a woman, now you can. Beyond the obvious, I mean.

Yury, too, had advice. —Or save it for a gift for another man, to get his help. You may never see another bottle of French perfume again.

Arkady stared at blue glass.

Yury raised his glass of water as if in a toast. —Too bad Misha's not here.

Vadym dropped his spoon; it clattered in the soup bowl. Kostya stared hard at Yury. So did Arkady.

Yury's eyes widened. —I mean, we're all together here, well, Katelnikov's new. Katelnikov. Isn't that a Doukhobor name? Has that not caused you any trouble?

Matvei shook his head.

Grinning to hide his anger, Kostya turned away from Yury to face Boris. *I won't forget that, Little Yurochka. I'll pay you back.* —Thank you, Comrade Captain. This is beautiful.

—Just make sure any woman you give it to merits such a gift.

As Kostya tucked the bottle into the pouch on his *portupeya* and then took out his matches and cigarettes, he pleaded in his thoughts with Vadym: *Don't ask if she cooked the mushrooms. Don't mention her. Please, don't.*

Vadym chuckled, and his eyes, while still sad from thoughts of Misha, twinkled. He took a breath to speak.

Arkady spoke first, clapping his hand on Kostya's good shoulder. —As if such a woman could even exist. You smoke too much, Tatar.

Boris smiled as he stood up to join Yury and Matvei at the other table. —Nikto, Stepanov, Katelnikov: you younger men would do well to learn what your elders, Arkady Dmitrievich and Vadym Pavlovich, with their sacred vows of chastity as priests of Cheka, already understand. A man might drown in women.

Arkady, Vadym, Yury, Matvei, and Kostya, each annoyed for his own reasons, suppressed frowns.

Boris finished his warning. —Cunt may ruin us all.

Yury nodded, and soup dribbled from the spoon onto his chin. —Amen.

Blowing out a long stream of smoke, Kostya stood up, stepped over to Yury, and chucked him on the chin. Then he shook a shred of carrot from his finger. —From each according to his ability, to each according to his work. You'll never get to drown in women with lunch on your face.

Blushing in misery, Yury joined the laughter of the men.

He is the true heir of the Tatars, not I.

Kostya lifted his gaze from the prisoner, slumped in a chair before a desk, and took in the pocked and peeling walls, the damp floor, and the caged electric light. Then he looked the other two NKVD officers in the eye. —Neither of you speak Kazakh?

—Not a word, Comrade Senior Lieutenant.

—I thought it was gibberish, Comrade Senior Lieutenant.

Kostya glanced again at the prisoner: bruised, bleeding, hand-cuffed. Nearly five hours had passed since Yury asked Kostya to look in on this prisoner. *Cuffed all that time, if not longer. Can't be helped.* —It's a gorgeous language, and you wouldn't know beauty if it gave you a blow job and then chewed off your cock. Free his hands.

—But he's dangerous.

Kostya glared at them. —I just gave you an order. Oh, I must show identification, yes? Stand at attention when I speak to you! Look at my collar. Look at my card. What do you see? Hey?

The guard who wouldn't know beauty stared straight ahead. —I see, ah, the rank of senior lieutenant.

His fellow glanced at the identification and nodded. —Yes, I see it, too: Senior Lieutenant Nikto. That's what it says.

—Right. Now free his hands and get out. Tell the guard outside I will bang on the door and call out when I am ready.

—Yes, Comrade Senior Lieutenant.

The heavy door clunked shut; the lock clacked into place.

As the sobbing man moved his stiff arms until his hands lay in his lap, Kostya walked behind the desk, pulled out the chair with minimal noise, and sat down. *Think. Think in Kazakh.* —Good day.

222

Battered and swollen eyelids allowed only a slit for vision. Tears leaked.

Kostya passed him a handkerchief. —My accent is heavy, I know, but do you understand me?

—Yes. Your accent is fine.

—Thank you. I'm out of practice.

—No, no, it's beautiful.

—What's your name?

—Abdulin. Nurasyl Abdulin.

Green eyes, like mine. —How long have you been in Moscow, Abdulin?

—Three months. What is your name, officer?

—How old are you?

—Nineteen last week.

Kostya noticed the date of birth in the dossier. —Happy belated. Why are you in Moscow?

—I can't hunt. I can't ride. I can't farm. I can no longer be a burden on my father. I came by train. Some of the way I walked.

—And where do you work?

—Shanghai.

Kostya nodded, recognizing the nickname for the city-within-a-city in Proletarsky District of tents, barracks, and dugouts for factory workers. —What is your job?

—I told the other men, I told them, I told them—

—Hush, hush. The other men cannot speak the language. The other men are gone. I won't hit you. You'll tell me now, yes?

Shaking, Nurasyl gritted his teeth against a wave of pain. —The Stalin Works. I polish headlights for automobiles.

—The other officers say you wrecked something.

—No.

—Did you drop a headlight?

—No!

—An accident. Glass is slippery.

Nurasyl grimaced. —I hate the noise of glass. Even when I got tired, I never dropped a light. If I break a light, I don't get paid, and if I don't get paid, I can't eat. And I'm hungry. I came all this way to work and become a good citizen. Why am I still hungry?

—If you can't manage your money, that's your own problem.

—I line up for hours for bread that's not there.

—Abdulin...

—I sleep on the bare ground. Where can I cook? I was better off starving at home.

—Abdulin.

—And you, officer, you speak the language, yet you understand nothing.

The chair scraped on the floor as Kostya stood up; Nurasyl cried out, clenched his eyes shut, and covered his face with his arms.

—Abdulin, take your arms down from your head.

Sobbing, Nurasyl obeyed.

Kostya returned to his chair. —Now, tell me what you wrecked at the Stalin Works.

Nurasyl detailed an impossible list of acts of sabotage. Had even a fraction of it been true, the works would have shut down. Kostya knew this. Nurasyl knew this. Yet Nurasyl confessed it, and Kostya wrote it down.

—Can you read, Abdulin?

—Of course I can read. I am not your savage of the steppes.

—Write?

—No.

Kostya turned his written notes around, and Nurasyl turned his head to peer at the page with his less-swollen eye, studied the pages. The Russian officer's written Kazakh, in the Latin alphabet, looked angular, shattered.

Nurasyl frowned. —I can't read it.

—Why not?

—The letters — no!

Kostya needed a moment to recognize why pleasure shot to his penis and why the prisoner screamed. His patience had frayed, and he'd aimed his Nagant at Nursayl's forehead, still held it there. He had no memory of drawing the gun, or of deciding to draw the gun. —I did say I'm out of practice.

Nurasyl stared at the muzzle, the chamber, the hand, the officer. Then he bowed his head.

Feeling sweat break out on the back of his neck, Kostya holstered the Nagant. His behaviour would provoke little comment, certainly no rebuke, from his colleagues, yet Kostya felt like a failure, a fool. So easily insulted by a comment on his handwriting? Drawing his weapon without thought?

He rolled his pen across the desk to Nurasyl. —Make your mark.

—How did you do it?

—The speed of the gun? Just target practice.

Nurasyl looked up, the green of his eyes almost hidden now as the swelling worsened. He trembled. Many prisoners at this point of an interrogation sounded craven, miserable. Nursayl sounded mystified. —No, I mean...the other men could have beaten me to death, spoken any language they liked, and I'd have died knowing I'm innocent. You made me believe I'm guilty. I believe it. I know I'm not, yet I believe it.

—Mark on the bottom line, please.

—You turned me against myself. I betrayed *myself.* How can this happen?

—Your mark.

—I hate you.

Kostya lit a cigarette; his hands shook. —Just make your damned mark.

—

Vadym, eyes shut, spoke on the telephone at his desk.

—I've told you everything I know. He was assigned abroad. It's a great honour to be allowed to serve abroad, and with all his languages, and you're proud, yes? I'm proud. What? Yes, I love him. He's my nephew. Of course, I love him.

In the corridor, Kostya stepped to the side of the door, out of Vadym's line of sight. He'd come to thank Vadym for the mushrooms, hoping Vadym would then invite him somewhere, even out for a quick walk, just away.

Away from Lubyanka.

Arkady's parties.

Everything.

Vadym covered his eyes with his hand. —Petya, please. I am doing everything I can... His work is secret. I am sure he will write to you as soon as he's able, and who knows how long mail might take, wherever he is, or if he's even allowed to write. Yes, the map is big. I know. I know. Petya. Petya, I'm your brother. I would not hide any word of Misha from you. My fault? I didn't force him to join NKVD. Do you really think... Kostya? Yes, he's... Petya, if Kostya Nikto knew where to find the slightest trace of Misha, if he'd even dreamed of him, he'd have told me right away. What? No! Petya, sometimes, in a war... Listen to me... do not call me at work like this anymore. Petya, please. Stop. I have no answers. Just stop.

The receiver clicked against the cradle.

Kostya stepped into the doorway, ready to distract Vadym from his misery, ready to break the spell.

Hands hiding his face, Vadym leaned on his elbows. His whispers of his nephew's name sounded like a prayer.

This noise of private grief, this naked despair: Kostya blushed.

Still unnoticed, he eased Vadym's door almost shut and returned to his own office.

[ ]

FEME SOLE 2
Wednesday 9 June

Sitting in the front room beneath the open window, hoping to catch a breeze, annoyed by the bright white walls, and very tired, Temerity rubbed her temples. Shards of memory glinted from the evening she left Hotel Lux, and she reached for them. The music on the unattended radio, the empty street, the two men. The smell of the interior of the car. The threats. *You love your papa, don't you?*

Love Edward West? Yes, she did. She'd also hated him, feared him, mocked him, admired him, and modelled herself after him. As a child, she'd seen him as a disappointing link to her dead mother, a man unwilling even to talk of Viktoria. Later Temerity understood he'd been not unwilling but incapable. She'd eavesdropped one evening when she was twelve, during one of her Aunt Min's visits home from India. Min asked her brother if he thought he might ever remarry, and Edward dismissed the idea with a snort. —No one would have me.

—Really, Edward. Why on earth not? You're rich, not too hideous to look at—

—Oh, thank you very much indeed.

—And you're kind. A woman could do much worse.

The soda siphon hissed. —Let me rephrase it, Min. I should not inflict myself on another woman. I'm not the same man who married Vika.

—We all change over time.

—It's not change. It's damage. I'm eaten out. I'm incomplete. A gorilla at the London Zoo is more of a human being than I am. A riot in the street I could understand. A war. A cancer. God's sake, even a runaway horse. But flu, Min? Wife and son to bloody flu?

Temerity heard a terrible noise then. Her father, all duty, love, and strength, stern voice and high expectations, cried.

Min's skirts rustled; perhaps she sat next to him. —Edward, listen to me. You lost Vika and Felix. You didn't kill them.

His voice shook. —But why did I live? Why am I still here? I got sick first, and she brought me tea, and I was so feverish that I thought she was a ghost, and I shoved her away, made her spill tea all over her dress. Even as my arm reached out, I knew it was Vika and not a ghost, yet she was both at once. When tea burned her, I laughed.

—You were ill. There's no fault here. No one is responsible.

Edward took a deep breath. —That's it. No one's responsible. The story makes no sense. And I can't love, Min, not again. Not like that.

Away at school that autumn, her first year at Roedean, Temerity saw that the failure to create a palpable memory of her mother was not Edward's but her own. She could gaze at photographs and listen to stories, but she could not make her mother live. She had no memory of Viktoria, and Edward had too much. Still, she often treated him and others with resentment, and her second year at Roedean played out as a disaster. Appalled by Temerity's marks and behaviour, insistent she could do much better, Edward pleaded with the headmistress to keep Temerity just one more term. The headmistress cited several examples of Temerity being disruptive, even violent, assaulting other girls with surprising strength. —We can't even have a Girl Guides meeting without her causing a fuss. And her such a slight little thing.

Edward reached an agreement with the headmistress and removed Temerity so that everyone might avoid the word *expulsion*. He was working in the city, Kurseong House closed until summer, and he now had to bring Temerity to his London flat. On the train ride, he planned a long letter to Min, electing instead to send a telegram. *T good as sent down. Advice?* Min replied with three words: *Languages. Prepare her.*

So began Temerity's intensive study of modern languages. She'd had tutors at home before, but this time she felt challenged and thereby respected. Dormant abilities woke, and the discipline she'd so resented at Roedean now felt natural and right. Edward told Temerity later that once she made up her mind to excel, once it felt like her own idea, her intellect seemed to ignite.

When Temerity asked to learn Russian, Edward balked. They argued for days, Edward evasive, Temerity infuriated and confused. Edward knew he must lose this dispute. His recurring dreams of Temerity lost in a huge country while looking for her mother: not the girl's burden, and certainly not her fault. Sometimes Edward wondered if the 1918 flu had damaged his brain, weakened it, leaving him prone to that Temerity-lost dream whenever he got so much as a sniffle. The dream's logic was simple and clear. Forbid Temerity from learning Russian, and she would never go to Russia. Of course, Edward could so no such thing — well, he could forbid it all he liked, but she would not listen — and he did not even try to explain his fears. Temerity would consider his dream utter nonsense and dismiss it with a laugh like Min's, that memsahib's laugh of certainty touched with derision, and she'd be right to do so. Besides, he'd already boasted of his daughter's abilities to his superiors in the Service, and they'd indicated much interest. A daughter of an existing polyglot agent, groomed for the work? What a gift — if she passed the interviews, being female and subject to a woman's weaker mind, after all. How many languages did you say?

So many arguments. Father and daughter loved each other with not just a shared understanding of how much they resembled each other but with a ferocity that startled them both. The arguments lessened as Temerity got older, but both Edward and Temerity remained primed, ready for dispute. Temerity worried that her father must be so disappointed in her and all her inadequacies; Edward worried that his daughter might be her own worst enemy.

They'd argued during their last conversation, back in early March. They'd just boarded a train at St. Pancras headed to Prideaux-on-Fen and Kurseong House. Temerity, already regretting her agreement to help get Kurseong House aired out for the summer, cursed the weather. —Bloody miserable rain.

Edward sat quite still as the train gathered speed. Rattling his newspaper, wheezing, he exposed an upside-down story on the worsening situation in Spain. —Temmy, have you seen this note on a lecture at the British Museum, on the death drive?

—Death what?

—The death drive, or so it says here. 'A lecture on the subject of the Freudian death drive as the primal force behind mankind's lust for war.'

Temerity sat across from Edward, deciphering the story on Spain. The half-column of text mentioned hunger and air raids.

Edward followed her gaze and stabbed a trembling finger at the story on Spain. After a coughing fit, he got the words out. —Damned Bosche.

—Don't excite yourself.

Coughing some more, Edward peered over the edge of the newspaper. With his blue eyes and white hair he looked nothing like Temerity, yet anyone seeing them together, observing body language and hearing voices shot through with expectation of command, knew them for father and daughter. —Herr Hitler's Luftwaffe at target practice, that's what this is, training Franco's boys. Marshal Stalin's no better, whatever side he pretends to take. God's sake, proxy wars. And I'll thank you, Temmy, not to patronize me like that again. Don't excite myself, indeed.

Apology ready, Temerity sighed, then said nothing.

Edward seemed not to notice. —We should strike the blighters now, while we still can, unless we want to lose the entire empire and perhaps even England itself, though India's just a matter of time.

Temerity thought of their family's wealth, how much they'd benefited from the commerce of the empire.

—Temmy, my dear, did I ever tell you why your uncle and grandfather stopped talking to me? I was twelve. All I said was that we

British might have shown some restraint in our reprisals after the '57 mutiny. My history master beat me. The headmaster beat me. Then he wrote to my father, and when next I returned home between terms, my father beat me.

Temerity suppressed another sigh, this story so familiar, often told. —Dreadful.

—And then, when I refused to apologize or go back on my word, for that's what it was, the old man expecting me to go back on my word, my pledge to justice, you see, I...where was I?

—You refused to apologize.

—Yes, so the old man gave me the silent treatment. Communicated by note, if you please. And your uncle, the rotter, he did the same, and when he inherited, he told me in a letter left atop my packed bags that I was not welcome in Kurseong House. Used the old man's stationery. From the Desk of Lord Fenleigh. Your Aunt Min pleaded with him, got nowhere, so then she refused to speak to him.

Temerity watched raindrops stream across the train window.

Edward rattled the newspaper. —Best thing for me. I had to make my own way in the world, me and my languages. I met your mother. And then your damned fool uncle died. It's all such bloody nonsense, Temmy, Kurseong House, the titles. Your grandfather only got elevated when Lloyd George had to recreate the House of Lords. Then he built Kurseong House on the dampest piece of ground he could find. Fen-leigh, indeed. All we sheltered were leeches and mosquitoes.

—It wasn't that bad.

—You never got stuck in the fen, did you? And the house is damp. You must concede that. I don't even know why we're bothering to open it. Freeman tells me you've transferred over from Five?

Abrupt changes of subject: one of her father's favourite tricks.

Temerity nodded. —I should like to put my languages to work.

—Good way to save face after that bother with the fascists and Brownbury-Rees.

Bother? Temerity's cheeks flushed. Every time, every bloody time, her father found some way to belittle either what she'd accomplished or what she'd endured. She felt at once cocky and inadequate, as if she'd exaggerated and bragged when in truth she'd understated. If she now corrected her understatement to the truth, she'd sound conceited, and her father would make short work of it. —I should never have told you about that.

—I'd have seen Brownbury-Rees go to prison. Nothing in the courts, mind, leastaways nothing to involve you. Stitch him up for theft, perhaps, find someone over in Five who owes me a favour. Easy enough to do. But his father's not well. Dying of shame, I shouldn't wonder.

Temerity snatched the newspaper from Edward, ink from the story of Spain smudging her fingers.

—What on earth is the matter with you, girl?

—Tell me, when France, bloody France, has taken tens of thousands of refugees from Spain, why is it that the greatest empire in human history can't be bothered to accept a mere fraction of the burden, indeed, can't even be shamed into it? All I can think of here, Father, is Queen Victoria: tell me not what is expedient; tell me what is right.

Expecting a lecture on the complexities of British foreign policy with a reminder of atrocities committed on both sides of the Spanish Civil War, ready to kick herself for even inviting such condescension, Temerity took a sharp breath.

Edward gently removed the newspaper from Temerity's fingers, resumed his study of an article, and then, after a long moment, turned a page. —I may install a shower bath at Kurseong House. All the comforts of a city flat back at the estate. What do you think?

—Did you not hear a word I just said?

—Mm-hmm.

—Father, I'll be leaving next week.

Edward finally looked up, his eyes glinting with the recognition of an argument already lost. Still, he'd fight. —I beg your pardon?

—I can't tell you where.

—I can bloody well guess it's Spain. Out of the question.

—I don't need your permission.

—I'll not have you gallivanting over half of Europe and in the papers every other day like Jessica and Unity Mitford!

—Unity? How dare you compare me to that gormless fascist heifer? And what would the papers know about it?

—Temmy, for God's sake, I've given you an excellent education, and you've got the bloody vote. What more do you want?

Tears pricked. —The freedom to take up my duty! If I were Felix—

—Don't you dare throw your brother at me, girl. Don't you dare.

—Aunt Min—

Edward dashed his newspaper to the seat beside him. —I only let her take you to India to test your mettle, see how you travelled, and she talked me into letting you attend those damned suffragette-su classes—

—Jiu-jutsu, Father.

—Withered old maids wielding Indian clubs—

—The correct term is Persian meels.

—You want to take up your duty? Languages, girl, your languages and that phenomenal brain beneath your thick skull. Decrypt. I've been telling you that for years.

Temerity sniffed, blinked at the few tears, folded her hands in her lap and studied her fingers. —Father, listen to me.

—That fool, Freeman, he's put you up to this.

—I can decide for myself.

—Decide to run off to a war zone, with bloody bombs falling from the sky? Women in the field, God's sake. Have your forgotten you're someone's daughter? Have you forgotten what that would mean to invading soldiers?

Temerity said nothing.

Edward stared out the window, thinking of the graves of his wife and son, long untended. —I've given the Service almost twenty-five years. All my languages, all my work, and now they tiptoe around my desk like I'm soggy ordinance ploughed up in a field and liable to go off. Worse than you with your *Don't excite yourself.* I'll not have it.

—Father, I don't like that wheeze. Have you been ill?

—I'm fine.

The compartment door squeaked open, and the train guard stepped in, seeking tickets. —Beg your pardon, sir, but as this compartment is reserved, I must ask...

Edward turned his icy gaze from the glass. —Ask what?

Temerity smiled at the guard. —My father is tired. Is the compartment reserved in the name of West? Or perhaps Lord Fenleigh and Lady Temerity West?

—Yes, that's it. If I might bother your lordship for the tickets.

Edward continued to stare, not, Temerity thought, at the train guard.

—Father, aren't the tickets in your inner left pocket?

—Hm? I don't think so, Temmy.

—Could you check? We don't wish to keep the guard waiting.

Edward patted his inner left pocket, retrieved the tickets. —Ah.

—Thank you, my lord.

—What?

The train guard deepened his tones of courtesy and respect. —Thank you, Lord Fenleigh. I hope you and the Lady Temerity have a pleasant journey.

Temerity hurried to fill the gap left by Edward's silence. —I'm sure we shall.

The door squeaked shut.

—Father, you—

—Damned odd, that. How did that fellow know the titles? If I've said it once, I've said it a thousand times, call me West.

—Perhaps a secretary reserved the compartment.

Edward folded the newspaper on a sharp line, and the newsprint squeaked between his gloved fingers. For just a moment, the left side of his face seemed to lag behind the right as he spoke. Then both sides matched. —Did you know Charles Dickens was one of the first in England to install a shower bath? I wonder if it helped him write.

—Father—

—He took long walks all over London, all hours of the day and night. Little wonder he wanted a wash.

Temerity shut her eyes and rubbed her temples. Edward's conversation would twitch and dance now as he changed the subject, and changed it again, until Temerity surrendered. Yet his manner seemed excessively careful, even brittle, like that of drunk man walking with a slow and forced grace.

Angry, worried, and confused, she said nothing else.

Neither did he.

Higgins, their aged butler and their only remaining servant, met them at the train station and drove them to Kurseong House. Edward asked Higgins about his rheumatism and about the village in general. Temerity pretended she did not notice Higgins wince as he took her light overnight case. To suggest she carry own case, she thought, would only insult him.

Young women from the village, hired for the week, aired the house and changed the dust sheets, in no need of Temerity's nominal supervision. Temerity stared out at the back lawns from her old bedroom window. Her father was right. This house, this utter folly of a house, built too fast on a fen, felt oppressive with damp.

Edward seemed not just tired but afflicted, even confused. He spoke of nothing more meaningful than the weather.

Sunday evening, Temerity returned to her own London flat; Monday evening she crossed the Channel. She'd left Edward a note on his own stationery. *I may be gone for some time. Give Higgins my regards.* How to sign it: Temerity? Love, Temerity? Your loving daughter, T? Yours, Temmy?

No: *TTW.*

The white wall interrupted, its sight reminding her of just where she sat, hidden in an NKVD officer's Moscow flat.

As sunlight streamed through the glass of tea and out past the filigree of the *podstakannik*, and Temerity tilted her head to get a better view, she thought of Kurseong House and her desire to leave it. The certainty of her desire felt old and distant, lost. After returning from Roedean, she'd lived year-round at the estate, tended by three servants. Edward visited every weekend, more when he could manage it. As much as she thrived on language study, she longed for some sort of work, something messy and intricate, difficult. Instead, privilege settled on her in layers, each one heavier than the last. Language study at home. Excellent food. Devoted servants. Beautiful grounds. Even tailored trousers, worn on the understanding she must change into a skirt or frock when leaving the house.

The suffocating summer of 1933: Temerity's debut, with Aunt Min back from India to chaperone. Temerity, tired from party and after party, event after event — that bloody flower show perhaps the most boring of all — and disgusted by the stunts of one or another Mitford sister, wanted only to resume her study of Russian.

One day, she asked her Russian tutor about his melancholy air. Was it true, then, those stories of sadness woven into the Russian Soul?

Count Ilya Yakovich Ostrovsky shook his head. —Miss West, you are more intelligent than that. Now, your Russian compositions. You speak the language well, very well. You're a perfect mimic for my voice, but if you truly wish to write in Russian, to communicate at all, you must first think in Russian. This composition is English in Cyrillic letters. Again, please.

She would dream in Russian some nights, then dream of her mother's book of Russian fairy tales with that illustration of Vasilisa the Beautiful. In her dreams, adolescent Temerity told herself not to push the book away, not this time, because if she behaved herself then she might hear her mother's voice, yes, her mother would be here any moment. She would wake in silence, her face wet.

Day by day, Ilya seemed ever sadder.

Again, please.

Again. Again. Again.

Of all the treasures Ilya had abandoned when escaping St Petersburg in 1917 — he never called the city Petrograd or Leningrad — he said he missed the enamel samovar and tea service the most. He described it one afternoon when Min invited him to join her, Edward, and Temerity for tea. Then he confessed he'd never quite adapted to drinking tea in the British style. —The teapot is tyrannical.

Min lifted the spout free of Ilya's cup. —Whatever do you mean, Count Ostrovsky?

—You, the hostess, control the tea. So you control the strength. All courtesy then demands I drink my tea as you would please.

Min placed the teapot back on the tray. —My dear count, if the tea is not to your liking...

—The tea is delicious. It is crisp and bright. From one of your own Darjeeling gardens. That is not my point. With the samovar, one makes *zavarka*, a tea essence, a concentrate, and then a guest may add as much or as little hot water to dilute it, as he pleases.

Edward, annoyed on Min's behalf, clinked his cup against his saucer and quoted a Bolshevik slogan. —From each according to his ability, to each according to his work?

Min raised her eyebrows. —Really, Edward? Count Ostrovsky, I apologize for my brother.

Temerity gazed at her tutor in this awkward moment and saw him for the first time as a person, a fellow human being, and one shaped by a different culture and a complex past. Posture straight and elegant, he wrapped his long fingers around his hot cup, as if in penance, and gazed into his tea. When he looked up, he caught Temerity studying him. Sunlight streamed through the window and caught the edge of his strong cheekbones and the few blond hairs left in the grey.

Moscow pipes rattled.

God's sake!

Standing up, giving her head a shake and demanding of herself a little discipline instead of this daydreaming, Temerity strode to the little fold-down table and cleaned it for the third time. Then she returned to the samovar.

Earlier that morning, Efim and Kostya, each irritating the other, had hurried to make tea for her, and their competition spared her the dangerous embarrassment of admitting she had no idea how to work a samovar, let alone puzzle out the best ratio for *zavarka* to water. So now she experimented. The first glass she dumped down the sink, expecting it to improve the drainage. The second, which gave up a colour much closer to red than brown, proved drinkable: smoke, wine, leather, flowers.

Ursula Friesen's voice: *You Britishers always want some tea.*

Memory trickled again, and Temerity found herself thinking of Roedean and the ram's head over a door, the way the light played on the tea-coloured glass eyes. She'd noticed this while rehearsing *Henry V* on a staircase, Temerity cast as self-sacrificial York and wishing instead she could be Henry and deliver his glorious lines. *Tell the constable we are but warriors for the working day . . .*

The samovar hissed.

These daydreams, Temerity told herself, *have simply got to stop.*

This time, Temerity pinched her forearm. Then she straightened her posture, checked locks, sought keys, checked locks again, read *Izvestia*, cut *Izvestia* into squares and took them to the bathroom, where the blue tiles shone.

The fat one's voice as he injected her hand: *Now, not a sound.*

She stifled a moan and placed the scissors on the table with great care. She knew, she knew perfectly well, she'd imagined the man's voice, for no one else in this moment occupied the flat. Just her. Locked in.

She slammed cupboard and pantry doors until she found scouring powder and rags, and then set to scrubbing the bathroom tiles clean. Her fingernails softened; her cuticles swelled and stung. Then, praying the futile prayer for sufficient heat and water pressure, she took a shower. She got a good three minutes before the pressure changed and the water cooled, best shower yet. Sighing, she tugged on her clothes: the same skirt and blouse for days now, and no underwear.

I still feel dirty.

She strode to the *stenka* in the front room, yanked opened a drawer, and took an undershirt and pair of shorts from Kostya's supply. In the bedroom, she removed her Temerity West passport from the blouse lining and studied it a moment. The same photograph and date of birth as in the Margaret Bush passport: a young woman with curly hair pinned up yet still escaping, and a look in the eyes that a Roedean history mistress had called pure spitfire. *It will get you in trouble one day, West, trouble you can't get out of. Mind yourself.*

Mildred Ferngate, Margaret Bush, Nadezhda Ivanovna Solovyova, and still, Temerity West.

She shoved the passport between mattress and bed frame.

Kostya's underclothes, too large, at least felt clean. She buttoned one of his shirts and then slipped on a pair of his civilian trousers, snug on her hips and gaping on her waist. Amused, she hunted again in the *stenka* and found a pair of frayed braces, affixed those to the waist of the trousers and adjusted them over her shoulders. It didn't help. Then she rolled up trouser cuffs and sleeves, rigged a clothesline in the kitchen from two high hooks, and set to washing her clothes in the kitchen sink. No mangle to be found; she must wring the clothes by hand.

Hands aching, clothes hanging to dry, she returned to the front room and stood before the white, white wall.

White. White silk dress for one's debut. White stationery marked *Kurseong House.* White vision when Kostya shot wide in the clinic and hit the tin of blood.

She recalled the touch of the Basque boys' cardboard name tags. *Why did I help him? I was another woman in another country. Is that it?*

The lock clicked.

Temerity checked her watch. Too early for Kostya or Efim to return.

The door opened. A little cough, as if testing for a response.

Vadym Minenkov?

A louder cough.

The door shut. Leather soles tapped beneath a heavy tread; the male visitor had not bothered to remove his boots.

Bloody hell. —Kostya?

The tread paused, then hastened.

He stood by the kitchen, and Temerity emerged from the front room to meet him.

She gasped.

The fat one with the moustache, the host of the party, and, according to Kostya, a guardian angel: Arkady Dmitrievich Balakirev. Today he wore his uniform, the clothes and their meaning adding menace and bulk. Temerity recalled her father's voice as he read to her of Mandeville's crocodiles: *And in the night they dwell in the water, and on the day upon the land, in rocks and in caves. And they eat no meat in all the winter, but they lie as in a dream, as do the serpents. These serpents slay men, and they eat them weeping.*

Arkady looked up at the blouse and skirt on the clothesline, then down at this petite woman wearing a man's clothes. Kostya's clothes. —So, you're the whore.

—I'm no one's whore.

Arkady stared at her a moment, eyebrows raised, astonished at not just her defiance but the speed of it. He almost laughed. —Get me something to drink. What's your name?

Brazen it out. —Solovyova, Nadezhda Ivanovna. Tea?

—If I must.

His quiet voice put Temerity at ease, which in turn made her tense up. She approached the samovar with a confidence she did not feel. *Zavarka,* she reminded herself, *then water.*

Arkady settled himself into the armchair in the front room—And how long have you lived here, Nadezhda Ivanovna?

She made her voice nonchalant. —Oh, just a few days.

—Come here.

She got close enough to pass him a glass of very dark tea.

He sniffed it, looked at her in some horror, and placed the glass on the floor. Then he stared at her throat. —Did you cook the mushrooms the way Vadym Pavlovich told you to?

Kostya cooked them. —Yes.

—Do you care for him?

—Vadym Pavlovich?

—Kostya.

—That's a very forward question, uh…I didn't catch your name.

—I think you know who I am, but, as I'll be arrested five minutes after the two of you are, fuck secrets. Here.

Arkady passed her a red leather wallet like Kostya's. She opened it and looked at the initialed photograph and the ornate form bearing the words Balakirev, Arkady Dmitrievich, Major, NKVD.

She gave it back. *Get him talking.* —You're Kostya's father?

—Is his surname Balakirev? Your papers, please.

She stared him down, no gasp, no plea, not so much as a twitch.

Arkady nodded in admiration. —I see why he's fallen for you.

Temerity did not drop her gaze, and Arkady read the danger in her eyes: something focused and determined. Disciplined. He'd seen it in women before, in the old Komsomol meetings. He'd avoided those women, called them hard, preferring the naive ones who understood that their duties to the Party included fetching tea, typing correspondence, and servicing the needs of male members.

He stood up and leaned in to kiss her cheek. —What a shame I didn't get to sample you first. But then you're so tiny I'd split you in half.

Queasy, she kept still. —What do you want, Arkady Dmitrievich?

He kissed her other cheek. —I know who and what you are, Margaret Bush: the ruin and death of Kostya Nikto. So, I want you to disappear.

She took a step back. —If I am arrested—

—If?

—If I am arrested, I will tell them about that night at your house.

He seized her by the face, pressing her cheeks and wrenching her neck. —No one will believe you. Even if they did, it would mean nothing. But that's the future. Right here, right now, you need to listen to me.

Wine, onions, fish, and something uric: the fumes on his breath sickened her. Faster than she knew, she broke his hold, kicked his ankle and ruined his balance, seized his arm — and refrained. She did not throw him, instead releasing his arm and darting out of reach. Her eyes sent a new message, one which withered Arkady's sense of himself as he stumbled upright.

Pity? Oh, there's venom in the spit of this old dragon yet, my dear. Fucking venom.

Arkady opened his hands and held them out, palms up. —I just want you to listen. Will you listen?

After a moment, she nodded.

Staring at a wall behind Temerity, Arkady murmured about a boy frozen to the ground. The story seemed rehearsed, a draft, part of something longer, a confession perhaps. Then Arkady looked her in the eye. —My turn to pity you, you so young and so hard, because you cannot win this. You're already dead. You and Kostya both.

His sigh shook.

Words fast, voice low, he might have said something about protecting Kostya as long as he could; Temerity no longer understood him. He might have said something about her beauty as, dry lips gentle, he kissed her on the forehead. Then he frowned as if in sudden pain, sneered the word *whore* again, spat at her feet, and left.

She got to the armchair and almost fell into it, wrinkling her nose. The scent of him clung. Then, disgusted with herself for crying, she acknowledged what she'd heard, or rather, not heard: a click of a key in the lock.

She peered down the little corridor to the door.

A sliver of light betrayed it: the door pulled over, not shut.

Just get outside, get oriented…

She ran to the bedroom, wrenched the Temerity West passport from beneath the mattress, and tucked it in the right pocket of the trousers. Then she tried on Kostya's shoes in the closet but tripped on them the second step she took. Glancing down at the trouser cuffs, she reasoned the long pants would hide her bare feet. Filth, cuts, lockjaw? Later.

No cringing. Off we go, then.

She stepped outside the flat.

No one called out. No one seized her arm.

She took note of the number on the door: seven. She glanced up: one more floor. Down: as the stairs seemed to disappear in the dun, she counted five other landings. Up again, and far beyond the landing and any human's reach, a single light bulb dangled from the seventh floor ceiling.

How in hell does one replace that? A seven-storey ladder?

A draft of fresh air wound round her ankles, and downstairs, far downstairs, something creaked.

Cool wood beneath her bare feet, the steps gritty with tracked dirt, Temerity descended.

One step, two steps.

One floor, two floors.

Below, the heavy lobby door opened, wood and glass. Keys jingled.

A hoarse voice called a greeting. —Good afternoon, Comrade Yaroslav.

—Good afternoon, Grandmother.

—You're home early today.

—Yes, Grandmother.

Yaroslav, a man in his twenties taking the stairs two at a time, soon passed Temerity. He ignored her. She watched him open his flat on the fifth floor; the door bore the same number as Kostya's.

Each floor has the same numbers on the flats?

—Who hides in the dark on my stairs?

Blast. Blasted blasted bloody hell.

—Come here, so I can see you.

Holding the trouser cuffs above her feet so she would not trip, Temerity stepped into the lobby. Then she let the trousers fall to their full length. —I do not hide, Grandmother.

The older woman kept rocking in her chair. Her dress, buttoned to her neck, draped down past her ankles and ended in a wrinkled mound. She kept her long hair in a low bun at the back of her neck, like Ursula Friesen. Her eyes, deep set and brown, seemed to be study-ing a different place and time. Then she smirked. —You're dressed as a man. And you're barefoot.

Temerity noticed the window which showed a reflection of the stairs. The older woman would have seen her hitch up the trousers. —Yes, Grandmother.

—I wondered when I'd see you. Come closer, child.

The light bulb in the ceiling high above flickered, darkened again, as Elena squirmed and retrieved an object from a pocket in her skirt: one of Temerity's shoes.

—Why, Grandmother, where did you get that?

—Left behind in my lobby. And this is the first I've seen of you. Where did you get the courage to come downstairs, out of a bottle? We have an NKVD officer living in this building. Shall I tell him about you? No, no, I'll likely forget by the time I see him again. He looks so handsome in that uniform. He must look even better naked.

I could sell these pretty shoes on the black market for a small fortune. I could sell them to the NKVD officers outside.

Temerity saw them: two uniformed officers leaning on their black car, looking up, smoking, bored.

Oh, God.

The officer on the right lowered his gaze to the lobby. He flicked the remains of his cigarette to the street, then ground it out with his boot. Then something distracted him. He saluted, then elbowed his fellow to do the same.

Elena tucked the shoe away. —Do you not hear them coming? Go back. Go. Go!

Temerity ran up the stairs, peeked at each landing; the flat numbers repeated over and over. *Which floor? Which blasted floor?* Gasping, ribs tight, she wrenched the doorknob of a flat marked seven.

In the lobby, Kostya held the door open for Efim. Both men nodded to Elena in the rocking chair. She, in turn, laughed.

Arms full of shopping packages and a bag from Babichev's, Kostya gave her a light bow. —You're jolly today, Grandmother.

Far above, someone's flat door clicked shut.

Elena nodded. —Yaroslav just got home.

Who the hell is Yaroslav? Kostya looked to Efim, who shrugged. Stifling a sigh, Kostya gave Elena a second light bow. —Thank you, Grandmother.

Efim started up the stairs, and Kostya rearranged his bags as he prepared to follow.

—Comrade Nikto?

—Yes, Grandmother?

—You need a perhaps-bag, one of those collapsible ones made from string. Then you can always carry it with you, and perhaps you'll see something you want to buy.

—I'll keep that in mind.

—You don't look well. Do you get enough sleep?

—Please don't worry about me, Grandmother.

—Ah. Welcome home, then.

His fever dream on the train into Moscow in 1918: Arkady had taught Kostya how to use the worry beads, to keep him quiet. Kostya got so cold, yet the amber seemed to shimmer and melt. Then the train ran on fowls' feet, and Baba Yaga spoke to him. *Welcome home,* bezprizornik, *welcome home.*

Elena laughed some more.

—I hope you have a pleasant evening, Grandmother.

—And for you, Comrade Nikto, I wish sweet dreams.

In the flat, Kostya joined Efim in admiring the ingenuity behind the kitchen clothesline, even as a flushed Temerity apologized for the sight of both her laundry and herself in Kostya's clothes. She left the room without saying anything else, and, in a moment, the shower ran.

Efim decided not to question why someone who needed a shower had already changed into clean clothes, just as he'd decided not to question why his key had slipped, why the door seemed to be unlocked. He beckoned Kostya into his bedroom. —Let me see your shoulder.

—It's fine.

—The pain scowl on your face could cut glass.

Scowling all the more, Kostya acquiesced, and closed Efim's bedroom door behind him.

Efim opened his medical bag. —If I invite you to call me Efim Antonovich, then may I call you Konstantin Arkadievich?

Kostya looked around the tiny room, much smaller than his: enough space for a single bed and one person to move around it, even then only with some care. He sat on the bed and extended his left arm. —Yes, of course. I'm not sure why we've not done that already. Don't bother with the patronymic. Not for me.

Efim moved Kostya's shoulder this way and that. —Konstantin, I must be blunt.

—Me, too. I can't keep taking morphine like this.

—Why is she wearing your clothes?

—You saw hers hanging on the line. She can't go naked. Besides, I told you, she's staying with us for a while.

Efim examined the ampoule: nearly empty. Then he drew the liquid into the syringe. —And she came with nothing? Your mistress is your own concern, but why does she not get the rest of her things and just move in? You're NKVD. You can jiggle registration and residency permits, update her *propiska*.

—Doctor...

—My name.

Kostya took a deep breath as the tourniquet tightened on his arm. —Efim, please. I don't want to see you come to any harm. This is a temporary arrangement, very temporary. Next month you'll have forgotten all about her.

Holding the needle away from them both, Efim sat down next to Kostya. —I am under significant pressure to take care of you, to keep you fit to work. Major Balakirev—

—I know. I know how he can be. Please, if you complain or even just comment to the wrong person, all three of us are in trouble. You live here, the logic goes, therefore you must know something about it.

—I know nothing.

—And I wish to keep it that way.

Sighing, Efim looked at the ceiling.

Kostya reached for Efim's shoulder and stopped as Efim turned to examine Kostya's other arm. —We understand each other, yes?

—I understand very little, beyond first my need to fear Balakirev, and now my need to fear you.

—I'm sorry.

Efim studied him for a moment. —Then I'm damned thrice over, because I believe you. Now keep still. I think I found a good vein.

As Kostya set out supper from the deli, a feast of *bubliki*, butter, yogurt, pickles, and shredded fowl, Temerity joined him. Her damp curls sprang up. —I'll get my skirt and blouse down right away.

—Are they dry yet?

She took her hand from her skirt. —No.

—Then leave them. You're shaking.

—The water ran cold. I caught a chill.

Overhearing them as he left his bedroom, Efim glanced into the bathroom; steam fogged up the shaving mirror. He joined them at the little table, saying nothing.

Bouts of chewing, bouts of silence.

Temerity paused to remove a bone from her mouth. —Is this duck?

Kostya swallowed. —Could be. Might be some pigeon in there, too.

He noticed Temerity and Efim had stopped chewing and now stared at him.

Kostya shrugged. —Diet of the *bezprizorniki*. I could bring home sausage next time, *doktorskaya kolbasa*. It's a bit bland, but easy to digest. Very nutritious. Efim would approve.

Efim shook his head. —It's full of pork.

Giving Efim a quick look, Kostya broke off a piece of *bublik*.

Efim stood up from the table. —It's been a long day. I think I'll go lie down.

As Temerity picked up the dishes for washing, Kostya stared at the ceiling. He felt peaceful, even dreamy. He watched Temerity run the water and struggle to get any lather at all from the scrap of soap, and then walked over to her.

Temerity thought his footfall seemed slower than normal. Less certain, somehow.

Kostya wrapped his arms around her chest and leaned his chin on top of her head. —I got you a present today.

Her neck stiffened. *Passport and papers. Please, God, please.*

He took his arms off her and opened the pouch on his belt. —Turn around.

In both palms, he held a bottle of Shalimar.

Not just a bottle of Shalimar in Moscow, but one with a chipped stopper.

She felt cold. —Where did you get this?

Smiling, Kostya wagged a finger as if rebuking a child. —Put it on.

Get him talking. —You like perfume?

Watching her draw the stopper down her throat, he nodded.

She dabbed perfume onto her fingertips and then fluffed the curls in her hair. —There. That's one of my secrets.

—And I didn't even need to raise my voice to learn it.

—I might tell you many things. Will you pour me some vodka?

He did this, no hesitation, his back to her. —I got something else nice on the way home.

Brown paper rustled; vodka glugged.

He turned around and gave her drink in a large and full glass. A wedge of lemon floated on top, and beneath that bobbed gooseberries and strawberries. —I got the gooseberries from Babichev, but I picked the strawberries near that cemetery by the well.

Then Kostya thought of the strawberries at the *poligon.*

So lush, so sweet.

Temerity held the glass up to the light. —Cristobal Zapatero liked strawberries. Something he told me as I sketched his portrait.

Kostya almost dropped his drink. Staring at the delicate tremor in his hands, he sounded polite. —Duty, Nadia. Right now it's your duty to change the subject.

Temerity took a sharp breath, fell silent. They both sipped their drinks. Then Temerity stroked Kostya's forearm. —I can't stay here.

He rubbed the back of his neck. —We've all got to die sometime.

—Pardon me?

—Not tonight. I hope.

—Kostya —

Hearing Vadym's voice, *I'm worried sick about Misha,* Kostya plopped down in a kitchen chair. —Can we just leave the past behind?

—It's the not past that worries me.

—I had a terrible day, just one in a series. Focus on the present moment, yes? Come. Come sit down. Now, look at me.

—Kostya, listen. Earlier today—

—No. I said leave the past. Right here, right now, we can be together.

—But—

He raised his glass. —Ssh. To love and safety. We can be safe. Just for one day.

After a moment, she raised her glass to meet his. —To love and safety.

Eyes closed, Kostya swallowed much of his drink. —I want to memorize this moment. Just the two of us, at the table after supper, when I can catch your perfume. I'll need this memory later.

She studied him, his chest rising and falling, his uniform spotless. Street sounds filtered through the open windows; water ran in the pipes. —Listen to me. Your Balakirev paid a visit.

Efim's bedroom door opened; the bathroom door shut.

—Not now, Nadia.

—Yes. Right here. Right now.

—Very funny. You want to drag Efim with you? He knows nothing of all this, of you and me. One wrong step, and all three of us are marched out that door. And then NKVD arrests Efim's wife in Leningrad. Do you want to be responsible for that, too?

—Kostya!

—Hush!

The toilet flushed, and the faucets ran as Efim washed his hands.

—Nadia, I am very tired. My shoulder hurts like hell. I must ask if I can sleep in the bed tonight.

Efim's bedroom door clicked shut.

Temerity finished her drink. —I'll take the floor this time.

—It's a double bed.

—One night on the floor won't kill me. I've slept rougher.

He sighed, then stood up from the table and moved to the front room, where he stretched his back. —Give me four hours. We'll switch later in the night, yes?

She imagined the passport falling out of her pocket as she slept. —Let me get changed first.

Kostya took some frayed pyjamas from the *stenka*. —No, your clothes are still wet. Here.

She stood beside him now, peering into the *stenka* drawer. —Wait, is that a book?

Kostya parted some more folded clothes, took out a towel and a pair of shorts for himself. —No need to sound so surprised. I grew up surrounded by my grandfather's books, Nadia. I'm not a complete savage.

—Correct. You miss complete savagery by the grace of this one book. Let me read it.

He covered it with undershirts. —It's dull.

—Then could you go to a library and—

—No! Hurry up and get changed while I take a shower.

—Kostya, please. I am bored witless in this flat.

He exposed Turgenev's *Fathers and Sons*. —Fine, fine. Take it.

In the bedroom, she closed the door and listened. Once the water ran, she stashed her Temerity West passport back under the mattress. Then she changed into the pyjamas, rolling up sleeves and cuffs, which promptly unrolled again as she folded the clothes she'd worn, and laid them on the closet shelf.

As Kostya's shower finished, Temerity settled herself in the arm-chair in the front room. She ran her fingers over the book's binding, then lifted the book to her nose to breathe in the scent of old paper. She also caught sweat, dust, and hospital disinfectant.

In the bedroom, Kostya hung up his uniform pieces and tucked the holstered Nagant and the amber beads beneath his pillow. As he pulled on clean shorts, he caught sight of the shirt Temerity placed on the closet shelf. He grabbed the shirt and pressed it to his nose to smell the perfume.

Temerity thought of the Lichtträger, the scent of kerosene.

Kostya stroked the shirt against his face, then folded it again and returned it to the shelf.

Temerity turned to the book's title page and struggled to forget the stench of tinned blood. Arkady's voice intruded: *I want you to disappear.*

The bed squeaked as Kostya lay down.

Temerity raised the book in the air, as if in a toast. *To love and safety.*

[ ]

PROPISKA
Thursday 10 June

Uncertain what woke him, Kostya checked his watch: seventeen minutes after two in the morning.

Five bangs of a fist. —Comrade, open the door.

Shit!

He felt the floor beneath his feet before he understood he'd gotten out of bed. Efim in the room next door cried out in fright. In the front room, the chair scraped against the floor as Temerity stood up.

Kostya grabbed his keys and identification wallet from the side table and his robe from the closet. In the hallway, he discovered that he'd taken a *gymnastyorka* instead.

Nadia, I'm sorry.

Five more bangs. —Open the door, comrade!

—Yes, yes, I'm coming!

Kostya hauled the *gymnastyorka* over his head, blinding himself to the sight of Temerity standing behind the chair. He lurched to the door and pressed his ear to the hinge to listen. He thought he recognized the voice.

—Comrade Yaroslav! At once, please. We've no wish to wake your neighbours.

A second man spoke. —Katelnikov, listen to me. We're on the wrong floor. That's the wrong flat. They're all numbered the same in this building.

—Oh, fuck.

—You'll be fucked if we don't make quota.

Kostya unlocked the door and stepped into the dirty light of the one hanging bulb. —Katelnikov?

Matvei whirled around, faced the man who called his name. —I...oh, no.

Nodding to Matvei and then to his partner, Kostya showed his ID. —Can I be of any help?

A third officer ascended the stairs, his voice stiff with embarrassment. —Nikto? Is that you?

Kostya recognized the third officer: an older sergeant, and one of his department colleagues, not that he could remember his name. So many new men. *Dobrynin, right.* —Good morning.

Dobrynin squinted at Kostya's *gymnastyorka* and undershorts. —Light sleeper?

—When fellow officers beat on my door, yes.

Matvei gave a little cry. Then he cleared his throat. —The numbers on the doors are all the same. On each floor. We're on the wrong floor. An accident, Comrade Sergeant Dobrynin, a simple oversight.

—A simple idiot. Who's on your list?

—Yaroslav, Nikolai Eduardovich, fifth floor, flat number seven.

—Then go directly below to the fifth floor, flat number seven, and arrest Yaroslav.

—Yes, Comrade Sergeant.

Dobrynin turned on the second officer. —And you. Find the other one, what, Petrovna, Elena Tikhonovna. Comrade Senior Lieutenant Nikto, permit me to show you the list. Now, which flat is Petrovna's?

Kostya felt dizzy. —This floor, flat number two. Down the hall. She's very old. I've no idea how she manages the stairs.

—There, you see? Comrade Senior Lieutenant Nikto can read the list just fine, and we just woke him up out of a sound sleep, so the problem is not with the list.

As the second officer found Elena's flat and beat on the door, Dobrynin offered Kostya a cigarette and matches.

Kostya lit the cigarette and took a deep drag. —Puppies.

Dobrynin nodded. —Once we're back at Lubyanka, I'll kick them up the arse.

—Telephone directories in flour sacks, yes? Leaves no marks, so the boys will look fit for duty.

They both chuckled and wished each other a good night.

As Kostya retreated into the flat and locked the door, the arresting officer called Elena's name.

Efim and Temerity stood near the kitchen, at the end of the corridor to the door, Temerity in Kostya's pyjamas and clutching Turgenev to her chest, Efim fully dressed and carrying a small suitcase.

Efim whispered. —Are they gone?

Kostya's laugh, quick and rough, sounded more like the yelp of a dog. —Not yet.

Down the hall, Elena screeched her protest, her loyalty to the Party. —I can prove it, comrade! These shoes!

Temerity dropped the book; Kostya and Efim flinched but kept quiet.

Matvei ran back up the stairs. —Do you need help?

Dobrynin sounded amused. —Shoes, Grandmother?

—The witch who lost these shoes cringes here. I saw her.

—Senile old sow.

Matvei disagreed. —With respect, Comrade Sergeant, take a look at these shoes, this lettering inside them. I think that's English.

Kostya stared at Temerity. He couldn't speak. Efim saw this and shut his eyes.

Dobrynin's voice approached the door. —Nikto knows languages. I'll get him.

Cigarette gone to ash, Kostya waved Temerity and Efim away, pointing to the bedrooms. They kept still.

Matvei almost shouted. —No! No, please don't disturb him again.

—You timid little rabbit. What, are you in love with him? Don't want to upset his beauty sleep?

—No, wait—

Elena's voice rang out. —Iosif Vissarionovich!

Temerity stepped close enough to Kostya to whisper. —She calls on *Stalin?*

Kostya nodded.

—Iosif Vissarionovich, help me! Help me! I am loyal to you! Iosif Vissarionovich, hear my prayer! Iosif—

A heavy thud.

Dobrynin laughed. —Pistol-whipping old ladies, Katelnikov? Nobody's rabbit now. Get her in the car.

Men grunted; feet dragged. After some noisy difficulty on the stairs, Kostya guessing that they allowed the unconscious woman to roll, Dobrynin returned to the fifth floor to collect Yaroslav.

The NKVD car departed.

Efim felt much of the tension leave his body. Yet even this relief corroded him, scarring his thoughts and feelings as much as shrapnel had scarred his patient's shoulder.

Not me, not me, not me.

Kostya ground out his cigarette in the ashtray with great care, then raised his right fist and struck a wall in the kitchen. —Fucking idiots!

Efim and Temerity flinched.

Kostya rustled in the cupboards. Glass rattled and clinked.

Efim winced at the racket, and his voice sounded higher than normal. —We don't keep the vodka there.

A pot clattered. —Good thing I'm not a drunkard, then. Where's the powdered milk? I'm sure I saw some.

—Second shelf in the cupboard left of the sink.

—How precise you are, Efim Antonovich, and how correct. Nadia, come here, so I can tell you a secret. Go into my closet and look to the left-hand side. On a hanger near the wall, you'll find an old woolen coat, dark blue. In the inner chest pocket is a packet of sugar. It's granulated and already torn open, so the sugar might run free. Be very careful, and cup the packet in your hands, yes? And next to the sugar, there's a string of beads. Bring me those, too.

Asking herself if she was truly awake, Temerity fetched the sugar and the beads. She gave them to Kostya, then sat at the little fold-down table with Efim.

—Thank you. Now both of you, please, relax. I know it's hard, but tonight you're safe. I promise.

Temerity and Efim looked at each other, then at the table.

Kostya placed the sugar and beads next to the stove. —I wish we had honey and cinnamon.

Wishing, too, that he could rid his mind of the noise of agitated dogs at the *poligon*, Kostya drew water from the samovar into a small pot and added powdered milk. He broke the lumps with precision and care, then placed the pot on the stove.

Then Efim laughed, shrill at first. —Look at us. Our night clothes. Ragbags, all of us.

Temerity chortled, worked to control it. Kostya's mouth twitched. Then all three of them laughed, hard. Thinking of clothes, Kostya almost told them how people might be arrested naked, during a sex act if necessary, and how he'd done so. He stopped, just as his first word got lost beneath the noise. *One must coddle laughter,* he thought. *Best keep that story to myself.*

Almost breathless now, Efim shook his head. —Hot milk, Konstantin?

—My grandfather would make hot milk for me when I had a nightmare.

Temerity pointed to the pot. —Don't let it boil.

—It's in no danger of boiling, Nadia.

Temerity nodded. Kostya had hesitated before saying Nadia; perhaps he'd wanted to say something else.

Kostya stirred the milk, then poured in sugar; white particles glistened as they fell. —This may interest you, Efim. He was a doctor. A good one, too. Semyon Mikhailovich Berendei. People came to the house all hours, and he treated them. He never turned anyone away, even when he knew damned well he wouldn't get paid. He charged on a scale. My grandparents raised me; I never knew my parents. My grandmother died when I was nine, and then my grandfather disappeared when I was twelve.

Temerity and Efim said nothing.

Kostya poured sweetened hot milk into three tea glasses. Temerity carried two of them to the table, gave one to Efim. Kostya followed her with his own glass and the beads. He set them down and tugged at his *gymnastyorka.*

Temerity sipped the hot milk. —Thank you.

—I wish I could give you something else. Nadia, may I sit near you? I'm cold.

Finding this formal courtesy odd for a man addressing his live-in mistress, Efim retrieved a light blanket from his drawer in the *stenka* and placed it over Kostya's shoulders. Then Kostya snuggled into Temerity, and she put her arm around him.

They drank the hot milk.

Rubbing beads between his fingers, Kostya sighed. —Cinnamon. It needs cinnamon. And real milk would be nice, too. I can't make it like he did.

—It's fine.

—It's terrible. You're a sweet liar, Nadia, but powdered milk is terrible.

Temerity kissed Kostya on the cheek; Efim stood up and returned to his bedroom.

Kostya smelled Temerity's perfume again and ran his fingers through her hair. Then he took his hand away. —Did you fall asleep in the armchair?

—Yes.

—I want you to lie down in the bed now. I'll go back to the floor.

She sighed. —Come to the bed with me.

—What?

—Just to lie down.

—You trust me?

She studied him for a long moment, standing there in his undershorts and a uniform piece, beads dangling from one hand. —It's almost three in the morning, Kostya. Try to rest.

[ ]

DOGS' HEADS AND BROOMSTICKS 2
Thursday 10 June

Evgenia shook her head. —You look terrible.

Kostya rubbed at his gritty eyes. —Didn't sleep well. Make my tea strong, yes? Please?

—And extra sugar. Here are your dossiers for review.

—Comrade Ismailovna, I need your help.

At the samovar now, she glanced over her shoulder, eyes wide.
—My help?

—Yes. Why not?

She gave him the tea, its scent so pungent that it tickled his nose.
—Ask away.

—Some of the confessions. They're nigh-on incoherent, and I know not every single prisoner is illiterate. Nor is every officer stupid.

Evgenia snorted and smirked, then made an effort to look serious.

—And the pattern of guilt: it plays out the same way, again and again. What if I wrote up three or four different styles of confession, and then you type them up...

Careful not to nudge a perilously high pile of paperwork, Evgenia dropped two pieces of sugar from the tongs into Kostya's hand.
—And if we don't use them as straight templates, at least they could be guidelines. It might speed things up.

—Ismailovna, you read my mind.

—No. But I am under the same pressure you are. More more more, now now now.

As Kostya thanked her, a smell reached him, iron, copper, and spice: old blood.

A large shadow blotched Evgenia's desk. —The famous Nikto?

Kostya turned around.

A broad and fleshy man, built like Arkady, squinted at him. —I thought I recognized you by the stories of the scars. How did you get those?

Kostya forced himself to keep still and look into the man's eyes, to ignore the fat fingers reaching for him. —An accident.

The broad man stroked Kostya's neck, fondled his ear, tapped his insignia. —You got off easy. And promoted to senior lieutenant. Well done.

Kostya glanced at the man's fingernails. *Blood in the cuticles?*

Evgenia's voice betrayed warmth. —We're very proud of him in this department, Comrade Commandant Blokhin.

He gestured to Kostya's dossiers. —Buried in paperwork?

—Yes, Comrade Commandant, aren't we all?

—Paperwork slows me down. You'll notice my hands are empty. And with that, he walked towards Boris Kuznets's office.

Evgenia took in a sharp breath. —Do you know who that is?

Kostya nodded. Vasily Mikhailovich Blokhin, Lubyanka's chief executioner and a man who loved his wet work. Blokhin, who would likely shoot Yagoda.

Evgenia stamped a form. —Nice of him to single you out.

—Yes. I need the smaller meeting room for half an hour this morning.

—This morning? I'm afraid you need to book that in advance, and then have the department head sign his approval.

Kostya slurped his tea. —Well, I just got this memo this morning, typed by no less than you, yes? I'm to enjoy a respite from arrest duties myself and instead take command of eighteen men, most of them new recruits. Where else can I put eighteen men if not in that smaller meeting room?

—There's not enough room for them to sit.

—They can stand. I promise you, Captain Kuznets would approve.

Evgenia dug beneath a stack of paper for a notebook, then flipped some pages. —The room is free, comrade. You're lucky.

Pretty and lucky, Misha had called him when they were cadets. *Lucky,* Yury had snarled, *schastlivyy, schastlivyy, schastlivyy.*

—Good morning, comrades. I am Senior Lieutenant Nikto.

No one raised an eyebrow at the surname, and all replied at once.

—Good morning, Comrade Senior Lieutenant.

—Let's make this quick, comrades, as we're all a bit busy this week. Grim chuckles.

—I shall divide you into six squads of three, and ... wait, who's not here?

A soft knock on the door. Seventeen men cleared their throats, sucked their teeth, clicked their tongues. Waited.

Kostya, too, waited, almost too long to keep his dignity. Then he recalled it was his task and privilege, as the commanding officer in the room, to order someone to open the door. He decided to do it himself.

—Katelnikov. Forgive me, comrade. I thought I scheduled this meeting for ten o'clock. You prefer it for five past, yes?

Red-faced, Matvei stared at the toes of Kostya's boots. —I am sorry, Comrade Senior Lieutenant. I only just got the memo. I had night duty, and I got delayed in the cells.

—Go stand with the others. I don't want to waste any more time. So, as I said, squads of three focused on a better plan. Yes, Comrade Sergeant Kamenev?

Gleb lowered his hand and cleared his throat. —I don't know about you, Senior Lieutenant, but I've got a timetable to meet.

Surprised at Gleb's interruption and surly tone, close to insubordination, Kostya inclined his head to the older man and decided to speak with deference and respect. —Do you refer, Gleb Denisovich, to the timetables Comrade Captain Kuznets handed out?

—Yes.

—And do you not think I attended that same meeting, Gleb Denisovich? That same meeting where Comrade Captain Kuznets gave me *two* timetables?

Some appreciative laughter. Gleb inclined his own head to Kostya, also in respect, and some apology. Matvei looked up from the floor.

Kostya ignored Matvei's gaze. —So we've established that everyone is busy, yes, with quotas to fill? Good. Now, sometimes when we're on a raid, it's inevitable we're going to wake someone up.

Matvei turned pale.

Kostya felt a prickle in his belly, almost like electricity. Easy, so easy, to hold Matvei Katelnikov up as an example, let his fellows laugh at him, let shame flog him to better results.

No.

—We're not here to frighten innocent citizens. So I want to see a redoubled effort on getting the correct flat number. Check our *propiska* lists against the *Directory for All Moscow.*

Silence.

A blond officer shifted his weight from foot to foot, pointing to a side table. —Ah, yes, well, with respect, Comrade Senior Lieutenant Nikto, I mean, which directory, 1936 or 1937? My last commanding officer kept complaining how the '36 directory is out of date.

Gleb stopped chewing on his moustache. —Has anyone even seen a '37 version?

Kostya noticed copies of the '36 directory on a side table. He knew what Gleb meant: the rumours about why no 1937 Moscow telephone directory had appeared, that too many people had disappeared. The '36 directory now functioned less as a guide to the living and more as a list of the disappeared and the dead. He let out a long breath, aware as he finished of perhaps sending the wrong signal. A competent commanding officer would not show exasperation or fear over something as trivial as a telephone directory. —Comrades, Moscow is growing rapidly. The publishers of the directory simply can't keep up. This is why we must also check the *propiska* permits. Now, comrades, check my list to find your new team—

Five bangs on the door: many of the men flinched.

Scowling, Kostya reached for the doorknob; he ended up catching it as the door swung open. —Comrade Captain Kuznets, good morning. Come in.

—Good morning, Comrade Senior Lieutenant Nikto. I have a treat for you men today, a distinguished visitor.

Vasily Blokhin entered the room. He held up his hands, palms out, as though blessing the faithful. —At ease, comrades, at ease. I just want a moment of your time. Comrade Captain Kuznets is new to this department, yet already he brags about you.

—A moment, Vasily Mikhailovich. I should introduce you. We've got so many new men. Comrades, this is the head of Kommandatura, Comrade Commandant Blokhin.

Kostya and the others saluted.

Boris clapped Vasily on the shoulder. —And I promise you, comrades, he does not enjoy his nickname.

Vasily frowned, then shook Boris off. —Nickname?

A muscle twitched in Boris's cheek. —Leather Man.

Vasily's laugh sounded dull, rehearsed. —Apron and gauntlets, right. Comrades, I must protect my uniform. Unless one of you has found a laundry service that can reliably shift blood?

More laughter, brittle and loud.

Boris's face relaxed, and Kostya could not tell which emotion induced his own nausea: fear, anger, or guilt.

Vasily gestured to the men, then to Kostya. —You're in good hands here with Comrade Senior Lieutenant Nikto. Don't disappoint him, or, well...

He extended his index and middle fingers and cocked his thumb to mime pointing a gun at Kostya's face.

Kostya stared back at him.

Vasily kept his hand steady; his eyes seemed to retreat further behind the heavy lids.

Boris released a word from his lips, as though kissing someone, so quiet: —Bang.

Vasily lowered his hand. —I've got another appointment.

—This way, Comrade Commandant.

They left, and Kostya closed the door behind them, taking a deep breath. *An exercise, just an exercise. For me, and the men.*

When he turned to the others, eighteen sets of wide eyes dropped their gaze to the floor. Embarrassed for their commanding officer, or frightened for themselves? Kostya could not tell.

Angry now, he pinned a list to the wall. He wanted to nail it there. The pin, bent, fell to the floor. Matvei found him another pin, handed it over.

—Thank you, Katelnikov. I've put you all in new teams, shaken it up. Maybe we can get different results this way, and even if we don't, at least when senior command asks us if we tried new teams, we can say why yes, of course, comrade.

Low laughter.

—Any questions?

Feet tramped on the floors outside and above, and water squealed in the pipes.

—We reconvene in seventy-two hours. Let's see some real progress on those tables, yes? Dismissed.

Relishing the solitude, Kostya leaned back in his desk chair. His officemates remained on schedules opposite his, and he rarely saw them. Even so, today he'd closed his office door to mute the racket of other people so he might concentrate. His right hand ached, distracting him from the fiery pain in his left shoulder. He'd written three different fake confessions to three different crimes, wrecking, espionage, and the all-purpose anti-Soviet activities, each confession just over five pages long, with blanks left for the names of anyone else the prisoner might denounce. The anti-Soviet activities confession had come out too balanced, too poetic, with compound-complex sentences no prisoner would utter after a beating. Kostya rebuked himself. *It's a tool, not a work of art. This is not story time.*

Scowling, he locked the templates in a desk drawer and took out his cigarettes. A timid knock sounded on his closed office door, one-two, one-two, like that of the tsar's servants in *Lieutenant Kizhe*.

Kostya shook his match dead. —Come in.

The caller turned the knob, met resistance.

Kostya hurried to open the door. —I am sorry, comrade. This door is tricky. Katelnikov. What can I do for you?

Matvei's eyes widened. The courteous, even collegial, tone in the senior lieutenant's voice after the fuck-up with the flats left Matvei feeling much more at ease. He passed Kostya a note. —Comrade Major Balakirev needs your assistance in the cells.

Drawing on his cigarette, reading the cell number, Kostya raised his eyebrows. —Balakirev? Must be languages.

—I only know what I was told, Comrade Senior Lieutenant.

—You'll go far. Wait, you had night duty. Go home.

Matvei looked at the floor and whispered. —She's still unconscious.

Elena Petrovna. Kostya offered him a cigarette. —So you've not left Lubyanka at all?

Matvei struggled to light the match. —I sat with her.

Kostya studied him a moment. —You're no doctor. Now go home and rest. That's an order.

Underground, Kostya navigated the maze. The corridors, designed to confuse and contain anyone who might escape confinement, could also baffle the most experienced officer. Kostya, who found these corridors easier than the Odessa catacombs, took note of scarce numbers, chipped paint, and leak stains: trail marks. *Go I know not whither,* he thought, *and fetch I know not what. Why can't I stop thinking about stories?*

The laughter of Vasily Blokhin floated on the air, spontaneous this time, joyful. Then a gun fired.

Kostya flinched, resumed walking. *Fucking Tokarevs.*

Noise faded as Kostya walked to the farthest cells. Not certain he had the right spot, for the unguarded cell door hung open a few centimetres, Kostya knocked and called out. —Comrade Major, you sent for me?

The heavy door opened a little further and Kostya stepped inside, just managing to avoid the large puddle on the floor. The puddle reflected back the image of the usual desk and two chairs, one for chief interrogator, one for prisoner, and the terrible brightness of one caged light bulb.

Arkady pulled the heavy door almost shut, then wedged a tiny opening with a ruler. —Is she still there?

—What?

—Your whore. I tried to send her on her way.

—Arkady Dmitrievich—

—The stool's behind you. Get up there.

Kostya looked around again, found no prisoner perched on the high stool. Arkady's voice unsettled him, too. He'd not spoken to Kostya quite like that, in tones of disappointment and contempt, for many years.

Arkady backhanded Kostya across the face. —I said, get on the stool.

Stunned by the violence, suspended in that cold moment of accepting the blow and yet believing no pain would come, not this time, Kostya obeyed. Steel touched his haunches, and his struck face blazed. —What the hell was that for?

Arkady backhanded him again, same cheek. —Don't make this harder than it needs to be. And lower your voice, unless you want to get us both fucking killed right here, right now.

Tears clouding his vision, Kostya slowed his breathing and calmed his voice. —How shall I explain this bruise?

—I don't give a goat's rancid fuck what you explain to others when first you must explain something to me.

Kostya slipped down from the stool. —I am not some adolescent you may beat when annoyed. I'm—

He staggered backwards until he hit the wall, and he wanted nothing more than to slide down to the floor.

Because Arkady had punched him in the belly.

Arkady rubbed at his knuckles. —Annoyed? I beat you because sometimes the only way to reach you is to pound the truth though that thick skull. You will get back up on that stool and perch there until I instruct you otherwise.

Spitting, Kostya obeyed. —Arkady Dmitrievich, please...

—Please what? What? Shall I not hit you? Shall I not worry about you? Shall I not wake up in a cold sweat from dreams of you packed in some shit-filled cattle car for a fucking *month* as it inches towards Kolyma? Look at me when I speak to you. Look at me!

Tears running down his face, Kostya looked.

Arkady cradled Kostya's face in his hands, and his voice dropped to a whisper. —What have you done to yourself? Intersections of power, Kostya. The steppe gives up in patches to forest, and the forest gives up in patches to tundra, yet in places where you see no change, all the differences blend. Survive. I taught you that.

Kostya said nothing.

Arkady caught some of Kostya's tears on his fingers. —You took her home from my party.

Voice quiet: —Yes.

—In the car Stepanov had signed out.

—Yes.

—And that's why Kuznets wanted to see the garage logs. Fuck. Kostya, you need to come up with a reason why you took a car signed out in another officer's name and then returned it in your name. A good reason.

—Stepanov was too drunk to walk straight, let alone drive. I did him a favour by bringing it back.

—Not bad, not bad.

Kostya wiped his mouth with the back of his hand and struggled to think. —Are you under investigation?

Arkady spat on the floor. —Do you know who sits in his own shit just a few cells away?

Kostya knew. He waited for Arkady to tell him, because Arkady needed to say it.

Somehow.

Arkady mouthed the name. —Yagoda. And do you know who's going to shoot him?

Kostya nodded. *Vasily Blokhin.*

—So no, I am not under investigation, not officially, yet I am. And so are you. NKVD purges the country, and it purges itself. You know this. So *do not* give Boris Kuznets, or that stunted little weed Yury Stepanov, any more reasons to come after you.

—Kuznets? He gave me a gift. The perfume.

—Kinder to give you a *kulich* bomb. Come on, Little Tatar, did you really think that was a gift? It was a warning. Here, take my kerchief.

Kostya looked to the floor as he dried his face. —Warning me of what?

—Warning *me*, Kostya. Warning me that he knows you took Stepanov's car and is willing to press the issue.

—What the barrelling fuck has perfume got to do with the car?

—That woman! I know what she is, and I am trying to protect you!

—By beating me?

—When necessary, yes!

Kostya shook his head. —And if I told you I love her?

Fast and hard: the blows, the fall off the stool, the water in his nose and mouth, the kick to his back. Kostya curled up tight, and the shame of this treatment magnified the pain. He couldn't fight back. Not Arkady. Even as the pain paralyzed him, devoured him, he told himself he had a theoretical choice but could not, ever, fight back against Arkady.

Puddle water splashed.

The blows ceased. Kostya had no idea why. Perhaps the old man got tired. Or perhaps Kostya's squealed plea embarrassed them both.

—Steal me, steal me, steal me.

Arkady dragged Kostya away from the puddle and propped him against the desk. Then Arkady leaned next to him, and they both gasped, wheezed, grunted.

Wept.

Arkady shifted his weight, then put his arm around Kostya's shoulders. Flinching, Kostya wrenched his thoughts from the chaos of fury and pain as a drowning man might launch his face at the surface of the water: a sliver of a moment, desperation. Anything. Anything to breathe.

He smelled Arkady's vodka flask beneath his nose, took several good swallows. Then, as on the train to Moscow in 1918, he snuggled into Arkady's side.

Arkady almost whimpered. The memory of that long journey and its clear purpose felt so distant now. *Time grinds me down. Please, keep this moment still.*

Then Arkady recalled the wounds in Kostya's left shoulder and eased the pressure of his arm there. —Get rid of her. Your duty—

Kostya spat the word. —Duty.

—That alone could get you twenty fucking years. Yes, duty, if to nothing else, then to your own safety. How many times, over and over... Should I have left you in Odessa? Left you for the Germans who cleaned the streets? I saved you, Little Tatar. I fed you. I made sure you had a warm bed, and I got you new identity papers and an education. I navigated the intersecting planes of power with you, for you. Konstantin Arkadievich Nikto, bright star in NKVD, and you'll piss all over it?

—Invasion of the psyche.

—*What?*

—Bekhterev. The neurologist.

—Bekhterev, the unperson. Don't say his name so loud.

Kostya whispered. —He taught us a few classes when I was a cadet. At least, I think it was him. Physical energy forces blood to the brain and affects not just thought but autonomic behaviour. We can manipulate that by diverting the energy to other parts of the body, along the nervous systems. Induce pain and suffering in the body and you deplete the energies in the brain. That makes the brain vulnerable to suggestion, and then suggestion changes behaviour.

—Old knowledge.

—Bekhterev proved the science of it.

Arkady rubbed his forehead. —Yes, yes, we do this every day, but we do it here in the cells, not in our homes and to our own whores.

—She's not a whore.

—She's—

—She is *not* a whore, Arkady Dmitrievich. Understand me yet?

Arkady scowled.

So did Kostya. —You say I'm conducting an experiment on her. If you're arrested first, you tell them that's what I told you.

—No one's going to believe that!

—It doesn't matter what we believe. It's about stalling for time.

—Stalling death.

—Arkady Dmitrievich, please, I don't want you harmed by this.

—A little late.

—She remembers you and your house. She'd speak of that right away under interrogation.

Arkady waved a hand. —Kuznets attended that party. He'd cover it up.

—Are you sure?

Arkady said nothing.

Kostya's sigh shook.

Rubbing the back of his neck, Arkady tried to smile. *Tell him I know he was looking for the papers. Tell him.* —Tatar, I need to tell you something. I've got to leave Moscow for a bit.

Kostya stared at him. —What?

—Temporary transfer. My expertise is needed in a rural station, just outside Sverdlovsk. Yes, I snorted, too. Still, I've always wanted to see the Urals.

—What the barrelling fuck? We've *got* agents in Sverdlovsk. It will take you two or three days just to get there.

—And Kuznets wants to borrow my house while I'm gone.

Shit. —Kuznets is just a captain. He's banishing you. How does a captain banish a major?

—Maybe someone higher's involved. Maybe it's a test. And he did promise to look after the cats.

Her papers. Ask about her papers. —Those brutal old toms? I've seen them bring down crows. Look, I can give the damned cats their herring. I'll take care of the house.

—Kuznets wants to throw some parties. He owes some favours, he said. He's not getting along with his wife, and his children want to use his dacha.

Kostya shut his eyes. Chilled now, he felt his teeth rattle.

Arkady kissed the top of his head. —I'll keep you safe.

—From Sverdlovsk?

Arkady said nothing.

Ask about the papers. —Arkady Dmitrievich...

—What?

Kostya found he could not speak.

Careful not to jostle Kostya, Arkady stood up. —Get yourself together. Say you slipped on the stairs.

He left the cell door ajar.

In his head, Kostya called Arkady back, called his name over and over. His mouth did not move.

He staggered up and grabbed the desk for balance. The pain told him stories of deep bruises and ugly welts and how they would need many days to heal.

A long time since he last beat me. Long time.

Adapting his walk, he found his way to the wire-caged stairs. Other officers, busy with their tasks, did not notice him.

And if the old man disappears on his way to Sverdlovsk? In Sverdlovsk?

Kostya pretended to stumble and slip and forced himself not to protect his face as he fell. The stairs bashed his right cheekbone. His performance, while awkward, convinced those who heard it and now ran towards him. The other officers blamed the poor lighting on the stairs, then reminded him to fill out the correct accident report forms, because the paperwork had changed. Again. Nodding, Kostya insisted he'd be fine.

—Kostya, we've got a problem.

He kept his back to Temerity for the moment as he finished locking the flat door. —Oh?

—Please, listen to — what happened to your face?

—Nothing.

She followed him into the bedroom. —Nothing?

—I fell on the stairs. Narrow stairs, all covered in with cage wire, poorly lit. Easy to slip. If you're so worried about it, get me a cold compress.

Resenting his tone of command while yet wishing to help, she scowled at him, then complied.

He added a word. —Please.

After a moment, he joined her in the bathroom, wearing only his *galife* pants and undershirt.

Temerity reminded herself of just how many steps separated the bathroom from the bedroom. *Get the revolver, girl. You know how to use it.*

Then what?

Movements stiff, Kostya blocked the bathroom doorway and took off his undershirt. She stepped closer to the shower to make room, fascinated, appalled, by the welts on his back and face.

The water ran.

—Kostya, this is far more than a fall. Who did this?

Closing his eyes, he almost escaped the memory of how Arkady had asked him the same question in 1918. He accepted a cold cloth from her and held it to a bruise on his side. —You don't understand.

—What is there to understand? Someone beat you.

He leaned on the edge of the sink. —It's nothing.

—Was it Balakirev?

—What?

—Well, that's who came to visit me yesterday, and he was full of foul threats then. You're aware he knows I'm not Russian?

Kostya shut his eyes. —Yes.

She pressed a cold cloth to his bruised face, wincing as he flinched. —You're afraid of him.

—Like hell I am.

—Then walk away.

Kostya stared at her, eyes huge. —Walk away? Think, woman. Arkady Dmitrievich taught me how to survive. To learn that, I needed to learn obedience. Because I had the good luck to meet him and the good sense to obey him, I survived a revolution, civil war, and two famines. Yes, I fear him. I fear him for my own good. And so I obey, for my own good.

Temerity refreshed the compress and once more pressed it to Kostya's face. —Obedience without thought?

—Yes, without thought. Defiance only causes trouble.

—First thinking about one's obedience is not defiance.

—It can be. At best, it is false obedience.

—Kostya—

—True obedience works faster. Or does the weight of duty mean nothing to you?

She almost dropped the compress. —Don't you dare lecture me on duty. I choose to follow my duty, just as I choose everything else in my life.

He laughed. —Choose? You hauled your sweet little privileged British arse all the way to Spain and then Russia, because you chose it?

—Yes.

—Right. The dragon, Zmei Gorynich.

—Don't change the subject.

—I change nothing, Nadia. I merely show you what else exists to darken the argument. Now, Zmei Gorynich is a fat old beast, yet still very fierce. So you're sent into battle against him, and you're told, over and over, do not cut off his head. You're not told why. Then Zmei Gorynich roars at you, and it's the easiest thing in the world to cut off his head. So you defy your orders and cut off his head. What happens? Two heads grow back where there was one.

—Ah.

—Ah, what?

Temerity leaned back on the wall, crossing her arms. —The Hydra. Greek mythology. It's the basis for all civilization, all our stories.

—Zmei Gorynich is ancient. Slavic.

—Yes, I know. And it comes from the Greek myths.

—No, it doesn't.

—Heracles and the hydra, cut off one head and two more grow back. Greek mythology is where it all begins, Kostya.

He rolled his eyes. —The story is Russian. Just because Britain thinks civilization began with the ancient Greeks, no one else's history matters?

—That's not what I said.

Each turned from the other, frowning.

Then Temerity ran more cold water and this time pressed the compress to a welt on his back. —Zmei Gorynich, indeed. Well, you'll never take Saint Dzhordzh from me.

—Nadia, the old coat of arms for the city of Moscow was Drzhordzh and his shield fighting the dragon, yes? You have no claim. Oh, save me, Saint Dzhordzh, save me from my captivity!

He found this quite amusing, and, despite the pain in his back and face, he laughed.

Listening to Kostya's laughter, Temerity considered the sound of names. Dzhordzh in English: George, a beautiful name, steady, certain, oak and stone. A variant of the same name in Russian, Yury, made her think of a dragon's tail coiling. The sound of the name

Kostya: soothing. Oh, not as reliable as George, to be sure, but the very meaning, the roots of it: constancy. She laughed, too, as the absurdity of her own name pricked her. *Temerity Tempest West, because my Russian mother liked the sound of it. God's sake, who am I?*

—Nadia, Nadia.

Kostya ran his fingers through her hair, invading the curls.

Temerity let him. Even his calloused trigger finger felt pleasant against her scalp.

—Nadia, how did this happen?

A curl caught on his fingers.

—Ow. Kostya...

—Sorry. I wish...

His pause felt deliberate, some snare of language and time, something an interrogator might try. Yet it also felt genuine. Desperate.

—I wish we could just stay like this.

Temerity untangled the curl. —Not quite like this, surely. We'd have to get out of the bathroom at some point.

—A language school. If I could be anything else, I'd become a teacher. We could open a language school, and teach everyone how to communicate, yes? Pretend we've got a map of the world on this wall, here to here. I've got my finger on Moscow. Now, I'll close my eyes and point at another spot, and that's where we'll set up our language school.

His finger landed far west-southwest.

Recalling Neville Freeman's isochronic map, Temerity smiled. —The British Empire.

—The sun never sets.

—Newfoundland, to be precise. We'd have our work cut out for us. I understand they don't even speak English terribly well.

—We'll start with Esperanto. I don't know a word of Esperanto. But we'll get everyone at ease in Esperanto. Equal footing, everyone must learn the new language, no conqueror's tongue imposed, and then, once we can all invite one another to supper and figure out what we all like to eat in Esperanto, we can start learning one another's languages, and share the poetry.

Temerity kept still. *He's serious.* She took a breath to speak and almost told him about her plans for Kurseong House, decided on the steamer to Leningrad: a modern language school for girls and women, and one generous with scholarships.

—Nadia, imagine if one could not tell a lie in Esperanto. One can always lie, of course, even drawing figures in the sand, but imagine if one could not.

—I think it's better if we can choose not to lie.

—And you run from the discussion again. Choice, choice, choice. When we enjoy choice, we fail.

—No, we don't.

He shook his head. —Let me tell you a story. It's a winter day, completely foul. Sleet falls. You can't get warm. So you move to the hearth, or the stove, where someone cooks, oh, I don't know, a roast of pork.

—I love roasted pork.

—Do you, now? Good. Then my example will mean something. So you're cold, you're hungry, and you're safe indoors, not a big house, no mansion, but two storeys, three bedrooms, a parlour, a dining room, a kitchen, a sewing room, and a library.

—Not a mansion, you say.

—No, not at all, just a nice tidy house. Strong walls, good roof. Sleet rattles the glass and irritates everyone, because they're already hungry and impatient for dinner. A knock on the door. Some adolescent. You've encountered him before and consider him a troublemaker. He says he's cold and hungry. Do you choose to invite him in?

Recognizing the story, she hesitated. —It depends.

—Horseshit. You drive him away.

—No, it depends. Is he alone? Is he hungry?

—He says so, but you've got only his word for it. And he's not had a bath in weeks. He stinks. He's confused. He looks so angry. He's misplaced all the good manners he's learned, all the courtesy, yet he does not want to be vicious and bestial. He wants to be a man. Can you see that?

—Kostya, wait.

—You enjoy a full and open choice here. Let him in, and the consequence is you have less to eat. Turn him away, and the consequence is nothing at all. Will you let him in to share your meal?

—Yes.

—Liar.

Her cheeks burned. —Yes, I would.

—His eyes glint like limestone. Perhaps he's dangerous.

—He's tired.

—His nose runs like an infant's, and you wonder, is he too stupid to wipe?

—He's got no handkerchief. I'll help him clean up.

—He smells like a goat, his feet wrapped in rancid socks and crammed into leather boots too small for him, and your father orders you to turn this filthy little bastard out of doors. Do you still think you'd let him in?

—Don't shout at me!

He smirked. —It is you who shouts, Nadia. I've not raised my voice. Now, do you turn him away?

—I just . . .

—See? You try to deceive me, and you try to deceive yourself.

—No!

—You're unable to answer the question right away. No obedience to either your instinct to drive him away or to your conscience to let him in. And therefore, chaos.

—Kostya, please.

—I thank you for proving my point.

She strode past him into the bedroom, sat on the bed, and leaned forward, elbows on her knees. The holster lay in easy reach; she ignored it.

Kostya followed her, then knelt before her. —Nadia, you look like you're about to be sick.

—How did you do that? How did you make me feel so guilty over a boy who...

—Who doesn't exist?

—Stop!

She sounded like a prisoner pleading in a cell.

Kostya looked to the floor. —Nadia, I only want you to see how far more than choice influences our lives. There is also chance, or design. So much of it. I'm never sure what to call it.

—Right. Chance. Like Apollo chanced to see Daphne?

—Who the barrelling fuck are Apollo and Daphne?

—You want design? Bernini got it right in his sculpture. Chance has nothing to do with it. Apollo's fingers sink into Daphne's flesh. She twists away and screams, and her hands and hair are already transforming into twigs and leaves.

—Nadia, you've lost me.

She was weeping now. —Apollo is stronger and faster, and he *chooses* to rape Daphne. To prevent that, to try to save her, Daphne's father chooses to transform her into a tree. A God damned tree! She's not changing; she's being changed. Where is the chance or design for Daphne when Apollo and her father choose to do these things to her?

—You're not making sense.

—Oh, my God! Kostya, *listen* to me.

—No, it's you who needs to listen. Chance or design. We met by chance or design. You saved my arm, perhaps my entire fucking life, by chance. Was it design?

—What?

He pointed to his scars. —The sulpha pills. These wounds never got infected. How did choice play out there, hey?

—I chose to help you.

—You, no more a nurse than a stray dog, had a duty to help me. You obeyed your duty. Why? Design.

—Choice!

—How? Where is the choice in duty?

Her voice got very quiet, and it shook. —Yes, I had a duty to help you, because I was posing as a nurse. Yet, despite my other duties, I *wanted* to help you, because you are a human being. Is that not enough?

Kostya considered the duty of executions, those he'd carried out in Spain and at the *poligon*. Obedience had shown him the boundaries between life and death, even as he'd shut down his thoughts. *It's not murder,* Arkady had said, *when it's the law.* —True obedience hurts less, in the end.

Eyes shut, she rubbed her temples. —Leave me alone.

After a moment, he got to his feet and picked up his holster, shirt, and *gymnastyorka*. He carried these with him to the front room and started to dress just as Efim returned.

—Nadezhda, are you here? It's just me. I'm home early. We needed a Special Clean at the lab. Konstantin, good God. Who did this to you?

Stalin gazed from his portrait, face smooth, hair dark and lush, moustache splendid yet still shy of decadence. He looked off to the right, thoughtful, perhaps amused.

Cunning.

Beneath the portrait, Boris Kuznets gave a little sigh, almost a snort. —Konstantin Arkadievich, I'm worried.

Bruises aching, Kostya sipped his tea. He'd observed other senior lieutenants enter and leave this office for their own meetings with Comrade Captain Kuznets; none of them ever carried a glass of tea. Twice Kostya had reported for his meeting without tea, and Boris, already sipping his own, had sent him out to Evgenia to get some.

The tea and the perfume: tokens of favour and respect?

Then again, *poligon* duty: a test of loyalty, a punishment?

Kinder, Arkady had said, *to give you a* kulich *bomb.*

Boris ran his fingers over the *podstakannik* filigree. —Young Katelnikov. He spent the night with one of his prisoners as she lay unconscious.

—Oh, her, yes, but that was hardly improper, more of a vigil. He's still young, tender-hearted.

Boris waved his hand as he swallowed some tea. —We've not got time for tender hearts and vigils. Katelnikov should have asked for help from a senior officer, or volunteered to assist another team, or presented himself for filing work, anything, anything but sitting on his arse watching an old woman sleep. Did she die?

—Yes.

—Make sure he fills out right paperwork.

—He did.

—And another thing. Single men interrogating female prisoners without a witness.

—With respect, Boris Aleksandrovich, we have so many prisoners and not enough officers.

—If NKVD, or at least our one little department, doesn't maintain minimal standards of common decency, then who will?

From each according to his abilities. Kostya wished he had more sugar for his tea.

Boris nattered on about toughness and efficiency, and Kostya found himself saying yes, yes of course, Boris Aleksandrovich, I agree.

—I'm glad to hear it, because I am not making a request; I am giving you an order. Katelnikov is the weakest of the men under your command, so start with him. Once his performance is satisfactory, task him to train another weakling, and then they will train other weaklings, and soon we'll see escalated efficiency as each former weakling outperforms his trainer. Accompany Katelnikov to every interrogation. Make sure you have a third man at all times. Show him how it's done. Either the weaklings toughen up, or we let them fall away. Is that clear?

—Crystal.

—Dismissed.

Kostya got to his feet and saluted.

Eyes on his paperwork, Boris pointed at his door. —Leave it open when you go. I don't want to give the impression I keep secrets.

[ ]

PARRHESIA
Saturday 12 June –Thursday 22 July

In the animal kingdom, Efim had said, *it's adapt or die.* Reminding herself she might well be in Lubyanka, or Kolyma, or a grave, Temerity day by day, sometimes moment by moment, adapted to captivity. She imagined nerves leading from her brain to her hands, her feet, her mouth, stretched taut, fraying. While Kostya still looked after obtaining food and bringing it to the flat, both he and Efim seemed to expect Temerity to cook and clean, as if paying rent with labour. Efim, still mistrustful of her and perhaps afraid, avoided her more and more, as he might avoid a stray dog in the street. Twice in two days she begged Kostya for a pencil and paper so she could sketch; he refused, saying her sketches could become evidence. His point, she acknowledged, lay beyond dispute, yet she asked him a third time. He refused a third time, shouting. She practised jiu-jutsu, and she washed and mended her clothes. She darned Efim's socks, with no particular zeal or skill, often throwing the work against a wall; the darning mushroom would roll away. She listened, rapt, to radio bulletins on Amelia Earhart's flight. The suffocation of skirts and expectations, the gleams of ambition and duty, the joyous risk of navigation: Earhart understood. In one three-day stretch, surprising herself with her new tolerance, Temerity started and finished a one-litre bottle of vodka. Kostya, annoyed by this sudden lack, turned his irritation into a performance of martyrdom and quickly obtained another bottle. After that, Temerity declined vodka and often wrecked her sleep with too much strong tea. On these nights she cleaned: cupboards, drawers, floorboards, and sinks. She rearranged the dishes. She unfolded all the towels and clothes in the *stenka*, folded them again, put them back. As the sun rose, she studied the patterns of shadow and light on the walls. Another night survived without a raid, another night endured without surrendering to her fears, she would sigh and then crawl into the bed next to Kostya, who seemed to sleep like the dead.

In truth, he slept like a man worried and in pain, mind busy with nightmares of the banal: seeking lost files, seeking Evgenia Ismailovna as Boris Kuznets bellowed for paperwork, seeking Arkady in the Lubyanka basement. When finished his shifts, he would take longer and longer walks on his way home, sometimes hoping to return to his flat and discover Nadia had disappeared, hoping for an end to this ordeal. His walks often took him to Arkady's house. He worked out elaborate plans to stalk Boris and then break into Arkady's house when Boris was elsewhere. Instead, he found himself exhausted from coaching Matvei Katelnikov and yet more paperwork.

Matvei did improve. Day by day, Kostya demonstrated proven interrogation techniques, most of them physical, demurring when Matvei asked about the business of offering cigarettes to women, the Nikto Touch. Soon Matvei could lead an interrogation, Kostya and a third man mere assistants. Kostya also drilled Matvei on his paperwork, pointing out that the better his reports and forms, the less work for his commanding officer. —One day, Matvei, paperwork might save you.

Kostya sought proof of any change in Matvei, something to match his new brutality, a coarseness of the voice, perhaps, or of the face. Matvei remained wide-eyed and sweet, boyish, smooth. Boris Kuznets congratulated them both.

One afternoon, Matvei invited Kostya to exercise with him at the gym after work, and Kostya, refusing to think of Misha and how they'd competed, yet thinking of nothing else, agreed.

Over and over, Matvei got Kostya in a leg lock or wrestled him to the mat.

A coach eyeballed their technique. —Comrade Nikto, Comrade Katelnikov is smaller, and he uses your own weight against you.

—I'd guessed that much.

The coach pointed to Kostya's scars. —Have you adapted?

—My shoulder's fine.

—Then why do you lose?

Sweat stinging his eyes, Kostya took a deep breath.

The coach knelt down beside him. —I can show you some newer *sombo* moves. I've taught injured Red Army men, as well as NKVD.

—I'm not injured.

—No, no, of course not, those scars are merely cosmetic. You ass. The whole point of *sombo* is skill over strength. Now, show some brains and stay behind.

Kostya obeyed, and the hard exercise allowed him to forget the galling secret of a British woman hidden in his flat. *Right here,* he told himself, *right now.* The coach defeated him, over and over; sweat flew; Kostya defeated the coach.

—Again.

They grappled; the coach won.

—Again.

They grappled; Kostya won.

—Again. Again. Again.

Both men lay on their backs, limp and breathing hard.

Kostya turned his head to face the coach. —Thank you, comrade. Thank you.

Hair and face slick, the coach grinned. —My pleasure. Now, never forget: an injured man must fight not just harder but smarter. I know, I know, you are not injured. But, should you ever become so, you know what to do.

—Yes.

Matvei, showered and back in uniform, stood over them.
—Comrade Senior Lieutenant Nikto, I must go.
—You're still here?
A flicker of hurt in Matvei's eyes, then a deferential nod: he extended a hand. —Let me help you up.

That night, the flat smothering hot, Kostya and Efim argued. Efim wanted official leave to visit his wife in Leningrad; such leave must be approved by the signature of Arkady Balakirev. Temerity, reading *Fathers and Sons* again, curious about the underlined passages, worked to ignore the quarrel.

Kostya wiped sweat from his face and smeared it into his hair. —Efim, I'm sorry, Balakirev can't be reached right now.
—Why?
—He's away.
—Where?
Kostya shook his head.
Efim left the flat, slamming the door.
Kostya snatched Turgenev from Temerity's hands. —You hide behind that book.
—Oh, do I? Funny, I thought I hid in this flat out of necessity while you hid behind cowardice and excuse.
Stung, Kostya almost called her a bitch. —What cowardice?
—Get me to the British Embassy.
—I can't do that.
—So you've said.
—Nadia, you have no papers and no shoes. I can't take you outside without papers and shoes.
—And whose fault it is that I have neither papers nor shoes? Cowardice and excuse.
He promised, insisted, swore he knew the location of her passport

and papers. Maybe, he muttered far from her hearing, just maybe, he could sign out a car and drive her to the British Embassy, papers be fucked. The desire and then the decision roared up, stalled. Signing out an NKVD car to cross the Moskva on the new Bolshoy Moskvoretsky Bridge, eight lanes of radiant future, and drop an undocumented foreign national at her embassy, yes, well, that might cause a few problems. Aloud, he said he would save her. That night, he believed it.

Temerity no longer believed. The day she surrendered her faith in Kostya, though not her hope, she also surrendered her refusals and allowed his touch. She'd just interrupted his medical consultation with Efim, and it felt intimate, shocking. Both men looked at her in some guilt as Efim pumped liquid into Kostya's vein, and the scars on Kostya's left ear and shoulder flushed deep red. When Efim left, Temerity traced her fingers over Kostya's scars, and Kostya turned to kiss her. He tried nothing else.

Temerity asked Efim about Kostya's wounds a few nights later.

Efim shook his head. —Shrapnel. He's lucky he didn't bleed to death or lose the arm. Or die of infection.

—Would a gunshot do something similar? One that glanced the shoulder?

—Depending on the wound, likely much worse, unless the patient got to a hospital in time. And then there's infection.

Her giggle sounded young and silly, nervous. —I mean, would it leave scars.

He peered at her. —That, too.

So, considering duty, the next evening Temerity murmured something Kostya wanted to hear. —I need you.

—What?

—Please.

After a moment, he stroked her shoulders, kissed her neck. —You smell so good.

—You finished all those sulpha pills?

—What? Yes, yes, of course.

She clasped his fingers and guided his hands.

He asked her twice, thrice. —Are you sure?

She touched his lips with the tips of her fingers.

He said it twice, thrice. —I love you.

He surprised her: urgent, yes, but also attentive, and as he kissed her thighs, she cried out.

He stopped, looked up. —Did I hurt you?

—No, no, it's fine, I just...

—Then let me speak in tongues.

—What?

He resumed.

She laughed. Then she gasped.

Later, Kostya woke up with terrible pain in his shoulder. He stifled a cry and shifted in the bed. Silent beside him and wide awake, Temerity listened to him breathe and recalled a dusty old play. *Fornication: but that was in another country, and besides...*

The second time, Temerity suggested, then insisted, that Kostya remain mostly on his back. Dubious, he acquiesced, and afterward slept much better.

After the third time, she asked for shoes.

Kostya shook his head. He could hide shoes in another package, wrap them up with his laundry, perhaps. Getting shoes up the stairs: not impossible. Getting Nadia back down the stairs and outside? —I don't know how to get you past the watchwoman. The new one, oh, Nadia, she doesn't miss a thing, who lives in which flat, which children are in which grade at school. Yesterday she told me I was late bringing my dirty laundry to the service this week, and then she complimented Efim on his haircut. I never noticed he got a haircut. Did you?

Temerity shut her eyes, unable to escape the memory of Elena Petrovna calling on Stalin as if calling on God.

Then Kostya spoke about his language school dream. —Maybe Finland? Get to Leningrad first. We'd have to swim. How are you in cold water? You said you can speak some Finnish.

Recalling Mikko Toppinen's *Babel Interior*, Temerity smiled with sadness and shook her head. —Danish. And nowhere near enough.

The days wore on. The flat got hotter and hotter, cooling at night only to ramp up at dawn, and Temerity always felt hungry — for food, for Kostya, for fresh air, for every word, however difficult, in *Pravda*, *Izvestia*, and *Krokodil*.

Kostya looked at her in growing worry, wishing he could explain why he dared not search Arkady's house, now occupied by Boris Kuznets. —A few more weeks, Nadia, and I can get this settled.

The night of the second of July, she had her first recurring dream of being lost in a flower garden, the flowers growing not from soil but flesh. The giant from *Ruslan and Lyudmila* pursued her. In the morning, the radio announcer, a woman, shared a sombre bulletin: Amelia Earhart and Fred Noonan had disappeared.

Efim worried more each day, each week. He and Kostya continued to use a laundry service, yet Nadezhda Ivanovna washed her clothes by hand. Efim and Kostya continued to come and go for work almost every day; Nadezhda remained in the flat. Efim could hear almost everything in that flat, every little whimper and thrust. What he could not hear: the words in those urgent whispers.

Who is she?

So Efim spent more and more time at the lab. A breakthrough, he'd say, we're near a breakthrough.

Sometimes, when Kostya worked a night shift, Efim and Temerity sat up late, talking. He told her funny stories from his time in medical school, and he told her about courting Olga. He even told her about some of his time on the armoured train during the civil war, omitting the coercion. Sometimes he described a deathbed vigil. He called it medicine's brittle privilege.

Had Olga's first pregnancy gone to term, the child would be about Nadezhda's age.

—Thank you, Nadezhda Ivanovna. I've always found it easier to talk to women.

Temerity smiled, said nothing.

Near mid-July, Efim confessed a great unhappiness: no letters from Olga, over a month now. His restless fingers hid his mouth as he spoke.

Temerity felt chilled, and her Russian pronunciation slipped. She sounded like an foreigner. —I'm so sorry.

Sighing, Efim shut his eyes and refused to remember the first morning, when Nadezhda Ivanovna asked for something in what sounded like English. *I heard no such thing.*

Temerity took his hand in both of hers, and he flinched.

She smiled. —Tell me about your wedding.

Efim looked away. He should refuse, at least demur, yet in that moment he wanted to think of nothing else, and she still held his hand. The wedding. All the food. The funny drunken guests. The joy. —You've not got the time to listen me ramble.

She let go of his hand and sat back, gesturing to the walls. —I'm not going anywhere.

He blinked several times. Then he started the story, this time entering it sidelong with observations of Olga's maiden aunt. —Of course, she's dead now, but Valentina Vladmirovna, like most women I know, had more backbone and fire than twenty young men...

Then he grimaced, as if in pain.

—Efim?

—I don't deserve this.

—Sometimes letters get lost.

—I mean, you. I don't merit your kindness. At the lab, we…test things. Compounds. Drugs. People die. It's no hospital. They're prisoners. They suffer, and they die. And then I tell myself that compared to Kolyma's slow death by hunger and cold, it's a mercy.

He waited for Temerity to sneer, to cry out in revulsion.

Instead, she took his hand again.

Efim sobbed. —I never wanted this. How can you even look at me? How can I do these things?

After a long moment, she answered him. —You're trapped. You want to survive, Efim Antonovich, and you're trapped.

He placed his other hand over hers. —If your parents had not named you for hope, Nadezhda, then they could have named you for mercy.

Temerity looked toward the door. —Thank you.

Kostya woke Efim later that evening to ask for a higher dose of morphine. —Target practice. It always hurts after target practice.

—Where is Balakirev?

—I told you, out of town.

—Perhaps you can go without a dose tonight.

Kostya shut his eyes. —It hurts.

—Will you be speaking with Balakirev anytime soon?

—How many times do I have to say it? He's out of town.

—The moment he's back, then.

Kostya studied Efim a moment. Tell him? Confess his stark fears that Arkady might not return?

Efim held the morphine ampoule to the light. —I write Olga twice a week, yet I've gotten nothing back. It's been too long. Surely someone else can approve my leave?

—If Balakirev's your case officer, then you simply must wait for Balakirev. I can't help you. I'm sorry.

Efim stared at him.

Kostya looked to the floor. —I can make inquiries here at the Moscow office, have them passed on to Leningrad.

—You'd do that?

—Of course.

—Won't that cause you trouble?

—I'll handle it.

After a moment, Efim lashed the tourniquet to Kostya's arm. —Make a fist. Good, good. And you'll tell Balakirev I need to see him?

—The moment I see him myself, yes.

Efim gave Kostya the injection.

Temerity overheard, and once Kostya closed the bedroom door, she took a breath to ask him about her papers.

Kostya placed his *gymnastyorka* and *portupeya* in the closet. He tucked the holster and gun beneath his pillow. —I am so tired. What is it, Nadia?

—Nothing.

Taking care not to jostle his shoulder, he lay on the bed. Soon, he dozed.

Too hot to sleep, the open window letting in only noise and not fresh air, Temerity stared at the ceiling and listened to nightingales. Other voices interfered: memories of Kostya and Misha at the clinic, the desperate parents in Bilbao, Cristobal Zapatero.

Freckles on your eyelids.

Can she speak Russian?

Kneel. Now!

Señorita Inglesa, Señorita Inglesa . . .

I like strawberries.

Sweating, she sat up, got her breath, listened.

Kostya snored; nightingales sang; the ceiling squeaked as a neighbour on the floor above paced his flat.

She hid her face in her hands.

The following night, after assuring Efim he'd made the enquiries to Leningrad, lying, Kostya spoke of his grandfather. —I don't know why I've been thinking about him so much. Today someone mentioned Koshchei the Deathless, and I almost got lost in remembering how my grandfather told that story. Every time he told it, he added something new. He said that we need to hear stories again and again, stories, especially the scary ones, because stories are how we rehearse for our lives. I always told the boys that.

Efim welcomed the distraction from his consideration of Nadezhda. Her manner of speech, the gentle accent at once suggesting Leningrad and also some other land, her bare legs and feet, all so easy to dismiss, and yet... He forced himself to look at Kostya. —Which boys?

—At one of the children's homes. I would visit and read them books, tell them stories.

Efim peered at him. —Really?

—Yes. Why not?

—I just don't picture NKVD officers doing that sort of thing.

Kostya inclined his head, acknowledging this. —Well, it has been a while. I spend most of my time listening to stories now. Confessions, I mean.

Efim raised his eyebrows.

Smile strained, Kostya took Temerity's hand as though inviting her to dance. He kissed her fingertips, and she did not pull away.

Later, Temerity turned around on the bed, got up on her knees, and faced the tiny open window. Birdsong pierced the rattle of the city. —So many nightingales?

Ignoring his memory of the coded messages in Spain, the phrase from Turgenev to signal liquidation, *even nightingales can't live by song alone,* Kostya knelt up beside Temerity. He wrapped his left arm around her shoulders, wincing. —Ilya Muromets fought Solovei, the thief who hid in the forest. When Solovei whistled like a nightingale, the woods fell flat. Ilya fought him, bound him, dragged him back to the tsar. You're trembling. Hush, hush, you're safe.

Temerity snuggled into him. *He's so warm.*

Curls tickled Kostya's face as he kissed the top of Temerity's head.
—Nightingales sing louder in the cities.
—Why?
Kostya kissed her again. —So they might be heard.

[ ]

FERTILITY RITES
Friday 23 July

Examining Kostya's shoulder, Efim used the word *narkomania*.

In the bathroom, where the shower ran, the stall empty, Temerity pressed an ear to the door and eavesdropped.

Efim said it again. —Narkomania, but not the morphine.

—Then to what am I addicted, Comrade Doctor?

—Deceit. Something's wrong with that woman, and yet you keep her here, when it's dangerous for us all.

—It's nothing. Once Balakirev gets back in town, I can...

—Even self-deceit. You grope for it as a drunkard for the bottle, or a child scared of monsters for his blanket.

—It is not deceit!

Kostya took a breath.

It's hope. I can't be addicted to hope.

Efim shook his head. —You'll kill us all. As sure as if you pulled the trigger yourself.

—Efim, wait.

Temerity placed her hand beneath the shower stream to break up the flow of water and convince the men she stood under it, unable to hear them.

Kostya emerged from Efim's room and stood near the bathroom door, by the telephone.

Temerity got the rest of her body beneath the stream and managed not to cry out as the water blasted cold, then hot.

Kostya returned to his bedroom. —It's fine. She can't hear us.

The piece of soap melted as water hit it. Temerity hurried to finish, and she recalled her Aunt Min standing beside her as she soaked in a bath in 1933. Min had returned from managing the West family business interests in Darjeeling to coach and chaperone mother-less Temerity through her debut and first social season. Temerity dismissed the entire exercise as a cattle market, mere theatre. Min agreed, then called it very necessary theatre, prattling on about white dresses and dance cards, calendars and rubber petticoats, the precise placement of ostrich feathers in one's hair, and the deferent elegance of the curtsy due to the king.

—Min, why?

—Because one must curtsy to the king.

—I know, but—

Min passed her niece a towel. —Come out, dear, you're pruning.

—Screw for survival, is that it? Marry some dolt of an aristocrat who's got money in the bank yet nothing in his head?

—An aristocrat with money in the bank? They're all skint, dear.

—Fine, fine, money tied up in the estate, and then nothing in his head.

—Surely one of these young men has some intelligence.

—None on my dance card. Min, I don't want to be the wife of Lord Gormless. I don't want to be a society hostess. I'll die.

Min helped blot Temerity's hair. —Die of boredom, yes, I shouldn't wonder, and all those languages you speak shall wither on the vine, drop to the soil, and rot, unnoticed.

—Min!

—Temmy, my dear, you know how your father serves king and country. Have you given much thought to how I do so?

—What?

Min peeked over Temerity's shoulder and met her niece's gaze in the mirror. —It needn't be the cattle market.

Only later, travelling through India for several months with Min, did Temerity discard the last of her contempt. Min had fooled her, as she fooled many people. Lady Minerva West, the avid photographer who now owned and used, at great expense, both a movie and a still camera and plenty of colour film, Min the sweet older lady who charmed others and got them to open up by speaking to them in their own language, Min who supplied long and detailed reconnaissance reports, photographs, and movies to the Secret Intelligence Service. No dotty memsahib here.

When Temerity admitted her mistake, Min only smiled. —I told your father you'd travel well, and that it might knock some sense into you. Now, remember what I said about making your mind like a steamer trunk, many compartments. No matter what you must pretend to be, so long as you remember your duty and your best self, you'll do fine.

Travel well. The phrase signalled more than grace under seasickness. On a rope bridge in Darjeeling, Temerity stared down between slats at the chasm below, aware of menstrual blood flowing into the gauze tampon Min had taught her to roll. Nothing to it, really. One bled, and one lived, all in the same moment. Temerity had reminded herself of that bridge during her last period at the end of May, as she arrived in Moscow, miserable with cramps.

May.

Breasts aching, Temerity traced lines on her left shoulder to mirror Kostya's scars. Min's voice: *Remember your duty and your best self.* Her own voice, on the Bilbao docks: *Don't let them forget their Spanish names.* Her fingers traced shorter lines on her shoulder now, letters of the Latin alphabet, her initials: TTW, TTW, TTW.

[ ]

CHILD. OF THE STRUGGLE
Saturday 24 July

A large and suffocating sound, yet disciplined and contained: swish-slap, swish-slap, swish-slap. Frowning, Kostya strode around a corner.

He knew he should recognize the noise, but it seemed off, even eerie, lighter than it should be. Then he saw why. Row on row on row of attractive and muscular young women dressed in navy blue shorts and white blouses marched past, their thin white shoes hitting the street in unison. The women all wore their hair in the same style, cut near the top of the ears, parted on the left. Brunettes, blondes, and redheads, hair straight, wavy, curly, upturned faces intent on some distant ideal, seemed to blend into one Soviet woman.

A practice march then, a rehearsal for a parade. He must wait. Even if possessed of the necessary rudeness to try, one could never cut across such a phalanx.

The women marched on, perhaps a hundred of them, in perfect formation, smiling, quiet.

Kostya waited another moment after the end of the parade passed, then crossed the street to a large house repurposed into Home of the Child of the Struggle Moscow Number Two Supplemental Number Three. The building looked even more dilapidated than it had the last time Kostya saw it, as though no one had so much as lifted a hammer for repair work because permits lay hidden on a bureaucrat's desk.

Over a year and a half since his last visit. He considered Efim's words: *I just don't picture* NKVD *officers doing that sort of thing.*

He knocked on the front door, and a woman in her early twenties let him in.

Kostya took off his cap and gave the woman a light bow to signal courtesy and, he hoped, the fact he'd not come to arrest her. —Thank you, comrade. I noticed the old sign on the lawn is gone.

Her voice wobbled. —What sign was that, Comrade Officer?

—The one identifying this building. Has the name changed?

—No, we just...no longer have a sign. We burnt it. In February. For firewood, I mean. But it wasn't my idea. I protested. With vigour. It was noted.

—I see.

—Vigour.

—Of course, of course.

She took a breath. —How can I help you today, Comrade Officer?

—I used to visit regularly starting in '33, before your time, once a week to tell stories to the boys, read to them. *How a Little Old Woman Obtained Ink,* that book was a great favourite.

—I did not work here in '33.

—Yes, that's fine. One of the boys—

The woman clasped her hands together before her waist. —I was still in school. Please.

—Yes, I understand. On one of my visits, I met an extraordinary young man. Timur. I don't recall his surname.

—Neizvestny?

—No.

—We've no one called Timur here.

—I'm sure he must have graduated by now. I remember him because he'd decided to keep an archive.

Her fingers tightened; her voice sounded airy and unconcerned. —An archive?

—Yes, records of each of the boys, their pasts, how they ended up here. Their stories. I thought it showed initiative and compassion. I'd like to see it.

—Comrade Officer, I have no idea what you mean.

—He wrote...

—Yes, I understand that, but I promise you, we have no archive. You may search the classrooms, if you wish.

—No, I—

—Please. Search them. We have nothing to hide.

—That's not why I'm here. The one Timur, can you tell me where he is?

Sweat shone on her forehead. —We have no one called Timur.

—Yes, so you said. Right here, right now, you have no Timur. But he did live here. Could you check your files? Ask another worker? Perhaps he's gone into the army.

—I can ask, but...

Kostya put his cap back on his head, tugged it into place. —Show me the files.

—Comrade Officer, please.

—Look, I first met him in '33, and he told me he'd arrived in '31. You must have records going back at least that far.

—Yes, of course, but—

—Then let me see them!

She paled.

He cleared his throat, softened his voice. —Please, comrade.

He followed her up the stairs to the room where in 1933 he'd once interfered with a French lesson. He'd noticed the teacher's error on the blackboard in a sample sentence. Timur had noticed the same error. His back to the door and the presence of a visitor, Timur raised his hand, stood in all courtesy, and asked about it. The teacher abused Timur for his presumption and called him names, finishing with dirty Tatar *bezprizornik*. Sergeant Nikto, his boots tapping on the floors, those taps like cracks of ice in the sudden silence around him, strode to the blackboard, praised Timur's knowledge and courtesy, erased the teacher's sentence and rewrote it without the mistake. Then he left the room. After telling stories to the younger boys, Kostya sought Timur, only to discover that Timur also sought him. Outside in the cool air, shielded by the racket of the younger boys at play, Timur and Kostya smoked, Kostya supplying the cigarettes, and Timur told Kostya about his archive.

The floor showed scars from bolts and screws; no student desks remained. A new portrait of Stalin hung above the blackboard; another portrait, identical, faced the first, hanging on the back wall above the door.

The woman cleared her throat, and Kostya flinched. He'd forgotten her. Then she opened the left-hand drawer of the teacher's desk and showed him the stack of ledgers within. —Our registers.

He knelt and lifted out all the ledgers at once. —Thank you, comrade. I'll come down when I am done.

As she strode away, boys in the next room recited multiplication tables along with their teacher. —Three times one gives three. Three times two gives six.

One page for each new boy, entered by year of arrival.

Nineteen thirty-seven. Nineteen thirty-six.

The pupils continued reciting. —Three times three gives nine. Three times four gives twelve.

Nineteen thirty-five: a page torn out. One page equalled one boy. Kostya said it aloud. —Sloppy.

Nineteen thirty-four.

—Three times six…

Nineteen thirty-three, two pages torn out. Two boys.

Oh, come on.

Nineteen thirty-two.

—Three time seven gives twenty-one.

Nineteen thirty-one, one page gone. He checked the other 1931 entries, found no page for Timur.

They tore him out. They tore out every mention of him.

And at least three more boys. Disappeared.

Where? If they'd gone to the army, they'd not be torn out. If they'd died in the orphanage, there should be some record of that. Wait. Drug experiments? Kolyma? Shot?

They're just boys.

Kostya placed his open left hand on the ledger, as if to push it away. He knew how torn pages could mean torn lives. He'd done it himself, if not with bullets then with complicities of paperwork. Until his travels to Spain, he'd not really considered the brutality of erasing names, of creating the unperson. In Madrid, staring at bomb rubble and scattered clothes and flesh, Kostya wanted to name the dead. People ran past him, infants and belongings clutched to their chests.

Shifting rubble clinked and rattled; blood pooled. Still, Kostya stood there, ears filled with the snarl of engines as more planes approached. He tasked himself: if he could not name the dead, he must count the scraps of fabric. Then he discovered he'd forgotten how to count.

The boys continued. —Three times ten gives thirty.

Kostya backed away from the desk and collided with the blackboard. Stalin, Father to All the Soviet Children, gazed upon him.

—Three times eleven gives thirty-three.

Scowling, Kostya replaced the ledgers in the desk drawer. Then he spotted a small book. He remembered seeing it here before: Russian translations of selected sonnets by William Shakespeare, English on the left-hand page, Russian on the right.

He looked up.

Stalin held his stare.

—Three times twelve gives thirty-six.

And what, my orphans, gives you '37?

He stashed the book of sonnets in his pouch and almost ran from the room.

Hands still clasped together before her waist, the woman waited for him by the front door.

Kostya nodded to her. —Thank you, comrade. You've been most helpful.

Jaw clenched, she nodded back.

He knew she'd not sleep well, and he wished he could explain that he'd not be sending colleagues. Pointless. NKVD well might bang on that door tonight, whatever Senior Lieutenant Nikto did or did not say.

A form darted from an upper window; someone else watched him in fear.

Kostya sighed. *I swear, I meant you no harm.*

[ ]

FEME SOLE 3
Sunday 25 July

As Kostya eased the bedsheet away from her, Temerity looked as pale and drawn as she had the first morning in his bed. —Go to hell.

Kostya blinked a few times, squinted. —What the barrelling fuck is the matter with you?

She tugged the sheet back over herself. —Don't touch me. I never said you could touch me.

For weeks now, he'd stroked, caressed, kissed, cuddled, nibbled, and pinched as he desired, and she'd always melted into his arms. And now, one soft touch on her shoulder, and this screech? —Hey, I've not once forced myself on you. You spread your legs all on your own.

—Must you be so crude?

—Well, what would you like me to call it? Natural impulses? Sexual intercourse and all its biological imperatives?

—Did you ask me, ask me even once, if I truly wanted to?

—Wanted to, what?

She made a noise of disgust and rolled over, her back to him.

His lips brushed her ear. —I think with you hiding here all safe and sound in my flat, it's the least—

He didn't finish his sentence; his impact with the floor interrupted him. Lying there on his back, he considered how this tiny woman had kicked him out of his own bed, when last night, delighted with the book of sonnets he'd brought, she'd wept and snuggled into his arms. Then she'd found the sonnet she'd recited at the clinic and read it to him again and again, helping him understand the tangly English.

> *Take all my loves, my love, yea, take them all;*
> *What hast thou then more than thou hadst before?*

No love, my love, that thou mayst true love call;
All mine was thine before thou hadst this more.
Then, if for my love thou my love receivest,
I cannot blame thee for my love thou usest;
But yet be blamed, if thou thyself deceivest
By wilful taste of what thyself refusest.
I do forgive thy robbery, gentle thief,
Although thou steal thee all my poverty;
And yet love knows, it is a greater grief
To bear love's wrong than hate's known injury.
Lascivious grace, in whom all ill well shows,
Kill me with spites, yet we must not be foes.

That was last night. Right here, right now, she'd just refused his advance and booted him from his own bed.

Rising from the floor, Kostya murmured first in English, then Russian. —By wilful taste of what thou thyself refusest? I admit, Nadia, sometimes you've got beauty in your language. Sometimes. But what does it mean?

Temerity tugged the sheets to her chin. —Efim is just finishing in the shower. Go get your injection.

—I don't need it.

She gave him an exasperated look. —The scars on your ear flush when you lie.

[ ]

SERVICE WEAPON
Monday 26 July

—Kostya.

Vadym sounded not pleased but annoyed as he turned from dismissing the choir. His greeting seemed to fall at Kostya's feet.

Kostya addressed him as Vadym Pavlovich and waited for the

choir members to file out of the room. Boris gave Kostya a look of knowing sympathy.

Vadym closed the door. —Twice you've disappointed me, Kostya.

—I'm sorry?

—No, when you apologize to me, you make it statement, not a question. Back in June, you forgot to tell Arkady about the supper invitation.

—Oh.

—And last night you forgot to meet me at the concert.

—Dima—

—I told you last week, Tchaikovsky, the full *1812*, box seats, even if we did have to share them with Kuznets and one of his mistresses. It took me weeks to get those tickets. And for the encore, a balalaika troupe performed *Flight of the Bumblebee*.

—Sounds amazing.

—A little busy on the balalaikas, maybe, but where the hell were you?

Kostya peered at him. Vadym never raised his voice, not with him. With Misha, yes, a thousand times, but he always spoke to Kostya in a gentle manner, even when in rebuke.

Vadym found that tone again. —I could swear something worries you. It's got its teeth in your neck and shakes you about.

Kostya found a most plausible lie, plausible because it formed part of the truth. —I'm worried about Arkady Dmitrievich. I've heard nothing.

—He's due back tomorrow.

—What?

—I got a telegram last night from some town I'd never heard of, likely not even on the map. I'd planned to show it to you at the concert.

—He's well?

Vadym snorted. —Did he look well when he left?

—But he is coming back.

—Yes. I doubt he can talk about it. But you'd know about that.

Misha's name hung in the silence between them.

—Dima, I'm due upstairs.

Vadym turned his back to Kostya and gathered up sheet music. Kostya watched how Vadym inspected each piece of paper and then added it to his pile. Each time he added a sheet, he tapped the edge of the stack against his belly. Once he'd collected all the sheets, he tapped the papers straight on a table. —You said you had to go.

Head bowed, Kostya returned to the corridor and, instead of climbing the stairs to his department, he descended. He would visit the garage, just to check if any new clerks worked in vehicle requisitions. A new clerk, unfamiliar with various officers and protocols, just might make it easier for Kostya, just might lend him the courage to sign out a car and then take an unauthorized trip to the British Embassy. Maybe.

In the dappled sunlight of the corridor of Laboratory of Special Purpose Number Two, Efim read over the chart. —Good results. We've cut the time down from fifteen minutes to just under eight minutes. I am impressed, comrades.

The younger doctors surrounding him, following him, murmured gratitude and deference.

He dismissed them with his usual courtesy. —Please, carry on. I'll join you later. I have some reports to finish.

Inside his office, Efim shut the door and leaned his back against it. Eight minutes from injection to death. Memory harassed him: conditions in the hospitals in 1918 and '19, no heating, no food. At Special Purpose Number Two, one enjoyed sunshine, a constant supply of tea in the monstrous samovar, free lunches at a nearby cafeteria. and clean lavatories. The prisoners, however, remained filthy and starved.

Efim wanted to bathe his face in cold water.

Or perhaps drown himself in it.

A gentle knock. —Comrade Dr. Scherba?

I've given dying patients that final dose of morphine. Is it not the same as what we do here? Morphine can be a poison, too.

—Comrade Doctor?

I'm just one man.

I'm full of shit.

—Comrade Dr. Scherba, please. May I speak with you?

Forgetting how a visitor could discern rough shadows through the frosted glass window in the door, could see him leaning there, Efim hurried to his desk. —Comrade Dr. Novikova, come in.

Anna Nikolaieva Novikova closed the door behind her and stood before Efim's desk. He'd avoided her, speaking to her only when necessary. Young and slim, with strong features that surpassed mere prettiness, she elicited from Efim both desire and guilt.

Scent wafted, Krasnaya Moskva, the same perfume that Olga wore. Efim wished he could shake the temptation out of his head, like water trapped behind an eardrum. Instead, he gestured to the chair before his desk. —Please, sit down.

She cleared her throat. —Comrade, I consider it a privilege to be working here.

Efim recalled her file, her excellent grades in medical school, and the psychological tests indicating fierce capacities for loyalty and hard work. —And we're lucky to have you.

—I wanted...well, I'm sure you've heard these stories a thousand times, the day the child decides to become a doctor.

Efim nodded. —Your story?

—Diphtheria. Myself and my younger brothers. The doctor held a lantern to my brothers' mouths and told my mother he saw the plaques in the throat. I saw them, too. He noticed me up and about, and he showed me. Then he told my mother to pray, if it gave her comfort. I would likely recover, but the boys looked bad.

—Blunt.

—Kind, in its way. My mother loved him for it. She knew what swollen necks meant. And yes, my brothers died, and I lived, and the doctor came to the funeral and apologized for what he called the obscure workings of God. At no point did he patronize my mother or belittle her grief. He only wished he could have eased our pain.

—And that's when you decided to become a doctor?

—No. I hated him. I blamed doctors for everything. Until I was about fifteen, when I saw another doctor attend a child who...

She scowled, took a breath.

—Who had suffered unfortunate malnutrition during a period of food difficulties. A common ailment. That doctor was brusque, and he had dark circles beneath his eyes. He delivered only bad news, over and over: the child will die; the child will die; the child will die.

—Yes, no one wants to hear it.

—No one wants to say it. He tried. Those children were too far gone. They couldn't even swallow water.

Efim glanced at the door, saw no shadow on the frosted glass. —The food difficulties must have been particularly acute there.

Anna read the poster on the wall behind Efim: *Only Those Who Work Deserve to Eat.* She'd seen many copies. —Yes, particularly acute. An exceptional scene.

Neither spoke for a moment.

Then Anna lowered her voice. —My problem, Comrade Dr. Scherba, is that here, in this place, I can ease no pain. I can't even acknowledge it. I do harm. So I must resign.

Efim let out a long breath. —Anna Nikolaieva, please reconsider. If you resign, the act may be perceived as ingratitude on your part, and it will affect...your future career prospects.

She passed him an unsealed envelope. —My letter.

Efim stared at the envelope in his hands. He must pass it along to Yury Stepanov. *Oh, dear God. Anna, no. No.* He gave the envelope a little shake. —Take it back, and I'll say nothing further on the matter.

Anna stood up. —I take nothing back, for I cannot do this work. I will not.

The low heels of her shoes clicked and tapped on the floor, fading out until swallowed by the creaks of the main doors and the sounds of the streets outside.

Her letter said nothing of diphtheria.

I, Dr. Anna Nikolaieva Novikova, resign from my position at Laboratory of Special Purpose Number Two.

Efim tucked the letter back into the envelope. *So brief.* In his younger days, such a letter might need an entire page for deferential greeting alone. She had done what he could not: said no. Declined. Refused. Walked away.

Her life now?

Efim dug for a handkerchief and dabbed sweat from his face.

So brief.

Evgenia glanced up as a white-haired officer from another department approached her desk. —Good morning, Comrade Major. My name is Ismailovna. How can I help you?

He flipped open his red wallet. —Minenkov, Vadym Pavlovich.

—Comrade Major Minenkov, welcome. Is Comrade Captain Kuznets expecting you?

—No, I'm looking for Senior Lieutenant Nikto.

—I've not seen him yet.

—Oh. I thought—

A wretched thud.

A male voice: —I've told you a hundred times!

Another thud.

Vadym followed Evgenia's wide-eyed line of sight: an older officer slamming a younger one against a wall. The older man, a sergeant in his late forties, looked tired and unwell, cheeks sunken, moustache limp, face ruddy from drink. The younger man, another sergeant, struggled beneath the hands pinning his shoulders. A third thud: the younger man's head hit the wall. The older man grasped him by the jaw and crumpled up the flesh of his face.

Boris Kuznets ran out of his office. Spotting the conflict, he strode up to the officers and clapped a hand on the older man's shoulder. —Sergeant Kamenev!

All the background racket of voices and movement ceased.

Boris's voice, though quieter, still carried. —Gleb Denisovich, what is this?

Gleb's words came frothed with spittle. —He harangues me. This young one. He would tell me how to do my job. Me, a Chekist who shared a dinner table with Felix Dzerzhinksy!

Vadym remembered. Yes, they'd all shared a table one night. *Kamenev. He taught Kostya and Misha when they were cadets.*

Boris clicked his tongue in sympathy with Gleb. —The younger officers sometimes show such disrespect for their elders. Deplorable.

—I fill my quotas like anyone else, and this, this *infant* who has infested my office, who'd not know a hammer and sickle if I drove them up his arse, wants to show me new and better ways.

—His face is gone dark red, comrade. Ease your hand a bit. No, don't let him go. Just let him breathe. There we are.

—Tells me my methods are antiquated and not good enough. Me, a career Chekist! Everything I've given... Everything I am is Cheka.

—Comrade Katelnikov's parents would be ashamed of his discourtesies.

Tears shone on Gleb's face. —Saying he'll report my paperwork for inspection and review.

The silence deepened as everyone considered the implications of this dire threat.

Matvei sounded hoarse. —I saw him lie about his quotas. I know he's behind.

Gleb dropped his arms from Matvei's body, took a few steps backward, and spat at his junior's feet. Then he strode to their shared office and slammed the door.

Boris looked Matvei up and down. —Quite a stunt you just pulled. If, *if* you've got proof of something so terrible as that, you come see a superior. You report your concerns through proper channels. You never confront and humiliate another officer. Is that clear?

Water rushed through pipes.

—Clear, Comrade Captain Kuznets.

—Report to my office at once and wait for me there, so we may discuss your discipline. I—

Gunshot.

Heavy thud.

Matvei stared at the just-slammed office door, looked back at Boris, then ran to the office, shoving people aside. He could only get the door open a few centimetres; something barred the way. —Gleb Denisovich! Gleb Denisovich, no, no, no.

Evgenia murmured into her telephone receiver, asking the switchboard to send for an ambulance.

Blood and other matter seeped beneath the door and around Matvei's feet.

Vadym wished someone could knock Matvei out, force his silence. He nodded to Evgenia, signalling he would come back at a better time; standing up, Evgenia nodded back. Boris took Matvei by the upper arm and guided him to a chair; they both tracked blood. Evgenia took some old rags from a filing cabinet and placed them at the office door, managing to dam the leak. The others retreated to their own offices.

Wishing Evgenia had been more shocked, wishing that of himself, Vadym made for the stairwell and descended. He took great care to watch where he placed his feet.

—Dima.

He looked up. Kostya loped toward him.

—Dima, are you all right? You look terrible.

—A man in your department just shot himself.

—Fuck, not again. Who?

After some difficulty, Vadym could speak. —Kamenev.

The shadows of the crisscrossed wire enclosing the staircase fell across Vadym's face, making Kostya think of a map in Vadym's office.

A winter's day in early 1936, Vadym had pointed on a map of Russia marked with lines of latitude and longitude, pointed to the far northeast: Kolyma. Misha and Kostya had feigned polite interest as Vadym spoke of the Ice Age discoveries there. *Dwellings. Subterranean dwellings. Signs of civilization, even anthropomorphic art, so old, so very old, and yet so human.* That night Kostya had dreamt of a thin black line on the map, this line enlarging to a long queue of people marching on a gunpoint pilgrimage. Then the line shrank back to a strand thin as a barb on a feather, only to shrink some more as the feather pricked out beneath a shirt cuff — the shirt cuff of the terrible man Kostya saw on his fevered 1918 journey to Moscow. Black feathers on his arms, black feathers on the back of his neck, he stood on the train platform, watching. Kostya had recognized him for what he was: a demon.

One could no longer see demons in 1937, Kostya told himself. Nor, unless poisoned with morphine, cocaine, alcohol, bloodlust, and fear, could one see angels. —Dima, what's happening to us?

A door creaked below, and another senior lieutenant started up the stairs. Kostya and Vadym parted to leave him enough room to pass; he regarded them both with some suspicion.

Kostya said it loud enough for the other senior lieutenant to hear, so he might understand how the strange meeting and the silence on the stairs meant not treachery but dismay. —An ambulance on the way?

—Your Comrade Ismailovna has sent for one.

The footsteps faded as the man left the staircase for an upper corridor.

Vadym looked up at the wire caging. —Not that an ambulance will help.

—He might —

—Too much blood.

Then Vadym reached out for Kostya's face. He cupped the younger man's cheek and stroked his thumb beneath Kostya's eye, as if to wipe away tears.

Kostya stared at him.

Vadym took his hand back. —I was in your department because I wished to apologize.

—You've nothing to apologize for, Dima. I was a thoughtless pig.

—I should let you get to work. Go on. You'll be late.

Legs feeling heavy, Kostya ascended a few steps.

—Kostya?

He looked back over his bad shoulder, winced.

—Kostya, please. Did you see Misha in Spain? Yes, or no. One word. Just one word.

A door opened, and several other officers descended the stairs between Kostya and Vadym. More men began an ascent from the floor below.

Kostya turned his back to Vadym and joined the press of bodies climbing stairs to some other purpose.

Queasy, Efim strode through the huge department store. He needed fresh air, not the strange stillness of high ceilings, shiny tables, and random consumer goods. His walk had left him feeling vulnerable, exposed, as though many people watched him through many windows.

Yury Stepanov's pursed little mouth, the lips wet: *Merely an informal chat. I just need to understand, Comrade Doctor, so I can explain to my superiors, did you know Comrade Dr. Novikova planned to resign? Did she talk to you about it at all? Had she seemed unhappy? Was her work focused and efficient? I'll need a detailed report on her workload and how she interacted with her colleagues.*

Defeated before he might even consider defiance, Efim had nodded.

Women's shoes filled his vision. Two shop clerks hurried to remove the shoes from one large crate, match them in sized pairs, and place them on a display table.

Nadezhda Ivanovna's bare feet.

Efim picked up a shoe: low heel, leather upper, rubber sole. He took up another, held it to the light.

—A present for your wife?

Efim flinched, dropped the shoe.

Arkady bent to pick it up, with some difficulty, and when he rose, his uniform looked rumpled and creased. —I'm sorry I startled you.

—What brings you here, Comrade Major Balakirev?

—Chance. I've been out of town, and I just got back. Though I have been thinking of you.

Chance? —Comrade Major, I need to speak with you.

Arkady gestured to a bench in the wide corridor. —And I with you. Let's sit down. Now first, tell me about Kostya.

Efim dredged up every scrap of professional dignity he could, but this Major Balakirev's voice: impossible to defy. Resenting his quick surrender, Efim bit the inside of his cheek. —Well, I had hoped to tell you about some real improvement by now, but these last six weeks in particular have convinced me that his injuries will get no better. He's still in pain. I expect he will have pain there for the rest of his life. He may experience progressive weakening of the arm as well.

—So you can't heal him?

Efim felt suspended in a moment of recognition, the moment of tottering toward a fall, and his speech sounded rapid and pressed. —Perhaps we'll see some progress in the next few months. Now, Olga.

—Who? Oh, your wife. What of her?

—I've heard nothing from her in weeks. I wish to go and see her. Please. I've waited for weeks. I cannot get permission to visit Leningrad without your signature.

—Is that all?

—Is that *all?* I had to leave her in the first place to come babysit your precious bastard orphan!

—You will lower your voice.

Efim did so. —And, as if this whole setup weren't absurd enough, I am expected to believe his surname is Nikto.

Arkady laced his hands across the top of his belly, said nothing.

Efim stared at the display of women's shoes, almost certain now he could pick out the right size.

Arkady shifted his weight. —You want leave to go to Leningrad and see your wife. It's a reasonable request. I'll see what I can do. Oh, before I go: that whore in the flat.

—Her name is Nadezhda Ivanovna Solovyova. There's an accent I can't place, very subtle. I thought it was Leningrad. She likes tea. And that is all I know about her.

Efim's words had rattled out at such speed that he could not be sure he said them. Yet he knew he'd said them. Trading likely dangerous information for a chance to see Olga? It seemed a most reasonable barter.

Arkady nodded. —Thank you.

Then he walked away.

Considering nuances of betrayal, Efim stared at the Stakhanovite display of shoes, this absurd surplus, more more more, until his vision blurred, until all the shoes became one black blob, gelatinous and shiny, something that would ooze.

Stakhanov's coal mixed with blood, perhaps.

Kostya hurried to Evgenia's desk. —Comrade Ismailovna, I'm sorry. I didn't realize it was so late.

As Evgenia shrugged on her jacket, her eyes once more signalled favour. *For you, I have sugar. For you, I would wait.*

He gave her a clutch of papers. —Here, more of the confession templates we discussed. I got behind on them. The upset earlier today ...I can't think straight. Perhaps some of the officers can make use of these.

Smiling, she glanced at his eyes. She liked to compare the hue of green to spruce in bright summer light. *And those long lashes, on a man? What a waste. Yet so beautiful.* —This could save me a lot of time with the paperwork. I'll type up some copies tomorrow morning. Do you want me to hand them out, or shall I give them back to you?

—Type them up and run them by Comrade Captain Kuznets first.

She unlocked one of her filing cabinets, tucked the confessions in a dossier near the front, and locked the cabinet once more. —I'm taking supper today at the new cafe on the corner. Would you care to try it with me?

What? —Oh. I wish I could. I'm due back at my flat. I mean... my girlfriend expects...

—Oh. Yes, yes. I'm sorry, Comrade Senior Lieutenant, I meant nothing improper. You should take your girlfriend to the cafe. They do wonders with herring.

Herring. —Thank you, Comrade Ismailovna. I will remember that. See you tomorrow.

—Right. Don't forget, we'll have a crew here to do a Special Clean by nine.

Sidestepping the remains of the bloodstain, imagining the racket of buckets dragged over floors, Kostya returned to his own office.

Evgenia stood behind her desk, furious with herself for not guessing that Konstantin Nikto must have beautiful women queued round the block, beauty with which she could not compete.

Furious with him, too, for seeming so surprised when she asked him out.

The walls echoed with the hum of voices and footsteps from earlier in the day. She glanced at the office where Kamenev had...

Just bring an end to this day.

An officer's boots in the hallway: the footfall still new to her, Evgenia looked up.

Boris Kuznets strode up to her desk.

Not again.

—Comrade Ismailovna, would you come to dinner with me?

The first time she'd declined, Boris had said nothing, and the following day two NKVD officers harassed her mother in her doctor's waiting room. The second time she said no, Boris said, *My grandfather spoke in proverbs. You remind me of one: fear has big eyes*, and the following day, her cousin disappeared. If she refused a third time? She took a deep breath. —Why, thank you, Comrade Captain. Yes.

—Perhaps you'll tell me the secret of your lovely skin?

Buttoning her jacket, she smiled at Boris, unaware of how defiant she looked to him, yet quite aware of how much Boris would enjoy crushing such defiance into shame.

[ ]

THE AIR RAID AND THE SNEEZE
Monday 26 July–Tuesday 27 July

—Just tell me.

—It doesn't matter, Nadia.

—Kostya, the scars write a story on your skin.

—How poetic. It's nothing.

—Will you just listen to me?

He finished his third glass of vodka. —What is it you wish to say?

—How did you get those scars, and how did you not bleed to death?

—Shrapnel in Gerrikaitz, and I've no idea.

—But it hurt.

—Of course it hurt.

—Like a gunshot?

—What?

—I said, like a gunshot?

Kostya could smell the lorry in Spain, the grease and oil, the dried sweat of both Misha and Cristobal. —Most of the gunshots I've seen are fatal. The head. Fucked in the mouth, why do you even ask me that?

—Kostya—

—Please! Shut up. Just shut up.

The bottle clinked against the glass. He poured another drink, knocked it back, and swallowed hard as the vodka shot back up his throat.

A few hours later, pain woke him. A hot bolt bore through his shoulder and pinned him to the bed. As Temerity slept beside him, her breathing regular and deep, the ceiling surrendered to the Spanish sky, and the low Junkers growled, the noise steady, mechanized, nothing like an animal's. So many planes. He stood outside an abandoned barn and farmhouse in Gerrikaitz, squinting in the sunshine. Dust-dimmed light of interiors: he'd been working inside the barn for many hours, working hard. Struggling with duty. Ready to scream. Misha had already screamed. Their conflict, their ordeal, now interrupted by the growl of those planes, fell away.

Luftwaffe? What the barrelling fuck?

Even as Kostya asked himself that question, he saw the answer; dark shapes fell from the bellies of the planes.

The whistle, the squeal: Kostya ran not from the sight of bombs and planes but from the noise.

The abandoned farmhouse was boarded and locked. The barn held problems of its own. The nearest other buildings stood a good half mile away.

The ground shrugged, threw him off.

Mouth crammed with dirt, Kostya rose on his elbows and craned his neck. Wood and metal and earth fell on him, cut him, beat him down.

Coughing, spitting, weeping, he crawled out from beneath the rubble and discovered silence, yet the planes still fouled the sky. He screamed at them. He heard nothing.

Pressure in my ears.

In the bed next to him, Temerity's breathing changed.

Deaf on his knees in Gerrikaitz, Kostya stared at the sky.

I acted like a panicked animal. I left someone behind. He said that to a nurse in Bilbao. She stroked his hand, saying, *These are difficult times.* Then, reminding him of the shrapnel and splinters embedded in the flesh of his left shoulder and ear, as if he could somehow forget that pain, the Bilbao nurse ordered him to swallow these few sulpha pills, and he laughed, laughed, laughed so hard that the nurse told him to lie down. When another patient asked what he found funny, and what he'd done to merit a scarce cot when so many in the clinic sat huddled on the floor, bloodied and miserable, he shouted about knowledge and destruction. After a moment he recognized that he shouted in Russian. Two men seized him by the arms, and the nurse injected him in the back of his left hand.

When he woke up, he felt the jostling progress of the wheeled cart beneath him. The man in front of the cart explained he must remove debris from this patient's shoulder, and the man pushing the cart pointed out that the clinic lacked any general anaesthetic. The first man growled in his throat, in disgust more than aggression, then said *He's Russian, most likely* NKVD, *and that means he's hunting and killing people. And we have to treat him. Mother of God. Get those rosary beads out of his hand. Where in hell's name did he get rosary beads? Fill him up with as much bromide as you can without stopping his heart, and I'll see what I can do.*

Never any mistreatment. Nothing of the sort. They gave him back his clothes and papers, all intact, yet Kostya knew no one at the clinic would believe his stories. Mr. MacKenzie the Canadian volunteer for the International Brigade, Tikhon the Russian war correspondent, Ivan the Russian volunteer: no one would believe him at all.

Kostya himself no longer believed. Not in his fake identities, not in his own identity, not in his entire purpose in Spain. Torture and murder meant only torture and murder, not love of country, not duty. Yet how could he stop? How could he disobey clear and direct orders? *By my own free will,* he thought, gagging as someone helped him drink water bitter and salty with bromides, *yet twice as much by compulsion.*

Despite medical advice, he insisted on standing soon after the procedure, then walking, however much he shook in this overrun clinic in northern Spain, a clinic reeking of blood and then, as days passed and other patients' wounds took infection, corruption.

Misha.

He caught the scent of Shalimar.

Temerity laid her hand on Kostya's chest. —Breathe. Breathe. In, out. Nice and deep.

Sweat broke on his skin. —Those fucking planes!

The bed rocked as Temerity got up and tugged on some clothes. —Breathe, my love. I'll get Efim. Just breathe.

My love? —Stay with me.

Temerity glanced over her shoulder at the man struggling to catch his breath, then darted to the hallway to knock on Efim's door.

The knocks hauled Efim out of an anxious dream of seeking bandages. —What? What is it?

—Kostya's shoulder.

Thoughts settling, Efim discovered Kostya on his back, pale and sweaty, scowl lines cutting deep into his face. —When we skipped your dose earlier this evening, I'd hoped you could do without it.

—The wounds are old. Why must they hurt so much?

Efim held the filled syringe to the light, tapped it. —One of my teachers in med school believed a chronic wound could become a prison for pain. If the wound can't heal, then the pain runs in a cage, burrows in on itself. Not a useful metaphor, I admit. Then there's the psychology of it. When we worry about pain, it can create a feedback loop, like that noise a microphone can make.

—How can I not worry about this pain? I can't fucking *think* past it. It's my own fault if it gets worse? That makes no sense!

Efim found a vein, gave the injection. —It may take a while now to get this settled down.

One-two, three-four, five-six... —Just give me a bigger dose.

—No.

—Please.

—Konstantin, I said no. If I give you more, then I make it all worse.

—Make what worse?

—The need.

Kostya shook his head. —I can't be addicted already. It still hurts.

—Keep still. Let the morphine work. There, some relief?

Kostya's voice sounded looser, less connected somehow. —Yes. Thank you. It's not enough, but thank you. Must you help everyone? Medically, I mean. If someone comes to you wounded or sick, and you don't like their politics, do you still help them?

I am the doctor who leapt from the train. —Why would you even ask me that?

—I was thinking about my grandfather. I like to think he helped anyone who needed him, no matter what side they were on.

Efim nodded. —Very likely.

Kostya rubbed his eyes with the pads of his fingers. And Dr. Cristobal Zapatero, would he have shown a stray Russian such mercy?

Sitting up, Kostya adjusted the sheets to cover himself better. —I feel I owe you both something after that little show. I heard this joke at the office the other day. Picture one of those big houses made over into flats, where everyone uses the one main door to get outside. So they're all sound asleep, and it's two in the morning, and bang-bang-bang-bang-bang, knocks on the door. Everyone wakes up, yet no one moves. Bang-bang-bang-bang-bang! Everyone has the same thought, that it's NKVD officers on a raid. Still, no one moves. The knocks get very loud: bang-bang-bang-bang-bang! Finally, the old man who lives on the top floor, the oldest of old men, says 'Well, my life is over, so I might as well be the one to answer the door and be taken away.' He gets out of bed and limps down the stairs. Everyone listens. The door creaks open. Voices murmur. The door closes. Everyone keeps so very still. Then the old man then shouts up the stairs: 'It's all right, comrades, nothing to worry about. The building's on fire, that's all.'

Efim laughed. Temerity, eyes huge, looked at the bed, the wall, the floor.

Kostya noticed. —No sense of humour, Nadia? Try this one. The Kremlin, big meeting of Politburo, and the Boss himself, our beloved Comrade Stalin, is about to give a speech.

Efim glanced over his shoulder, knowing, even as he did so, no one else stood there.

Kostya continued. —Just as the Boss straightens his papers and opens his mouth, someone sneezes. Achoo! The Boss is furious! He demands: 'Who sneezed?' Silence. The Boss orders the guards to shoot the entire first row. Thump-thump-thump-thump-thump. The smoke dissipates, and the Boss clears his throat, ready to address his beloved comrades, when, wait for it, somebody sneezes. Achoo! Terror shoots through everyone, faster than electricity, and more than one old revolutionary fears for the state of his shorts. And the Boss glowers at the entire assembly, and he thunders out: 'Who sneezed?' Silence. 'Guards,' orders the Boss, 'shoot everyone in rows three to nine.' The guards obey. Bang! Too many thumps to count. And when the smoke clears, everyone can see the Boss still stands at the podium, still waits with the infinite patience of a kind and loving father. He takes a breath to speak, and once more, Achoo! 'Comrades,' roars the Boss, 'this is too much! Who sneezed?' A rustle in the silence as one man, one tiny man in the very back row who can bear his guilt no longer, stands up and waves, and he says, 'I did.' The Boss fixes his yellow eyes on the man...and says 'Bless you, comrade.'

Efim laughed some more. So did Kostya. Each man's laughter fed the other's, and the harder they tried to stop, the harder they laughed.

Temerity stared at them both. —That's not funny.

Efim dabbed at his eyes, deciding he now had an excellent excuse to make his accusation. —If that's not funny, then you're not Russian.

Kostya smirked at her.

Temerity kept her back to Efim as she smoothed some of Kostya's hair from his forehead. —Lost in translation, perhaps.

Still chuckling, Efim wished them both a good night.

Back in his own room, about to lock his door, Efim considered what Nadezhda Ivanovna had just said about translation. He visited the bathroom, urinated, then looked at himself in the mirror.

The doctor who leapt from the train was a much younger man.

Temerity took care not to rock the bed too hard as she got back in it. —Still hurts?

—Not as bad.

—How did it happen?

Kostya let out a long sigh. —Gerrikaitz.

—What were you doing in Gerrikaitz?

—My duty.

She took the risk. —Cristobal Zapatero?

After a moment, he answered. —I lost your sketchbook in the hospital. I lost his beads, too. I left you out of my report.

She waited, knowing that if she pressed him, he'd stop talking.

—And you, Nadia, what dragged you to Gernika so you could get bombed?

—Nothing dragged me. I chose to go to Gernika so I could get a message to London.

—Misha and I forced the issue. You chose nothing.

—Not this again. I chose duty.

He turned over to stroke her face. —And you got nothing worse for it than a bruise on the forehead.

—Nothing to show. Bad dreams. Then I got to Bilbao. I had to get home, or at least report in. And, ah, well, I was hardly the only one in Bilbao. What happened to those boys?

Kostya wanted to shout at her, tell her to shut up, demand she get him some vodka. He lacked the strength. —I don't know. It was a trial run. No one made a sound about it in the press.

—A secret evacuation?

—I was waiting for orders in Bilbao. Down by the docks I heard someone shout for anyone who spoke Russian, and I said, 'Here I am.' And this man told me he was a colonel and now I had to escort a dozen boys out of a war zone to Leningrad. And he just left them with me, twelve boys wearing cardboard name tags. Not one of those boys spoke a word of Russian. I hadn't slept for three damned days, and suddenly I'm looking after all these boys. The younger ones cried for their parents. I told them and told them they'd be safe, but they kept crying. I wanted to kick them, shove them aside, fuck, call them *bezprizorniki*. I told myself to do that, to help them toughen up, yes? I also wanted to hold them, calm them down, listen to them. My right arm was still bruised, and the left was useless. I couldn't even hold the pencil, let alone a crying child. Then I saw you. After you wrote their name tags, something in my mind collapsed. I was afraid of you, and I couldn't say why. The boat set out from Bilbao, and I tried to get the boys settled. I told them in Spanish they'd come back one day, when the war was over, but for now they were on an adventure. Two of the boys spoke only Basque. Some of the other boys could interpret. Yet if I just let them cry, that worked better than words. So I let them lean on me and cry. I tried to pat their shoulders, stroke their hair with my good arm. Fuck, that hurt. Then I organized the older ones and set them up as squad leaders, and we put the younger ones into squads. I made sure we kept brothers together. I demanded the cook feed them only the plainest rations, because otherwise they'd be sick the whole damned time. They got only hard bread, boiled peas, potatoes, and Narzan, and that's all I took as well. Solidarity, comrade. The steamer made it to Leningrad, and as we stood on the docks, swaying on our sea legs, I put them through some language drill. Then I heard the boots. The boys froze when they saw the uniforms, and my esteemed colleagues separated us. Some of the boys cried out to me, and I could not go to them. The oldest boy took this as a betrayal, and I saw the anger play out on his face. He blamed me. I got bundled onto a train to Moscow, and they got marched away. Those children are the reason I got home. It was an accident. I was in Bilbao at the right moment. The captain of that little fishing boat was Red Army Intelligence, working hand in hand with NKVD. Chance.

Temerity tapped her mouth with her fist.

Kostya touched her fist, loosened the fingers, kissed them.

She took her hand back.

He sat up, found his cigarettes on the side table, lit two, and passed Temerity one. Cigarette smoke curled around their faces, making Kostya think of both Odessa fog and a fired Nagant.

—Kostya. This can't continue.

—I know.

—Please, just get me to the embassy.

He said nothing.

—Kostya, I'm begging. Help me.

Recalling the sensation of the ashes in Arkady's furnace on his fingers, Kostya ground out his cigarette, unfinished, and lay down.

Temerity waited another moment. Then turned onto her side, facing away from him, and flicked off the lamp.

He stared at where the ceiling should be. —Nadia? If I could protect you here...

—You can't.

—If I could.

—Kostya, please.

—If I could protect you, if you were in no danger here, would you stay with me? Run that language school with me?

—Duty, Kostya.

—If duty didn't matter.

—If, if, if.

—What if there's no *if* and you are meant to be here? We should never have met at all.

—If everything is meant to happen, then why did you choose to take me from that party?

He said nothing.

After a moment, she rolled onto her back. —The nightingales are loud.

—The what?

—The nightingales, my gentle thief. The birdsong.

He frowned. —Are you saying I should have just left you at that party?

—You stole me.

—I saved you.

Temerity turned over on her side again, her back to him.

Kostya wept.

[ ]

A RADIANT FUTURE
Tuesday 27 July

Wrapped in a towel, Kostya answered the telephone next to the bathroom door and just kept himself from sighing as the operator told him to stand by for a call from Lubyanka. Expecting Evgenia Ismailovna to inform him of an extra shift, he smiled as instead he recognized Vadym's voice.

—Kostya, can you come see me in my office?

—I have the day off.

Static on the line, for it must be static, made Vadym's voice tremble. —Kostya, please.

Riding the metro to Dzerzhinskaya, Kostya knew he must face certain things, perhaps even the moral need to tell Vadym about Misha in Spain. Kostya's final report, while initially delayed by his convalescence, was long since approved and filed away. It was also incomplete. He'd said little of Misha and nothing of the British nurse. Any discovery of such omissions could get him arrested. If he told Vadym about Misha, he'd implicate Vadym in his faulty report. If he continued to refuse to tell Vadym about Misha, then he'd gall a man he loved with the torment of uncertainty.

Kostya did not see the two young women on the bench opposite him, wondering at the tears on the face of this uniformed NKVD officer.

Dima, I am sorry...

He thought of the story 'The Maiden Tsar,' of the moment when Baba Yaga complains of the hero's Russian smell and then asks him: *Are you here of your own free will, or by compulsion?*

He muttered the hero's response. —Mostly of my own free will, yet twice as much by compulsion.

Then he noticed his tears and hurried to wipe them away. As he glanced up, the young women watching him looked down.

At his desk in Lubyanka, Vadym felt confused by how little, yet how much time sagged between his hanging up the phone and hearing a knock on the door. —Come in, Kostya.

—Vadym Pavlovich.

He looked up. Not that he needed to look up to confirm the rich voice of Boris Kuznets.

Uninvited, Boris sat down and spoke in a quiet manner, almost an enemy's mutter, almost a lover's croon: a difficult task, comrade, a heavy need in these troubled days of widespread corruption when we must investigate comrades we thought we could trust, your closeness to the man in question and your simultaneous loyalty forged in the fires of revolution...

Vadym looked out his window.

—Vadym Pavlovich, please understand. I must pass on orders for you to assist in the investigation of Arkady Dmitrievich Balakirev and Konstantin Arkadievich Nikto for cronyism.

Vadym shut his eyes. *Cronyism* meant nothing. Yet it could mean everything.

Boris continued. —I'm compelled to point out that if you refuse or even hesitate to assist, then the investigation would widen to include you. If it hasn't already.

—My nephew.

—What?

Vadym opened his eyes again and met Boris's gaze. —Misha. Mikhail Petrovich Minenkov to you. You promised to find out what happened to him.

Boris leaned on the desk as he got out of the chair. —I've no idea what you're talking about, or why you think I'd barter information.

—Is he coming back?

—Speak with care, Vadym Pavlovich. To an outside observer, this conversation might sound close to cronyism. We could both be charged.

—Tell me if he's ever coming back!

—Ask Nikto. He was the last to see him.

Vadym stared at Boris and refused to look away.

After a moment's silence, Boris drew his index finger across Vadym's desk. —Dust. And a messy pile of dossiers. I've never seen your desk in such a state.

As Boris left, Vadym shoved himself away from his desk and strode to his office window.

I shot other men's sons for the good of this country.

Any moment his desk telephone would ring: his brother, asking for news of Misha. Despite Vadym's pleas, Pyotr would call again and again. Any moment he would call, and the cacophony of the wretched telephone bell would slice into Vadym's ears.

He leaned his forehead on the glass.

Any moment.

Wishing, as ever, that Dzerzhinskaya felt less grim, less grey, Kostya hurried to emerge. *Back to heaven, Odessa bezprizornik.*

As he strode toward Lubyanka, the racket of cracking glass made him look up.

A wooden chair fell from a third-floor Lubyanka office, and it shattered into sharp pieces on the ground: legs, arms, slats.

Then a uniformed officer leapt through the broken window and ran through the air.

No one cried out.

The officer fell atop the broken chair.

Kostya ran to him as others stared. Then he saw the shock of white hair.

Vadym had fallen onto his chest, face turned to the left. His jaw worked, and his right fist clenched and twitched. Blood flowed towards it.

Kostya hurried to kneel besides him. —Dima? Uncle?

—Misha?

—Kostya. I'm Kostya. Hush, don't move.

Vadym spat up blood.

—Dima!

The gathering crowd, so quiet, threw shadows.

Boris Kuznets touched Kostya on the upper arm. —Come away.

Other men pried Vadym's body from the asphalt, revealing wood, blood, bone.

Boris kept his hand on Kostya's good shoulder as Kostya gave his statement to other officers, described what he'd seen. Then Boris guided Kostya inside Lubyanka, up to the department.

Evgenia gasped when she saw Kostya's face.

Boris eased his office door shut. —Sit down.

Kostya obeyed. He studied the large rocking blotter on Boris's desk as the older man poured two stiff measures. The blotter reminded him of the one on the clerk's desk in 1918, when Arkady took him for identity papers.

Here you are: Nikto, Konstantin Arkadievich.

Boris offered a glass.

Kostya kept staring at the blotter.

Boris took Kostya's right hand and placed it around the glass.
—Drink.

—Yes.

Kostya knew he sounded young, impossibly young. Then he drank.

—Finish it.

Kostya obeyed that order, too.

—More?

Kostya nodded, drank the second dose.

—You knew him well?

—I call him uncle.

—You're his nephew by blood?

—No. Vadym is an old friend of Arkady Dmitrievich.

—And neither are you Arkady Dmitreivich's son. Yet you're so much alike.

Shock and vodka stifling his fear, Kostya told the story of his name.

Boris raised his eyebrows. —Arkady Dmitrievich saved you? Why?

—I... oh, God, Dima is dead.

—Yes.

—Dima is dead. He ran as he fell.

—Impossible. Bodies tumble.

Kostya stood up and slammed his glass on Boris's desk. —He ran!

Boris studied the splash of vodka, noticed how it missed his paperwork. —I am sorry you had to witness it. These are difficult days.

—He called me Misha.

—Sit down. That's an order. Now Kostya, listen to me.

—Do not call me that!

Boris stared at him.

A dozen apologies ripped through Kostya's mind only to fail in his mouth. He softened his voice. —With respect, Boris Aleksandrovich, you may not use that name.

—You're in shock, so I'll let that go. Nikto, you cannot work today. Go home.

—No, wait, I—

—Senior Lieutenant Nikto!

Kostya stood to attention.

—You will not work today. Is that clear?

—Yes, Comrade Captain.

—At ease. Now sit down.

Kostya almost fell back into the chair.

Silence.

—In a few moments, Konstantain Arkadievich, once you feel ready, we shall leave this office and descend to the garage, and I will drive you home myself.

Playing with his glass, Kostya shook his head. —I want to take the metro.

Boris blinked several times, then brushed his hand over his eyes. —Nikto, don't crack on me. Not now. I never expected this from Minenkov. I'll drive you home.

Kostya's voice sounded clear, precise. —I'll be fine. I like riding the metro.

—What's your station?

—Vasilisa Prekrasnaya. My flat's a short walk from there.

—Very good. I want you to sit here for a few moments while I confer with Comrade Ismailovna, and then I'll walk you to Dzerzhinskaya. You will stay here until I come back.

—Yes.

And he did that, aware of Boris's departure and return, aware of how his knees ached as he stood up from the chair, the same sort of chair Vadym had hurled, aware of how Evgenia Ismailovna and Matvei Katelnikov looked at him, aware, too, of the dozens of other men jostling him and Boris as they descended the stairs and emerged from Lubyanka.

Boris took Kostya's arm again and guided him away from the Special Clean crew. —I'll telephone later to check on you.

Kostya rode the metro past Vasilisa Prekrasnaya. Annoyed, he told himself to pay attention. Then he noticed the train had returned to Dzerzhinskaya. Kostya changed his seat, hoping to keep himself more alert. The vodka served as a fine bulwark against any harder emotion, and he nodded as if to a friend beside him. He reminded himself of the number of stops now until the train returned to Vasilisa Prekrasnaya; he counted them on his fingers.

After enduring another little chat with Yury Stepanov about the team making no progress on the newest poison, Efim told himself to expect arrest at any moment. A giddy peace descended on him then, and, in a mood of defiance, of one giant shrug, he left the lab to visit the department store in Red Square. As an ambulance siren howled, the vehicle heading for Lubyanka, he said a quick prayer for the ailing, something he'd not done for many years, and then he chose a pair of women's shoes. He paid, wishing the clerk a good morning.

On the metro, he recalled the day he leapt from the moving train. The tunnel walls seemed close enough to scrape the window glass.

Sometimes, he decided, face impassive, no different from the faces of the other passengers, *sometimes defiance looks like nothing at all.*

He did not, however, present the shoes to Nadezhda Ivanovna right away. He got distracted when he found her puffy in the face, dark around the eyes, and slouched in the one soft chair.

—You're home so early, Efim. Are you all right?

—I'm fine. I feel better than I have in months.

—What's it like outside?

—Hot.

She sighed. —Hot in here, too.

—Do you sleep well, Nadezhda Ivanovna?

—No.

—Bowels all right?

—I need more exercise.

—Here.

She stared at the shoes.

—Try them on. Doctor's orders.

—Efim Antonovich, please. I don't want to cause you any trouble.

He looked her in the eye. —How is it trouble for me that you need shoes? Must I kneel and put them on you?

She stood up and slipped her feet into the shoes. Then she took a few steps. They'd chafe her heels without stockings, but they fit. —What do I owe you?

Skin tingling, Efim turned his back. —Nothing.

Then he walked to the bathroom and locked the door.

That sound made Temerity glance down the little corridor to the main door.

Efim had left his key in the lock.

Temerity blinked a few times. Then she patted her blouse to check for her passport.

A few quick steps, the soles of the shoes tapping against the floor, a quick turn of the key, and she stepped outside the flat.

The air smelled less dusty than inside the flat, less close, yet hardly fresh. A draft from the lobby wafted up the stairs.

Holding the rail, steps deliberate, Temerity descended the stairs.

In the lobby, the watchwoman dozed in the rocking chair, her chin bent to her chest.

Temerity opened the main door and strode out to the sidewalk. Scents of tar, diesel, rivers, and stones, and such bright light, over-whelmed her for a moment, and she stood still.

A woman with her arms full of shopping bags made a point of offering a sarcastic apology as she veered aside.

Temerity peered down the narrow street lined with what looked like old houses made over into flats, unlike the new building she'd just exited.

A woman leaned out an upper window in the building across the street, scowling.

Temerity felt herself tremble. *I'm lost. Already.*

The shoes pinched and rubbed. The sun shone so bright.

No, not lost. Here. He parked the car here the night he brought me. The deli. Find Babichev's, then you can find Hotel Lux. God's sake, no, that's the last place to go. There'll be a map in the metro station. Walk with confidence, girl. Walk like you've got every right to be in this city.

As she entered Vasilisa Prekrasnaya and peeked down the stairs, the station's beauty seized her: ceramic tiles in the walls and ceiling; marble pylons, marble repurposed, perhaps, from the 1931 destruction of the Cathedral of Christ the Saviour; wrought iron sconces for electric lights; a colourful mosaic mural of Bilibin's illustration of Vasilisa outside Baba Yaga's hut, Vasilisa holding up her lamp of holy fire and a skull.

She's too small, Temerity had said, shoving the Russian fairy tale book from her father's hand. *She can't win.*

Now Temerity wanted to touch the mosaic, touch Vasilisa, reach her mother...

A sign interrupted her thoughts: *Fare 30 kopeks.* As Temerity considered how she might charm the fare guard into letting her pass, the sudden draft and a rumble of an arriving train distracted her.

Squeaking and squealing, the train came to a perfect halt, and the doors released a dozen passengers, including a uniformed NKVD officer. The other commuters gave him space as he ascended the steps.

Kostya stared at Temerity.

She stared at him.

Pale, he glanced down at her feet, looked back up. His eyes glittered. —How nice of you to meet me here, darling.

She took a step back.

Kostya offered his arm, and as various strangers passed them by, walking close to the walls to avoid the NKVD officer, she took it. She craned her head to get one last glimpse of the mosaic; columns and other people blocked her view. She and Kostya returned to the surface and walked the short distance to the block of flats, Kostya chatting about how much of a headache he felt coming on, how much he looked forward to a drink.

In the lobby, the old watchwoman slept on.

Temerity struggled to keep pace, slipping on the stairs. —Kostya, wait.

He wrenched open the flat door, shoved her inside, slammed the door behind them. She scrabbled to get out of his reach.

Efim, in his bedroom, gasped and flinched at the noise.

Kostya's eyes seemed to shrink. —You stupid bitch!

—Kostya, please, lower your voice.

—You've got no fucking papers!

She stood up, backing towards the kitchen counter. —And whose fault is that?

He backhanded her across the face. —Stay down!

She fell against the counter.

Efim ran to the kitchen. —Nikto, the neighbours.

—Fuck the neighbours!

A blow from the side of Temerity's hand struck the right side of his neck, interrupting the carotid. Vision greying, he fell against the table and got himself into a chair. Then he hooked his ankle around hers and tripped her, and she fell, her full weight thumping against the floor.

—Nikto, stop! I gave her the shoes.

—What?

As Temerity got herself beyond Kostya's reach, Efim touched Kostya on his good shoulder. —I gave her the shoes. I don't know who she is, or where she comes from, or why I had to get tangled up in this, and I don't want to know. But I gave her the shoes.

Temerity's voice, words quiet and low, carried. —I can't stay here.

Kostya whirled round and punched a wall. Shaking plaster from his hand, he left the flat, and his shouted profanities echoed down the stairwell.

Efim turned to Temerity. —Where did he hit you? Not your eyes? Good. Tilt your head so I can see.

—He's got no right!

Efim wanted to hold her, protect her. —No right at all. Wait here. I'll get a cold compress.

As Efim ran water, Temerity tried to stand. Her legs refused.

Efim knelt before her and eased the compress onto her cheek. His touch, so soft, made Temerity think of Cristobal Zapatero and his gentle movements as he rolled bandages. Then she remembered his rosary beads and how he'd dropped them in fear.

Efim, his fingers damp now with Temerity's tears, took her hand and guided it to the compress. As she held it in place, he sat on the floor beside her. Then he wrapped his arm around her shoulders.

Back stiffening, Temerity wanted to shake him off, shove him away like the illustration of Vasilisa the Beautiful. Instead, she leaned onto his chest and sobbed.

After a moment, she pulled away and patted the compress over her eyes. She wondered how best to thank him, whether to call him Efim or the more formal Efim Antonovich, or whether to pretend nothing had happened, when a key clicked in the locked main door.

Efim murmured about Kostya coming back to apologize and stood up.

On a slow and heavy stride, Arkady Balakirev emerged from the little corridor leading to the door. His face looked both drawn and puffy, and his eyes seemed sunken and small. When he took his spectacles from his pouch and placed them just so on his nose, the lenses magnified his eyes to something huge and absurd. —Where is he?

Efim now stood between Arkady and Temerity. —Who, Nikto? He left a few minutes ago. I don't know how you missed him.

—Did he tell you?

—Tell me what?

—Vadym Minenkov is dead.

Temerity got to her feet. —The one who brought the mushrooms, Efim. I don't think you met him.

As Efim gestured for Temerity to stay behind him, he felt very small before Arkady. —My condolences, Comrade Major. Is this someone close to you and Nikto?

—My oldest friend. Kostya called him uncle.

—What happened?

Arkady fixed his gaze on Temerity. —Hurled himself out a fucking window.

Silence.

Turning away, Arkady sniffed a few times. When he spoke, his voice sounded hoarse. —If you see Kostya before I do, look after him.

—I look after him every day.

Then Arkady faced them again, removed his spectacles, jostled Efim to one side and leaned in close to Temerity. —When he comes back, get him to telephone me. I don't care what time it is. Understand me yet?

She nodded.

He peered at her injured face, drew the pads of his fingers over the mark. —A good start. I should like to finish it.

Then he left.

Efim let out a shaky breath. —I am sorry he said that to you.

Struggling with more tears, she shook her head. —I'm fine.

He glanced at her feet. Fluid had collected round her ankles. And, Efim now noticed, around her eyes, wrists and fingers. She seemed puffy all over. —Nadezhda Ivanovna, are you nauseous at all?

She said nothing.

—Any dizziness? Any change in your breasts?

—How dare you ask me that?

—I'm a doctor.

She muttered something Efim did not catch.

He opened his medical bag, took out a stethoscope. —Let me listen.

After a moment, Temerity unbuttoned her blouse.

A faint smell of perfume reached Efim as he noticed the freckles on his patient's shoulders. The fabric of her blouse, save some staining in the armpits, seemed clean. She wore the same blouse almost every day. —Your heart rate's a little fast, Nadezhda. Do you feel anxious?

—Yes, I feel anxious! Kostya just beat me across the face, then that wretched old man threatened to beat me some more, and all I want is some fresh air…

She looked into his eyes and held her hand over her lower abdomen, much as Olga might.

Efim nodded.

Temerity took her hand away. —I can't do this. Not here. Not with him.

Efim plucked the stethoscope buds from his ears. —You're far from the first woman in this difficulty.

—Screw for survival.

He studied her. Arrest and interrogation might induce miscarriage, or Nadezhda and her fetus might prove resilient and robust. And when she showed? Could even a hardened Chekist kill a pregnant woman and thereby murder two at once? Of course he could. If Nadezhda was sent to Kolyma, she would starve faster than the others as the fetus sucked every calorie. And where would she give birth, in the barracks, in a mine? Incarcerated mothers brought young children with them. Perhaps the guards built nurseries in the women's camps. Yes, they must.

Efim shut his eyes and felt the constant rattling sway of the train in 1918. Then he remembered Olga's farewell: *Be a good doctor.*

—Nadezhda.

—I can't.

—I know. Do you want my help?

She stared at him.

He nodded. —Twenty-five years, if we're caught. Possibly death. I've got very little to offer you for pain, and we'd need to work fast. It will be unpleasant.

—Yes.

—Are you sure?

She stood up and straightened her blouse. —Yes.

Kostya had not spent so much money in cafes since the night before he left for Spain, out with Vadym, Arkady, and Misha. Nor had he gotten so drunk, worse even than the night of Arkady's dessert party. He staggered out of the cafe, discovered daylight still blazed, and then, after urinating in an alley, caught sight of one of his street contacts. *One of my own* bezprizorniki. —Andrei!

The boy turned to look over his shoulder. Then he nodded, signalling he'd heard, and hurried to Kostya.

—Andrei, Andryushka, how are you?

—Better than you.

—There are corpses buried five deep at the *poligons* who are better than me today.

—What?

—I need some wine.

—Wine's been scarce.

—Horseshit. I know you've got some in your little hideaway.

Andrei frowned. Senior Lieutenant Nikto did know that. Andrei had shared that information when Kostya asked how Andrei and his group of street children managed in winter. Kostya had paid for that information with more wine. And cigarettes, many cigarettes.

—It's shared, Senior Lieutenant. We're a collective. I can't just take something from the others. It's stealing.

—Shall I send the other officers here to round you up, your little collective? Hey? A children's home, is that what you want? Home of the Child of the Struggle Moscow Number Two Supplemental Number Three is not far from here, Andryushka.

Andrei took a step back. He knew the rumours. Orphans entered the state homes; doctors injected them; orphans disappeared. Senior Lieutenant Nikto had confirmed some truth to these rumours, adding that orphan boys might also join the army and be sent who knows where, or they might take sick and die all on their own, simple bad luck. —I'll give you the wine, Senior Lieutenant. Wait here.

Kostya smoked two cigarettes, waiting.

Glass clinked. Andrei ran to him, his jacket bulging.

As he gave Andrei cash and cigarettes and took the two bottles of wine, Kostya knew he'd just destroyed an important friendship. The boy's eyes confirmed it; Andrei would never trust him again.

And in that moment, Kostya did not care.

Besides, he'd discovered a much more pressing problem: his lack of a corkscrew.

Andrei carries one. Next to his knife. —Hey!

Andrei closed his eyes, sighed, and turned to face the drunk NKVD officer. The drunk, armed NKVD officer. —Yes, Comrade Senior Lieutenant?

Kostya held the bottles out before him. —Open these.

—Both at once?

—Now!

Andrei obeyed, struggling with his corkscrew as Kostya refused to let go of the bottles.

Kostya gulped down a quarter of a bottle; some of it dribbled past the edges of his mouth. —Now Andrei, where can I drink this in peace?

—This way.

He followed Andrei into an alley, one slimy with refuse and excrement. Leaning against a rough stone wall, he drank from the first bottle, vomited, waited a few moments for his head to clear, drank some more. Then he dropped the bottle. Green glass shattered; red wine spilled.

—Fucked in the mouth!

He'd still got the second bottle by the neck. And he knew, oh, he knew, just where to go and enjoy it. Not too far of a walk. Not far at all.

Dampness seeped through Kostya's clothes, into his skin, as he worked to recognize the voice saying his name. He stared up at the concerned face of Matvei Katelnikov. Even in civilian clothes, the young officer seemed very out of place here in Arkady's flowerbed.

Matvei's voice sounded crisp. —Nikto?

Kostya's own voice sounded like a cooling sauce, clotted and thick. —Katelnikov.

—Comrade Major Balakirev found you here.

—Here in the irises, yes. Lovely night.

—Can you stand up?

—What time is it?

—Just after eleven.

—Oh. Lovely night.

—So you said. Comrade Senior Lieutenant, please, I need you to stand up.

—Arkady Dmitrievich is such a fussy old woman about his flowers. If I've broken any, I'll never hear the end of it. Fuck, did I spill the wine over myself?

—The wine, and some puke. You're lucky you didn't choke.

—Laundry service will...Katelnikov? It's Katelnikov, right?

Sighing, Matvei extended a hand. —Yes, it's me.

—You look younger every day.

—Comrade Senior Lieutenant Nikto, please. I need you to stand up now.

—I don't think so.

—If you don't stand up, then I shall have to call Comrade Major Balakirev down here.

Kostya squinted at Matvei. —Wait, he called NKVD because of someone in his garden?

—I was in the area. He shouldn't try to lift you on his own. He also told me that if I must call him back down here, then I must arrest you for debauchery in a drunken state, in a garden, while in uniform.

—The old man really said that? Is that even a charge?

—Well, it might fall under anti-Soviet activities. And you are in uniform.

Kostya giggled. —Then I'll save you the paperwork, yes?

Leaning on Matvei, Kostya managed to stand, and the pair of them staggered and dipped to the back door of Arkady's house.

Arkady had been watching through the study window. He met Matvei and Kostya at the door, opening it before Matvei could knock. —Good work, Katelnikov. Help him inside, first room on the left.

Kostya winced. —Don't shout.

—I've not raised my voice. Over there, Katelnikov, just get him as far as the bed. Good. You may go. The front door, please, over there.

Obedient, curious, Matvei gawked as he moved through the parlour, and he found himself outside again before he could ask Comrade Major Balakirev if he might assist in any other way.

Then he let out a long breath, relieved he'd not been compelled to arrest Senior Lieutenant Nikto in a flowerbed. Such an interaction and its results would be, well...

He got into the NKVD car, started the engine.

Difficult.

—

Just over an hour later, Arkady opened his front door, this time to Efim Scherba and the NKVD driver who'd delivered him. —Took you long enough. Dismissed.

The driver saluted and left.

Efim followed Arkady inside. —I'd like to know why you sent NKVD to knock on my door. He frightened the hell out of me.

—Why? Have you got something to hide?

—It's late, Comrade Major.

—Kostya needs you. In the study. Follow me. We found him drunk and passed out in my garden. I got him stripped down to his pants, but the stench on him.

Kostya lay on the bed, insensible, halfway turned onto this right side, his right arm bent across his chest. His breathing lapsed into snorts and snores.

Efim gave Arkady a smug half-smile, feeling, for the first time, the man's equal. Here, Scherba the doctor could do things that Balakirev the Chekist could not: ease someone's misery and call it his job. —The wine fumes are enough to knock me over. Any idea how much?

—We found only one bottle on him, but I'm sure he drank more.

—Has he said anything about his shoulder?

—Nothing I could understand.

Efim took up a thin rug from the desk and chair, intending to drape it over his patient. —Not much to be done for him until he wakes up.

—Not the Persian! If he pukes on that, it's ruined. Don't look at me like that. It was expensive. I'll get you something else.

As Arkady strode upstairs, his tread and breathing heavy, Efim glanced around the parlour and the study. All this space, this entire house, for one man? A cat flap squeaked, and soon a large tom sauntered over to Efim. The animal eyed the strange human in apparent disdain. Efim called to him, rubbing his fingertips against his thumb, and the cat, eyes wide, trotted over and accepted a fondle around his ears. Then he wound his body around Efim's ankles.

Returning with a worn grey blanket, Arkady noticed the cat. —He normally avoids people.

As Efim took the blanket for the patient, the cat leaned hard against his lower legs and purred. —Cats like me. What's his name?

—Tchaikovsky. The other two are Borodin and Rimsky-Korsakov. Well, why not? They live with Balakirev.

—I didn't know you liked music.

Arkady adjusted the grey blanket over Kostya. —Vadym would say I only recognize *The Internationale* because everyone stands up. He named the cats. Come to the parlour. I'll get us something to drink.

Efim thought of his medical visits when he'd just graduated, of how a doctor's call, once the patient settled, could become something of a social occasion. Sometimes a family had paid him for his services with food and drink. Efim often learned valuable information about his patient this way, and about how the family functioned. This visit? Efim wanted only to run and escape his dread, escape this man. Was it evil? Was Arkady Balakirev evil? Nothing so simple. Corrupt? This idea felt more accurate yet more difficult, because corruption meant something good had once existed there and might, with intervention and care, exist again. Survival, then? Had Balakirev turned himself cold and hard because all around him had gone cold and hard?

Eyes reddened, Arkady passed Efim a glass of vodka. —We must be about the same age, Efim Antonovich, the same sort of man.

—Is that so?

—Old enough to remember the horrors of the tsarist days. Instead, I give you the Party's promise of a radiant future.

Each man emptied his glass.

Arkady gestured to the table. —Try the diced cucumber. I'm sorry, the bread's gone. I think I've got some crisp biscuit here somewhere. I eat out more and more. The NKVD cafeteria is quite good, you know, balanced meals.

—Nutrition is important.

—Never know when the next bout of food difficulties might come.

Efim detected a uric scent then. The tomcats? No, cat urine smelled very different, and the animal had wandered off. —When was your last medical checkup?

Arkady wiped yogurt from his lips. —I'm fine.

—A devoted servant of the Revolution like yourself, pushing body and mind so hard...

—It's Kostya who needs you, not me. Did he ever tell you how we met? He was a *bezprizornik* in Odessa, one of hundreds. At least I thought I saw hundreds. I don't know the numbers. Dangerous place to be lost, Odessa. Then the Germans took Odessa, cleaned up the streets and solved the *bezprizorniki* problem. They hanged them. The boys, I mean. I don't want to think about what happened to the girls. Leave children alone. Why is that so difficult? I once had a photograph of those gallows. I kept it to remind Kostya and myself what I'd saved him from. I burned it last year. It was hard to guess the boys' ages, because their faces looked so tough, all cheekbones and scowls, yet those baggy smocks belted round narrow waists as they queued told me they were starving. Why do we photograph such things?

—I wouldn't know.

—An execution should be efficient and humane, quick and clean, for condemned and executioner alike. Too much terror in a hanging, too much temptation into theatre. That is why I approve of guns. Instantaneous.

Efim considered the impact of a bullet on a brain. —As close as we can get.

—I got Kostya out of Odessa just before the Germans took it.

—Kind of you.

—Completely unplanned. I simply had orders to return to Moscow. Kostya begged me to take him with me. When I saw those photographs years later, I knew I'd been right to do so. More?

—Please.

Arkady poured vodka. —We'll drink to beauty.

—Women?

—Confession.

—Very well. To the beauty of confession.

The vodka burned Efim clean of worry and fear.

Arkady put down his glass and laced his fingers over his belly. —It's good for the soul. My own father was a doctor. There now, you've seen one of the stains in my file: my petit bourgeois background. Use it against me, if you wish. I didn't have the good sense to hide it when I joined the Cheka. I didn't boast about it, but I didn't I hide it. It gets worse. My mother came from wealth. We took holidays in Odessa. The climate, you see, it agreed with my mother. So when I had a chance in the Cheka to visit Odessa, reconnaissance, set up a Cheka depot, I leapt for it. And despite everything, at first I felt so happy. That changed. Odessa felt desolate, boarded-up windows and bread queues, carriages and trains, and *bezprizorniki* everywhere, like they heaved out of the gutter. That's how they smelled. They all begged. Kopeks or cigarettes. They always wanted cigarettes. Smoking kept them from feeling hungry.

Efim thought about how much Kostya smoked.

Pouring more vodka, clinking the bottle neck against the rims of the glasses, Arkady smiled. —Kostya wasn't begging. I found him almost frozen to the ground. Someone had doused him in water, in January. I helped him up. Just another sign of the struggle, I thought, one who would have to find his place in the new order or die, but when I heard him curse, I knew then he must be special.

—Because he cursed?

Arkady tilted his head to one side, then put on his spectacles. The lenses magnified his eyes, and Efim could not look away. —In four different languages. A born polyglot. He's fluent in six languages now. He'll tell you it's seven, but his spoken English is not very good. He's got gifts to burn, so when he drinks himself to oblivion, or risks his career and his life for some whore, I confess, I tend to worry.

Prying cucumber loose from his teeth with his tongue, Efim considered how much he'd scrubbed his hands earlier in the evening, how difficult he'd found it to remove Nadezhda Ivanovna's blood from his cuticles.

Vodka glugged and splashed as Arkady refilled his glass yet again. —Kostya's shoulder. The pain is eating him alive. I can see it.

—If you want his pain controlled, then I need to increase his morphine dose, and that starts us up the ladder to narkomania.

—That's not good enough.

—Some shrapnel wounds never heal. I repeat what I said when I first examined him: proper convalescence, and then, if he must work, a desk job only.

Arkady shook his head. —I can't do that. Too much attention is dangerous.

—More dangerous than severe pain or raging narkomania? What will that do to his judgement and career? What has it done already?

—A crippled officer is an easy target in a purge.

Efim had nothing to say to that.

Arkady stood up. —Let's get you comfortable, Efim Antonovich. Pick whichever chair you like, or the couch.

—What? I can't stay here.

—So inject him now.

—While he's unconscious and liable to vomit? I might kill him.

—Then you must stay. No doctor wants to kill his patient.

Efim clenched his fists and stifled a cry. Laboratory of Special Purpose Number Two. How many more? Certain he could smell blood from his fingers, and certain Arkady could, too, he reached for his medical bag. To calm his thoughts about the lab, he imagined the inventory of his bag: stethoscope, tongue depressor, reflex hammer, tourniquets, bandages, syringes, morphine. Speculum, dilatation rods, curettages, and a wooden dowel dented from the recent pressure of Nadezhda Ivanovna's teeth.

Risk of hemorrhage. She should not be left alone.

Arkady settled himself into an armchair. —Take the Persian rug from the study so you don't get a chill.

Near half-past two in the morning, pain tearing a hole in his sleep, Kostya cried out. Efim followed Arkady to the little room, and, like Kostya, squinted and frowned in the sudden light.

Arkady took his hand from the light switch and stood close to Efim, leaving Efim little room to work.

Efim ignored him as he picked up Kostya's wrist and took his pulse. —Shoulder?

—What the fuck else?

Arkady snorted. —Kostya, you will not make the doctor's work more difficult than it needs to be.

Kostya sat up. —Arkady Dmitrievich. Why are you here?

—It's my house.

—Right, right, debauchery in the iris bed.

Arkady flinched.

Missing this, Efim took equipment from his medical bag and prepared an injection. —He's still drunk.

—He'll be drunk for days, at this rate.

Efim tied a tourniquet on Kostya's left arm. —Lie down. No, not on your back, in case you vomit. On your good side. You'll feel a pinch.

Arkady watched the liquid flow into Kostya's vein. Then, careful not to jostle the injured shoulder, he tucked the grey blanket around Kostya.

Efim fastened his medical bag shut and thought he should admire Arkady's tenderness, yet all he wanted to do was spit. —I need to get back to the flat.

—Rest here, at least until the metro is running.

—No, I can't impose. I should go.

—It's half-past two in the morning. If NKVD see you out on the street, they will want to know why. I will call for a car and driver.

—Comrade Major, that's not necessary.

Arkady had already picked up his telephone's receiver and now spoke to an operator.

After an awkward wait of twenty-three minutes, during which Efim tried different ways to sneak a peek at his watch, headlights shone on the front window. Arkady walked Efim to the waiting car and ordered the driver to bring the good doctor home. The officer stepped out and held the door so Efim could climb into the back seat. Efim looked over his shoulder; Arkady nodded, so pleasant, so courteous. The air smelled of iris.

Fucked in the mouth, what did I do to my head?

Snow fell from a white ceiling. Then Kostya got his eyes open further, chasing away a dream of snow at his wedding, a wedding that proceeded despite the unacknowledged absence of the bride. Annoyed by the dampness of the sheets, he sat up, and that worsened his headache. The stink of bile and wine from his soiled *gymastyorka* and undershirt on the floor added to his nausea, which then got urgent. Despite a difficult journey of staggering gait and burning eyes, he ascended the stairs and reached the bathroom in time. Then he sat a while on the floor, resting his face against the cool toilet bowl. His memories of the day before settled like silt.

What did I say to Andrei?

Irises.

I hit her.

Dima's chair.

He turned and retched.

Shoulder aching, he grasped the sink, hauled himself up, and splashed some water on his face. Arkady's razor and shaving soap lay in their usual spot, and Kostya picked them up, just as he'd done after release from hospital, recalling the fever dream on the train in 1918: Baba Yaga and her menacing comment on his Russian smell.

He said it to the mirror. —I smell like a Chekist because I use the Chekist's soap.

He got himself back to the study, noticing the good Persian rug, the one he'd wrapped Nadia in at the party, rumpled on the couch in the parlour.

—Arkady Dmitrievich?

The cat flap squeaked; one of the toms, Borodin, slinked through the porch.

Kostya ignored the cat, and the cat, as ever, ignored him. Then Kostya called louder, up over the stairs. —Arkady Dmitrievich, are you still here?

Nothing.

Back in the study he found a note on the desk.

Good morning. Or afternoon. I telephoned Kuznets.
You're on leave for bereavement. The funeral is
tomorrow, ten o'clock. The cleaning women are due
at four today. Be certain you leave nothing on the floor.
Do not make their work more difficult than it needs to
be. You've already done that to me. Once you're clean and
civilized, make yourself useful and fetch the items listed
on the other sheet for the funeral reception. And do not
disgrace me with any more sloppy drunkenness. We all
mourn here, Kostya. Grief entitles you to nothing. You'll
find some civilian clothes in your old closet and some
bromide salts in the pantry for your headache.

Kostya opened the curtains and stared out at the garden: so much greenery, so much space, not another human being in sight. That meant nothing, really, but in that moment, he believed in the garden's offer of privacy and peeled off his *galife* pants, shorts, and socks. Naked, he strode upstairs to the bathroom again, recalling first he must visit the linen closet for a towel.

He passed Arkady's bedroom, hesitated.

He'd not dared to look for the papers and passport there.

Boris Kuznets had come and gone from this house as he pleased over the last six weeks.

Kostya checked the dresser drawers, the clothes in the closet, the mattress, the bedding, the pillows, the rug, and the high closet shelf. He flinched when the telephone rang, then ignored it, wondering again if Arkady had buried the passport and papers in the garden.

The dessert parties: the one thing he knew he hated about Arkady, and yet he craved invitation. Once allowed to attend, he'd always chosen a woman, always enjoyed himself.

Blood weighted his penis.

A memory of sensation: the surrender of Nadia's cheek beneath his fingers as he backhanded her face. He'd enjoyed it.

No, it's not like that.

Forcing her to sit on the stool in the Lubyanka cell.

Duty.

Arkady forcing him to sit on a stool in a Lubyanka cell.

He cares about me.

Arkady beating him as an adolescent, as a grown man. The conversation with Arkady after the last beating, the absurd attempt at a bargain.

His erection twitched.

He shut his eyes, picked up the towel and held it to his face.

A long shower washed away nothing.

—

The watchwoman in the lobby slept on as Kostya climbed the stairs to his flat. He fumbled his key in the lock, grateful he'd not lost the key last night, and heard the jangle of the telephone. He strode past both a note on the table and the closed door to his bedroom and picked up the receiver by the bathroom door.

—Yes, this is Nikto. Yes, yes, I just said that.

The operator asked him to stand by for a call from Lubyanka.

A woman's voice, not Evgenia Ismailovna, greeted him with a crisp efficiency that made Kostya wince. Then she informed him he must report to work.

—What, today? Comrade, I'm...German, yes. Italian, yes, very close to Spanish, but can this not wait until...Fine. Yes, thank you. Give me...I'll be there as soon as I can.

He eased the receiver into its cradle and sighed, further irritated by the darkness in the hallway. —Nadia?

Nothing.

The air in the flat seemed heavy, stale.

Slow and careful, he eased the bedroom door open, padded to the closet, and took uniform pieces from their hangers. Asleep, Temerity did not move.

In the kitchen, he found some bread and cheese and a note on the table. As he took a small bite of bread and picked up the note, he caught another whiff, another touch of that heaviness, a scent he knew.

Old blood.

The note read: *Let her rest. Come see me at the Lab.*

Struggling to swallow the dry chunk of bread, Kostya considered the mysteries of women's courses, of which he knew very little. Sometimes, women in the Lubyanka cells smelled of blood, even when no one had struck them. In Spain one night, Kostya had wondered how women in the field managed, or the nurses in the clinics, and he'd wondered this in moonlight as he flicked a cigarette butt into the spreading pool of blood at his feet. Trotskyist, tsarist, Red, White: all blood smelled the same. In defiance and pride then, Kostya had lit a second cigarette, baiting any sniper who might be nearby, daring him.

Go on. Take a shot. Kill me.

Nothing.

The men he hunted in Spain: he'd shot most of them. Once he'd cut a throat — quiet, but more difficult than he'd expected, as his target heard him and lunged almost out of reach. When he shot the five-litre tin of type O-negative in the clinic, the spatter reached his mouth, his nose, even the curves of his ears. Blood, blood, blood.

How much does a woman bleed?

He got himself into uniform.

Questions of menstrual cycles irked him all morning, providing a merciful distraction as he emerged from Dzerzhinskaya and strode towards Lubyanka and most certainly did not study a boarded-up office window on the third floor. Inside, he strode to Evgenia Ismailovna's desk, ready to report in and enjoy the solace of tea, except a different woman sat there. He asked for both Evgenia and Boris. The new woman explained that Comrade Captain Kuznets was busy elsewhere and that Comrade Ismailovna was ill. Kostya nodded, accepting paperwork. *Her courses?* Former girlfriends had complained of sore breasts and cramps, and refused sex, but, in the end, they'd explained nothing.

How does it feel, to bleed like that, bleed to a purpose, bleed without injury?

These stubborn questions also interfered with his concentration as he interrogated some Comintern members accused of spying, an Italian woman called Nina Fontana who kept asking after her husband and children, and a German woman called Ursula Friesen. Both women spoke passable Russian, despite their injuries. Kostya played his game, addressing each woman in a soft voice, in her own language, offering cigarettes: the Nikto Touch. Everyone in his department marvelled at his skill with foreigners, especially the women. Get Nikto on it. Let handsome Nikto finish it. Call Nikto. Other officers had tried the business with the cigarettes, got nowhere.

The cigarettes, Kostya knew, accomplished little.

It's the language. Their own language breaks them.

He ached to be anywhere else, free of bare walls and heavy doors, yet here, burrowed in Lubyanka's basement, burrowed in duty, he felt safe, safe from Vadym's death.

Ursula and Nina both signed the confession forms, new ones based on Kostya's templates. Nina extracted a promise from Kostya that she'd be sent to the same camp as her husband, a promise Kostya could not keep and indeed soon forgot. Nina didn't even try to read her confession form. Instead, she looked her interrogator in the eye and insisted the Soviet government take responsibility for her children. —You've a duty, now, comrade. Believe what you like about my guilt, but you know, you *know*, that my children have done nothing.

Andrei.

Timur.

Timofei.

Enrico, you are now Genrikh. Miguel, you are now Mikhail. Perhaps they'll call you Misha.

—My children, comrade!

Kostya straightened papers. —I'll see that they're looked after.

He ate lunch in the cafeteria, taking his time, the taste of the *shchi* a little too sharp today, the noise of people eating a little too loud.

Matvei Katelnikov sat at his table and offered him a cigarette. Kostya accepted, and the two officers smoked together, in silence.

Yury Stepanov, eyes bright and strange, as though he struggled with some deep thought, offered him condolences. He sounded sincere. Kostya thanked him. That, too, sounded sincere.

Back in the department, Evgenia's substitute called out to him, her voice nasal and high. —Comrade Senior Lieutenant Nikto. You're required for *poligon* duty tonight.

—What? Why?

She gave him a stern look, almost a warning. —Languages. The commanding officer has asked for help with the paperwork, and you were named.

—That should have been cancelled. I am supposed to be on bereavement leave.

—Your orders are right here. Comrade Captain Kuznets signed them.

—When?

—Earlier this morning.

As Kostya shut his eyes, he saw text dance, and he heard pleas in different languages. —Words, words, words.

—Pardon me, comrade?

Walking away, he called over his shoulder. —I'll be there. Of my own free will, yet twice as much by compulsion.

—Comrade Senior Lieutenant Nikto!

He froze, and others looked up from their work and conversations. The rebuke and accusation in her voice: a civilian to an NKVD officer? How dare she?

Kostya refused to turn around. —I am busy, comrade. What is it you wish?

—Look at me when I speak to you!

A man's voice from somewhere behind Kostya: —I will not tolerate this!

Yury Stepanov.

He strode to the woman and slammed his open hands on her desk. —You, comrade, will not presume to command any of us. Comrade Senior Lieutenant Nikto works very hard under extremely difficult circumstances, and you—

—We all work hard, Comrade Sergeant, and I will not—

—Shut up! Shut up, you stupid bitch!

Other officers joined Yury now, and their deep voices rose in a collective until the woman's higher voice collapsed in tears and defeat.

Kostya got to his office and slammed the door behind him. His startled officemates, subordinate in rank, hurried to their feet, addressed Senior Lieutenant Nikto in tones of respect, apologized that they hadn't expected him, and explained they could leave. Wishing he'd got the strength to tell them to stay, or even invite them out for a drink, Kostya stood out of their way.

He sat at his desk, almost frantic with paperwork, for hours. Then, not bothering with supper, he signed a car out of Garage Number One and drove himself to the *poligon*.

Metriks: surname, first name and middle name, for those lacking the cultural habit of patronymic.

Age.

Address.

Hair colour, eye colour, height, weight, ethnicity.

Kostya tugged on a clerk's sleeve and pointed to a blank on the form. —This one's German, not Dutch.

—Are you certain, Comrade Senior Lieutenant?

—Can you speak German?

—No, Comrade Senior Lieutenant.

—I can. So I am the one to be certain, yes?

—Yes, Comrade Senior Lieutenant.

Kostya leaned over another desk. —That one's French.

—Thank you, Comrade Senior Lieutenant.

A third desk and clerk. —Italian.

—Very good, Comrade Senior Lieutenant.

Eyes shut, Kostya rubbed his temples. *Welcome to Iosif Vissarionovich's Butcher Shop. Today's special: international cuts.* —I need some air.

The master-sergeant heard him. —Don't go far. We'll start soon.
—What?

—The squad is short a man tonight. Is that not why you're here?

Kostya broke a match, took out another, lit his cigarette. —Of course.

Outside, in view of a grassy area perfect for picnics and games, another officer leaned on the stone cottage wall. He wore an old leather coat. —I remember you. Earlier in the summer, one of the Nagants. I'm Lev.

All expectations of etiquette and rank had departed, this *poligon* its own world now. —Konstantin.

Lev took a packet from his right pocket and pressed it into Kostya's right hand, whispering the street value of the cocaine inside it.

—Why are you giving this to me?

Lev grinned. —Because you'll need it tonight. And someday further on, I may need a favour.

Kostya nodded, tucking the little envelope into his pouch. —Handsome coat. Old Chekist?

—Yes, my father's. I had a cough last week, so he insisted I wear it to work, keep warm. I'm almost cooked. If I take it off, you won't tell him, will you?

—Your secret's safe with me.

Cigarette done, Lev headed inside, where the barrels of vodka and Troynoy stood ready, where other executioners prepared for the night's work.

Kostya followed him. Then he measured out some cocaine and sniffed it, making sure Lev could see him.

Dogs whined and barked. Tractors idled. The sergeant dipped a tin cup into the vodka barrel and raised in a toast. —To your stamina, comrades.

Feet shuffled; prisoners and executioners got into their final queues. Kostya checked his Nagant for the third time: loaded, ready.

Noises of clunking switches and electricity: outside, searchlights shone.

The sergeant blew a whistle.

Kostya looked to Lev. —Is that new?

—A few weeks ago he lost his voice shouting orders at us, and we got behind schedule.

Another whistle, and the men of the squad stretched fingers and limbs, touched their toes, ran in place.

Warm-up at the gym, Kostya thought, and he rolled his shoulders, stretched his back, turned his head from side to side.

Third whistle: the executioners marched into the bright light.

As Kostya's vision adjusted, the squad formed before a new open grave, and the first line of prisoners joined them.

—Kneel!

The prisoners knelt.

—Aim!

The squad lifted weapons.

—Fire!

Noise and smoke.

A whistle blew. The next line of prisoners took their places.

The scene played out seven times; the Nagants reloaded while the Tokarevs mocked; another row; the Tokarevs reloaded while the Nagants jeered.

Again, again, again.

Kostya recognized Friesen and Fontana, the women from the morning's interrogation.

Just this morning?

Kneel. Aim. Fire.

Kick a corpse.

A recess: return to the stone cottage for vodka and cocaine, no shortage. Celebrating this bounty, some of the men sang 'Yablochko.'
—Ekh, little apple . . .

Lev turned from his sniffing as someone called to him, and the powder fell from the back of his hand. Alerted to this loss by another man, Lev only laughed.

Telling himself this would not, must not, become a habit, Kostya sniffed some more of Lev's gift. A numb clarity returned, a great comfort: purpose and duty, unsullied by emotion, shone as clear beacons.

It didn't last.

A whistle.

A return.

—Kneel!

On Kostya's left, the gaunt form of Pavel Ippolitov, tall even as he knelt...

—Aim!

On his right, a flash of purple silk near a woman's neck...

—Fire!

The purple left his line of sight. Vodka and bile shot into his mouth; he swallowed it back.

A whistle...

Blood and clots gushed as Temerity sat up and so tilted her pelvis; the flow soaked the padding. Efim had left to find more bandages, more wound dressing, more of something, anything, she might use.

As instructed, she rinsed the bloodied wads in the shower, wrung them out, then wrapped them in layers of *Izvestia*. Setting aside the last of the clean padding, unsteady, she stepped into the shower. She did not linger, careful to be thrifty with the soap, and, once dried off, packed, padded, and dressed again, she placed the package of *Izvestia* in a suitcase that Efim kept under his bed. He would dump the bundles in the incinerator at the lab.

No stains on my skirt, at least.

Finding the walk to the front room taxing, she sat in the soft chair. She dozed for a while, waking when Kostya stumbled into the flat. Fear jumped in her belly; fatigue pinned her down. That stink again: cordite and cigarettes and cologne and sweat and blood. His face and *gymnastyorka* looked dark grey, almost sooty, and his hair, which often shone with pomade, seemed dull as a shadow. He lurched toward the bathroom.

Temerity waited for him to call to her.

Not a word.

Instead, he strode back to the front room, fumbled in the drawers of the *stenka*, returned to the bathroom, and flicked on the electric light. An odd noise then, interrupted, brief, something between a hiss and hush.

Then Kostya yelped. —Ow! Nadia?

—A moment.

—Nadia, please.

—Yes, I'm coming.

Illuminated before the mirror, Kostya pried clippers away from a clump of hair on his now patchy head.

Bloodied hair.

He shook the clump free and resumed cutting. Rough. Random. The clippers made their shushing noise as Kostya left some spots incomplete, others bare, still others alone.

He glimpsed Temerity in the mirror. —The fucking showers don't work!

Hush-hush-hush.

—The work we do, and no showers?

Hush-hush-hush.

—And now the car's got to be taken out of service to be cleaned.

Hair fell to the floor. Temerity studied the waves and curls, and she wanted to cover the bloodied clumps with a towel.

Kostya dropped the clippers into the sink.

Wincing at the noise, Temerity rubbed her belly. She knew what she should ask. She also knew he might hit her again. —Where were you?

He took up the clippers again. —The *poligon*.

As Temerity struggled with the word *poligon* and considered geometry, the clippers jammed on another clump, and Kostya wrenched the lock of hair from his head.

—Fucked in the mouth!

—Let me do that.

—Don't touch me.

—Kostya, please. You'll hurt yourself.

—I don't feel a thing. Oh. Look at that. More filth. More fucking filth on this filthy fucking night.

She said it in English. —God's sake, you're bleeding.

Tears cut little paths on his face, startling him when he looked in the mirror. —My name is Konstantin Arkadievich Nikto, and I am a senior lieutenant of state security. Tell me you love me. Tell me it's still possible to love me. I'll never be clean.

Temerity met his gaze in the mirror.

Behind Temerity, Kostya saw Gavriil, tall and fair, wearing a black peaked cap, little round spectacles, and a Chekist's leather coat like Lev's, like Arkady's. He looked like an effete intellectual desperate to prove his revolutionary devotion and credentials, except he looked like nothing of the sort. Revolutionaries might have long and thin faces, and the old Chekists might wear those coats, but Gavriil, for all the order of the disguise, meant chaos. Gavriil shed the coat and revealed NKVD uniform, then shed that so that he looked like the ikon of the Novogord Gavriil, only with eyes of flame.

Kostya's knees buckled, and he caught himself on the sink.

Temerity's voice reached him. —Get in the shower and get that mess out of your hair. Then I can finish the cut.

—Get rid of it. Clip it off. All of it!

—Fine, but you'll have to wash it first. I'll turn on the water, get it warm.

She did this, disgusted with herself. *Shall I hold Tam Lin tight?*

Kostya watched the water flow from the shower head. —Nadia, I'm sorry about your face.

—Yes, I'm still quite angry about that. The water's warm now. Get in.

He stood there.

Sighing, she tugged at his *gymnastyorka* and *portupeya*. —Take these off.

He writhed out of his uniform, dropped the lot on the floor, and stood beneath the water. Temerity glanced at the holster, then at the scars on Kostya's shoulder.

—Nadia, pass me the soap.

She did. Then she put the toilet seat down and perched there.

Water ran, ran, ran.

—Nadia, I'm so sorry I hit you.

Staring at the wall, she said nothing.

—That will never happen again. I swear it.

She studied the clumps of hair on the floor.

—I've not been my best self. I don't even know who that is. I'd like to think he's better than the man who hit you.

She moved some of the locks and clumps aside with her toes.

He rinsed. —Arkady Dmitrievich says my grief entitles me to nothing.

—He's right.

Kostya turned off the water, accepted a towel from Temerity, and dried off. He touched his scalp. —What have I done to my head?

—How's the shoulder?

—Fucking recoil. Did Efim say when he'd be back?

—No.

—Please.

Please, what?

He stood there, arms limp. —Nadia, please. Just... touch me. Tell me I'm real. I still exist.

She stared at him.

—I am a ghost. I'm already dead. And I've killed you, too.

Temerity touched the skin near the scars of his bad shoulder. —You're quite warm for a ghost.

Gentle, he took her hand, placed it instead on his good shoulder, then lifted it to his lips and kissed it.

Then he let go of her hand and picked through his clothes for cigarettes and matches. —Recite something and help me fix my head. Please?

Almost line by line, interrupting herself with pauses as she got better control of the clippers, she whispered Shakespeare's sonnet 40 in English and cut what remained of Kostya's hair.

The English words and rhythms soothing his ears and his mind, even as meaning flew past him, he sat on the toilet seat and watched his hair fall away. Gavriil, still standing by the wall, eyes no longer flames but caverns, refused to explain anything. Then he disappeared.

Temerity lowered the clippers. —Done.

Kostya ran his hand over his scalp: the faintest stubble. —Good. We'll clean this mess up later. Right now I need a drink.

—I think you've had enough for tonight.

—Far too much. But just one drink, for just one story, yes?

Big green eyes stared up at her.

Tapping the clippers clean of hair, she gave a tight little smile. —All right, Kostya. One drink.

He sipped his vodka. —Vadym had a nephew my age, Mikhail. Everyone called him Misha. When Arkady Dmitrievich first brought me here to Moscow, in '18, we both had flu. Vadym looked after us. After I got a bit better, he introduced me to his Misha. He thought we might be friends. Arkady Dmitrievich never liked Misha, called him a rebellious angel and said he'd come to a bad end. Misha was determined to solve every problem himself, and he was braver than me, not that I ever told him that. I loved him. We competed in everything, especially at the gym. He played better bandy, but I could row faster. He leapt hurdles, but I could run the long races. I could shoot better, and that pissed him off. Neither of us could be best in wrestling. Coaches called stalemate after stalemate. We graduated from school and ran straight for the NKVD. We competed there, too. In the end I got the better grades, and I was always the better shot.

Remembering where she'd heard the name Misha, remembering Cristobal Zapatero, Temerity felt nauseous.

Kostya swirled his drink around in the glass. —We both ended up in foreign intelligence because of the languages, and we got sent our separate ways. Except we met up again in Spain. All these international communists poured in to fight the fascists, winds of change, flames of revolution, blah blah blah...

—I know what you did in Spain.

—And I enjoyed it.

Temerity took a good swallow of vodka, hoping to block her memory of Cristobal's rosary beads hitting the floor. She failed.

Kostya raised his glass to her, in a silent toast. —I got homesick. I never expected that. When you spoke Russian to me, you knocked something loose. I knew my duty. I knew I'd have to shoot you, leave no witness. But you spoke Russian, and you told me about your Russian mother. Was that true?

—Yes.

After a moment, Kostya shrugged. —I met up with Misha again just a few days before in Bilbao. I was so happy to see him. All the troubles of Spain, and there's Misha. Things made sense again. He even remembered my birthday was coming up. He had vodka. He'd saved it, one little flask, carried it from Moscow and then all over Spain. It felt like years, and yet it felt like only a minute passed as we drank together, and we spoke Russian, and we laughed. Later told everyone we were Canadians.

Temerity snorted. —Canadians?

—Mr. MacKenzie and Monsieur LeBas of the International Brigade who came all the way to Spain to the fight the fascists. I didn't have time to carve any princes out of butter, so I wouldn't call it a very good Canadian disguise. Misha spoke better Spanish, so I let him do most of the talking. Even if anyone guessed we were Russian, no one wanted to believe we might be NKVD, or would want us to know they'd guessed, so it worked. Then we got the orders to liquidate Zapatero. I needed to see a doctor anyway, so I thought I could get treatment first, and then kill him. Except I met you. And Misha fucked things up. Misha should have shot Zapatero in the head. Simple execution job, but no, he had to miss. And I knew right away it was deliberate. No way, no fucking way, could he miss from so close. I gave him hell. Misha and I had a spot in Gerrikaitz, this abandoned barn, and we took Zapatero there. Misha said we should question Zapatero. We had no orders to question him, but what the hell, Misha argued, we had him, so we might as well use him. We packed his wound, but once we moved him he started to bleed again. I could see we didn't have long. So we got him to the barn, tied him down. Misha's big chance: interrogate the captured POUM member and glean useful intelligence. 'Fine,' I said, and I stood back.

That Spanish fucker... Three hours we worked on him, and all he said was, 'Take the bullet out.' Told us to free his hands so he could do it himself. Then he started babbling. At first Misha thought Zapatero was giving us names, but he was just calling on the saints. I aimed at Zapatero's forehead, and Misha got between us. 'Listen to him,' said Misha. 'Just listen to him.' We both looked to Zapatero, but he'd passed out. 'Then listen to me,' Misha said, 'because we're killing our own.'

We argued for hours. We drained the last of the vodka, and some of the wine I'd stashed there. I got so fucking sick on wine and sulpha pills. I'd retch, and nothing would come up. I looked around. Solid, well built, big rafters in the ceiling. Various pieces of gear stored there, scythes and ropes and shovels. Big hooks.

We talked some more. At least, Misha talked. He asked if I ever had doubts. 'No room for doubt when there's duty,' I wanted to say, but the words wouldn't come. All I could think of was how I hadn't shot you and how that could get me killed. Then I thought that Misha would understand.

Before I could say that, Misha admitted he missed Zapatero's head on purpose. 'I wanted you to listen,' Misha said. 'I wanted you to listen to someone in POUM and then make up your own mind.'

'Enough,' I said, and I got in front of Zapatero and shot him through the right eye. 'You want mercy for the enemy,' I said, 'there it is. He's out of his misery.'

Misha leapt at me. He knocked me over, pinned me to the floor, and he looked so hurt and betrayed. Misha, the rebellious angel. Arkady Dmitrievich said he could see it in Misha's eyes, a reflection of fire. He'd come to a bad end.

He got up without hurting me. Then he reached out his hand to help me up, and we drank.

Misha had no head for vodka, never did. He passed out, snored through the dawn. I got things ready. I had to save him. Misha was my best friend, and I loved him, so I had to bring him back and save him. It was all I knew. He fought me all the way, but I'd surprised him. Good strong rafters. Pulleys and hooks. Misha hung from his wrists. He kicked at me, and he spat on me, and I kept calm and hit him in the ribs with a spade. When he cursed at me again, he sounded afraid. That got me. Until I'd hit him with the spade, we could still back out, pretend somewhere in our heads that we were competing at the gym, playing a game.

He told me I'd broken something, and I let him hang there a while, asked him some more questions about his time in Spain. He gave me a pile of horseshit about infiltrating POUM and then coming to agree with them. At least, I think it was horseshit. Misha and his doubts... I just had to find some way to make him promise to run and be silent. I would let him go. So I got down on my knees, beneath him, and as he begged me to let him down, I begged him to forget me, forget his own name, forget everything we'd ever shared, and never to return to Russia.

Then I heard the growl. The planes. So many of them. Low. I ran outside. Junkers, the fucking Luftwaffe, in tight formation. I knew. The way I know languages. I just knew. And I stood there, and I stared at the sky, and the bombs fell.

Twenty minutes, I've been told. It felt much longer. I ran. I knew I had to get back to the barn, get Misha down, get him out.

The shrapnel hit my ear, my shoulder. I only felt the impact, like a really hard shove, and then everything fell on top of me. I got up, but it didn't matter, because the barn had collapsed. I screamed, and still I could hear nothing. I screamed for Misha. I ended up in a clinic. I don't know how. Someone pushed me part of the way in wheelbarrow, I think. There was so much fire. And that, Nadia, is how I ruined my canvas jacket and killed my best friend.

Temerity stared into her glass. —Kostya...

—So do you see it now?

She looked up. —See what?

—Why I took you from the old man's party. All that death and waste. All that blood. I nearly shot you, and still, still, when I called for help with those damned name tags, you answered. It was you. You had every right to ignore me or scream at me or shoot me where I stood, and instead you helped me with those children.

She said nothing.

He gave a long sigh. Then he drew his palm over his scalp, pausing at the likely entry point for an executioner's bullet. —It feels so strange.

—It looks strange.

New cigarette between his lips, he smirked. —I look old?

Smiling, wiping tears, she shook her head. *Condemned.*

She stood up. Pooled blood gushed. She scowled and grasped the table.

—Nadia, you're exhausted. Please, go to bed.

Back to that bed, where she'd lain all day? His bed, the centre of her ever smaller world, all meaning there found and lost?

In the bathroom, she checked her padding.

God's sake, how much more must I bleed?

[ ]

DOGS' HEADS AND BROOMSTICKS 3
Wednesday 28 July

Arkady embraced Kostya, careful to be gentle with the bad shoulder, kissed him on each cheek, and stroked his shorn head. —Tatar, what have you done to yourself?

—The showers at the *poligon* are fucked.

—Shh, we're in a church.

Kostya almost laughed at that. The Revolution drove out superstitions of God, and bullets extinguished priests, yet here they all gathered, for the funeral on an NKVD officer. —I got material in my hair. I clipped it off. Why a church?

—Vadym's brother insisted. Wait, *poligon* duty? Last night? I told Kuznets—

—I got called in. Languages.

Arkady fixed the lapels on the leather coat. —And this old thing of mine?

—I wear it out of respect.

Respect for you and Dima. Respect for what you both tried to do, that you both tried to save me. Respect for the loyalty of Pavel Ippolitov and Evgenia Ismailovna. Respect for the priests I shot last night. Respect for the truth: I kill people to survive.

Arkady's laugh had a shakiness to it. —It will cook you in this heat. Did you remember my groceries for the reception?

—Oh, God, I'm sorry. I—

—Kostya, shh, just breathe. Breathe.

In Arkady's arms, leaning on his chest, Kostya gasped, gasped again. —I'm so sorry, Arkady Dmitrievich. I watched him run. I watched him fall.

—I know. I know. Breathe, breathe. There, that's it. Better?

Kostya stepped back. —Better.

Boris Kuznets cleared his throat. —Arkady Dmitrievich, Konstantin Arkadievich. My condolences.

Both men flinched, then spoke at the same moment; Kostya deferred to Arkady and stopped talking.

—Thank you, Boris Aleksandrovich.

—Please introduce me to Vadym Pavlovich's family, so I might pay my respects.

—Of course. This way.

—Before we do that, come closer to me, both of you. I made certain that the coroner arrived at a verdict of a heart attack.

Kostya stifled a laugh.

Arkady glared at him, and he struggled to keep his voice low. —Heart attack?

Boris kissed Arkady on the cheeks. —In his confusion and pain from his heart attack, Vadym Pavlovich broke his window and fell. Easier for the family.

Arkady and Kostya both nodded, acknowledging this mercy.

Then Boris embraced Kostya and kissed him on the right cheek. —Some paperwork has gone astray. Our former secretary may be responsible. She had other paperwork snarls, quite suspicious. Uncooperative, too.

The purple silk. —Boris Aleksandrovich, do you mean Comrade Ismailovna?

Arkady took in a sharp breath.

Kostya continued. —Ismailovna is well organized, thorough, and most co-operative. With respect, Comrade Captain, I find it hard to believe you'd think otherwise.

Boris's eyes seemed to communicate surprise, respect, and satisfaction. —I find this funeral hard to believe, in a church, no less, yet here we are.

—What the hell is she guilty of?

—Contaminating the sacred trust of confession. She showed me her templates, these ready-made confessions. It will save time, she said. 'Why, Comrade Ismailovna,' I said, 'such laziness masquerading as efficiency could lead to false confessions. At no point can the NKVD tolerate such a practice. You've heaped a galling duty on me.' She begged for my protection. I could protect her from nothing.

Enough! Kostya expected to shout. Instead, his voice sounded quiet and young. —She can't be guilty. She can't.

—You must be mistaken, Konstantin Arkadievich.

Kostya shook his head. *I designed those templates. Say it. Say it's me, not her.* Then he felt Arkady's grip on his forearm, as though Arkady tried to hold him back from a fall.

Boris's eyes seemed to twinkle, as though he and Kostya now shared a delicious secret. —Handkerchief? Your face is wet. You're shaking, let me help. Now, the Minenkovs.

After clearing his throat a few times, Kostya introduced Boris to Vira and Pyotr. Then he noticed how sickly Arkady looked. No hiding it here: light danced on Arkady's cheekbones, once hidden beneath ample flesh, now sharp in defeat. Then he followed the older man's line of sight: the pedestal, the urn.

Absence.

Vadym, Dima, gone.

And so many others.

Kostya put his arm around Arkady's shoulders, and Arkady did not pull away or shrug him off.

The service, its old words and gestures, even the smells — incense, tobacco, cologne, perfume, stone, sweat — comforted Kostya, and that comfort startled him. Most of the women wore scarves on their heads, the ancient deference. Most of the men wore NKVD uniform. The elderly priests, eyes darting, seemed to shrink into their robes, and Kostya wondered about funerals in Kolyma.

A priest caught his eye, held his gaze.

At once moving forward of his own desire and shoved by people behind him, Kostya joined the procession out. As he saw Misha's parents, his knees buckled. He managed to steady himself, and then Pyotr and Vira Minenkov fussed over him, so fond, asking after his wounds, his state of mind, saying how they'd recognize him anywhere, never mind the haircut, adding how much Vadym had loved him and Misha both.

Kostya could only nod.

Vira understood something in Kostya's eyes. —Of course, we are prepared for Misha, too. We presume he's dead.

Pyotr almost barked it. —We don't know that.

Vira stroked his husband's arm. —Blood pressure, dear. Kostya, you're very pale. You should sit down.

Pyotr took a deep breath, counted to ten, and greeted the next mourner.

Moving away from the Minenkovs, Kostya did not genuflect to the huge ikon of a big-eyed Christ. Nor did he kneel or make any other gesture. The old ways had gone, the Revolution's cleansing now twenty years old. Priests starved in the camps and died at the *poligons*. Despite the funeral taking place in a church, the old ways meant nothing, so he must ignore the massive Christ, even as the ikon not only commanded the entire space but created a new one, a space infinite and at the same time intimate, only for Kostya. Commanding this warp of physics and time, Christ's eyes emptied of pigment and paint, sockets dark and deep, becoming the limestone catacombs beneath Odessa. Children hid there.

Kostya cried out. No one noticed.

Christ's eyes filled again with ancient colour, ancient mystery, asking, as Gavriil's eyes had asked, *Who are you?*

The Moscow clerk's abuse: *Tell me your surname. Tell me your surname.*

Nadia's disbelief: *Your name is really Nikto?*

Arkady's rebuke: *At least sit up straight. You slouch like some sneaky* bezprizornik.

Baba Yaga's taunt: *Welcome home,* bezprizornik. *Welcome home.*

Christ's eyes demanded response.

Arkady caught Kostya as he fell and made it look like nothing more than a stumble.

Leaning into Arkady's strength, Kostya noticed Boris and Yury studying them. He felt this should mean something: a warning, perhaps, a signal. —Arkady Dmitrievich, it's Zmei Gorynich.

—What?

—When Dobrynya Nikitich fights Zmei Gorynich, his feet get stuck in spilled blood. He's trapped.

Arkady pressed his lips to Kostya's forehead, seeking fever. —You're tired, Tatar. I'll drive you home.

—All the way to Odessa?

Scowling, Arkady grasped Kostya by his forearm again, navigated a path around the knots of people, and hauled him out of the church.

Outside, in the bright sunlight, safe from all the eyes, Kostya took a deep breath, then another. He obeyed Arkady's instructions to get in the car.

—Arkady Dmitrievich, they changed the forms again for Garage Number One. Did you sign this out with the correct form?

—My paperwork is fine.

They drove.

Kostya thought he caught sight of Andrei. —How often do women bleed their courses?

—What? I missed your street. I've got to loop back. Every month, you know that. It stops when they get pregnant. It's the most vile thing about them: bleed for a week and live. Worse than bitches in heat. At least when a bitch bleeds, it signals something.

A month is four weeks and a few days. —Signals what?

—Signals she's in heat... Kostya, no.

Arkady forgot the clutch and stalled the car. It juddered and died.

—It's fine, Arkady Dmitrievich, it's fine. She bleeds now. It's fine.

Arkady felt his limp hands slip from the steering wheel. —She has killed you. That whore has killed you, and I hate her for it, but when I'm arrested, I'll say nothing about her. For you. I promise that.

—They'll beat it out you. They'll fucking *beat* it out of you, because it's what we do.

—Wouldn't the Odessa herring merchant laugh now?

Kostya snorted. —The first time I held a Nagant, you told me it's not murder when it's the law.

—Go and rest.

—Arkady Dmitrievich, please. Let Scherba take a look at you, yes?

—I have fifty-odd mourners on their way to my house, expecting food and drink. Not the time. Wait. Did...

Kostya watched Arkady's hands tighten into fists.

—Kostya, did Dima say anything?

Kostya sighed, wiped his face with the back of his hand. —He was a good man.

—But did he say anything?

—He called me Misha. Then he died.

The little dings and cracks in the car's windshield filled Kostya's vision: Nurasyl Abdulin and the sacred weight of an auto's glass. *I came all this way to work and become a good citizen. Why am I still hungry?*

A tremor took Arkady, starting in his hands and climbing upwards until it seemed to escape out of the top of his head. Then, taking a deep breath, he seemed his old self. —This will end soon. Call me this evening, once you wake up.

—If you're under investigation, others will listen on the line.

—I don't care. Just call me, so that I know you're still here.

As he climbed out of the car, Kostya noticed various people watching him through windows.

Or perhaps, lost in their own worries, they stared at nothing.

Arkady drove off.

In the lobby, a new watchwoman stood by her rocking chair, her face stiff, not quite allowing herself to relax yet after a terrible fright.

The uniform, Kostya told himself, *the car.* —Good afternoon, Grandmother. I live on the sixth floor, flat number seven, Nikto, Konstantin Arkadievich. Do you wish to see my identification?

Avoiding his eyes, she shook her head. —I believe you are what you say you are, Comrade Nikto.

—Nadia?

Temerity stood still, arms raised in graceful defense. Ignoring Kostya, she finished the move.

—What is that?

She smiled. —Just a stretch.

The vodka bottle made a sharp clink against a glass. —I know *sombo* when I see it.

—The correct term is jiu-jutsu.

Looking to the ceiling, Kostya sighed. Then he sounded friendly, warm. —Come sit with me.

She joined him at the little table, accepted a drink.

His voice stayed warm as he lit two cigarettes. —Did you feel a kick? Here, take it. Hey? Answer me, Nadia.

Her brown eyes glittered. —Why?

—What do you mean, why?

—I mean, why in hell should I answer you?

—Because I deserve to know.

—Oh, do you?

—Yes. I deserve to know, before a bullet crashes through my brain, if—

—It was far too early to feel a kick.

After a moment, he sneered and ground out his cigarette. —Efim?

—Well, it wasn't Elena Petrovna, now, was it?

—Nadia, please.

She kept her voice steady. —Should I be happy? Should I recite some Shakespeare? Should I make this easy for you?

—I only—

—You did this to me!

—Nadia, you came to me!

—You! The man who's kept me in his flat to please himself!

—To keep you safe!

She ducked, shielding her face with her arms, and Kostya saw he'd raised his arm, ready to backhand her.

He chose to reach for the cigarettes.

Temerity heard the scrape of the match, then opened her eyes and lowered her arms. —Kostya, just get me somewhere near the embassy. I'll run.

Drawing hard on his cigarette, he shoved himself away from the table.

—Run with me. I'll vouch for you, tell them you've been kind. I can get you out of here. Kostya, please.

He wrenched open the door and strode into the corridor.

—Please!

She expected him to slam and lock the door behind him.

Instead, he eased it shut.

Then locked it.

The early evening gave no respite from the heat. Standing in the kitchen, his jacket and tie in a heap on the hinged table, Efim plucked his sleeves from his sweaty skin, rolled them up, and told himself the heat was no bother. Neither was his likely sentence of twenty-five years when found guilty of providing an abortion. His attempts at self-deception provided no real distraction. Once NKVD hauled him in, he'd confess it. He knew this. A matter of time, and perhaps of pride, but mostly time. *I'll babble it in the car before we even reach Lubyanka.*

As he sterilized his gynecological instruments by boiling them on the stove — he'd not dared to use the autoclave at the lab — Efim confronted a deeper recognition. Not only had he broken several laws, but he'd chosen the safety of this patient, however desperate, over the safety of his wife.

What kind of man am I?

He'd asked that question earlier in the afternoon at Laboratory of Special Purpose Number Two, testing refinements on a new formula with which he and the other doctors murdered two young women, twin sisters with frizzy blond hair, each pleading pregnancy.

He told Temerity he must examine her.

On Kostya's bed, towels beneath her, Temerity sweated in embarrassment and fear: the difficult pragmatics of tilting her pelvis at a good angle to allow Efim a view, of exposing, once again, a part of herself both violated and loved.

—No sign of infection, Nadezhda.

—I need to be sick.

—Did this come on suddenly?

She rolled on her side and retched.

Efim took a thermometer from bag and shook the mercury down. —Once you're done, we'll see if you're feverish.

Her temperature reading normal, Temerity tugged sheets up over herself. *I'm going to die here.*

Efim studied the bruise on Temerity's face. —I think you fell in love with the wrong man.

She sat up, making her nausea worse. —You think I chose this?

—Shh, your voice.

—My voice? I should scream. Isn't that what captives do? I should have stabbed him after I kneed him. I should—

The telephone rang; they both flinched.

Temerity listened to Efim answer the caller's questions: yes, yes, no, no, no, yes.

He stood in the doorway. —I have to leave.

—Wait, I need money.

He shut his medical bag and shook his head.

—Efim Antonovich, please, just thirty kopeks.

—You shouldn't be on your feet yet. Get some rest. Doctor's orders. He left the flat.

After a moment, she checked the door.

Locked.

She arranged fresh bandages for herself. Then, in the front room, she switched on the radio. A shrill report on production quotas for iron concluded and gave way, for the education and betterment of all, comrades, to a live performance of the first movement of Johann Sebastian Bach's *Partita for Solo Violin No. 3 in E Major.* —Please welcome violinist Comrade Orlova.

Temerity knew the piece well. Bach's vigour and clarity in this partita always made her heart beat faster, and she gasped in pleasure. Static interrupted yet failed to obscure the insistent, almost frantic beauty as the violinist reached beyond the state-induced Stakhanovite aesthetic of faster-faster-faster, more-more-more, and begged — dared — the listener to keep up.

Temerity felt her ribs ache, her lungs twitch, as if she'd forgotten to breathe. She'd last heard the piece performed at a concert three years before, accompanied by her father and Count Ostrovsky. Tears pricked.

A click: the announcer informed the audience that he held a stop-watch close to the mic. The first movement of that partita often took three and a half or even four minutes to play. Comrade Orlova had just finished in three minutes and thirteen seconds.

—Have you anything to say, Comrade Orlova?

—Oh. Ah, just thank you.

She sounded much as Temerity imagined Amelia Earhart would: not frightened, but exhilarated. Despite the menace and threat of the Purge, despite the risk of drawing the attention of those who might sense her resistance and strength and so wish to harm her, Orlova had reached for beauty. In this moment, she could be both loyal and, for those who had ears to hear it, subversive. Of course, she pursued excellence for collective joy and the glory of the motherland, nothing self-interested, bourgeois, or formalist here. And yet, in the same moment, she pursued excellence as a private devotion to something greater than mere survival. In that decision, perhaps more instinct than choice, she stood defiant.

Patting her left shoulder, Temerity smiled.

—No sign of him?

Efim placed his medical bag on the sofa. —None.

Pacing, Arkady gestured to his large table: cheese, bread, and some cold roast fowl, little bowls of chopped cucumber in yogurt, and three bottles of wine. —Leftovers. I hosted a funeral reception today. Help yourself.

Resenting Arkady's hospitality after his command to come to the house, no explanation given, Efim studied the table and its offerings. —Please accept my condolences once more.

—I told Kostya to stay at the flat and call me.

—Nadezhda Ivanovna says he got upset and left.

—Nadezhda Ivanovna can rot in Kolyma and then take a holiday in hell. Nadezhda Ivanovna Solovyova: you do know that's not her real name. At least, you suspected. And she's not Soviet, either. I've seen her passport.

Efim felt dizzy. *How could I not know what I know?* —Why do you tell me this?

—So that now we shall all tumble into the meat grinder hand-in-hand, singing folk songs that celebrate the triumph of the workers. Drink?

Nodding, Efim sat down. A cork popped; wine splashed; Efim looked up. As Arkady returned to Efim, passing through patches of shadow and light, a sheen glistened, then dulled, on his forehead, like a salt stain, like a frost.

Efim accepted the wine. —When did you last consult a doctor? For yourself?

—You're here now, aren't you?

Efim peered at him. This big Chekist, free of his uniform, seemed smaller. His cheeks sagged, and his eyes betrayed something new, something besides fear and corruption and expectation of command: sacrifice. Balakirev, Arkady Dmitrievich, Major, NKVD, his desires and motives wrinkled and obscured, had reached a decision.

Arkady sat near Efim. —Let me tell you how my father died.

Efim listened to this story as he studied Arkady's face, eyes, hands. Then he asked permission to listen through his stethoscope.

The lungs crackled and wheezed, air fighting with fluid. The heart beat too fast.

Arkady shuddered as though chilled. —I itch all over. Worse at night. Get that thermometer away from me.

Efim stroked Arkady's cheek with the backs of his fingers and found no fever. To make sure, he pressed his lips to Arkady's forehead. As he retreated, he tasted his lips: salty, uric, foul. —You've no pain with this, Comrade Major?

—None.

Efim washed away the taste with a sip of wine. —That may change.

—I don't care.

Efim believed him.

—I don't care. I just want Kostya looked after, and for the first time in my life since I became a man, I can do nothing. Too much works against him. I cannot save him. And I'm afraid he cannot save himself.

Efim's practised speech for the dying, his gentle encouragement to detach from worldly concerns and visit the church of the mind, failed. Taking a deep breath, he told himself to use the diminutive, for in this moment he'd intruded on something intimate, as a doctor must. —You need to let Kostya worry about himself.

—Kostya, alone? Him, and that whore? Even if I can't save him, I will still protect him. I know him well; I know how he thinks; he'll be here soon. And then I may need you all the more. I don't want him to know you're here, though, so when I tell you, wait in the study.

—What?

A wheeze sharpened Arkady's sigh. —Efim Antonovich, I've been presumptuous. I ordered you here instead of inviting you. Vadym said I treat every encounter as an interrogation. I think he was right. Will you stay a while?

Not a command but a plea, a plea from a sick man. Confused, Efim nodded. —Of course.

As Arkady topped up their drinks and started telling a story of Kostya as an adolescent, the trouble he caused with a friend called Misha, Efim saw how he must counsel two violent Chekists on the inevitability of death. He laughed at the thought, just at a moment where Arkady's story invited laughter. Then he recognized a deeper truth: he must prepare a loving son for the loss of his father.

Ears ringing and arms stiff from too much target practice, Kostya struggled to write his name on the correct line to sign out a car. He passed the forms back to the clerk, who, eyes down, eager to return to the magazine he'd hidden when the officer had approached his desk, wrote his initials next to Kostya's signature. Then the clerk stood up, stretched his lower back, and plodded to the new display of keys. They dangled on tiny metal rings, the rings themselves hanging on individual nails. Above each nail: a careful entry in pencil of numbers matching key to automobile. Several spots lay empty. The clerk stood there a moment, as though watching a confrontation play out and deciding whether to intervene. Then he returned to his desk and glanced at the form again.

Kostya rolled his eyes. *Just pick one.*

The clerk plucked the key from its nail and gave it to Kostya. —Car number forty-two, Comrade Senior Lieutenant Nikto.

—Thank you, comrade. Goodnight.

In the garage, where the cars waited in their numbered spots, a driver opened a car's rear door, and Vasily Blokhin emerged. —Good evening, Nikto. On your way home?

—Just finished some target practice.

—Excellent, stay ready. I've got night duty, myself. How's your shoulder?

—Oh, fine, fine.

—You knew Minenkov. Vadym Pavlovich.

A statement, not a question. No tinge of accusation.

—Yes.

Vasily bowed his head. —My condolences. These are difficult days.

Then he left, his walk slow and steady, and his purpose, it seemed, clear.

Behind the wheel of car number forty-two, Kostya removed his Nagant from the holster and studied it. Such a practical design, elegant: the inviting curve of the grip. Seven rounds nestled the chamber. A thing of beauty, a joy for the permanence of revolution.

Ready.

As was he.

—Not yet.

Kostya's eyes glittered as he hung up the phone from talking with Arkady. —Why not?

Behind the bathroom door, Temerity adjusted padding. —Just a minute.

Studying his wristwatch, Kostya leaned against the wall. He'd done it. Signed out the car. Kept his promise. He'd get her to the embassy.

Temerity touched his good shoulder. —You mean it? In truth?

One of those spells again: asleep with his eyes open. —Yes, my Marya Morevna, in truth.

She blinked away tears.

He leaned down to kiss her cheek. Then, tasting salt, he whispered in her ear. —The car's just outside the lobby. I'm your driver. We make it look right, yes? I'll open the car door, and you get in the back. Even the watchwoman can't object to that.

Her rapid nod brushed her curls against his nose and mouth, tickling him. He held her tight, inhaled the scent of the top of her head, let her go.

Outside the flat, at the top of the stairs, expecting this dream to shatter, Temerity hesitated. Up so high, such a fall, the watchwoman at the bottom...

Kostya offered his arm.

Temerity took it, and they descended together.

In the lobby, Kostya pressed his palm to the seat of the empty rocking chair. —Still warm. She's not gone far. Move.

Dusk. The air seemed to patter on her face, like raindrops. Temerity took in a deep breath. —Oh, God, it's so fresh.

Holding the car door open for her, Kostya shook his head. —It's hot. The whole city stinks.

Temerity took in the smells of the car: leather, oil, steel. Kostya peeked at her in the rear-view mirror, then adjusted his cap, too big now for his bald head.

As they passed Vasilisa Prekrasnaya, Temerity remembered some of the drive from the party to the flat, remembered screaming at Kostya about the car being all over the road. Unaware she did so, she patted her blouse where the Temerity West passport still lay hidden. —Just get me across the bridge and drop me near the embassy. I'll be fine. You don't even need to stop the car, just slow it down. I'll run.

Curious about why she patted her blouse, Kostya wanted to caution her: growing accent, rapid speech. *You sound loose.* —We'll take the Bolshoy Moskvoretsky across the river. It's fastest.

Steady the Buffs. —Thank you, thank you. I'll never forget this. Thank you.

—But first I need to say goodbye.

—What?

Headlights played on the curtains; a car engine shut off. Arkady, sitting in his favourite armchair, in uniform with his *gymastyorka* unfastened, informed the cat in his lap that he must stand up.

The cat only purred and seemed to get heavier.

—No, Tchaikovsky, I have guests. I must answer the door.

The cat spread his paws and kneaded Arkady's thigh; two people outside approached the door.

Arkady resumed scratching the cat around the ears. —Then again, he has a key.

The cat jumped away. Wincing at the pricks of Tchaikovksy's claws, Arkady flicked on electric lights and plodded to the door.

The lock released; the knob turned; that British woman with the bruised face stepped inside. Kostya, in uniform, walked right behind her, either to protect her, or block her exit. Which one, Arkady could not say.

Kostya greeted him. —Arkady Dmitrievich.

Voice hollow, quiet, Arkady gestured to the parlour. —Leave your boots and shoes on. Sit down.

Temerity's memory strengthened with each click of her heels. *This room.* She recognized the chair Arkady now offered her, even as the light glared on his spectacles and hid his eyes. She shook her head.

—I'll stand.

—You'll sit.

Kostya nudged her towards the chair, and both men watched as she obeyed.

Then Arkady turned to Kostya. —Just what do you hope to accomplish with this stunt?

—I need to get her to the British Embassy.

Temerity closed her eyes. *God's sake!*

Arkady snorted. —Sometimes we tell lies not to save ourselves but to comfort ourselves. You're not going to drive her anywhere, Little Tatar, because you're not that stupid.

—Arkady Dmitrievich, please. Let's say goodbye.

—What?

—I'm going with her.

Temerity stared at him. A vision, a desire, a delusion: a sweet summer evening at Kurseong House, in the library, Kostya in his fifties, hair gone grey, face lined from laughter and cigarettes, sitting beneath the Novgorod Gabriel print with a book. Nightingales sang.

After a moment, Arkady managed to speak. —Just steal a car and cross the Moskva like nothing matters?

Kostya gave a crooked smile, acknowledging the absurdity. —The car's not stolen; I signed it out. And I left once before.

—You can't come back, not this time. Even if you make it across the water, even if the British take you, you're done. You will turn your back to me, which doesn't seem to bother you—

—Arkady Dmitrievich—

—You will turn your back on your home, yes, your home, because however fucked up this country is, it's still home, and you'd abandon it for a bit of cunt—

—No.

—And you'll abandon yourself. Kostya, you're a Chekist. You're NKVD.

—I am more!

—Everything you are is tangled up in the NKVD, and you'll run to the British? They'll interrogate you for weeks, and then they'll fucking kill you.

—And if I stay, my own friends and colleagues will interrogate and torture me for weeks and then kill me. Oh, sorry, fucking kill me.

—No. No, Kostya, please.

—Arkady Dmitrievich...

Temerity got to her feet and crept around the edge of the room until she stood outside Arkady's line of sight.

Unaware of this, Arkady drew his Nagant and pointed it at Kostya. —Don't. Not after everything I...no.

Working to ignore the gun, Kostya took a shaky breath. —Then just give me her passport and papers. I'll drive her there, and I'll come right back and turn myself in.

The Nagant trembled. —Do that, and you've killed me, too.

—A British passport and travel papers. The name is Margaret Bush. She lost them here, at the dessert party.

—I don't know what you're yapping about.

—Yes, you do!

—Tatar, Tatar, listen to me.

Kostya perceived two forms moving around the edge of the room: Nadia, and Gavriil. *Not got time for either of you right now. Please stand by.* —Arkady Dmitrievich, please. I've torn holes in this house looking for that passport.

—That was you? I thought...I heard you in here one night. You scared me.

—I thought you'd gone out.

A glow distracted Kostya: the two small fiery holes of Gavriil's eyes.

The ikons on Grandfather's beauty wall.

This time the Angel Gavriil's NKVD uniform bore a senior lieutenant's insignia.

As Kostya raised his hands in surrender, a shadow changed. Arkady lifted his Nagant from Kostya and whirled to face Temerity.

She seized his arm, broke his grip on the Nagant, and flipped him.

The crash of Arkady's heavy body on the floor seemed to rattle the whole house. His spectacles landed near Temerity's feet, and the lenses shattered. Breathing hard, Arkady shifted his weight to rise. As he looked up, he saw Temerity aiming the Nagant at his forehead.

Kostya took a step back. —Nadia.

She kept her gaze on her prisoner.

—Nadia. Don't. Please, don't.

She kicked Arkady's spectacles away. —Balakirev, where are my papers?

—I don't answer whores.

—You may address me as Nadezhda Ivanovna Solovyova, or as Margaret Bush. Pick one. And then you may tell me the location of my papers and passport. After that, I will decide whether to shoot you.

Kostya paled. —Nadia.

She refused to look at him. —Kostya, I can't rely on you.

—No, no, please, please understand. Arkady Dmitrievich can fix this. He knows people. He can fix it all.

Eyes still on Temerity, Arkady shook his head. —Kostya, Kuznets knows you took a woman home from the party in Yury Stepanov's car. Peeked out a window at just the right moment, he told me, then put the rest together when Stepanov couldn't find his car and you, of all people, signed it back in.

Kostya blinked a few times, then stared at Arkady.

Arkady could not meet his gaze. —He's been saving the knowledge for just the right moment. But that's all he knows about her.

A floorboard squeaked beneath Temerity. —Kostya, who is Kuznets?

Arkady answered. —Captain Boris Aleksandrovich Kuznets, Kostya's immediate commander, and one of my party guests. He'd recognize you on sight.

Temerity held the Nagant steady.

Arkady admired her nerve. —Kostya, he came to me with a basic corruption charge against you, except, as I pointed out to him, any investigation into my last party would compromise him, too. He nodded and apologized for his folly, and I knew then he wanted more. He pressed me. I'm sure he pressed Vadym. I gave Kuznets the handbag, with the perfume and the cash in it, a mirrored compact, too, I think. Oh, and a cloisonné cigarette case, very pretty. Then he gave you the perfume and probably sloughed off the rest to a mistress. It wasn't enough. He wanted you. He wanted to destroy you the way a perverse child wants to smash fine china. And while I was gone, he tore this house apart. He found nothing. Do you know why he found nothing, Tatar?

—Wait. Dima? He hurt Dima?

—The steppe gives up in patches to forest, and the forest gives up in patches to tundra.

Kostya said it with him. —Yet in places where you see no change, all the differences blend. Survive. Nadia, I want to kneel. Don't shoot. I want to kneel down, next to Arkady Dmitrievich, yes?

Sweat shining on her forehead, Temerity nodded.

Click and swish of the flap: a cat arrived. Grind and squeak of the brakes: a car parked. Chatter and trill of the whistle: birds sang.

Kostya heard only his own voice, much the way he heard it in a Lubyanka cell, not always certain who spoke. —Arkady Dmitrievich, no more lies. No more games to distract me. Tell me why.

—Duty. Duty and compulsion

Duty and compulsion? Is that why I hurt Misha? —Tell me why!

—Why, what?

—Why did you save me in Odessa?

Cheeks burning red, Arkady looked from Kostya to the floor, then to Temerity. He could no longer ignore the sight of his own Nagant pointed at him, and when his voice broke, he sounded defeated, craven. —I don't know. I don't know. I don't know!

Each man closed his eyes.

Arkady's voice cracked again, leaving him hoarse. —Kuznets found nothing because *I've* got her passport and papers. I carried them with me. Kuznets searched my house, but no one searched my clothes. I outplayed him there, at least, and I kept you both safe.

—What the barrelling fuck? Arkady Dmitrievich, if anyone had found them on you—

—No one found them.

—Then just give them to me.

—I expect Kuznets is in the car outside. He's had a surveillance detail on you. You did notice them, right, your little followers? Katelnikov in the flower bed? He might get a promotion for it.

Kostya stared at the worn edges of Arkady's *gymastyorka* cuffs and the black hairs peeking out beneath them.

—You should have kept going, Tatar. You could be halfway across the bridge by now.

A clock ticked. Kostya's heart pounded. He looked up.

Temerity had lifted the Nagant away from Arkady and toward herself.

Kostya leapt. The Nagant fired.

Efim ran in from the study, and Boris, Yury, and Matvei ran in from outside. As Arkady sobbed, Matvei and Yury wrestled Kostya from Temerity, and Efim shouted for better light. Boris knelt near Arkady and took his pulse, urged him to sit up. Yury and Matvei shoved Kostya into the big armchair. One of the cats, crouched and ready to retreat, watched the blood pool.

Eyes shut, Kostya heard much.

Train tracks rattled in the fever dream from 1918, and the rattle became laughter as Baba Yaga said, *Welcome home,* bezprizornik, *welcome home.*

Efim murmured, shouted. —God, she's still breathing. Ambulance, now! I can't see, too much blood. Stepanov, get over here, help me.

Boris's deep voice rumbled into the telephone as he ordered the operator to send an ambulance, then almost sang as he asked Arkady the terrible question. —Who is she?

Arkady whispered. —Nobody. Nobody. No one at all.

Clothing rustled as Matvei pinned Kostya to the chair by his shoulders, leaning his full weight into his hands. —Keep still.

Kostya opened his eyes and glanced at Matvei's hand pushing on his bad shoulder. —That hurts.

Boris stood before Kostya now, beside Matvei, interrupting the light. —It's all right, Katelnikov. Take your hands off him. He'll stay.

Kostya nodded. *By my own free will, yet twice as much by compulsion.*

[ ]

DO NO HARM
Friday 30 July–Saturday 31 July

Chance. The young NKVD guard, distracted by the pretty nurse, took no notice of Efim leaning over his patient to check the dressings over the new plate in her head. Efim blew gently in her ear, hoping to rouse her. Then he whispered. —I've got your blouse.

The guard heard the noise. —No talking.

Calm, Efim faced the guard. —Head wound patients mutter.

The guard gave a little snort, then resumed chatting up the nurse. —We could meet for a drink after work. When does your shift end?

Temerity's whisper almost cracked. —Embassy. Say...flu.

Efim flinched, tried to hide it.

The nurse stepped away from the guard. —Wait, I'm to report anything she says.

Efim gave the nurse a sorrowful look. —Then report nonsense. The patient is still delirious after surgery. Her good eye is still bloodshot. You can make a note of that.

From behind, the guard grasped the nurse by the elbows.

She shook him off. —Pig.

—Hey, hey, don't be like that. I can show you a good time. A really good time. I wouldn't want to see you have a bad time, not because of some misunderstanding.

Ignoring the plea in the nurse's eyes, Efim asked to excuse himself from the room, and the guard nodded his thanks.

The light in the hallway, so bright, hurt his eyes, and the bare white walls bounced back the echoes of so many voices. Efim heard suffering, patients and doctors alike as they confronted their own helplessness before some terrible disease, but he also heard compassion.

So very different from Laboratory of Special Purpose Number Two.

Several white lab coats hung from a coatrack near a closed door. Not breaking stride, Efim liberated a lab coat from a hook and shrugged it on.

No one noticed.

Then he almost gasped. For he'd found one: a telephone. On a desk. In an office. Door wide open.

So easy?

Shoulders back, he entered the office in all confidence. He eased the door shut, then picked up the telephone handset.

The switchboard operator asked for the number.

He said it with ease, not quite sure he said it at all. —British Embassy.

A pause. —Could you repeat that, caller?

—British Embassy, please.

Another pause, long enough, Efim reasoned, for the operator to make a note or start a recording of this strange call, too long for her to refuse outright.

Light glinted on a brass nameplate on the desk: Annenkov.

—Connecting you now, Comrade Dr. Annenkov.

The rings on a crackling line sounded so far away.

Answer, answer. Hurry.

Any moment, strong hands would grab his arms, strong voices would command him to come along. Any moment.

A male voice spoke in accented Russian. —Embassy of Great Britain.

—She...

Efim cleared his throat.

—She's hospitalized with the flu.

—Say again, please.

He gave Temerity's room number. Then he hung up.

Outside, in the corridor, boot soles tapped.

Efim emerged from the office to face his future.

The two NKVD officers ignored him, striding to some other task.

He found a lavatory in time. Dizzy, he washed his hands, lamented the lack of any sort of hand towel, and rubbed his fingers against the borrowed lab coat.

Olyushka...

As he returned to Temerity's room, he noticed a woman searching the coat rack. The lab coat collar, now warmed by his neck, gave off a scent of Krasnaya Moskva. The woman called to her colleagues in banter, accusing them all of robbery, and then strode back into the office: Anna Novikova.

Efim almost called after her. Yet what to say? *Anna, I thought you were dead. Anna, I thought you'd be arrested.* She'd resigned from secret work at Laboratory of Special Purpose Number Two, and survived? Found another job? Still had her medical licence?

Who protects her? Is she just lucky?

Just outside Temerity's room, the nurse, eyes bright with angry tears, nearly ran into him. The NKVD guard poked his head through the door, looking peeved. When he noticed Efim, he stepped aside to let him in. He spoke of frigid sluts and their moods, then resumed blocking the open doorway.

Efim sat beside Temerity's bed, his feet nudging his doctor's bag. As he bent over and retrieved the bag to check for the blouse and passport, still there, he whispered to her. —They know.

No response.

He snapped shut the bag, placed it by his feet, and stroked Temerity's hand.

Starlings and crows swooped and dove in Moscow-Leningradksy Station, and a locomotive hissed. Efim remained beside the stretcher, near Temerity's head. British men in suits and hats, very natty, spoke to him in decent Russian, and they spoke to one another in quiet English.

A crack in the floor jostled the stretcher.

—Have a care!

—Isn't she sedated?

—Sedated, not comatose. Now be gentle!

A new voice, deep and rich, one Efim recognized from Balakirev's house. —Comrade Dr. Scherba.

The British men, startled, stopped talking, then tightened their grip on the stretcher.

Efim only sighed. —Comrade Captain Kuznets.

—A word?

Efim touched one of the British men on the arm. —Take the utmost care getting her on that train carriage. Wait, what's she saying?

—She's asking for you.

Efim gave him a sorrowful look and stepped away from the stretcher.

Boris put his arm around Efim's shoulders as they kept walking. —My balls are in a vise.

—Mine, too, Comrade Major, and I have a train to catch.

—And I have nothing left to lose. Do you understand me? Balakirev was my case to investigate. I expected some everyday cronyism, some favours done for Nikto, the business with his *propiska* and flat. Not this. Never this.

Efim looked back over his shoulder to the train for Leningrad, where the British men struggled with the stretcher. —Oh?

—My father always spoke in proverbs. I swear the man knew no other language. Laws, he said to me, laws catch flies, and hornets go free. That's what this whole purge is about: find the hornets. I never even saw the hornet. I look incompetent.

Efim had nothing to say to that.

Boris gestured to the train. —And now I'm also overruled. The orders to get her home come from the highest diplomatic channels. It seems the Boss has a soft spot for women who shoot themselves. He's full of surprises. And you want to go with her.

—By British request. It's been approved. I witnessed the injury, and she needs medical escort.

—Aristarkhova needs her husband.

Efim felt only exhaustion. —How do I even know she's still alive?

—She's fine. There's been some trouble with the post, but she's fine. Waiting for any word of you.

—I can't trust you on that.

—What will you do once you reach Leningrad, Dr. Scherba? Leap off the train, scream your goodbye in the street, and hope she hears the echo?

Efim noticed the approach of three other NKVD officers. Behind them, a cleaning crew dragged pails, brushes, and mops across the floor.

Boris waved them away. —You can't go.

—The British are expecting me.

—The British can't have you! The arrogance—

—It's all been approved. Believe me, no one was more surprised than I was. And you said yourself, no one wants a diplomatic fuss, least of all Comrade Stalin.

—Over her, yes. You are a very different matter, and I'm surprised I need to explain that.

The Leningrad train whistled, warning of departure.

—Dr. Scherba, you are still a Soviet citizen on Soviet soil. Answer me. You contacted the embassy, did you not?

Efim said nothing.

—And you made this call from a hospital telephone assigned to one Dr. Annenkov. You've never even met Annenkov. He's in Lubyanka now, charged with treason, execution scheduled for tomorrow night. You've cost him his life. Don't cost Artistarkhova hers.

Efim snorted. —I can't protect her. If I've learned nothing else, it's that I can't protect her. I can't protect anyone.

—Yet you'll try to protect this foreign woman?

—She's my patient.

—She's a spy and a whore.

The train whistled a second time. One of the British men filled the carriage doorway, watching Boris and Efim.

Olyushka...

Efim recalled the touch of her cold fingers on his face just before she kissed him. *Be a good doctor.* She'd also said, *Spare me a martyrdom.* The night of the mistaken raid, when Kostya made the hot milk and spoke of his grandfather, Dr. Berendei: *People came to the house all hours, and he treated them. He never turned anyone away.* —Comrade Captain Kuznets, without medical oversight, perhaps even with it, that woman on the stretcher could die.

—Isn't that what she wants? She did shoot herself. I'm sorry you're entangled in this, Comrade Doctor, but I have a duty here.

—So do I. And I must go.

Anger glittered in Boris's eyes. —Why?

—Because I'm a doctor.

After a moment, Boris took a few steps back. —Then go. As I told you, I have nothing left to lose. And I am not afraid of the paperwork.

—What?

—Go.

Legs weak, Efim wanted to grab onto Boris for support. Then he turned to face the train to Leningrad, where one of the British men waved at him. He nodded. Took a step.

Three steps.

—Comrade!

A stranger's voice, male, commanding.

Not for me. Not me.

—Comrade, stop!

Not my business. Someone else. I'm free to go.

Third and final train whistle.

—Comrade, stop, or I'll shoot!

The train lurched forward; Efim ran toward it.

A hammer blow: bullet to the thigh. As Efim fell, the train lurched again. Boot soles tapped as NKVD officers ran towards him, and a bucket clattered and clanked as the Special Clean crew dragged it over the floor.

—Open your eyes now, comrade.

Four pairs of legs blocked the light.

Boris watched Efim's blood pool. Then he spoke with vigour so all could hear. —We told you to stop, comrade. And you ran. Only traitors run.

Efim stared at the muzzle of the Nagant.

As Boris aimed at Efim's forehead, the other three offices understood something dire: the hassle of cleaning leather. They hurried to step clear.

Blood spattered their boots.

[ ]

WRINKLED ICARUS
Sunday 1 August–Wednesday 4 August

In a shadowed corner of Arkady's hospital room, Kostya imagined his body fusing with the slats of the wooden chair. His eyelids, heavy and hot, refused to part, and his shoulder, despite the doctors here injecting him with morphine every twelve hours, burned, burned, burned. He wondered what sort of tree had fallen for his comfort. Spruce? Pine? Birch? Vadym's chair, what had that been?

Then he thought of Nadia and her story of Daphne.

Bernini got it right in his sculpture. Apollo is stronger and faster, and he chooses to rape her. To prevent that, to try to save her, Daphne's father chooses to transform her into a tree. She's not changing; she's being changed. Where is the chance or design for Daphne?

In the hospital bed beside the chair, Arkady took the shallow breaths of the dying, stubborn function of the brain stem, oxygen moot.

Kidney failure, the doctors said, silent disease, many years' ambush, mental and now physical functions impaired by accumulated toxins. Perhaps Comrade Nikto had noticed some mood swings, some paranoia? —We'll keep him comfortable.

Arkady had glared at the hospital room ceiling. —My father died the same way. Don't waste your tears on me.

Kostya wiped his face. —I'm not.

—You stink of tobacco, Little Tatar. You smoke too much.

Not long after that, Arkady slipped into his strange sleep.

Footsteps approached the private room.

A nurse, Kostya thought, eyes still closed.

A wash of light as the door opened, closed, and a man's soft yet heavy tread.

He stood there a moment, waiting. Then he scraped another wooden chair across the floor, sat down, and grasped Arkady's hand.

Kostya kept still. *He knows I'm here. He must.*

When Boris spoke, he kept his voice quiet. —Arkady Dmitrievich, can you hear me? I never wanted it to end like this. I swear it. A game. You played me, even as I thought I had you by the balls, telling myself every morning as I shaved that you'd do the same to me. And you just lie there like Scherba, sacrifice meaningless. You knew. You knew how sick you are. You had to know.

Sacrifice? Kostya allowed one eye to crack open; the shadows of the day had changed and now obscured him in the corner. Perhaps Boris had not yet noticed him.

—Your Kostya's not left your side these three days.

Then he thinks I'm asleep.

Boris whispered now. —I once said we've not got time for vigils. I regret that. I do. Yury Stepanov asked me why your Kostya's not arrested yet, why I've told the others to hold off and wait. I had to explain vigil, Arkady Dmitrievich, explain it, to a grown man. You're right: Stepanov's a stunted little weed. And when this purge is done, he'll be the best of what remains.

Arkady's breath rasped, stalled, rasped again.

—You did get your revenge. I had to fight off the British Embassy. Fucking diplomats. I still don't know who the hell she is. We should have taken her straight to Lubyanka, but I was worried she'd die before she could tell us anything. See where mercy gets me?

Arkady's lips sputtered.

Boris sighed, then grinned. —Here's the best part. She had two passports, two different names. Both British. The travel papers only matched one.

Kostya's eyes flew open.

Just in time to greet another wash of light as a nurse opened the door and peered in to see this NKVD captain bidding goodbye to his dear friend. Boris kissed Arkady's hand and took up a song as though he'd just paused long enough for a few tears. His voice, so quiet, yet so rich, the best of those coached by choir leader Vadym Minenkov: the perfection of performance. Kostya almost laughed.

Ay-da, da, ay-da,
Ay-da, da, ay-da,
Now we fell the stout birch tree!

Touched, the nurse left, and the door swished the light and the dark.

Boris let go of Arkady's hand; it flopped to the bed. —How did he hide her? How did you help him?

The vibrations, the pressure of Boris's voice and question, his breath, touched Kostya's cheek like a feather. This moment, right here, right now: likely his last chance for silence. He struggled not to speak.

—Scherba is dead.

Kostya gave a little grunt, as of a man stirring in his sleep.

Boris smirked. —Nice try, Nikto. You had me, for a moment.

Kostya opened his eyes. —Scherba? Was that necessary?

—Yes. Shot him myself. She might be dead by now, too. I don't know. The last I saw, she lay strapped to a stretcher on a train to Leningrad.

Leningrad. Steamer back to England?

Boris leaned over Arkady and smoothed his hair. —Shall I tell you both what gushed down the pipe yesterday and splattered at our feet? Order four hundred forty-seven. We must now make special renewed efforts against foreigners and spies and other anti-Soviet elements, and we must speed up interrogation and trial. Vigour, vigour, vigour. Beat the horses to the bone. How much faster can we go?

Arkady seemed to sigh.

Boris patted Arkady's hand. —When I came here, I wanted to say something else. I rehearsed it in the back of car number forty-two;

my driver is waiting outside. Here it is. You are finished. So am I. You get the easy way out, Arkady Dmitrievich. And you, Konstantin Arkadievich, this is your portrait, the flower and roots, you and him. This deathbed is how I shall always remember you.

Another wash of light: Boris departed.

Early the next morning, Arkady died. Kostya signed some paperwork consenting to cremation of Arkady's body and acknowledging the state's seizure of Arkady's house, received a morphine injection, and worked to understand his orders. No funeral for Balakirev, the message read, just the cremation already arranged, and for Kostya himself, informal medical and bereavement leave. Do not report to the department, the message concluded, but still consider yourself on call.

On the way back to his flat, aware of the weight of his service weapon, Kostya took a guess why.

They want me to shoot myself, save them the trouble.

So he sat in the soft armchair in the front room, turned on the radio, and practised his aim. Temple? Over the ear? Roof of the mouth? *Quick,* he reminded himself, *quick and easy. How many times have you squeezed a trigger?*

His wrist ached.

He dropped the Nagant, caught it in his lap, tucked it back into the holster. Then he stood up and returned to his bedroom, where he removed each piece of his uniform and hung it up with precision and care, placing the amber worry beads on his bedside table and his underclothes in the hamper. Naked, he got into bed and dozed, sleeping and waking, for almost eighteen hours, missing his evening injection appointment. He woke up with his nose blocked, his face and pillow wet.

He sat up in bed. Any moment now, his colleagues would come arrest him. Any moment.

The paint on the walls rippled and danced like amber beads between his fingers.

No one came.

The fifth day after Temerity shot herself, Kostya reported to the hospital and received another morphine injection. He also received a stern medical lecture for missing his previous evening appointment.

Kostya fastened his *gymnastyorka*. —How much longer must I come here?

The doctor, a slender young man with dark circles beneath his eyes, waved a form. —As long as the paperwork holds.

Kostya returned to his flat, where he'd left the radio on, changed from his uniform to civilian clothes, and cooked and ate some kasha. Then he slept some more, waking up every hour when the radio announcer gave a time check, except for six and seven o'clock. Once again, he missed his evening injection. Once again, he sat up all night. His skin twitched. His shoulder hurt; his thoughts raced; his fingers numbed as he stroked the amber beads. The paint on the walls, at least, kept still.

And once again, NKVD did not come.

The doctor plucked the needle from Kostya's arm. —I reviewed your new X-rays. That's a lot of shrapnel. You're lucky you kept that arm, let alone got use of it back. Do you know that?

Kostya tugged his *gymastyorka* straight. —I exercise the hand with worry beads. Here.

The doctor accepted the amber beads and held them to the light. —Beautiful.

—Are we done?

The doctor handed back the beads. —How's your appetite? Are you eating?

—Kasha now and then.

—Washed down with vodka and wine?

—What of it?

—Any patient who uses morphine for a long time is at risk of narkomania. The risk grows if the patient is also addicted to alcohol. That you're standing up after the dose I just gave you makes me think you've developed a dangerous tolerance.

Kostya tugged his cap onto his head. —I drink no more than any other officer.

—That does not reassure me, Comrade Nikto.

Kostya considered how the doctor had just insulted the entire NKVD. *Such an easy arrest, this one, a clear example of an anti-Soviet activity.* He sighed. —You're just out of med school, yes? Twenty-five?

—Twenty-four.

—Married?

—Engaged.

—Live at home?

—With my mother. My father's dead, but—

—But you've not reported that to all the right places because you and your mother want to keep the flat, what little space you've got?

The doctor raised his clipboard as if to shield himself. —She can come live with me once I am married, once my wife and I find a larger flat of our own.

—And your comment about drunken NKVD officers?

The doctor stared at him.

—I've got you on two different offences: *propiska* fraud, and abuse of an officer of state security. Let's throw in some anti-Soviet activities. Perhaps your mother—

—Wait!

Kostya shook his head. —Kolyma gets cold, so cold that sound and light warp and your heartbeat feels like a scream. The commandants sometimes keep doctors out of the mines so they can do the amputations. Frostbite, you see: fingers, noses, toes. Cocks.

Perhaps your own. So unless you want ten to twenty-five years to find out, *do not* say you presume every NKVD officer to be a drunkard. Understand me yet?

The doctor's voice shook. —By my silence, I give consent.

Kosyta laid a hand on the doctor's shoulder. —Shove your heroics up your arse and shit them out in the morning. If not for yourself, then for your mother and your fiancée, yes? Promise me that, and I'll keep quiet.

After a long moment, the doctor picked up the ampoule of morphine and rocked it back and forth. —And in return? What do you want?

—Nothing you can give me.

In Gorky Park, grass and sky shimmered, and so did the light.

Here, Kostya decided. *I'll sit here.*

I told the old man we should visit the parks more often, or even go on holiday. Told him and told him...

Kostya leaned back on the bench, arms outstretched, amber beads in the fingers of his left hand, and stared at the sky. As someone squealed in delight at the parachute tower, the sunlight got too bright, and Kostya closed his eyes.

For a moment, and for a moment within a moment, he allowed himself to believe he lay in the sun near the water, on holiday with Arkady, in Yalta, or in Sochi. And for a moment within that moment, he believed he lay on his back in an Odessa park, that grassy bit by the oaks, as his grandparents fussed with the picnic basket and called each other, even in their mutual exasperation, fond names.

Misha never understood sunbathing. *I can't just lie about and get burnt.*

Kostya shoved back his cap. The sun's heat felt like a fond caress on his face, and his fingers reached for a cloisonné cigarette case.

Just a memory. Is the sun so bright in England?

When he opened his eyes, dapples and smears hovered a moment, to remind him that they existed.

Gavriil? No.

His visions of the angel had long deserted him.

As Kostya straightened his cap and took cigarettes and matches from his pouch, his sight cleared some more. Footsteps approached the bench: adult and child. The boy, maybe four years old, slowed his stride to admire Kostya's uniform.

—Mama, the cap!

The mother turned to see, and fear rippled through her face. —Don't bother him.

—I want a cap.

A click, then several clicks: a twitch had run through Kostya's hand, and he dropped the beads. They fell beneath the bench.

—I get them!

The boy ran to the bench and bent to retrieve the beads, motions graceful. He held them out for Kostya.

Smoke curled around Kostya's face as he took the beads. *What would we have named the child?* —Thank you.

The boy returned to his mother, narrating his just-completed quest. —I helped, Mama! I found the man's beads. I found them, and I gave them back. I helped.

His voice thinned out as his mother, the breeze stirring her brown curls, hurried him along.

Kostya took a deep drag on his cigarette and stood up. —Stop.

The woman froze; the boy looked to her for guidance and copied her posture.

Kostya strode up to them. —Comrade, have I not seen you in this park before? Jumping from the parachute tower?

—Very likely. I often visit this park.

—Mama?

Kostya stroked the boy's hair. —It's all right.

The woman spoke with forced cheer. —Yes, it's all right. We visit the park. We jump from towers. After all, our business is rejoicing. Am I free to go, Comrade Officer?

He nodded. —Take care of your son.

At ten to three in the morning, as Kostya sat at the little fold-down table wearing civilian trousers and an undershirt and finishing a bowl of kasha, men murmured outside the flat. They had yet to knock, so Kostya stood up, unlocked the door, and swung it open.

A team of two: Yury Stepanov, wearing a junior lieutenant's insignia, fist raised to pound on the door, and just behind him, Matvei Katelnikov.

Kostya spoke as though greeting expected friends. —Come in, come in.

Yury looked disappointed. —Ah . . . thank you.

Matvei, red in the face, followed Yury into the flat and then closed the door behind them.

Yury stood by the kitchen, looking around. When he spoke, he sounded spiteful. —All this space to yourself?

Gesturing to the front room, Kostya made his way to the soft chair. —I'll sit here while you work. You'll want to collect some evidence. Bedrooms are that way. So is the telephone, right next to the bathroom door.

Matvei raised his eyebrows. —By the bathroom?

—Moscow flats, what can you do? Don't get me started on the light switches.

Matvei chuckled.

Snorting, Yury pointed at Matvei, then at Kostya. —Keep him there while I look around.

As Yury opened drawers in the *stenka* and tossed items about, Kostya closed his eyes and told himself to remember how this chair felt. He'd be sitting in hard wooden chairs soon, perhaps bound there, hard wooden chairs before desks while struggling with consciousness and pain as fellow officers beat him. But right here, right now: the give of the cushions, the curve of the arms...

Yury strode to the bedrooms; Kostya took the beads from his pocket.

Click. Officer, or prisoner? Click. Criminal, or innocent? Click. Lover, or murderer?

His shoulder wounds burned.

Then he understood what Temerity had done. A shot in the upper arm or shoulder would cause enough of an injury to need a hospital, and from there she'd try to contact the British Embassy. The risk: if Boris Kuznets had not called an ambulance? If Efim Scherba had not been there? If Kuznets had ordered her straight to Lubyanka? A shot as risk, as defiance, even optimism?

Her duty.

He wept. *I knocked her off balance, and the bullet hit her head.*

Svyatogor's wife drowned in a river while locked in a box. Vasilisa the Beautiful crafted a lamp from a skull and holy fire. Marya Morevna fought Koshchei the Deathless.

Matvei passed Kostya a handkerchief; Kostya dropped it on the floor.

Yury returned, carrying an old newsprint photo of the battleship *Dobryna Nikitich* docked in Odessa, a menu from Babichev's, and the bottle of Shalimar. He passed the items to Matvei, who held them in his cupped hands. Then Yury's face filled Kostya's vision: snub nose, squinty eyes, three kinked hairs sprouting from the top curve of his left ear. —You're done, Nikto, you're fucking done. I will harness you to a chair and break your arms doing it. I will hammer your gut until you puke blood, and I will crush your cock until you can't even piss yourself. Beg. Beg me now, because in the cells you'll be so deaf with blood in your ears that you won't hear your own voice. And all this from Little Yurochka.

Kostya clicked another bead. *I never had her courage.*

—Fucking *look* at me when I speak to you, Nikto. Nikto!

Kostya met Yury's gaze. —My name is Berendei.

—What?

Matvei shut his eyes in dread. —Oh, fuck. The paperwork.

Is courage ever enough? A final bead clicked. —I am Konstantin Semyonovich Berendei, and I love her.

1957

PODMOSKOVNYE VECHERA
Moscow
Sunday 4 August

Muscles tense and defined, faces determined, arms pointing, no doubt, to that elusive radiant future, young Soviet women had balanced on angled boards attached to moving motorcycles. Considering it now, and how the image would likely haunt her, Temerity shook her head in some awe. The parade, part of the opening of the World Festival of Youth and Students, intended as spectacle, to be sure, most carefully planned theatre, artificial despite the truths of athleticism — how long had those women trained? — had somehow also presented itself as a study in defiance.

Defiance of what, Temerity asked herself, *gravity? Wait. Is it joy despite command, joy in their own strength? Here?*

As the fading daylight played on the faces in the crowd, Temerity felt at once exhausted and energized, even feverish. On top of the hundred thousand Soviet citizens invited to the city, over thirty thousand foreigners attended the World Festival of Youth and Students, coming from North and South America, Europe, Africa, Asia, and Australia. Many of them wore their culture's traditional clothes; others wore Western dress, collars open against the summer heat. The streets in and around Red Square smelled of sweat and musk, honey and smoke, pepper and wine, and sounded of laughter, shouts, and happy conversations. Temerity smiled as she paused near a brick wall to allow a crush of raucous and happy young people speaking in at least three different languages to pass by. This sense of freedom in Red Square, of all places, felt otherworldly, even dangerous.

Intoxicating.

Temerity wondered how her charges, two of her students from the West Language School being groomed for intelligence work, felt about this version of Moscow, so different from what they'd been taught. Both young women had stayed by her side during the festival's opening night back on the twenty-eighth, but after that they kept getting lost in the crowds, or so they said. So long as they made it back to the hostel each night by twelve, Temerity refrained from complaint. She'd lectured them on not expecting men to remember any promises to obtain and use condoms — Soviet prophylactics did not enjoy a good reputation — or, God's sake, to pull out in time. Temerity also made sure her students knew how to use their cervical caps, devices she'd helped them obtain without their parents' knowledge. The students' blushes and squirms, their frank disbelief that greying Miss West would know of such things, had made Temerity laugh.

Many cafés and bakeries lined the streets, some of them looking very new and bare, and almost all of them kept tables and chairs outside. As she considered her choices, taking in displays of food, Temerity caught her reflection in a window. She wore a white scarf over her hair, a short-sleeved white blouse, dark blue trousers, and brown Oxfords with a low heel. Many other women also wore trousers, giving the lie to her handlers' warnings — an attempt at tact, perhaps — that she might stick out in a crowd. Temerity understood something her handlers did not. Despite the dark glasses and the scars, despite the dent in her head, she could more or less disappear. Few men noticed a woman unless she could offer them something, even just the pleasure of her prettiness. Temerity, long past pretty and, she told herself, long past caring about it, might as well be invisible.

Another wave of young women and men passed by, very close, and Temerity found herself hemmed in. She stumbled. A fair young man speaking German turned to ask Temerity in Russian if she'd twisted her ankle; she answered in Russian that she was fine. Walking faster, the youngsters soon passed on, and Temerity considered how twelve years before that young man would have been her enemy. Of course, he'd been a child during the war, hardly an enemy, a view of accident and innocence that Temerity had learned to keep to herself during the forties. Perhaps this young German man survived the attacks on Dresden or Berlin. Perhaps he'd been conscripted to fight in those final days; she'd seen photos of German boys too young to shave, wearing baggy uniforms and holding weapons, eyes huge. Perhaps his parents remained quiet Nazis while he rebelled. Perhaps he was related to Ursula Friesen. Nothing, Temerity told herself, would surprise her anymore.

She adjusted her dark glasses as two uniformed KGB officers strolled past, faces not stern but mildly interested, helpful if asked, there only to maintain order, comrade. They'd changed their uniforms since the days when they were called NKVD, and no doubt many officers infiltrated the crowd in plainclothes. How many? Did they feel overwhelmed by the sheer number of people in Moscow for the festival? Temerity just kept herself from smirking. KGB feeling helpless? A delicious thought. Then again, a nervous and threatened KGB could be more dangerous. The Khrushchev Thaw, with its relaxed censorship and widespread release of political prisoners, who then saw their convictions expunged in a process called rehabilitation, had also eased, however slightly, international relations. Temerity, like many in the SIS, watched these developments with caution and muted hope.

It's still Moscow, Temerity told herself, echoing the warnings she'd given her students. *Khrushchev is desperate to prove he's not Stalin, but it's still Moscow.*

A group of people of all ages, children to elderly, dressed in various manners, now placed their arms around one another's shoulders, formed a circle, and began to dance, two steps right, one step left. Most of the dancers smiled, though one frowned when he saw Temerity.

Suspicious of the dark glasses, perhaps.

A scent of freshly baked bread wafted, and Temerity followed it to a nearby bakery window. A young woman who gazed at the crowd with a mix of longing and fear, a samovar steaming behind her, hung *bubliki* on a string. The first *bublik* collided with the wooden *X* at the string's bottom, and then the others quickly piled on. Then the young woman tacked the string to the ceiling. Temerity, reminding herself of her doctor's orders to cut back on starches, paid for a *bublik*. She first declined, then accepted the offer of an extra honey drizzle and a dip into poppy seeds, almost dizzy with anticipated pleasure. The long war years and her demanding work, both at Bletchley Park and then with MI19, interrogating prisoners of war, had left her thin. Since the end of rationing on meat and cheese a few years before, she'd gained nearly two stone. Her body seemed determined to store every possible calorie as fat. She refused to admit that the changes in her waist and hips bothered her — mere vanity, as silly as worrying about the grey hair. Her thickened ankles, however, she preferred to hide under loose trousers.

Biting into the *bublik*, she smeared honey and poppy seeds over her lips. Then she found a table and sat down. A tram passed, packed with yet more young people who stuck their arms and faces out the windows and called happy greetings to all. Visitors to the festival enjoyed free travel on the buses, trams, and metro. Temerity had even travelled the 1935 Sokolnicheskaya metro line, one stop at a time, getting out at each station to sketch. As the train pulled into Vasilisa Prekrasnaya, she almost decided to stay aboard. Then she peered at the huge mosaic; Bilibin's Vasilisa still dominated the space. Just as the train doors started to close, Temerity leapt out. The train departed, people streamed past, and soon she stood alone. She considered following them up the stairs to see if Kostya's block of flats had changed; sweat chilled her armpits. Then she stretched out to touch Vasilisa's hand, the one holding the lantern made of a skull and holy fire.

She could not reach it.

It was never Vasilisa who was too small, she decided. *It was me.*

Unable to ascend those stairs, unable to sketch, imprisoned by her failures, Temerity had waited and then caught the next train.

A man on stilts and dressed in a top hat and tails passed by, leaning over and greeting everyone he met in French, English, and Russian. —I am Pierre from Cameroon. And who are you? I am so happy to meet you. Yes, hello, I am Pierre from Cameroon. Who are you?

A young woman replied in French that she was Joie from Laos, supplying the obsolete term French Indochina when Pierre frowned and said he did not know of Laos. She climbed up on Temerity's table then, her feet among ashtrays and crumbs, and took Pierre's hands. —We have shrugged off the chains of imperialism. Someday soon, your country will, too.

They held hands and stared into each other's eyes.

Wobbling on his stilts, Pierre blinked back tears. —Let me get down from these things, and we can talk properly.

As Joie helped Pierre remove the stilts, Temerity stood up to leave them the table. Neither of them noticed her. They already stroked each other's hands.

Honeyed *bublik* filling her mouth, Temerity sat down at the next little table. The energy from the crowd took on a new edge, one delicious and dangerous, as sexual attractions blossomed and inhibitions fell aside. The circle dance stopped, and the dancers parted a moment to allow two violinists, a man and a woman, to inhabit the centre space. The woman, about Temerity's age, gave spectators a demure smile. The man, balding with jowly cheeks, kept his face neutral. Temerity thought she recognized him; the memory of his name slipped away. Both musicians raised their violins; the man nodded; the woman began.

Bach's *Double Violin Concerto in D Minor*, first movement. Without orchestral backup, it sounded bare yet courageous — exquisite.

The violinists, sharing glances, seemed to know and trust each other. Sweat glistened on the man's bald head and dripped down the back of his neck; a flush reddened the woman's cheeks and throat. They finished, and in the silence before the crowd could react, the man addressed the woman as Comrade Orlova, and thanked her.

Temerity joined the applause.

A man placed a glass of tea before her, the *podstakannik*'s filigree dulled steel in the shapes of comets and stars. —*Bubliki* are too dry to eat plain.

As she flinched, she noticed his withered left arm first, then the old wounds on his neck and ear. The cheekbones looked stronger, the flesh beneath them sunken and seamed. His hair had thinned, though not receded much, and the pomaded waves showed as much white as black. The skin of his face looked very coarse, as if pockmarked, or left unprotected for many winters. He wore a white shirt, collar spread and sleeves rolled up past his elbows, old black trousers, belted tight and much too big for him, and thin-soled shoes.

He held a second glass of tea. —May I sit down?

After a moment, Temerity nodded.

Kostya settled himself in a chair opposite Temerity, lit a cigarette, and angled his chair so he, too, might look onto the crowd.

Neither spoke for several minutes.

Temerity struggled not to stare at him. By far, the safest thing to do: walk away from him and not look back. *As I should have done at the Bilbao docks.* Pretend her memory had flared: thoughts of Kostya not always welcome, might interrupt Temerity several times a week. Pretend she felt nothing, give him only the cool appraisal due an enemy. Pretend she understood and embraced her duty in this moment and not only acknowledge Kostya's existence but also glean information from him. Yes, that would be her only interest in this strange matter. Information, the reason she'd come to Moscow in '37, and the reason she sat eating a *bublik* in Moscow now.

Still looking at the crowd, Kostya spoke first. —It's happened. It took a while, but it finally happened. I've lost my mind. Maybe it's flu. Fever dreams. Either way, you're not real. You don't exist.

The strength of her voice surprised her. —Oh, I exist.

Then she reached across the table to stroke his hand. He flinched, glancing at her in fear, then looked away as he lit a second cigarette from the embers of his first.

Temerity found herself wishing he'd instead light two cigarettes and offer her one.

He exhaled, and smoke curled around his face. The crowd before them surged, the violinists and dancers of a moment ago now gone. —What the barrelling fuck are they doing?

Temerity felt quite defensive and protective of the youngsters. She snapped her answer. —Celebrating.

—Celebrating what?

—Being alive.

He looked at her, eyes cavernous, then resumed studying the crowd. So did Temerity.

A young couple in front of them embraced, kissed. Those around them smiled and cheered them on. Then someone shook the kissing woman's shoulder and warned her of the approach of police officers keen to disrupt such displays. The couple separated and blended into the crowd, and seconds later, two more young men in KGB uniform approached at a stroll, eyes focused on the middle distance as if unconcerned.

Temerity took a good swallow of tea before she spoke. —I thought you were dead.

—Yes, I'd guessed that much. You're crying.

—Tea's too hot. Scalded my mouth.

He passed her a dingy handkerchief. —You weep over tea?

She accepted the handkerchief and dabbed at her face around the glasses. —I suppose you think I weep over you?

—No.

Another group formed a circle around two American delegates who offered to demonstrate something called boogie-woogie. They announced they'd need more room. A third American took a harmonica from his pocket and played a fast tune.

Kostya stroked the table near Temerity's hand. —When I got too hungry or cold to sleep, I would imagine your eyelids and count the freckles there, and then I'd imagine how more freckles appeared over time and count them, too. I'd draw little constellations. Let me see your eyes.

—No.

—Nadia...

Her voice deepened. —I said no.

Ignoring the dancers, Kostya bowed his head. Then he looked up and stared at Temerity, seeking something.

Noticing this, she twitched some of the headscarf aside so he might see the dent in her skull. —Steel plate.

He said nothing.

She faced him again, almost smiling. —I was hospitalized for two years. I couldn't talk for a while. When I got my speech back, I kept slipping into other languages. Oh, and I had to take rather a lot of sulpha.

He laughed. Just once. It sounded like the yelp of a beaten dog. Then he spoke in a lighter tone as though resigned to a joke at his expense. —I shouldn't even be here.

—Alive?

Kostya gestured to the crowd applauding the American dancers and lowered his voice beneath the noise. —That, too.

—I...Kostya...

A smirk tugged at his mouth. —A Britisher lost for words?

—What happened to you?

He answered in a workaday manner, drumming his fingertips against his cigarette pack. —Kolyma. Twenty-five years. I served eighteen. I'm rehabilitated now. Please stop crying.

—How can you be so calm?

—You know nothing of life here. Nothing.

—That's not true. I—

—Wolf ticket.

—*What?*

Kostya tapped out another cigarette. —See? You still have trouble with the idioms. In all this...freedom, is that what we call it? In all this, I'm stuck with a wolf ticket, my record of conviction. I'm pardoned for the crimes, yet can't shake off the conviction. I can't get a permit to live within a hundred kilometres of Moscow. I live in Voronezh and work in a factory. I check other people's paperwork. It's calm. I've got my own flat. Well, it's one room, but it's my room. I don't share it with anyone. I like that. Someone found out about my languages. I think I know how. Two men came to see me at work and told me to come with them. First, they brought me to my flat to pack a bag, then they made sure I got on a train to Moscow, where two more men meet me and escort me to...where I used to work. I'm a roaming interpreter. I check in twice a day to report anything interesting. Once the festival is done, it's back to Voronezh.

—Check in with whom?

—Whom do you think?

Then Kostya nodded toward a man of maybe thirty-five, his face stern, his civilian clothes ill-tailored. He looked fearful, as though examining a leak that might become a flood.

Plainclothes KGB, Temerity concluded, and he might as well have it stamped on his forehead. Then she recalled how she'd entered the country in 1937 as Margaret Bush—but had she left under the name Temerity West? Was there a record? *God's sake.* —Wait, they took you back? Did you tail me?

—Fuck, no! No, I just...found you.

—But—

Kostya beckoned her closer, and he murmured. —Listen, will you? I'm Berendei now, just a low-level informer. Nikto and his papers no longer exist. Only trouble is a man I knew back in the thirties. Little Yurochka's done well for himself. He's a major now. He tracked me down in Voronezh and told me how things would work. If I don't deliver reports, either in Voronezh or Moscow or anywhere else he wants to send me, I'll be shot. Specifically, I'll be shot in the gut first and left on the floor a while before getting shot in the head. Turns out I don't want to die. I thought I did. I've had a long time to think about death. They didn't arrest me right away in '37, so I had a chance to shoot myself, get it over with. I couldn't. In the camps, I stopped eating. They had us damn near starved anyway; I thought I'd just hurry it along. The first time I surrendered to a bowl of fish bone soup. The second time...why am I even trying to tell you this? Fucked in the mouth, what does it matter? Eating felt like too much trouble. I got very emaciated, a *dokhodyaga*. I didn't care. The camp doctor told me I was days from death. He got me assigned to work under him, like an orderly. Sometimes I'd take dictation. He convinced me to eat again. All those chances to die, yet here I am. Efim told me I was addicted to deceit. I thought it was hope. I refused to let myself die, Nadia, because I felt such joy with you in those moments when we could pretend not to worry. Because I love the freckles on your eyelids.

His voice cracked out, and he sipped some tea.

Temerity remembered all the smells of that Moscow flat, the whiteness of the walls, and her vision of Kostya living with her in England. Overwhelmed, she dropped the *bublik* to the ground. Pigeons surrounded it. When she spoke, she surprised herself. —I'm not quite the same person.

—Neither am I.

At the next table, Pierre parted from Joie, promising to meet her later as he got his stilts back on. Then he smiled at Kostya. —Hello. I am Pierre, from Cameroon.

—I'm Konstantin. Welcome to Moscow, comrade.

Pierre's wide smile seemed contagious, for Kostya smiled back.

Temerity recognized how little she'd seen him smile. She also noticed his missing teeth and the length of those that remained.

As Pierre and Joie left, and more people took their table, Temerity faced Kostya. —You said your surname is Berendei?

He smiled again, though not the happy smile he'd just given Pierre. —It caused a snarl with my paperwork. The arrest forms were in the name of Nikto, and I told them my name was Berendei. No one would believe me, of course. How many prisoners screamed we had the wrong man? But Matvei Katelnikov, this younger officer I was training, he took my Nikto identification, and it never made it to Lubyanka. People knew I was Nikto, but no one could prove it. The paperwork had to be accurate, and they couldn't just let me go, so they had to charge me with something. Twenty-five years for anti-Soviet activities for Berendei, Konstantin Semyonovich. I saw Katelnikov again about a year later, in the camp. He didn't last long. He told me about my Nikto identification, said he buried it. Then he told me he loved me. A few weeks later, someone found out he was former NKVD, and, well, I hadn't expected to dig a grave for Matvei Katelnikov. Perhaps I should have. At least it was summer, and we could break the ground. Cigarette?

The flame of the match danced between them. Then they each took a deep drag, Temerity coughing.

—Too strong for you, Marya Morevna?

—Out of practice. I gave it up during the war.

—Let me see your eyes.

—No.

—Please, Nadia.

—You're supposed to be dead. All of what happened here is supposed to be dead. Another country.

He reached across the table and clasped her hand.

She clasped back. —You're awfully warm for a ghost.

He squeezed, hard. —I've dreamt and dreamt about seeing you, and now I don't know what to do.

—First, let go of my hand before we draw an audience.

He did this.

Underarms slick with sweat, she took a deep breath. —I think I can get you out.

A sudden rise of laugher from the crowd obscured her voice; startled, Kostya looked towards a whoop of joy.

She tried again. —Kostya, listen to me. I, uh...I own a language school.

His eyes brightened, dulled. —Where? Newfoundland?

Despite it all, she laughed, then leaned closer to his ear. —England, you fool. Maybe two hours by rail from London.

He shook his head. —Shut up.

Temerity waited a moment before continuing. —Kostya, you once told me you felt great forces you couldn't understand influenced your life. Do you remember that?

He nodded.

—And you told me you surrendered to that idea. *I submit,* you said. Finding me here today, does this feel like an accident to you? Do you not feel you should submit to it? Because I do.

Mouth twitching, he stared at her.

Whoops and cries as another circle dance began, two steps left, one step right.

After a long moment, Kostya stroked the table near her hand again. —Did you ever tell your service about me?

—I said you were very kind.

He considered that.

Temerity's hand tensed. —Are you married?

—No. There's no one.

—Plainclothes again, ten o'clock.

Kostya sipped some tea, then spotted the two men. In their late twenties, they each wore ill-fitting grey suits. Their faces looked stern, yet their eyes looked fearful. Back in '37, he'd have called them puppies.

Longing for the delicate and defiant joy of the violins, Temerity craned her neck. She could not see the violinists. They could be half a mile on by now.

Kostya coughed, long, wheezy, and wet. —I harmed you.

—What?

—When I tried to help you...This is difficult. Let me finish. I don't know how I thought I could fix it. I couldn't just leave you at that party. I'm sorry. I've wanted to say that for years. I've rehearsed saying it, and I made these bargains with myself that if I ever saw you again, just seeing you would be enough. Just to know you're alive would be enough.

He took a deep breath, and his right shoulder relaxed. His left shoulder seemed paralyzed.

Temerity swirled the tea glass in her glass. —Enough? Like hell it is.

—What?

—Kostya, let me help you. I think I can get you out.

For a moment, and a moment within that moment, he admitted to himself that he might, just might, understand what she meant. Get out of the USSR? And how, precisely? Behave like a traitor and change sides?

—Kostya, you were going to come with me in '37. To the embassy.

Blushing, he shut his eyes and twisted his body away from her. —Nadia, I lost everything, fucking *everything*, because I loved you.

Temerity took a deep breath, said nothing.

Tracing a finger over the *podstakannik*, Kostya felt the old skills return, the desire and the ability to wound with language. —Efim died a few days afterwards. Or had you forgotten him?

Glancing at her sidelong, Kostya noticed her frown. The Nikto touch. He still had it.

Temerity sipped tea. —I hadn't forgotten. How did he die?

He tucked his matches back into a pocket as if preparing to leave. —I'll tell you another time.

—What? No, no, no, you don't pull that stunt on me, Kostya.

He felt startled and worked to hide it. —Too many people.

—You said, tell me another time. You want to see me again?

He gave her an exasperated look.

Temerity dropped the handkerchief on the ground, hoping Kostya had enough sense to bend over with her and help her retrieve it.

He did.

She murmured near his ear. —I need a clear answer. Do you want to get out?

—Shut up.

Temerity knocked the handkerchief farther under the table. —Paperwork in Voronezh too enticing? Kostya, listen to me. I can help. I need a Russian teacher at my school.

Kostya snatched the handkerchief from the ground and sat back up. His eyes, huge now, shone with tears. —I'm too small. I don't matter. And I'd never get the papers.

—We *both* matter. We—

A man in his thirties passed by and gave them a glance. He approached the table and spoke Russian to Temerity. —Is this man bothering you?

—Not at all.

—You're weeping.

Temerity dabbed at her face again with Kostya's handkerchief. —Tears of joy for the celebration in the streets, comrade.

The man glared at Kostya, then looked back at Temerity. —If you're sure.

—Quite sure, thank you.

He left.

Kostya tapped his cigarette package and discovered it was empty. —My handler. He'll expect me to file a report on you.

Temerity felt cold. *Bloody hell. Move fast.* —Can you get more cigarettes? I mean, are there shortages?

—We don't discuss shortages with foreigners. This is a land of plenty.

Temerity could not tell if he might be joking. —Be here this time tomorrow evening. If you want to be left alone, keep your cigarettes hidden in your pocket. If you want to come teach, put the pack on the table. I can't be here, but someone else will notice.

Kostya refused to look at her. Then, seeking clarity, he shut his eyes. —Nadia, I'm not sure I'd be a very good teacher.

He got no answer.

When he opened his eyes, he saw her empty chair.

He got to his feet, almost knocking over the table. Dozens and dozens of happy people penned him in. He wanted to climb on his chair for a better view, but that would draw too much attention. Instead he stood on his toes, scanning the crowd for a woman in a head scarf.

Several such women moved in all directions.

He turned back to the table, then brushed his palm over the seat of the chair opposite his.

Warm.

Oh, I exist.

Voices chattered; dusk thickened; nightingales sang.

A deputy head of SIS's Moscow Station stared at the middle-aged nuisance of a woman before him. —You really shouldn't be here, Miss West, except for the gravest of emergencies. What if you were followed?

—So you would prefer to explain to London how you declined to lift a defector who's former NKVD and currently attached to the KGB? No use at all, is he?

—How the bloody hell do you even know him? We had no briefing.

—Signal for Neville Freeman. He knows this file.

—Freeman? He's about to retire.

Temerity suppressed a sigh. —Well, he's not dead yet, is he? Please signal London.

He stood up. —On your say-so?

—On my recommendation. Request, if you like.

—Miss West, this is most irregular. We need to plan these things. It can take months. And we can't embarrass the Soviets with a lift during the festival. The damage to Khrushchev's credibility—

—John, isn't it? I expect your mother called you Johnny.

—What? Don't change the subject.

Adjusting her glasses, Temerity released her memsahib voice. —Now listen to me, Johnny. Back in '37—

—You were here in '37? Why?

—Need-to-know, that, and you don't. Back in '37, he helped me. He protected me. He risked everything to do so.

John blinked a few times. —You feel you owe him?

—How many times must I say it? He's not only tangled up with the secret police, but he's also a former political prisoner. He's only in Moscow by accident, and any moment now he'll be sent back to Voronezh. Surely he's got something to offer us.

Nodding, John considered that. —How long was he in the camps?

—Eighteen years.

John winced. —So much of his knowledge of the secret police is out of date.

—His knowledge of the camps is fresh though, isn't it? And how much can KGB have changed? God's sake, Johnny. Is this really your decision to make?

—Well, it's not yours.

Temerity decided to remove her dark glasses. What had Neville Freeman said after they'd interrogated an Abwehr agent together? *You do look fearsome. It's all about the theatre, you know. Squeeze them dry with theatre.* She stared directly at John, letting him take in the blinded eye and the scars. —This Russian saved my bloody life one night. He was willing to leave with me then, and I think he's willing to leave now, except he's too frightened to say so. And every defector we can take evens the score, just a little.

Neither of them had to mention the shame of the defections to USSR of British SIS agents Burgess and Maclean, and the ongoing fear of a yet undiscovered mole.

John could not hold Temerity's gaze, and his speech collapsed into a mumble. —If this blows up in our faces, I'll make sure it's you who gets the blame.

—Coward.

He sighed. —No, I understand pragmatics. Welcoming an enemy into the fold? Miss West, you have no idea what you've just opened yourself up to.

She put her glasses back on. —Then shouldn't you signal London and get some guidance, like I asked?

Heathrow Airport
Thursday 8 August

Only when they emerged from customs did Temerity address her two students about their recall and rapid return to London. —I'm sorry. This should not have affected you. You'll need to be debriefed. For God's sake, tell them everything you might know. Don't give them any reason to think you're hiding something. Don't even think about trying to protect me, not in any way. Clear?

Her pale and jet-lagged students only stared at her.

Then she spotted three men waiting in a row, each standing about a yard from the other. The men wore suits and doffed their hats when they saw the women. One of them was Neville Freeman.

Temerity gave a wan smile. —Right. One for each of us. Off you go.

Each man escorted each woman into a car with a waiting driver. Neville joined Temerity in the back seat of hers.

Nausea and fatigue kept her in a sickly doze as they drove to what looked like a military base. Armed men wearing battle fatigues guarded a gate and opened it only after conferring with someone else via walkie-talkie.

Temerity sighed. —Freeman, the students know nothing. Let them go.

Eyes on the road ahead, Neville kept quiet.

Temerity glanced over her shoulder at the closing gate, and she said nothing else until inside a long and low building that might once have served as barracks. Inside a dim room, grey paint peeling from the walls, she followed Neville's gestures and sat before a desk. He sat opposite.

—Miss West—

—Freeman, the students—

—Why have you proposed this defection?

—Freeman, please. Let them go.

—Out of my hands. Abundance of caution, and all that, and we can't just swan about Moscow cherry-picking Soviet citizens to lift. We help Soviets who have first helped us with useful intelligence. What makes him so special? I know he tried to helped you once, but is that it?

Is that not enough? —Might I have a cigarette? I seem to have run out.

—No. I've asked for a few hours alone with you before I report to my superiors, and if I can't convince them, then they will come to question you. They may do so regardless. You've not just tainted yourself and your students with suspicion in this enterprise but me as well, and you're still young enough to send to prison. Now please, I need to know anything and everything that could compromise you here.

—I am not compromised!

—Then why have you not told me everything?

For a long moment, she kept silent. The ticking of her wristwatch seemed to get louder, louder.

Neville did not move.

She took off her glasses so she might see better in the dim light and gently placed them on the desk. —Right. He had gonorrhea and a bad toe.

1958

THE BEZPRIZORNIK
Woking, England
Monday 7 October

Shipr cologne. Temerity often smelled it in her dreams, the resinous and sharp scent worn by Kostya in 1937. Except what those two young men leaning against a lamppost wore as cologne — carried on the mist, it seemed — was unlikely to be Russian. The young men gave no sign they noticed her as she passed. Then the heels of their boots clacked against the street as they detached themselves from the lamppost and hurried to catch up with her, one on either side. She saw now they might be sixteen or seventeen, boys, really, yet no less a threat. One of them asked for a cigarette as the other tried to snatch her newspaper and handbag.

A tall bobby rounded the corner, recognizing the boys, and he ran towards them. —Oi!

The boys turned to look. Temerity seized the distraction, sweeping one boy's ankles with a kick and sending him to the ground, and striking the second in the sternum with her elbow. The boys writhed at her feet.

The bobby reached out to touch Temerity on the shoulder, then thought better of it. —You all right, Madam?

—Fine, thank you.

One of the boys got his breath back. —Bitch!

Swift and graceful, the bobby reached down and hauled up the two boys by their collars. —No way to speak to a lady. Right, lads, off to the nick. You know the way. Madam, you follow me.

Adjusting her glasses and head scarf, Temerity noticed the bobby's preoccupation with handling the boys and decided to ignore his instructions. Instead, she continued to the address she'd been given in a crisp telephone summons. The boys' cologne and behaviour had stirred deeper memories of Moscow, memories already polluting her dreams and thieving sleep. One dream recurred. The beginning varied and over time became grotesque in its absurdities of just how Temerity found herself back in Moscow and compelled to find Kostya. She might glimpse him in a crowd, hear his voice, catch a whiff of Shipr. After long and complex quests, sometimes interrupted by another recurring dream of Gernika fires, the dreams ended the same way, with Temerity running to a train platform and arriving too late. She knew, knew as much as she knew that she existed, that Kostya had just been forced aboard.

She'd not seen Kostya after the 1957 evening at the Moscow café, and she knew nothing of his possible defection. After her friendly debriefing, as it got called, with Neville Freeman and then his superiors, she'd lost her security clearance. *Just temporary,* Neville had said, his cheer brittle and forced, *just until we get a few things sorted.*

She knew better than to ask about her former students and thereby further compromise them. Still, she ached to know, ached to apologize.

So Temerity had concentrated on her West Language School. Administration, recruitment, and scholarships, on top of teaching, filled her days, yet she felt empty, adrift. This limbo, this shadow existence of imperfect loyalties and exclusion, left her more lonely than she'd thought possible. Neither love nor duty drove her life. Purpose had fled.

Sometimes she wondered if she'd seen Kostya in '57 at all, wondered why she'd bothered with hope. So much risked…

Yet now, obeying a strange phone call, she stood in the worsening drizzle outside a dingy tea shop in Woking. The window bore spatters of mud and the remains of children's sneezes round the smudges of nose prints. Inside the window stood a display of bright cakes and sweets — dusty cardboard, Temerity discovered inside as she passed the tables nearest the window for one closer to the kitchen.

She sat with her back to the wall and facing the door, glanced around for other exits, and took a compact from her handbag to check her lipstick. Then she ordered tea for one with a slice of Battenberg cake. Stale and dry, the cake crumbled to a parching mess in her mouth, and the tea tasted muddy and weak. Milk only made it worse. She sighed. Lowest grade Ceylon, none of the sparkle and bite of Simla or Darjeeling. She unfolded her newspaper and turned to an obituary she'd read twice on the train. She now read it a third time, waiting for the thrill of *schadenfreude*. William Brownbury-Rees, who'd disgraced himself during the war and endured imprisonment as a fascist, had died after a long struggle with cancer. His attempts to return to politics in the early 1950s had failed. His estate, mortgaged in 1939 to support the British Union of Fascists, would go to the National Trust. Of Brownbury-Rees's now penniless widow, the obituary said nothing.

No *schadenfreude*, Temerity told herself, only sadness.

On her third cup of tea, now cool, Temerity asked the waitress for the location of the ladies' room. She could not risk missing the rendezvous for something as silly as a full bladder, yet whomever she was expected to meet was almost an hour late.

The waitress offered Temerity another pot of tea, stressing the word *another* in a voice loud enough for a music hall performance. —Or are you just about to leave?

Temerity's memsahib voice, much quieter, seemed the stronger. —Another pot would be lovely, thank you. And do your best to scald the pot first this time.

Temerity smiled to herself as the waitress departed. *She'll probably do her best to spit in the pot, after that.*

As she stood up to visit the ladies' room, cold and damp air swirled around her ankles. An elderly man stepped inside the tea-shop, tall and slim, elegant, using a silver-topped cane. She'd last seen him before Christmas, by chance, at a London performance of Shostakovich's *Symphony No 5*. They'd not spoken. Now, as he re-moved his hat, strands of his fine white hair stuck to the fabric, then fell, and his bright blue eyes looked sad. Spotting Temerity, he made for her table. The waitress noticed him, too, and she almost tripped over herself, addressing him as sir and asking if he'd like some of the reserved Keemun today. He agreed, his accent as crisp and aristocratic as Temerity's own. As the waitress left, he commented to Temerity on the dreadful rain. Perhaps aiming for non-rhoticity, perhaps over-compensating, he seemed to swallow his *R*s.

Temerity nodded to him. —Count Ostrovsky.

—Mister will do. It is pleasant to see you again, Miss West.

—It's been a long time. I'm surprised you recognized me.

—I knew about the injury. A pity about the scars. You had such a pretty face. I would worry about you when I was your Russian tutor, because your other tutor, Freeman . . . well, I did not approve of how he looked at you. And then I did not approve of how later he handled you.

Temerity gave a polite smile. Ilya had just as good as told her that he worked for one of the services, mostly likely in domestic counterespionage for MI5. Five, whose agents had tailed her openly since she'd lost her clearance. —Do you come here often?

Ilya frowned at the Battenberg crumbs on Temerity's plate. —Yes. Why?

—They must like you here. Keemun's not on the menu. The last time I drank any Keemun was well before the war.

—Your family preferred Indian tea.

As Temerity considered Ilya's rebuke, the reminder of empire, the waitress arrived with a large pot and fresh cups. —There you are, sir.

I know the lady's had quite a lot of tea already, but no doubt you want to share.

Ilya waved the waitress away with a flick of his hand. Temerity, forgetting her own imperious manner earlier, wanted to apologize for him.

Neither of them spoke as the tea steeped.

After checking his watch, Ilya poured, first for Temerity, then for himself. —You require a Russian teacher for your school?

For just a moment, Temerity thought Ilya meant himself. —I'm sorry, Mr. Ostrovsky, you've caught me off guard.

Ilya stirred sugar into his tea. —When he told us about the day he struck you on the face, I almost struck him myself.

Pulse quickening, Temerity inhaled the scent of the tea. *Struck my face? Brownbury-Rees?*

Oh my God. Kostya?

Face neutral, Ilya studied her. —Please think hard before you answer me, Miss West. Do you need a Russian teacher?

—I could certainly use one.

Ilya took two good swallows of tea. —That will warm my bones. Do you want a Russian teacher?

—I just said—

—Do you *want* him? Not just to see him over tea and cakes, but at your school. In your life. After everything he's done.

She felt chilled. *Everything he's done. By his own free will, yet twice as much by compulsion?* —Where is he?

—Answer my question.

—You've got him. You've got him locked away. Taking your revenge for history, are you? He had nothing to do with you leaving Russia in 1917.

Ilya's eyes shone with anger. —I shall be honest with you. I said I wished to strike him. Then I wanted to shoot him. In the thigh first. Then the testicles, then the gut, and finally in the face.

Temerity felt grateful for the cup, for something to hold. —He served eighteen years in the Gulag. Eighteen bloody *years*. Tell me, Mr. Ostrovsky, when will he be punished enough?

Ilya kept his voice soft. —Answer my question. Do you still want him?

—Yes, I want him. Where—

—Why have you taken such risks for one man?

Adjusting her glasses, Temerity let out a long breath. —Duty.

—To what?

She didn't answer right away. —To love. Or at least to the idea of it. Not that you'd know it.

Ilya turned pale. —I've never told you what the Cheka did to my children in 1917. I had a daughter your age. And it was not very long ago. Not for me. Do not presume to lecture me on love.

Cups clinked against saucers.

Ilya picked up the teapot and poured more for them both. —This has been a difficult case. He's cleared.

—What?

—We needed to confirm his claims. He's cleared now. So are you. He's free to go with you, if you will have him.

—Wait, I'll be reinstated?

—So long as this Russian is in your life, you look compromised. At least one of my colleagues still thinks he might be a double agent, or that you are.

—But Freeman—

—Has retired. Quietly. In some disgrace. You must not forget, Miss West, that we've had traitors who hid their activities in the thirties, and you omitted a great deal about 1937.

Temerity studied the fork she'd used to eat the Battenberg and imagined stabbing it into Ilya's neck. *We. Who is this* we? —How did you get involved?

—Language. I'm an interpreter, and his English is appalling.

Questions tumbled in her mind, yet she could not speak.

Ilya tapped his right temple. —He's damaged. We were hard on him. We had to be. The debriefing might have been too much, after everything else.

Hearing the sound of running water from the kitchen, Temerity watched a stray piece of tea leaf sink to the bottom of her cup. —When can I see him?

—Whenever you wish.

—Now.

Ilya laid coins on the table to pay for the tea. —Come with me.

As they passed the window, Temerity noticed a car parked on the opposite side of the street. Ilya took her elbow and guided her there, opening a back door so she might step inside. Then he sat in the front passenger seat. The driver said nothing. Kostya, gaze fixed on the drizzle-smeared windshield, waited in the back. He wore a badly fitting suit, with a white shirt and no tie. More of his scalp showed, and the greying hair that remained defied comb and pomade and still fell in waves. His broken nose sat at a strange new angle.

Temerity sat next to him.

No one spoke.

She shifted her weight in the seat.

Still, no one spoke.

She sighed. —Gentlemen, I've drunk rather a lot of tea, and I need to find a ladies' room. The one at the train station will do.

The driver stifled his chuckle as Ilya glared at him.

Temerity spoke with muted irritation and certainty. —Off we go, then.

Ilya gave a slow nod. The driver started the car.

Kostya said nothing until they'd boarded the train and Temerity closed the compartment door. He spoke in Russian. —Is this first class?

—Yes. We might even have it to ourselves. It's just over two hours to Prideaux-on-Fen. Then we'll take a taxi to the school.

He drew his fingertips over worn upholstery.

Outside, the train guards blew whistles and waved flags. The train lurched.

Temerity sat down, then retrieved cigarettes and matches from her handbag. — Here, I bought these at the station. Woodbines. The closest I can get.

Kostya sat across from her, lit a cigarette, a took a deep draw. —Not bad. A little weak.

She smiled. Then she considered his broken nose. Behind the glasses, her eyes widened.

Kostya, reading her raised eyebrows as disgust with him, gave a half-smile. —I was afraid you would turn me away.

—What? No, no.

—I worked so hard to stay in the present. The doctors kept advising that when I got back from Spain. *Your past is your enemy. Stay in the present.* I got through some of…in Lubyanka, I could sometimes slip into the past. Not this time. The only comfort in my past is the ghost of what I wanted for you and me. Why didn't you tell me they would imprison me?

—How long have you been in England?

The train lurched again and pulled out.

—Kostya?

Tapping ash into a tray, he stared out the window, then at her. —I never knew when it was night. They always kept the lights on. I told them everything, every little thing I knew, right down to Little Yurochka and the size of Arkady Dmitreievich's boots, and still they don't trust me. Why didn't you tell me?

She had no answer for him.

Kostya almost smiled. —I got him, in the end, that old White interpreter.

—Ostrovsky?

—Yes. You know him? The contempt for me in his face…he'd reduced me to tears and snot, and I said, *Whether you believe me or not, I can never go home again. At least in Kolyma I was exiled within my own country, but now, I can never go home. Neither can you.* He turned pale as snow and had to leave the room.

—He—

—Fuck him. I never want to hear another mention of him. I hope dogs eat his corpse.

—I can't hate him, Kostya. He taught me to speak your language.

Kostya stared at her, then snorted. —Let me see your eyes.

—No.

—Why not?

—I said, no.

—Please?

After a moment, she pried off the glasses, looked at him.

He took in the scars, the damaged eye, and shrugged. —I've seen worse.

She put the glasses back on. —Ever the charmer.

—What is your real name?

She hesitated, said nothing.

—Nadia, please don't cry.

—I can't believe you're here.

—I'm here. Right here, right now, I am with you. Let me prove it to you. Tell me your real name.

She took a breath. —Temerity.

—Doesn't that mean—

—Yes, I know what it means. My middle name is even worse. Temerity Tempest West, in part because my Russian mother liked the sound of it.

Kostya leaned forward, clasped her hands in his, and tried out the name. —Temerity. Temerity.

—Without the Russian *R*. Call me Nadia, if it's easier.

—No, I will call you by your name. Temerity. Temerity. Temerity.

He trilled the *R* harder and harder, keeping his face stern, until she laughed.

He lifted her right hand and kissed it. —I love that sound. I want to laugh, too, but I keep thinking of the dogs. In Kolyma. When it got to minus fifty, we did not have to work. We never saw a thermometer. One day, it was bright and still, I'm sure it was only minus twenty, yet we did not have to work. The guards let the dogs off leash, and they played in the snow. Romped and barked and chased one another. Yet they stayed within the barbed wire. Even the dogs knew not to run out to death. I feel like that. If I stay within the wire on this one special day, I'll be safe. After sunset, it's back to that White Russian interpreter, or the camp.

She couldn't answer right away. —Kostya, I'm so sorry.

He answered in English. —No. Do not be sorry. You tried to save me. You did not steal me. I stole you.

Then he let go of her hands and looked to the floor.

She touched his face, on the left cheek, near the scars on his ear. —*I do forgive thy robbery, gentle thief.*

His back and shoulders shook.

—Sit beside me, Kostya. Come on, squeeze in closer.

He did this, his face wet, and his spine seemed to surrender as he slumped. Temerity placed her arm round his shoulders, careful not to jostle the left one, shifting in some discomfort to herself so his head might rest on her chest. She inhaled the scent of his scalp, kissed a bald spot, shut her eyes, and smiled.

Later, Kostya would remember hearing neither the racket of the tracks nor the mutters of Baba Yaga but the steady beat of Temerity's heart.

ACKNOWLEDGEMENTS

Early in this project, tired, intimidated, and nearly broke, I rolled my chair back from my desk, rubbed my eyes, and said 'What I need here is a detailed social history of Moscow in the year 1937.' I couldn't bear to look at my computer screen any longer, so I took a trip to a bookstore. I meandered over to the history section, where I spotted a thick hardcover called *Moscow, 1937*, by Karl Schlögel. I took a step back from the shelf, looked again: yes, it existed and yes, it offered up invaluable details of everyday life in 1937 Moscow—details of everyday life colliding with the brutal realities of the Great Purge. It was precisely what I needed. I couldn't afford it, yet there it sat, as if waiting for me. My next paycheque several days away, I had to choose between the book and food. I chose *Moscow, 1937*. I owe Karl Schlögel and translator Rodney Livingstone a great debt.

I also owe a debt to Vadim J. Birstein for *The Perversion of Knowledge*, his study of Soviet doctors and scientists working on poisons, to Alexander Vatlin and translator Seth Bernstein for *Agents of Terror: Ordinary Men and Extraordinary Violence in Stalin's Secret Police*, and to Jeffrey Keith for his *MI6: The History of the Secret Intelligence Service 1909-49*. Of course, writing about characters in complex historical settings risks historical flubs. Any such errors in the novel are due not to my research sources but to my own limitations.

Somewhere around draft six, I recognized I did not have a full grasp of Temerity West. I'd assumed she would be easier to write than the Russian characters, as she is English and I grew up in a culture informed — perhaps dominated — by British habits and views. I'd forgotten something crucial: the British Empire. The 2002 TWI/Carlton TV miniseries *The British*

Empire in Colour was a huge help. This documentary explores the empire's miseries, complexities, and legacies — and the footage is fascinating.

I also studied, and continue to study, a work that felt like a quiet invitation into the realities of Soviet life in 1937: Dmitri Shostakovich's *Symphony No. 5*. Shostakovich composed the symphony during the summer of 1937 while in official disgrace and terrified of imminent arrest. The symphony confronts the listener with fear, dark comedy, subversion, and tragedy: with truth. Listeners at the symphony's premiere in Leningrad in November 1937 gave a half-hour standing ovation. Many wept. My favourite recording is the January 2015 concert performance by Orchestre de Paris, conducted by Paavo Järvi.

An earlier and thinner version of this story as a one-act play called *Aphasia* benefited from the 2007 Women's Work Festival and dramaturgy from Robert Chafe and Sara Tilley. I also acknowledge financial support for *Constant Nobody* from ArtsNL.

Warm thanks to Bethany Gibson for her thoughtful edits, Jill Ainsley for her sharp-eyed copy-edits, and Antanas Sileika for reading a manuscript version and suggesting a change that I first resisted but then welcomed. Thanks also to Christine Fischer-Guy, Christine Hennebury, Ami McKay, Sean Michaels, and Trudy Morgan-Cole for manuscript reads and helpful advice. Loving thanks to my husband, David Hallett, who read every draft, and to my children, Oliver and Kendall, who endured hours of me chattering about this or that historical tidbit, sometimes grotesque, over supper.